THE EQUINOX

A NOVEL OF HORROR

M.J. PRESTON

WILDBLUE
PRESS

WildBluePress.com

THE EQUINOX is a work of fiction. Any resemblance to a person, or persons, or historical events is entirely coincidental.

THE EQUINOX published by:

WILDBLUE PRESS
P.O. Box 102440
Denver, Colorado 80250

WILDBLUE PRESS is registered at the U.S. Patent and Trademark Offices.

ISBN 978-1-948239-19-6   Trade Paperback
ISBN 978-1-948239-18-9   eBook

Interior Formatting/Book Cover Design by Elijah Toten
www.totencreative.com

THE EQUINOX

For Stormy.
You are my love, my life.

TABLE OF CONTENTS

IN SPIRIT WOOD

By MJ Preston

Gather young children, hush now and listen
Do you hear the call of skin, the walker within
Its head filled with hunger, its heart filled with ick
Walk softly my children and pick up the stick

Where are the guardians, what came of their glow?
Why have they abandoned us, to die in the snow?
Its shriek brings us sickness, its calls brings on fear
Walk softly my children the walker is near

No man but the hunter can slay this great beast
No man feels the pull of its mark from the feast
Our future was bartered that day for a life
And children of Chocktee have paid a high price

It knows only hunger this walker of skin
It hunts for mere pleasure and scares you within
When night and day are equal the walker shall rise
And the children of Chocktee will meet their demise...

✝✝✝

PROLOGUE · THE HUNT BEGINS

1

Spirit Woods, Chocktee Nation Village

1995: One Day after Spring Equinox

He was packing the small knapsack with provisions for the trip, yet he really had no idea what to take. At his side, his mother wept. Once so upright, so proud, now she was barely a skeletal shell of the woman she had once been. Cancer was consuming her, had turned her thin, gray. The death of her father, coupled with her son's erratic behavior, drained her even further, and he was too entrenched in his own selfishness to appreciate the depth of her pain.

The freshly bandaged cut on his cheek was swollen and had been stitched closed the night before. Small dots of crimson peppered the cotton dressing. Pulses of fire radiated from the gash, stopping maybe an inch below his right eye. Not being able to touch it only made matters worse. It hurt just to blink.

He picked up his knife from the bed, wrapped a piece of cloth around it and placed it into the bag. Then the dreamcatcher and feather. Suddenly his hand reached up and tugged at the medicine bag hanging around his neck. Grandfather had given it to him. That was more than he could take.

This is all so unbelievable. Only yesterday morning the old man had been smiling and joking around, and now he's gone! Gone! Anguish rose above all else and anger pushed him into a tantrum. Let this be a dream! Fuck! Please let this be a dream! Tell me I didn't get my Grandfather killed!

But he had.

Janice Blackbird finally broke her mournful silence. "You don't have to leave. I will talk to the Elders. They will let you stay."

He stopped what he was doing, turned in her direction, his voice sharp and spiteful. "I'm not doing it for them! I have to go, Mother."

Her eyes welled up with fresh tears, her voice quivered. "Daniel, this is crazy."

Finished packing, he fastened the straps, not wanting to look at her. "I can't stay here. I have brought disgrace to your name; to Grandfather's name."

"I know all about disgrace, Daniel. When I brought you back here, I faced their looks of disapproval, but I knew in time that they would come around. Our people are good. They will forgive you. It is in their nature to forgive." Her voice rose and fell, rife with anxiety. But it was futile: she knew, no matter what she said, he would not change his mind.

Again, he stopped, but this time his eyes met hers. With gentle care – so as not to harm her feeble form – he reached out and pulled her toward him. She was so frail; this brittle body hardly contained her strong spirit. Physically she looked that of a woman twenty-five years her senior.

She cried harder in his arms, her body convulsing gently, knowing that she would never see him again and that there was a distinct possibility that he may die before her. She tried to take solace in his arms, but there was no use: his embrace only epitomized the sheer hopelessness of the situation.

Gently he caressed her back, feeling the bones protruding through the light sweater she wore, and he felt hopeless and conflicted. "I have to go, Mother. I don't want to, but I must." He shoved away the urge to cry. "I need to speak with the

Elders. They won't even acknowledge me, but if you talk to them, maybe they'll listen. There are many things I don't know. I need their counsel."

Janice Blackbird had been a Den Mother of the Chocktee people for three years and was now a respected member of the nation and its council. They would grant her son an audience if she asked, but that would be the last of her political clout. They would do it because of her Father, but only grudgingly. With their help and magic he had a chance; without them, he would be going to slaughter.

She pulled away from his embrace. Her long, silky black hair, flecked with grey, flowed down over the protruding collar bones which poked through her sweater. Even now, in the throes of this terrible disease, she still held onto her beauty. She mustered her strength, wiped the tears with the heel of her hand, and then used her sleeve to rub her nose.

"They will see you, Daniel. They will give you what you need. I will make sure of it."

2

He met with them that afternoon, standing in shame, before their dissecting and accusatory eyes. They were seated behind a large wooden table. Crafted from cedar, it was engraved with Chocktee symbols and the names of all the Elders who sat before them. There were five seats – but one stood empty, and the remaining occupants shifted inward. In the center sat Jake Toomey in what was, until yesterday, his grandfather's chair. Now Old Jake Toomey had assumed the position of Chief Elder. Toomey had been his grandfather's closest and oldest friend.

They talked amongst themselves in Ancient Chocktee, and though Daniel tried to interpret their words, he was unable to equate it to the modern language of his people. Chocktee dialect was similar to Cree, but the Elders' tongue was of the ancient times and indecipherable to Blackbird. Only the chosen were taught the ancient language.

The four men barked back and forth, raising their voices over each other, but among the four one voice held stable in its tone – and that was Jake Toomey's. He was Blackbird's only hope. The remaining Elders – Fortier, Machino, and Monias – cast an angry glance his way as they individually waved their hands, making their points and pontificating. Daniel could only guess they were making arguments for putting his head on a stick. But Toomey was calm, patient. While all Elders oversaw the good of the Nation, the Chief Elder reigned supreme, and his word was law.

Finally, Toomey raised his hand to silence them and turned his attention on Blackbird as the others listened. "Daniel Blackbird, you are wepinikewin." (One who walks alone) "You cannot return to Spirit woods unless you undo this. Here are the things we can give you."

Fortier passed a leather roll made of deer hide across to the Chief Elder; he unrolled it on the cedar table. Blackbird stood motionless, his eyes fixed upon the objects before him, afraid to move. But Toomey motioned him forward, and he did so cautiously. An old crossbow, collapsed and dismantled, sat next to ten small arrows. The tip of each arrow sparkled with amber, the fire inside the room reflecting off the precious metal they had been dipped in.

"Silver is said to be hard enough to break the icy heart of wendigos and skinwalkers, but this creature is more dangerous and powerful than others. Use these arrows only for protection. If the time comes when you think you can trap it, you will need our help." Toomey rolled the hide up and handed it to Monias, who then passed it across to Blackbird. His face was an expressionless mask. Like the others, his anger was muted by the Chief Elder's authority.

Blackbird started, "What can…"

"Close your mouth and listen to the Chief Elder!" Fortier's voice was venomous, laced with spite. Toomey remained silent, his expression plain. The Elders were the enforcers of discipline in Chocktee, and he would not second-guess them, even if he felt they were heavy-handed.

"You are omachiw," [a hunter] Daniel Blackbird. You accept this burden?" The light from the fire flickered across the span of Toomey's wrinkled forehead, setting his curly grey hair ablaze with amber.

"I do."

Blackbird waited to see if the others would scoff or grunt. They did not. At least not with their mouths—but their eyes were angry spheres that did not require words to convey their sentiment.

"You bear its mark." Toomey touched his index finger to the pocked landscape of his cheek, drawing an imaginary cut from eye to cheekbone. "As the wound heals you will feel a pull taking you in whatever direction it moves. You are a hunter now, and it is your quarry. The walker is fast and smart, but a slave to its hunger. You must make this weakness your weapon and try to catch up to it. Have you any questions?"

Blackbird had a thousand but limited himself to only those that were most pressing. This conversation alone was a blessing, one that he would not sniff at. "Are there any signs it will leave behind or clues to its whereabouts?"

Toomey looked at the other Elders then cleared his throat. "It must feed daily. It will eat animal. But craves to eat of man. In its wake you will find many bodies, the organs removed. Read the signs and concentrate on the beckoning. You have many roads ahead of you, Omachiw. Trust the pull as it guides you."

Monias reached across and handed him an envelope. In it, Daniel correctly speculated, was a sum of money. "Spend this wisely. Live as a man who has but the clothes on his back."

Blackbird took the envelope and lowered his eyes.

"You are done, Daniel Blackbird. Leave us now," Toomey said.

Daniel had not expected to be turned out this way. The sudden finality was akin to the death of his grandfather, in that he could not argue or undue his misfortune. He sighed—but minutely, so it would not draw criticism. He stowed the items they had given him, lifted the knapsack, and exited the shelter.

Toomey watched the young man go as the others spoke amongst themselves. He had known this young man and his cousin, Johnny Proudfoot, their entire lives. He took no satisfaction in banishing him, but as Chief Elder, he had a duty to his people.

Watch over him, Nekoneet. Protect him with your wisdom, he thought sadly.

The hunt was on.

***

CHAPTER 1 - RITUALS AND INTERSECTIONS

1

Chicago, Illinois

October 2001

Roosted on a building high above the city's red-light district, a group of pigeons congregated, trying to ward off the autumn cold. The ledge where they gathered was spattered with droppings that wafted the vile stench of ammonia. Below, the cityscape was filled with the noisy activity of cars and people moving along the gridwork of streets, illuminated by the fluorescent glow of night lighting. In the distance, adding to the chorus of sound, an ambulance siren cried out.

Not far from where the pigeons huddled together, a lone raven stared obsessively down upon the nightlife. But this was no typical raven. It was not a parasite content to pick over the remains of the dead, but a predator always hungry, always stalking. It was a magnificent creature, with a wingspan that spread four feet across. It was slightly ragged looking, its feathers unkempt, and it had eyes that were as cold and silver as steel ball bearings. The streets below reflected in those shiny globes as it scanned the panorama for new prey.

The pigeons cowered. They saw through the chameleon cloak, right into the grotesque and macabre thing it truly was. They saw the embryonic monster pulsing beneath the black feathers and skin, felt the spiral of madness pulsing from it in waves.

Must eat! So hungry! So very hungry!

It cast a fleeting glimpse their way, and they squawked huddling together even tighter; though they had nothing to fear, because the creature's appetite could not be sated by the meat on their scrawny bodies. It smelled the air hungrily, tasting it – and a scent caught in its nasal cavities. The giant bird spread its wings and took flight, descending from the ledge, down towards the ignorance of its prey.

2

Kerry McNeil had been on the street for five years now. She left home at the age of fifteen. Nobody wanted to hire a teenager in the city, so turning tricks became the only alternative. Now, at twenty years old she was what many would call a seasoned sex trade worker; a streetwise working girl who knew how to handle herself – although she had come by this wisdom as most people in her profession: the hard way.

Before turning 16, she had been beaten up and raped twice. As a result, she kept a fresh supply of condoms in her purse and a four-inch blade in her boot. Both used as weapons against HIV and the occasional bully. Some 'Johns' would insist on having sex without a condom, and this almost always led to confrontation. In one incident a guy grabbed her by the hair after she had argued with him. He changed his tune when she pressed the blade from her boot against his inner thigh, only a few inches from his scrotum.

"Understand me, asshole," she whispered. "I know what it's like to get beat up and I will cut off your balls before I let you do that."

He relented and left without much of fuss.

Her other life seemed a thousand years ago. The abusive drunk that had been her father was fading from her memories. But the ghost of those memories would always linger that memory as a reminder that this life was better than the one she had left behind.

Gay prostitutes and transsexuals worked the east side of 22nd and the straight girls worked the west side. You didn't dare step into somebody else's territory. This was something Kerry found out in her first month as a working girl. She wandered onto the wrong corner and got slapped around by a tranny named Carla. Carla – Carl in her former life – could have easily given Kerry's father a run for his money.

Kerry stood alone. It was cold, and she wanted to get off the street. Goose pimples rose on her legs: despite the autumn air, she stood kitted out in a black leather miniskirt and matching boots.

Soon she would have to resort to jeans. Something she didn't look forward to. Blue jeans didn't draw as much attention as a miniskirt, and as a result, business would suffer.

Cars approached, slowed, and then moved on. Many of them were just onlookers, getting a cheap thrill at her expense. Drunken college kids out for a Saturday night or married men trying to work up the nerve to cheat. So far, she'd only turned one trick tonight, blowing a guy in his car for $30. That wasn't enough. She needed to turn at least two more tricks tonight so she could eat and put a bit away for the rent.

Another car slowed, and she walked out toward it putting on her best smile – but as she got closer, it sped off. "Fuckers," she cussed. The cold pinched at her legs. "Fuck it." If there was no action in the next hour, she would pack it in for the night and work twice as hard tomorrow.

So she stood back and continued to wait. And as she did, what she did not realize was that she was being watched.

3

Detective Sean Woodman sat sipping coffee inside the surveillance van while watching the suspect. The suspect was a native man, a little taller than six feet, sporting a braided ponytail which ran down the length of his back. He looked to be approximately twenty-six years old.

"What's our mystery man doing tonight?"

Woodman's partner, Brad Rosedale, was just sitting down beside him with a fresh cup of coffee.

"He likes to watch," Woodman remarked. "Beyond that, not too much." He adjusted the video camera and zoomed in a bit.

"Three days I haven't seen him proposition one girl."

"He's just working up his nerve," Rosedale said.

"At this rate, the guy is going to be a virgin for life," he said and took a sip of his coffee. Just then, their suspect began to walk towards one of the girls. Woodman lowered his coffee, leaned forward in his chair. "Hello, looks like cold feet just got his nerve."

4

She was ready to give up when a friendly male voice spoke up from behind her.

"Hello," he greeted, "how are you doing this evening?"

A tall man stood on the sidewalk to her left. He was dressed all in black. Like that old Country singer, Johnny Cash, but this guy was an Indian, not a cowboy.

"Better now," she replied, a smile forming on her face as she sized him up. He wasn't a bit like what she was used to – he was good-looking, for a start. Most of the guys who frequented the red-light district had some kind of baggage. Fat, ugly, shy, mother issues – so the odd good looking 'John' was definitely a red flag. Good looking guys had issues; odds were that a 'Looker' was either an abusive asshole or a cop.

"What's your name, sweetheart?"

"Franklin. And you?" The tone of his voice had an air of sexuality in it that she couldn't quite explain, but it turned her on.

"Kerry." She drew her fingers across her breast provocatively. *God, he's charming! She almost felt hypnotized by his gaze.*

"Chilly evening Kerry." His eyes moved over her from top to bottom, a shameless smile across his lips. He had a soft accent which she could not place, and it was clear that English was not his mother tongue.

"Too chilly to be outdoors, Franklin." She looked behind him. "I didn't see your car."

"I don't have a car. I'm here on business." His smile broadened. A sudden uneasy shiver pulsed up and down her spine.

This guy is a cop. He could have any girl he wants at a club. IIc's too charming, too good-looking. Walk away, Kerry. Don't take the bait.

"My hotel is a block from here. Would you like to come with me?" he asked. Before she could answer, he continued, "I know what you're thinking, Kerry."

Yeah, I'm thinking all sorts of things: that you're a cop. A women beater. Or maybe even a biter. You have no idea what I'm thinking, Franklin.

Though her mind argued, her mouth invited. "Oh really? What am I thinking, Franklin?"

"Well, you think I'm with the police, that this is some kind of set up," He picked a bit of lint off his black shirt. "But you're wrong."

This was a new approach, she thought, and said, "Well, a girl can't be too careful, Franklin. Maybe you could show me some I.D.?"

"I don't carry a wallet on me. Too dangerous – especially when I'm talking working girls."

Fuck this! I'm not spending the night in jail or the emergency room! She turned and began to walk away without saying a word.

"Wait," he called after her. "I have an idea."

She spun around, her expression solemn, her mind screaming, *Don't be an idiot! It's a trap! Fuck, Kerry, what are you doing?*

He pulled out a wad of green notes and removed a 100 dollar bill. Kerry's eyes froze upon it, transfixed. "This is a gift, Kerry," he said, handing her the bill. "I am not paying you for any services. I am just giving you a gift."

Maybe he's an eccentric rich guy who likes getting down with the whores on Saturday night. She reached out and took the bill from him. *Yeah! Sure! I'm a goddamned no-brain idiot.*

"Now, here is what I am proposing. I am going to give you another gift when we get back to my hotel room. You are not obligated to do anything but come back with me and talk. I find you very attractive, Kerry, but where our friendship goes from there is up to you. We can talk, and if it goes beyond that, it will because it was what two consenting adults wanted. There is no financial transaction attached to it. Therefore no crime has been committed, and no chance of arrest."

She'd already tucked the hundred away.

Are you a bad guy, Franklin? Will you hurt me?

If she went with this guy and he decided to give her more money she could sock a bit away for a rainy day. She still felt uneasy, but it was cold, and it was only going to get colder. *Maybe he'll give me four hundred instead of two. Screw it!*

"Okay, Franklin. Let's go to your hotel and get to know each other." She reached out her hand, muting her internal voice of reason as she did. Maybe he's okay. There came no response: just indifferent silence. She was on her own. The voice of reason would be back later to gloat if this all went terribly wrong.

"I'm glad you saw it my way," he said taking her hand in his. It felt smooth and cold, devoid of lines or callous, almost like plastic.

Then he suddenly released her and began to walk away, leaving her to chase after him and the money. As he walked something small flapped about on the back his shirt, just below where his long hair swept across his shoulder blades.

When Kerry caught up with him, she snatched it up and showed him the tiny black feather. "What's this, Franklin?" she asked. "You're not into kink, are you?"

He plucked the feather out of her hand and for a moment she thought she saw something flicker on his face. Or was it his eyes? But an instant later it was gone, and that seductive smile returned. He tickled her chin with the feather. "That, sweet Kerry, is yet to be seen." Then he tossed it, retaking her hand and leading her down the street.

As they walked away, the small feather danced in the autumn breeze back and forth, back and forth, drifting gently down as it fought gravity. At last, it fluttered down, settled in the gutter next to a condom wrapper and Popsicle stick. Then it began to crystallize, tiny diamonds of frost sprouting across it. By the time they were 15 feet away, it had become hard, frozen, and too cold for human touch.

5

If Daniel Blackbird were a man to complain, he most certainly would grumble about his feet, because they ached horribly. But he muttered not. He had not been raised a complainer. He was not a full blood Chocktee like his mother or grandfather and bore the brunt of judgment from not only the prejudices of white men but his own people. In any other circumstance, he may have become bitter and weak, but his grandfather would have none of that.

"You must always be strong, Daniel. Never take umbrage with the shortcomings of others. Instead, draw strength and show them that you are unaffected by the blindness of their judgment," his grandfather counseled.

That was a voice from another time. When his grandfather was alive. When he had been welcome: not cast out by the Chocktee or spirit woods. He had disgraced himself and carried with him a burden no man would want to carry.

Focus. He's here somewhere. Stop mucking around and figure out where Skin is, before he smells you and runs again, he scolded himself and tried to concentrate on the tug that had brought him to the city.

6

Woodman lifted out of his seat. "Where did he go?"

Rosedale leaned in and scanned the monitor. "Christ, he was just there a minute ago."

Woodman's heart began to pound in his chest. "Where the fuck is he, Brad?"

"I don't know. He just vanished, like smoke."

"Fuck!" Woodman picked up the radio. "All units, this is Team Leader. We have lost contact with the subject, report status."

The reports came in. "Team Alpha no visual. Team Bravo no visual."

Woodman got up and put on his coat, adjusted his shoulder holster, then zipped up. His face broadcasted panic, his words were jittery. "Jesus Christ! Alert them I will be doing a walk by."

"All Units, be advised that Team Leader is doing a walk by."

Rosedale scanned the street anxiously. If the subject was their man and they lost him there could be dire repercussions, especially if he killed someone.

"Let's hope we can un-fuck this, Brad," Woodman said. He opened the door and stepped out of the van.

Carefully, he stepped out onto the sidewalk, first looking left, then right. The crisp night air cooled the hot panic he felt by a fraction. Stay calm. He's only been out of sight for a few minutes. Besides, he might just be a Looky Lou, anyway.

But he doubted his own reassurances: he was pretty sure this was their guy.

7

Kerry and Franklin turned the corner down an alley between a warehouse store and an apartment building. "It's a shortcut," Franklin insisted, but halfway down he stopped. There on the ground, he saw what he needed. This place would suit his needs finc.

"Come on, Franklin, I'm freezing. Let's get to your hotel." Kerry tried in vain to pull the miniskirt down over her legs. Goosebumps prickled up between her thighs.

He turned and caught her eyes in his hypnotic gaze. It disarmed her: suddenly she felt calm and disconnected; as if she had just smoked some premium weed.

"It's not cold, Kerry. It's actually quite warm," his voice soothed.

Yes, it is warmer.

She could feel him holding her there using some strange telepathic anesthetic to control her. Yet she was strangely at ease—and aroused. She was being seduced, as a vampire might lull its victim or a leech will inject numbing chemicals into its prey, readying itself to feed. *He's feeling me; touching me inside.*

"It feels good, doesn't it, sweet Kerry?" he asked, as he had so many times before.

"Yes." There was a slur to her speech: minute, but there nonetheless. "Please don't stop."

"I wouldn't think of stopping."

He began to change physically. His copper skin washed out, becoming grey and translucent. His eyes fell back in his head, growing and warping until they were steel balls, while his nose melted into the flat alien landscape of his face. His dark grey lips now exposed the tombstones protruding from his – its – grey rotted gums as the cloak he wore melted away.

A witness would have turned, run in terror. This creature was a man, but not a man: grey, without a nose, and three talons on each hand for fingers. Its eyes glowed fiery white in the darkness of the alley.

Kerry could not see the physical change; she only felt the immense loss of control as it anesthetized her. She could not feel its talons wrap around the nape of her neck.

Then it began cutting off its anesthesia and bringing her back, and she came down at an incredible rate. She was unaware that it was holding her in its clutches. Her eyes still closed, she tried very hard to hang onto the high that enveloped her – but reality loomed.

"Open your eyes, Kerry," it urged her.

I don't want to. I want to stay here. But she sensed something was wrong.

It needed her fear to sate its appetite. "Open your eyes."

She tried to fight it, but couldn't: the calm tide was receding. She heard a hollow whistle of labored breath and smelled a stench she could only compare to rotten meat or garbage.

Please let me stay; feels so good.

"Open your eyes. Open them now." The words came from inside of her somewhere, pushing.

At first, she saw a reflection of herself in the chromium spheres set before her, and then her most vivid nightmare came to life.

"Hello, sweetheart," her father, Rodney McNeil, laughed.

She tried to pull away, unable to scream, but he held her in a death grip. "You're not going to make Daddy pay, are you?"

He grinned layers of jagged teeth set neatly within black infected gums. Terror cut through her, and before she could cry out, he unscrewed her head. There were crunching sounds as bone and ligament cracked and tore, but she was sure it could not be her. Then it elevated her up, and she felt weightless, her body numb. In the millisecond it took for Kerry to compute that her head had been removed, her world went black as the synapses in her brain fired their last electrical pulses.

Her head thudded on the dirty concrete, bits of grit embedding in her cooling cheek, the last bit of blood expelling from her lifeless brainstem mixing with oils and grime. Then the monster lifted her torso, opened her belly with its razor toe, and began to feed.

8

Blackbird was a block away when the Walker he tracked pulled Kerry McNeil's head off. He knew he was close, but he had no idea just how close – all he could feel was it pulling him down the street, calling to him. The scar on his face tingled. His body pulled westward, like a magnet.

9

Louise Weatherton would never forget what had drawn her to the window of her third-floor apartment that night. It was a grating sound. A sound everyone knows but hardly gives a second thought. The sound was that of a heavy manhole cover being dragged across pavement. She might never have heard it except for the fact that the low-income apartment she rented had no air conditioning. The night air might have been cooler outside, but the 10-story apartment building was a humid chamber, heat retained within its brickwork and hollow cavities.

She was just finishing up the dishes when she heard the noise.

It's a little late for city workers.

She looked toward the window, folding the tea towel she'd been using, and laid it on the countertop. At that moment she was about to go into the living room and watch Jeopardy. Then she heard it again.

Louise was a nosy woman in her mid-forties. She did not deny this fact, nor did she feel ashamed. She had little to do but inject herself into the lives of others. Which, much to the chagrin of her neighbors, she did often.

She opened the curtains on the kitchen window as carefully as possible – because, like most voyeurs, she did not want to be spotted watching.

When she peered down into the alley, she suddenly lost her ability to breathe. Somebody had removed a manhole cover, but it wasn't the Department of Works.

Am I really seeing this? Is this real?

She reached blindly for the phone, which was just out of reach, unable to tear her eyes away from what she was witnessing. In the alley below, a creature that could only be described as a monster held before it a disemboweled and headless body. The beast stood about seven feet tall, skin grey, rotten. It was bald and had long arms with claws for fingers on each hand. Its face was smooth, and its eyes glowed. Its blood-smeared mouth opened and closed as it fed, revealing two rows of top and bottom teeth. It reminded her of the things from the movie 'Alien' – except this thing was uglier.

She fumbled for the phone and somehow managed to grab it. She mashed 911 into the keypad without looking.

"911. What is your emergency?" the voice on the other end of the phone asked.

In any other situation, her response would have been comedic – but the monster heard the operator and turned its fiery gaze upon the window.

Louise let out a shrill high-pitched scream.

10

Daniel Blackbird heard the scream and picked up on its direction instantly. He reached up and touched the scar that ran from eye to cheekbone, an ugly wave of white skin on a sea of unblemished copper. He felt the tug inside him, the tingle in his face, and began moving in the direction of the scream.

By the third stride, he was running.

11

Frozen with fear, Louise stood there at the window as the monster dropped the body into the sewer. All the while it never took its eyes off her.

Louise was paralyzed. She could not move no matter how hard she tried.

A thousand miles away she heard a voice saying. "Miss? I have dispatched police to your location. Please stay on the phone."

She couldn't respond – but she thought, *Oh please, tell them to fucking hurry!*

Stay there, the monster told her. Its command came from right inside her head. It was now at the base of the building and bashing its claws into the masonry as it began to scale the wall.

I'm going to die, she thought.

Yes, you are going to die, the monster echoed.

"Oh my God," she whimpered.

The monster was ten feet away now. Its horrible teeth grating as the stench of rot filtered upward to the open window. The blood from its last victim was already coagulating on the corners of its mouth.

Don't move.

She could feel its hunger, a spinning lust coalesced with madness. A desperate prayer rocked through her: Let it be quick.

It let out a low, guttural shriek.

Only a few feet away, the stench was overpowering.

She wanted to close her eyes, but it would not let her.

Be afraid! This is going to hurt! Be afraid!

The phone fell from her clutch onto the counter, and when she was face to face with the abomination the masonry beside her window exploded. At first, she thought it was the monster, but then she realized that someone below had fired something at the window. It turned and looked below, breaking its hold on her.

Shoooooooooothunk.

Again something ricocheted off the brick wall.

The monster turned its attention on the man below. He was holding some kind of bow and arrow. But Louise didn't stop to contemplate why. Its grip on her was suddenly gone. She broke from the window and dashed for her bedroom, screaming all the way.

Blackbird knocked another arrow into the crossbow and armed it. It dropped from the wall and landed on the ground. It stood in front of him, unfurling its long arms and extending its deadly talons. Blackbird had never been this close, except for that one night. It was huge; much larger than he remembered.

"You," it growled, and let out a screeching bray of laughter that echoed through the alley. "I thought I left you shivering in your boots up north."

Blackbird took aim.

Toomey's words rung out in Blackbird's mind: "Do not engage in dialogue with the walker; he will trick and seduce you."

He released the arrow, which had been blessed by the Elders. It flew straight and true. For the brief instant of its flight, he wondered what would happen when the silver pierced the creature's skin.

He didn't get a chance to find out. It snatched the arrow from the air and bent it in half.

"Your blood will be sweet."

It moved on him, as he tried to get a fourth arrow into the bow.

Above them, Louise Weatherton was back at the window. Now she was prepared.

Crack! Crack! Crack!

Gunfire erupted from the apartment window as she hammered the trigger wildly. To her, the explosions from the Browning 9mm were deafening, but a passerby could have easily confused them for firecrackers.

The monster stopped again and turned toward the woman in the window. Blackbird sensed the opportunity and tried to notch another arrow into the bow. But before he could, the monster turned back toward him – even as another bullet clipped its shoulder, sending a spray of black mucus up into the night air.

The Walker advanced like it had never even been hit, and as it closed the distance more bullets exploded from the barrel of the Browning.

Unable to seat the arrow, Daniel Blackbird raised the crossbow up like a Louisville slugger in a final attempt to protect himself.

One more bullet found the creature's thigh. This time it let out a horrific screech – but it was more anger than pain.

It reared up, about to bear down on Daniel – then it stopped. It paused, listened to some unheard noise that neither Blackbird nor Louise could hear.

"Another time," it invited, black ooze spilling from its mouth. Its eyes burned brightly as dirty smoke began to engulf it amid electrical pops and flashes. Then there was a crash and a liquid sound as it contorted and transformed before their eyes into a large Raven. It hung there a moment, like a toy on a child's mobile, but before either of them could seize the opportunity, it flew toward Louise's window, darted left and was gone into the night.

Police sirens filled the air.

"Shit," Blackbird cried, and dropped his bow to the ground.

"Are you okay?"

For the first time, Blackbird looked up and realized it was a large black woman who had been firing from the apartment window. She had very likely saved his life. He gave her a thumbs up, then added. "Nice shooting, Tex."

"You an Indian there, Hon?" she called down.

"Yup."

"An Indian with a bow and arrow?" she said, giggling nervously. "Imagine that."

"And a black woman with a gun," he laughed. "I'm Dan Blackbird; you must be Foxy Brown."

At that, they both broke into a fit of nervous laughter. Both were still laughing when police cars surrounded the alley. Then the police took up defensive positions and yelled for the Indian to get down.

"What have we got?" Woodman asked the uniformed Sergeant who had secured the scene.

The Sergeant opened his notepad. "We've got three bodies; one fresh, two in various states of decay."

"Three?" Woodman looked up. "Same MO?"

"Yeah, same."

The Sgt. thumbed through his notepad. So far, they had discovered nine bodies in the Chicago sewer system including the three tonight. Fortunately, the Chicago Police had been able to keep the grisly details out of the media. Good thing, too: it wasn't until the initial discovery of four bodies that the police knew they had a serial killer in their midst.

Detective Rosedale came walking up beside his partner, nodding to the Sergeant. "Sean, you'll never guess who they've got in custody."

Woodman turned from the Sergeant to Rosedale. "Virgin for Life?"

"Yes, sir," Rosedale nodded. "Our very own Native Voyeur."

"That would be witness number one," the Sergeant said.

"Witness?" both detectives said in unison.

"Yes; Daniel Blackbird. The other is a black woman who witnessed the perpetrator dumping our last victim down the manhole. Her name –" he thumbed a page back – "Louise Weatherton."

Woodman rubbed his right eye with his knuckle. "Hang on, Sergeant. This Indian guy is a witness? We have him pegged as a suspect."

"We've been watching him for three days now," Rosedale echoed.

"That might be, Detectives, but both stories from Weatherton and Blackbird are pretty cozy. As far as we know so far, they have never met before tonight. Although you'd think they were the Lone Ranger and Tonto with all the bows and arrows and gunplay that went on in this alley." The Sergeant waited for a reaction but got none.

"Okay, standard OP on the scene. Keep the witnesses apart, give me a walkthrough and then you can explain what the hell kind of mess we've stumbled onto. That work for you, Sergeant?"

"No problem, Detective, but I can pretty much guarantee that after I explain this shindig, you're gonna think I'm pitching some kind of screwed up Quentin Tarantino script. Can you take notes on the move?"

"I can do better than that." Woodman produced voice-activated tape player and then turned to his partner. "Brad, get the team canvassing the area and secure the witnesses. Most of all, keep the press at bay. I don't want anything leaked before we've got a handle on this."

"Alright, I'm on it." Rosedale didn't need anything further. He was a twenty-five-year veteran of the Chicago PD – eight of those spent in homicide. He was off and running.

Woodman reached down and put a fresh micro-cassette into the recorder. He hated putting pen to paper; he was slow at writing, and it made his fingers ache. He pressed the record button then put it on voice activation.

"Okay, Sergeant, let's do this."

***

CHAPTER 2 - BREATHING EXERCISES

1

West of Thomasville, MB

14 August 2009

Little Derek Wakeman set out that morning across his daddy's field, unaware of the terrible thing he would stumble upon. The Wakemans were farmers, and this year a crop of canola swayed in the field musically to the easterly breeze. The yellow flowering plant was waist height on an average man, but for young Derek, it touched his cheeks.

His mother had insisted he wear his outside clothes today. His chores were all done, and Daddy was pulling stumps with the tractor and didn't need him, so he told Derek that he could play on the property.

Derek was a typical farm boy: his life was often solitary, apart from his parents, especially when school was out. In the fall he and his father hunted deer, and when the biting cold of prairie winter set in they ice fished up at English Lake. Occasionally he could have a friend over, but the fact that he lived so far away from his schoolmates made sleepovers and visits infrequent. His best friend Cameron was in Florida with his parents: they were going to Disneyland.

He wished that he could go on a vacation with his mom and dad, but summer was the time of farming and Daddy could never get away. So today, like many others, he set out to make his own fun with the greatest toy a nine-year-old boy has: his imagination.

Derek's father, Donald Wakeman, was a tall man with a serious side that often rubbed people the wrong way. He loved his family dearly and took as much time as he could with Derek, but he was always focused on the crop. A strong Christian, Wakeman insisted that the family give thanks before every meal, that they say their prayers before bed and that God's word be practiced. Although not as strict as his own father, Donald believed genuinely that the end times were upon them. "We must be ready for when Jesus returns," he often said to Derek. As Derek made his way through the field, he could see the copse of woods that separated his father's farm from Mr. Hopper's. Daddy's rule was that Derek could not go beyond the small wood line or into the adjacent woods to the north.

2

The search party, headed by Sgt. Mick Collins, worked their way along Filmore Creek looking for some sign of ten-year-old Tommy Parkins. He had gone missing two days before after setting out with his fishing pole on a bright summer afternoon, intent on pulling a few trout from the muddy creek water.

The search party was made up of thirty residents from the town of Thomasville including Tommy's father, John Parkins. As they proceeded in an extended line on either side of the creek they called out his name, a cacophony of voices.

"Tommmmmmmmmmeee!"

While the searchers and families held out hope, Collins suspected the boy was probably dead. More likely drowned or a victim of exposure. He had seen enough of these searches in the last ten years to realistically assess what the outcome would be. But he did not, would not convey his doubts. Instead, he kept upbeat and urged the search on. It was essential to keep everyone in the frame of mind that they were looking for a live child, not a body. In the meantime, he and his colleagues would continue to wish for a miracle. It was rare, but just the same they would hope to find a boy with a busted leg or a broken arm instead of the tragedy these cases usually dished up.

There was another reason Collins kept his thoughts to himself. He knew the missing boy, and the boy's father was a longtime friend. He felt guilty for his analytical side, wanted to be unprofessional, but it had been two days.

While Collins covered the search party his boss, Chief David Logan was chained to the desk sorting out the small department's fiscal budget.

3

Derek snatched a stick up from the ground and pretended it was a rifle. He took aim at imaginary targets and began making mock firing sounds. As he entered the wood line, he dropped onto his belly and made believe he was an army Sgt. caught behind enemy lines. Sometimes it was fun playing alone: you could be anything you wanted, and nobody made fun of you. Cameron could get that way sometimes, ridiculing him or being mean for no reason at all. Just the same, he couldn't wait for his friend to come back from summer holidays.

The tree line which separated his father's farm from Mr. Hopper's was connected to Spruce Woods. Spruce Woods stretched endlessly northward and was easy to become lost in. Derek knew this because last fall he had ignored his father's rule and set out as boys often do, to explore the secrets of the unknown area. He had been up there deer hunting twice, but he was told never to venture into the woods alone.

On the day he became lost, Derek had only intended on going a few hundred yards into the woods, but that was all it took. Before long he became disoriented and ended up completely lost. The towering spruce trees overhead blocked out the path of the sun, and as he attempted to work his way back out of the canopy, he was venturing even deeper into the forest. By four o'clock in the afternoon, he decided to stop and wait for help. He had been wandering for five hours.

Donald Wakeman found his lost son on the same day just after suppertime. He was wearing his orange hunting vest and calling for him when Derek stood up and shouted, "Daddy?"

"Derek?" his father called back.

Excited, he ran toward the sound of his father's voice and saw the flash of orange between the rows of tree trunks. He dashed through them and stood face to face with his father. For a moment Donald Wakeman smiled, relief washing over him, but then he wiped his eyes, and his expression soured.

"Get over here, boy," he commanded.

What followed was a quick spanking, but the smacks hardly measured up to the three previous times his father had used his hand to teach a lesson. Nor was it the pain inflicted by the spanking that cautioned him from ever venturing into the forest alone again. It was tears he saw in his eyes. He had never seen his father cry, had always thought of him as indestructible. He knew that he had been the cause of those tears, and he vowed never to venture into the woods again.

Today, a year after his misadventure, he was restricted to playing in the copse of trees that bordered his father's and Mr. Hopper's farm. It ran roughly a mile downward between the two farms like a peninsula off the big woods to the north and was about three hundred yards across.

Mr. Hopper was a newcomer to Thomasville; he had bought the farm from the Angus family after Mr. Angus died of a heart attack in 2007 and Mrs. Angus moved away. The

Anguses were friendly people, and Mrs. Angus always had a bit of candy and a smile for Derek.

Mr. Hopper was what Daddy called a 'Hobby Farmer'; something Derek didn't quite understand. What he did know, however, was that his father did not care for his new neighbor, and Derek felt the same way by proxy.

Mr. Hopper was a stout man with a fine horseshoe of hair that rounded his wrinkled and pudgy head. Derek's mom remarked more than once that he looked like Lou Grant. Derek had no idea who Lou Grant was but guessed he must have been a grouchy man who swore a lot.

Crows cawed, enthusiastically feasting on Mr. Hopper's corn as Derek scanned the woods for enemy soldiers while crouching silently in the low brush. Just ahead of him he could see where the tree line opened up. Advancing on his belly, he moved forward. Soon it would be time to turn around and head in another direction. Mr. Hopper would not take kindly to someone mucking about on his land, nor would his father.

As he crawled forward something caught his eye. Lifting himself up on his elbows he saw that it was Mr. Hopper; he was doing something just beyond the trees. For reasons that only a young boy can explain, Derek decided to sneak forward and watch what it was Mr. Hopper was doing. He pretended that Mr. Hopper was an enemy soldier setting a booby trap for advancing troops. He, Derek, was a reconnaissance man pinpointing the booby trap and observing the movement of the enemy.

He crawled with remarkable stealth to a better vantage point and climbed up a nearby spruce. A metallic ping sounded: a shovel hitting rock. Slowly he scaled the spruce and sat down on a branch about eight feet above the ground. He was approximately thirty feet away from the unsuspecting Hopper. Derek peered at him. Hopper was digging a hole on the edge of his cornfield.

The hole was approximately four feet deep and long enough for a grown man to lie down in. To one side sat a giant pile of dirt and a black garbage bag. He's burying garbage? Why doesn't he just burn it like Daddy? Derek's thoughts shifted to the time he and Cameron had dug a hole half that size. He also remembered his father making the two of them fill it in before they were allowed to have supper.

As Mr. Hopper dug, the sweat between his broad shoulders stained the dirty grey plaid shirt he wore. Unaware of the young boy who watched, he picked his nose freely and rolled the ball of snot between his fingers, then flicked it off. Good thing Mr. Hopper didn't eat it: if he had, Derek would not have been able to contain himself. Reaching into his back pocket, Mr. Hopper pulled out a handkerchief and wiped the sweat from his brow, and then he looked about for any signs of life. There was none, so he continued to dig.

4

John Parkins was at the lead this afternoon. He had been out beating the brush for Tommy since the day he set out for Filmore Creek. Even before the search party had been formed, he had known that something was wrong. Tommy was a good boy, never late, always thoughtful. He and his wife Olivia had raised a very polite little boy who was not prone to forget himself or the clock. So when he did not come home for dinner, John and his wife were instantly concerned.

The night before, he and Mick had walked both sides of Ortona Road calling for his boy long after everyone else had left. He dared not ask Mick what he thought, terrified that he might answer honestly.

As he walked looking for any sign of his son he remembered he had been under the hood of his Chevy changing the alternator. Tommy had come along and asked him to go fishing, and he had said, "I can't, Tommy. This is my only day off and if I don't get this alternator in we won't be eating next week."

"Seriously, Dad?" A look of concern fell over his face; he was not your usual ten-year-old.

John Parkins smiled at his son, and for a moment he almost said, "I'll fix this later; let's go get some trout." But he didn't. Instead, he promised Tommy that next weekend they would get out and spend a morning at Filmore or head up to Linden Lake to catch some fish.

"That sounds great, Dad," Tommy replied, and set off down the road.

John watched his son walk away, fishing pole in hand and not a care in the world. He felt the love wash over him and again almost called to Tommy to stop and wait – but the alternator nagged at the back of his mind, stopped his words from even forming. John worked at the Feed Mill as a private contractor and used his truck to fill orders for the local farmers. While he could have missed a day of work, he did not want to tempt fate. There were a lot of folks out of work, and John Parkins subscribed to the philosophy that you have to take work while you could get it.

That was three days ago.

Now, as he trudged along, he beat himself up for being so shortsighted and stupid.

5

Up in the tree for about ten minutes, Derek was regretting the decision he had made. He sat there, his butt falling asleep, and began to think how angry Mr. Hopper would be if he caught him spying. His father's reaction would be even worse.

Below, Hopper finished the hole and climbed out. He was soaked in sweat and mumbled something to himself in between grunts. This frightened Derek for reasons he could not understand, but he held onto himself hoping that soon the fat man would finish burying his garbage, or whatever it was, and move along before Derek lost his balance and fell from the tree.

Hurry up!

Hopper stood at the foot of the hole and did something that made Derek even more uncomfortable. He unzipped and shamelessly began to piss on the ground. The noise reminded Derek of the pigs his family kept. Looking down at the sweaty fat man he noted he had more in common with their pigs than how he peed.

After zipping up, Hopper stood there a moment, took another look around and then reached over and grabbed the big black garbage bag and heaved it into the hole. Derek watched it tumble end over end as it fell and listened to the dead weight of its thump when it hit bottom. Just as he was about to ponder what was in the bag when it split open: a small pale hand fell out and into view.

Derek almost screamed, almost lost complete control and fell from his vantage point. He wanted to cover, to shield his eyes. A hand! Oh my God, a hand!

But Derek didn't cry out. In fact, he didn't move at all, because he understood almost instantly that if Mr. Hopper now discovered that he was spying on him, he would be digging another hole. Instead, he thought about deer hunting in Spruce Woods and what his father had taught him.

"There are three rules of thumb for being a good hunter," his father's voice echoed. "First, if you see a deer, you can't go off ranting and raving, or you'll lose the animal before you even get it in your sights."

Derek focused on Daddy's voice, pushing away the horror of Mr. Hopper and the pale bluish hand.

"Secondly, breathing is a vital part of hunting, my boy. If you don't control your breathing, you will lose your concentration, and your shot will be wild. Practice your breathing. Take a breath in and let half out, then relax as long as you can. Once you take your shot, expel the second half of your breath and follow through on your target." Derek practiced breathing in, exhaling halfway, holding it then expelling the remainder.

He focused hard, pushed every distraction aside. As he did so, his father explained to him that this was an excellent time to assess his surroundings. It took a day spent in the bush, but he soon found his breathing method, and Donald Wakeman said, "You're a natural. The third rule is that if you shoot something, you own it. Never let a wounded animal suffer. If it bolts, follow the blood trail and finish what you started."

While Derek's initial reaction was to scream and take flight, he instead began to breathe and take stock of his situation. He envisioned a deer in a clearing and inhaled a full breath ever so slowly, aware that sudden movement would draw attention. He pushed away from the side that was screaming for him to run and watched Mr. Hopper as he began to heave shovels full of dirt back into the hole and on top of the bag.

His bum had fallen asleep. He loosened his grip on the branch above him, shifted minutely, to relieve himself from getting a cramp. Then he expelled the second half of his breath and began the exercise all over again. He locked away his want to scream, to run – instead he focused on Mr. Hopper and pretended he was a deer through his rifle sight.

Mr. Hopper scooped another shovel of dirt and heaved it into the hole. When it hit the plastic, Derek again exhaled the remaining half of his first breath. He scooped; Derek inhaled. He heaved; Derek exhaled. Derek worked his breathing to perfectly match this routine.

For the next fifteen minutes, Derek Wakeman sat motionless on the tree branch like a chameleon. Occasionally Mr. Hopper would stop, wipe his brow, and Derek would hold his breath until the work resumed.

Finally, after what felt like an eternity, Mr. Hopper was padding the soil with his shovel, and for a short while, Derek was able to breathe freely. Mr. Hopper looked as though he was ready to leave – but then suddenly he began to move toward the tree line, and Derek.

He could easily have screamed and dropped from the branch but continued his meditation pushing away the urge, focusing instead on the imaginary deer that had got him to this point.

Ten feet directly below him, Mr. Hopper surveyed the tree line and began to pull bits of brush and branches from the ground. He carried the first handful back to the grave and started to camouflage it.

Go home.

Mr. Hopper examined his work and moved back to the edge of the tree line again.

What if he looks up? Panic was finally starting to dig its claws in. *Daddy is always checking the sky for clouds! Please, Jesus! Please, I beg you! Please don't let him see me!* But though his mind reeled, he sat perfectly still, eyes forward.

Hopper picked up an old log and dragged it back. He threw it across the grave, arranging brush and branches, trying to make it look natural. Finished, he examined his work again.

Go away!

Mr. Hopper began to gather up his tools and tossed them in his wheelbarrow, where they clanged together. Derek took this opportunity to shift ever so slightly, causing the branch to tremble. Mr. Hopper stopped dead in his tracks.

Oh, Jesus, no!

Derek's heart began pounding uncontrollably, and again he almost lost control. Making matters worse he could feel the pressure of a much-needed pee rising in his bladder. He thought the beating of his heart was loud enough for anyone to hear.

Don't look up! Please! Don't look!

Mr. Hopper began to raise his eyes upward – and a miracle occurred. Just then a crow burst from the tree line and landed on a fence post to his right. It cawed with delight, catching the fat man off guard and startling him. For a minute he gawked at the bird, almost as if he recognized it – then he shook his head and cussed. "Fucking crows."

Derek watched, continuing to breathe slowly, mindful not to make any more noise as Hopper grabbed the handles of the wheelbarrow, spun around and walked back down the path into the cornfield. He waited until he was out of sight a full five minutes before he carefully climbed down from the tree. His heart was still thumping madly to the point that it hurt. He gasped for air and looked around desperately. No longer the composed statue that melted in with its surroundings, he was now the terrified little boy digesting an unwanted taste of the macabre.

He was running now. Branches whipped his face as he ignored the trail and sprinted in a straight line toward his father's field. He could not feel the slashing; the pain muted by his terror, his dread that Mr. Hopper was going to reach out and lob off his head with his shovel at any moment.

He tripped. He hit the ground, scraping his hands on an old root, but he did not stop to check his wounds. Instead, he was up and moving at breakneck speed for Daddy's field.

Gotta keep going! Not safe, gotta get home!

6

Donald Wakeman saw the movement in his canola just as he was about to eat his lunch. The yellow flowers swayed in the opposite direction of the wind, which was blowing from the east today. Wakeman watched curiously. The moving object was coming straight at him from about 200 yards out. He was still deciding what kind of animal it might be when he realized it was Derek.

"What the heck is that boy doing?" he muttered, a smirk forming on his face. He could barely see the top of Derek's blonde tangle of hair as he cut a trail through the crop.

The smile on Wakeman's face began to slip away when his boy tumbled, got up and dashed forward. He started climbing down from the tractor, his lunch forgotten.

7

Derek got up and started running again. He had lost complete control and had forgotten to breathe. He didn't dare look back. Daddy was in sight now, walking towards him. He pumped his legs even harder.

Almost there!

When he reached his father, he fell to the ground.

Safe!

Donald Wakeman looked down at his son. Derek's face was smeared with yellow and covered in welts from the branches and canola. Beneath the colorful smears, he was red, almost purple, and he wasn't breathing. His eyes were wide, terrified, and darted madly back and forth. Donald reached down, but the boy pulled away almost instinctively and looked crazily from left to right.

He's choking, Wakeman panicked. Swallowed something?

"Breath, Derek!" he urged.

Derek could not hear his father's words. The horror of what he had seen was into much.

His father reached down and slapped him on each cheek.

"Breathe, Derek! Are you choking? Breathe!"

Daddy looked scared now, like the day he found him in the woods. Tears were welling up in his eyes.

He slapped Derek a little harder, and that was enough. A rush of breath escaped Derek's lips, and he began to convulse and hyperventilate.

"What happened to you?"

His mouth flapped, but no words came.

"Who did this to you, son?"

"Ddddd," was all he could manage.

"What?" Donald was lifting Derek up.

"Dddddeee," he stuttered.

"I can't understand you!"

"Deeeeeeerrrrrrrrr! Deer," he cried shrilly, and then there were no words, no stuttering – just the terrified screams of a boy who had seen something which no boy should ever see, even in his darkest nightmares.

He was still screaming when his father picked him up and carried him into the house.

8

Thirty minutes later Donald Wakeman was loading his shotgun as his wife protested. He could not hear her; rage unlike anything he'd felt in years beat through him. Derek had eventually told him what had happened.

"Donald, we need you here," his wife insisted.

"Francine, I need you to do two things. Get our son to the hospital and call the police."

He walked out the door bound for Stephen Hopper's farm.

***

CHAPTER 3 - CONFRONTATIONS

1

Chief David Logan was shuffling through manpower reports for the Mayor's quarterly fiscal budget. He had been Chief of Police in Thomasville for ten years, and this was the side of the job he honestly hated. Being a Police Officer was all David Logan had ever wanted to be, and although he had always been ambitious about getting his own command, he had never thought through the bureaucratic end of running a department.

Every three months he had to submit justifications for overtime and acquisitions. Mayor Locke was a good guy but would have the department of 10 Officers and one dispatcher working with a shoestring budget. Logan learned early on that you had to cross your "t's" and dot your "i's" or the Mayor's office would strip your funding. Therefore, instead of searching for a missing boy, Logan was doing what was necessary to keep his department out of the red. His second-in-command, Sgt. Mick Collins, would be leaving Thomasville in approximately six months to broaden his horizons in drug enforcement. Although he would miss Collins, both as 2IC and friend, he supported his decision to leave and further his career. Thomasville did not have a lot to offer in the way of career advancement other than the odd marijuana grow operation. For an ambitious police officer, Thomasville was not where you wanted to spend your career: it was more like where you'd want to end it.

Logan admired Mick, partly because his 2IC reminded him of when he was a young, ambitious homicide detective many years before. Ambition was fine, as long as you were willing to make sacrifices. Logan knew all about sacrifice. He had given up his marriage for his career, and now only saw his children during holidays. He hoped that Mick's wife, Nancy, would be able to endure the sacrifices imposed by her husband's ambitious career path. A plus in their favor was that they had no children, but that would likely change. Mick would have to be replaced, and there were two suitable candidates: Corporals Don Steel and James West. Both were capable young lads with a nose for police work, but when you got them together, they acted like juveniles. For the last three months, Logan quietly observed and took notes, but did not alert either of them to the possibility of promotion – although there was speculation that one of them would be taking the reins.

He realized that he had let his mind wander and picked another manpower report to log into his computer. Just as he was about to go over the numbers the dispatch line rang. He picked it up, already reciting. "Sabrina, what is it?"

"Sorry, Chief. I have Francine Wakeman on the line, and she's frantic," she replied.

"Uh. Can't the duty officer handle this?" Logan responded.

"You sent Peter out to get lunch." Sabrina was looking at him through the office window from her desk.

"Okay, put her through." There was a beep. Logan said, "Chief Logan."

"Chief, he's going to kill him," Francine Wakeman cried.

Logan sat up. "Hold on a second, Francine, who are you talking about?"

"Donald... My husband; he's gone over to kill our neighbor Mr. Hopper. You have to get over there!" She was in hysterics.

Logan was already up and out of his seat, attaching his holster to his belt. "Listen, Francine, I am getting ready to go, but I need you to calm down and tell me what's going on. You said that your husband Don is going over to Mr. Hopper's house. How do you know he's going to kill him, and why?"

She took a deep breath and began to explain. "Derek came home this afternoon in a horrible state, screaming, and when we finally got him calmed down, he said that he had seen Mr. Hopper burying a body."

"Are you sure he wasn't kidding around, Francine? You know kids –"

"A child's body! Chief, a child!" she cried shrilly.

Logan tapped the office glass to get Sabrina's attention. The sixty-year-old dispatcher got up and came to the door. "Okay, Francine, I'm going to head over to Mr. Hopper's place. Was Don carrying a gun or any weapon?"

"He had his shotgun. Oh, dear Lord," she cried. "Please don't hurt him."

Logan was more worried about getting accidentally shot by Wakeman than hurting him. "Alright. I'm going to put you on with our dispatcher, Sabrina. You stay on the line with her, and she'll get the rest of the information."

Constable Pete Kennedy was just walking in the door with lunch when Logan alerted him to get his gear. "Drop the bags, Pete! We've got a 10-54d and a civilian with a gun." 10-54d was police code for possible dead body.

Kennedy put down the bags and followed the Chief out to the parking lot.

2

A thousand things ran through Donald Wakeman's mind as he drove his pickup over to Hopper's farm. His first thought was that the man had hurt his son and for all his Christian goodwill, he could not find it in himself to get past that. He was a kettle of rage, and that blinded him to the fear he should have felt.

He turned into the cul-de-sac dirt driveway in front of Hopper's three-bedroom farmhouse. Originally covered with cedar strips and shingles, it was now grey and old. The Anguses took far more care around the place – but that was not why he was here.

He stepped out of his Ford pickup and grabbed his shotgun. Carefully he tucked his arm under it and held it casually so as not to draw suspicion, then walked toward Hopper's doorway, preparing for what he would do next.

3

Mick was going over a county map when the radio call came through to clear all traffic. A couple of other officers stopped and listened to their remotes. Thomasville Police, like most other police departments in North America, had abandoned police code to avoid confusion during transmission. In this case, Logan used a combination of the old system because he knew that most of his officers were near civilians. "All units be advised we have a 10-54d, I am en route to the location. Have Paul Sam contact me via secure means for a briefing."

Paul Sam was phonetic for Patrol Sgt. Mick pulled his cell phone out, dialed Logan's number and placed it to his ear. It barely got off a single ring before Logan picked up.

"Mick, are you alone?" Logan asked.

"Copy that," he replied looking around to make sure.

"Okay, it looks like we may have located the missing child. Unfortunately, the details don't look promising, but we have bigger problems. A neighbor is on his way over to the suspect's house with a shotgun. The address is 4987 Van Dyke Rd, suspect's name is Stephen Hopper. Neighbor with the gun is Donald Wakeman. Have you got that?"

"Copy that."

"I need you to get all officers moving to that position ASAP. Have two Officers block both ends of Van Dyke to keep traffic out of the area."

"Copy that." Mick was scribbling madly while turning over the situation in his mind. "ETA to that position is twenty-five minutes. Send rendezvous location."

"RV will be on site. I have Constable Kennedy in tow; he'll be my back up. Send everyone you have." He paused, then, "Wait!" Logan set the phone down to turn the corner; he was ten miles from Hoppers Farm. "Is John Parkins still on site?"

"Yes."

"Shit! Okay, have one officer escort, Mr. Parkins, back to his residence and keep him there. Someone that he knows. Your prerogative, Mick. Inform all available that radio traffic is to be kept to a minimum. I will keep you informed on the cell."

Logan got on his radio. "Constable Hardy, come to the command post." All officers within sight were looking his way. They had heard the transmission and understood a portion of what was going on. Sandra Hardy was about 900 yards away when he sent the call through, and she began jogging back across the field toward him.

4

Stephen Hopper opened the door to see his neighbor standing on the porch with a shotgun under his arm. "Hello, Mr. Wakeman. What brings you over here?"

"Hi. Well, I had a couple coyotes get at some of my chickens, and they headed this way a few minutes ago, so I jumped in my truck; thought we might head them off before they do any more damage." Wakeman smiled thinly.

"Head them off?" Hopper was still looking at the shotgun.

"Yeah, they were running for the woods between our farms. I think I've got them beat. If we get into the woods, we might be able to kill them before they do any more damage. Can you grab your gun?"

Hopper looked unsure but stepped out onto the porch to take a look. He moved almost mechanically. He couldn't see the copse of woods from the front of the house and was about to walk around to the side as he spoke. "Okay, well –"

Wakeman brought the gun up and planted the double barrel squarely against his neighbor's neck. "Do not move or I will kill you where you stand."

Logan was only minutes away now. Van Dyke Road was twenty-four miles long and stretched over three jurisdictions. It was a concession road connecting farmers to their fields and to each other, but it was also a secondary highway. Logan guessed that Donald Wakeman was already over at Hopper's, and hoped that he and Kennedy weren't walking into a disaster.

5

"Get on your knees," Wakeman ordered.

"Mr. Wakeman, why are you doing this?" Hopper was shaking.

"I'm not screwing around!"

Wakeman shoved the double barrel into his neck hard enough to break the skin. Hopper pressed down onto his knees. His mind reeled. His neighbor must have seen him, and now the crazy fuck was going to execute him right on his porch. He stared down at the boards ready to surrender himself to death.

"Now lay down on your belly."

Hopper lay down. Inside he felt some relief that this would end and that he would no longer live in fear. He didn't protest: he just put his hands in front of him and prepared for the end.

"What did you do to my boy?" Wakeman asked.

Hopper didn't respond, instead waited for Wakeman to shoot him.

"I asked you a question, Hopper!" He shouted and cracked the side of Hopper's head with the gun barrel." What did you do to my boy?"

"I don't know what you're talking about," Hopper croaked. His eyes were ringing.

"Did you touch him, you depraved freak?" Wakeman screamed.

"I barely know your son. There must be some kind of misunderstanding, Mr. Wakeman! The last time I saw your son was when we talked a month ago at the feed mill," he managed, and then thought, Why would he think I touched his son? There was a moment of silence. When Wakeman spoke again, his voice edged with doubt. "You never touched him?"

He fell silent for almost a minute. Hopper remained perfectly still, mute but for his breathing.

Could Wakeman be having second thoughts?

If so, Hopper decided to drive them home. "No, I haven't. In fact, I have no idea what you're talking about." He started to climb back up to his hands and knees.

"Not so fast!" Donald Wakeman planted a heavy work boot into Hopper's back and shoved him back to the floor. Hopper grunted. "Let's talk about what you were burying in the back of your property."

Oh my God! His boy must have seen me!

"Well? How 'bout it, Mr. Hopper?"

"I don't kn-"

"Lies!" Wakeman thundered and shoved the gun hard into the back of his neck again. "You'll tell me, or I'll shoot you."

Lying there on his belly, close enough to see the paint peeling in flecks from his deck, Hopper thought ridiculously, I was going to strip and repaint this in a week or so. *I guess I won't have to worry about it now.*

"The police are on their way. Question is whether or not they will be arriving to a prisoner or a corpse."

"That's murder," Hopper mumbled.

"It will be self-defense. It will also be justice served." Wakeman's voice became cold and calculated. "My boy saw you burying a body in your cornfield, Hopper. Was it Tommy Parkins?"

Hopper said nothing. Oh, for fuck sake.

"Here's the thing, Mr. Hopper: my boy saw you, but you are going to confess it to me before the police arrive. My boy has seen enough horror to last him a lifetime. What you have put him through is more than I can bear, so if there is to be a trial, you will confess to me so that my boy does not have to face you. If you don't, there will be no trial. Just the body of a murderer who tried to overpower his neighbor after the discovery of a crime."

"Look. Mr. Wakeman. Donald. I don't know what —"

"Lies," Wakeman thundered again, and this time cracked Hopper in the cheek with the barrel of his gun. "My patience is wearing thin! Maybe I'll just blow your balls off and be done with it." Then he booted Hopper in the side.

"Okay, okay. Stop," he wheezed. "I'll talk!"

"Was it Tommy Parkins?" He cracked him a third time. "Was it?"

"Yes," he barely managed, thinking his skull might be fractured. I'll probably die before the cops get here anyway.

"You killed and buried him?"

"Yes." Hopper was shaking now. That last crack in the head had done most damage: now he swam in and out of consciousness. His eyes blurred. Part of him — a small part that could still somehow maintain his thought processes — wished that Wakeman would just shoot him. He didn't care whether he lived or died; if he did live, the price would be hefty.

The last thing he saw as he retreated into himself was a drop of his own blood splash down on the weathered deck. As it did, the dried wood absorbed the crimson tissue, and it spread like the grisly stain of a madman.

I wonder how long blood would protect deck board from UV rays, he mused.

6

Put down the gun now!" Logan yelled. He hadn't drawn his pistol yet. With his lowered left hand, he motioned Kennedy to stay calm.

Donald Wakeman didn't see or hear the cars skid into the driveway when he cracked Hopper in the side of his skull. Standing over the man he might have killed with the barrel of his rifle, he felt adrenaline started to course out of him, and he began to shake.

"He confessed," he said and stepped away from Hopper. "He killed Tommy Parkins."

"Step away from him and hand Constable Kennedy your gun, Mr. Wakeman. I'm not gonna ask you again." Logan reached down and placed his hand on his sidearm.

Wakeman blinked, stepped back and moved toward the young constable's car, his arms stretched out, the shotgun in his right hand.

Kennedy grabbed the gun first and had Wakeman lean over the hood of the car as he placed the shotgun in the front seat of the cruiser. He came back around, cuffed Wakeman, and said, "I'm only doing this until we figure out what's going on, Mr. Wakeman."

Logan stopped over the body on the deck. "Mr. Hopper, can you hear me?"

Hopper stared at Logan. Without changing his expression, he said, "Yes."

"Can you get up?"

For a second, he didn't move – then he rolled onto his back with a deep sigh. A moment after that he managed to sit up. His head still swimming, but it was easing up. The cut on his cheek stopped bleeding. The side of his bald crown had swelled up turning peroxide brown.

"Can I have a smoke?" he asked.

Logan was ready to knock him down if he tried anything. "Okay, go ahead."

He reached into his breast pocket and produced a pack of cigarettes and a lighter. The first three cigarettes he pulled out were broken, but the last was flat and bent like a hockey stick. He straightened it out, then lit up and inhaled.

Logan stood over him, waiting for the big man to gain his bearings, checking how Pete Kennedy was making out with Wakeman from the corner of his eye. This had been the strangest afternoon he'd ever seen, one he thought would not be topped.

"Crush out your cigarette and place your hands behind your back, Mr. Hopper."

Logan pulled out his cuffs as the fat man snuffed the cigarette out on the porch. He snapped the bracelets on him and had him get up. He was leading him back to his own cruiser when the cavalry came in lights ablaze and sirens wailing. There were four cars in all, Mick in the lead. The dust of Van Dyke Road swirled in the air dramatically around the screech of tires.

With Hopper secured in the back of the car, he went and spoke to Wakeman. Mick stood behind Logan, listening as the farmer recounted the story about his son coming home. The tale the child had told and what Hopper had confessed to him. Logan scribbled this all down on a notepad. "Could you take us to the body?"

"I'm not sure of the location. I could probably find it," Wakeman said.

"Could Derek?"

"No! Absolutely not," Wakeman exploded.

"Okay, Don, calm down," he said, then looked at Mick. "I guess it's plan B."

Mick didn't understand. "Plan B?"

Logan turned and walked over to his own car. Hopper sat quietly in the backseat, looking straight ahead. Mick stayed with Wakeman and watched his boss open the back door of the cruiser. He was leaning in, talking to Hopper – and then without any announcement to his Officers or his 2IC he got into the cruiser and began to drive it around the back of the house toward the cornfield.

The other Officers watched and waited.

Logan maneuvered the cruiser through a narrow pathway in the cornfield, one side of the cruiser knocking down a stalk now and then. For the most part, the path led the way, and Hopper didn't have to say much.

When they came out on the other side, there was a wood line that ran parallel to the field. It was here that Hopper told him to stop: if he hadn't he would have been right on top of it.

"This is it?"

"Yeah."

Logan got out of the cruiser, opened the trunk and pulled out a roll of yellow police tape. Looking down he saw the fallen branch Hopper had dragged there only an hour earlier and used it to anchor the tape. The wind was coming up, and in the distance, he could see the threatening black clouds. He leaned in and picked up the handset.

"Base, you have a copy," Logan asked.

"Go ahead, Chief," Sabrina replied.

"I require 11-44 at my position immediately. I will be dispatching the Duty Officer back to your location with a prisoner. Ensure that you use Land Line to pass the relevant info. Copy?"

"Copy that, Chief."

Sabrina was a professional. She would contact the Coroner and have him moving immediately. Logan hoped that some of the locals with police scanners had missed the commotion, but he doubted it. In no time, word would spread like wildfire.

He climbed back into the cruiser and drove back around front to get on with the business at hand.

As he stepped out of the car, he could feel their eyes upon him. He took a brief glance at Hopper, then walked back up to the porch, and called his Officers into a scrum. He lit up a cigar as they gathered around. Collectively a sense of loss enveloped them, evident on their downturned faces.

"Okay, I'm not going to mince words. We have a gravesite on the west end of the property, and I would speculate that it is the missing boy, Tommy Parkins. However, we haven't confirmed this, so I want everyone to act like professionals and stay focused. I want rotating sentries on the hour at each end of Van Dyke Road. Nobody gets in except police and officials. Who we got out there right now, Mick?"

"Nero and Hill," Mick replied.

"Okay, Mick, you brief them when they come in."

"Okay, Chief."

"Pete, I want you to transfer Hopper into your cruiser and take him into town and keep him in holding until we're done here. Jim West can accompany you. I don't want anybody letting their guard down. Two officers accompany the prisoner at all times."

"Chief, I've got Mr. Wakeman in my cruiser," Kennedy reminded him.

"I know. Cut him loose; he probably wants to get over to Emergency to see his boy. Get him into his truck if he can drive. If not, one officer can accompany him. You can tell him I want his butt planted in a chair in my office tomorrow morning." Logan paused. "Questions?"

"How many men are you going to require for the recovery?" Mick asked.

"Nobody is allowed on the crime scene except me, Mick and the Coroner until we've secured it. Also, I want the house secured. No one enters until I give the word."

"Do we have a motive, Chief?" Corporal Steel asked.

"This pure speculation, folks, but I'm guessing that the motive was sexual in nature. That said, Pete, you get onto the wire and start checking the background on this Hopper, see if he has any priors. Check VICAP, and run him through the Predators database." Logan relit his cigar, which had gone out during the scrum. "Okay, that's it for now. We have our work cut out for us, folks, so the last thing I want to do is be chasing people. Get to work."

The scrum broke off, and Collins began assigning tasks to each officer. Once detailed, they wasted no time getting to work, mindful that they were now a cog in the gears that drove this investigation. As they went about their tasks, there was a looming awareness that a dark chapter in their town's history had been started and things would likely not be the same for some time to come.

Logan watched his officers with a certain amount of pride. Even at this moment in time, he could take comfort in the fact that they were professionals and that the investigation was now their focal point. He crushed out the cigar and took control of the crime scene.

***

CHAPTER 4 - THE EXCAVATION

1

The crime scene was secure. Officers were positioned at either end of the road, and a parameter had been set on the other side of the woods connecting to Donald Wakeman's land. All officers from the Thomasville police department were on site except for Sandra Hardy, who had the onerous task of escorting John Parkins home. There, she waited with John and Olivia Parkins, who understood that the search for their missing son was now out of their hands. John Parkins had wanted to come, but Mick told him in the kindest terms that it would not be possible. Now all they could do was pray that they were wrong.

"How long were you in Homicide, Dave?" Mick asked.

"Ten years." Logan tapped the cigar on the window ledge. "When we get in there, keep your eyes peeled. I only want the three of us there to keep our people from trampling all over the place. If you see anything in the area we are working, don't touch it: let me know, and we'll mark it."

Mick nodded and scanned Van Dyke Road for the coroner's vehicle. It was set to arrive any minute. He must have looked at his watch at least fifteen times since Logan informed him that the three of them would be on the recovery party. Constable Nero had commandeered Mick's vehicle to provide an escort for Donald Wakeman to get to the Emergency and see how Derek was doing. As a result, he sat beside Logan in his cruiser.

Logan told him everything he knew, which was not much more than he'd already put together. He knew Tommy Parkins very well. He had, in fact, gone to school with John Parkins and played Softball with him in the summer. He and wife Nancy had just been to dinner with the family two weeks before Tommy had gone missing. John Parkins was a decent guy, never a wrong word to say about anyone. Tommy was a good kid, too; always polite, even-tempered, and certainly not deserving of this – but then what kid was? Two weeks ago he gave the boy ride into town and now it was almost a certainty that he was buried beneath the soil of Hopper's farm.

Logan was puffing away on one of his rancid cigars. Mick cared a great deal for Logan, but the cigar smoke was something he could do without. He was an ex-smoker, which in Logan's book made him worse than a Jehovah's Witness.

Mick cracked the windows an inch or two, and a relieving flow of fresh air whispered in. Logan just sat there puffing and puffing, not saying a word. Mick wondered what was running through his mind. He was tough to judge sometimes. In one instance Logan could be extremely jovial, but at times severe and dark – not surprisingly right now, really, given the circumstances. Regardless, he had grown to admire the man who replaced Chief Jim Spencer. Most of the townspeople had not taken to an outsider, but Logan came into Thomasville and turned it around by expanding the force and prying more funding out of the always frugal City Hall.

There had been whisperings within the usual sewing circles. Many of his friends insisted that the town council should have appointed Mick to the position of chief, but Mick just smiled and kept silent. On a whim, they may have been willing to place him in power, but they would have scrutinized him for his age. And besides: it really did not fit into his career plans.

On the day Logan took over he invited him into his office for a sit-down. He took a seat as Logan looked over a file that sat on his desk. "You have been on the force for six years? From what I see here you have an exemplary record. I also see that you've taken a couple of extra criminology courses."

"Yes," Mick answered, "and thank you."

Logan looked up from the file, and an unexpected seriousness fell over his face. "Alright, I just wanna make sure that we're on the same level here. I know that some people think you should have been up next in line for Chief Spencer's job. But you and I both know that there is no way that an Officer with less than ten years' service would be considered for such a position. Seeing that I've taken that job, I want to make sure this won't create some kind of an issue between us."

Mick sighed, irritated by the question. "Look, Chief, I'll be frank with you. Even if I were offered the position, I would have turned it down. I plan on staying in Thomasville for a few more years, gaining experience and advancing my education. My career plans are outside of here. So, to answer your question: we're not going to have a problem."

Logan sat quietly for a moment or two. Then he smiled, stood up and stuck out his hand. "My friends call me Dave."

"Mick," he replied shaking his hand vigorously.

"Alright, Mick. On Chief Spencer's recommendations I am appointing you my 2IC – and from now on you're Sgt. Collins, so get that uniform changed up by tomorrow."

From there, things ran very effectively. Logan fought hard to get all of the officers a pay raise; he took the drug problem in the high school serious and gave Mick full rein to organize the officers how he saw fit. There were differences of opinion, but overall, they became friends very fast. The people of Thomasville had warmed up a little as well, but they still turned to Mick when it came to more personal matters such as family disputes.

Logan became the liaison to the town council and Mick the link to the people. This was not to say the Logan did not get out and meet the residents of Thomasville. In that regard he made himself available to all of the community, volunteering at the schools, giving lectures on crime prevention and of course regular duties. When a wildfire threatened to destroy Bob Anderson's farm, Logan had been there. When Filmore Creek overflowed, turning many farms into wetlands, Logan was there with a sandbag in hand.

He quickly gained respect throughout the community, but he was an outsider and always would be.

2

The black station wagon came over the hill, and Logan crushed out his cigar. "Time to go to work."

The wagon pulled up beside them. A yellow circle emblazoned one door, and in that circle printed in large white block letters: Thomasville City Coroner. Logan got out of the cruiser to meet Jeff Henderson, and they spoke briefly as Mick watched. Henderson was also an outsider; he had come to Thomasville six years before.

Mick was preoccupied with the fact in a very short while they would be excavating a young boy's body from the ground. At the moment he craved a cigarette desperately, yet was thankful that Logan smoked those smelly cigars. He didn't know who it was that stated once you've been off cigarettes for thirty days it was over. He still got the urge after meals and on the occasions when he took a drink. Never mind extreme times of stress, which just happened to be now.

"Let's go, Mick." Logan was getting back in the car. "Henderson's gonna follow us."

He put the car in gear and followed the wheel ruts Logan had forged only an hour before. Logan gave verbal directions, but there really was no reason to. The tracks from the cruisers first trip were well entrenched within the field's damp soil.

Logan didn't want to waste any time. The sky had shifted from pastel blue to depressing grey. That meant one thing and one thing only: a storm was coming.

They rounded the bend pushing through Hopper's cornfield, knocking down the few stalks that had not been bulldozed in the first trip.

Mick did not feel well at all. This was not his first exposure to a tragedy, but the circumstances and the child sent a wave of panic through him that was alarming.

Tiny droplets of rain started to fall on the windshield.

"God damn it, not now," Logan griped. "Tell me you packed the modular tent."

"It's in the trunk, but it'll be a bitch to set up." Mick turned on the wipers, and the rain responded by coming down just a little harder.

"It'll be a bigger bitch if we're up to our knees in muck," Logan responded.

He was right of course, but the modular tent was a heavy canvas that weighed better than 200lbs, and Mick worried that he hadn't packed all the aluminum poles. Couple that with what a pain in the ass it could be to put up and take down made Mick hate the old surplus tent.

"There it is," he said, tent leaving his mind. Anxiety throbbed like a dull ache in his stomach. What the fuck am I doing here, he thought, ignoring the obvious reasons. He then wondered what kind of shape the body would be in. You mean Tommy, don't you?

Just ahead a single strip of yellow police tape flapped back and forth in the wind. Mick looked over to see that Logan was staring at him. Does he know what I'm thinking?

"I know this stinks, but what we are about to do is very important," Logan said.

"I hear you," he agreed and wondered if Logan had sensed his anxiety and was propping him up.

They waited a minute for Jeff Henderson to get the coroner vehicle up beside them. The rain intensified, went from a minor sprinkling and ramped right up to an all-out downpour. The three men got out of the vehicles and gathered at the hood of the cruiser.

"Keeps raining like this and we're gonna need a tow truck to get out here," Henderson said, staring up at the sky.

"Bite your tongue, Jeff," Logan spat. "We brought the modular. Probably best we get that set up first."

"I don't think we'll need any picks; the ground looks pretty soft. Are you guys ready?"

"Ready as we're ever gonna be," Mick said.

He left them and went around to the trunk of the cruiser. Logan looked down for a moment, then gave Henderson a glance. At least Mick's words were truthful – and if they did not get moving, he was going to lose his nerve.

This was not Mick's first body – but he knew this kid, and that made it different.

Setting up the tent hadn't been as bad as Mick thought it would be, and thankfully all of the parts were there. The shelter was approximately nine feet at its peak and big enough to park a mid-size car in. The olive drab canvas had a front and rear opening so that it could be joined with other sections. The three buttoned one side – the other they left open to make use of the graying daylight.

Logan took numerous digital photographs of the site before they disturbed it. Not one of these three men could put their professionalism ahead of the fact that they would be unearthing the body of a little boy. Then, finally, with the tent erected, tools laid out, and photographs were taken. Each man grabbed a shovel and prepared to dig. Henderson looked at the two of them, let out a deep sigh, and scooped the first shovelful of dirt.

They worked in shifts. Henderson was first, Logan second, and then Mick. As they dug Henderson told them to move slowly so as not to damage the remains.

"The remains have a name," Mick said, removing another scoop.

"We don't know who it is yet, Mick," Logan interjected and waved his hand at Henderson to leave it alone.

You're only saying that because it's protocol. We know exactly who it is, Dave.

Twenty minutes in and they were all covered in mud up to their waists. Small muddy rivers ran down the tent and into the grave. Mick scooped slower now. He knew it would have been worse had they not erected the mod, but it was still miserable work.

Henderson was just about to take over when he felt a shovel slide across a smooth and slippery surface. He fell back against the edge of the grave and said, "Jesus, I think we're there."

"Stop! Get out of the hole," Henderson ordered. "I'll take it from here."

He climbed out thankfully as Henderson slid in and tossed a shovel out.

"Hand me the bucket and the garden shovel."

At the opening of the shelter lay an arsenal of tools Henderson had brought with him. Logan grabbed the bucket and garden shovel, then handed them down and watched, fascinated.

"I take it you've done this before, Jeff," he said.

Mick held onto the tent's aluminum frame, feeling dizzy. He did not look well at all.

"Murders in Alberta," Henderson said, nodding. "Four women, all strangled and buried in an abandoned strip mine. They never caught the guy." He scooped out one full pail of dirt after another, exposing the cocoon that encased the body.

"Jesus Christ, he put him in a garbage bag," Mick cussed.

"As terrible as that is, he may well have done us a great favor.

I guess that the bag has helped preserve the evidence." Henderson continued cleaning the mud around the black plastic. As he did Logan took each full pail and dumped it just outside the doorway.

Mick watched in a state of shock, wondering whether or not he was going to be able to keep from vomiting. He felt nauseous: not because the sight was particularly gory, but because of the gravity of the situation. He kept telling himself, *Don't puke; they'll look at you differently.*

Logan spotted his 2IC wavering. "You okay, Mick?"

"Yeah; just a bit dizzy."

"There's a plastic bag in my toolbox, Dave. Grab it and hand it to him," Henderson said. "Hang on, Mick. Try not to throw up. This is a crime scene!"

Logan fumbled through the coroner's bag, and Mick tried desperately to keep from puking. He watched Logan pull out the bag and felt his stomach retract, sending a gush up his esophagus. When it got to his mouth, he swallowed hard, forcing it down, but his stomach waged a counterattack and contracted even more.

"Take it," Logan shouted, handing over a clear plastic bag marked medical waste in bold letters.

Mick almost laughed at this – but his stomach beat him to it, and he emptied his lunch directly into the bag in two convulsive heaves. He noted perversely that there were still large pieces of pepperoni from the cold pizza that he'd eaten a couple of hours ago. *Guess I better start chewing more*, he thought, and threw up again, filling the bag to the halfway mark.

Henderson was out of the hole and Logan beside him, rubbing his back, saying, "Get it all out."

He had never been so embarrassed in his life.

Logan handed him a napkin, and he wiped his mouth. Once he was sure that he wasn't going to get sick again, he dropped the paper rag into the bag and tied it up. He stepped out of the tent and into the fresh air. That gave him some relief. Then he felt a hand pat his shoulder.

"I feel like a fucking idiot," he griped.

"Why? Think you're the first guy that ever puked on a crime scene?" Logan whispered.

"No, but..."

"No, but nothing! The important thing is that you didn't contaminate the scene and none of your subordinates saw a thing. Jeff and I won't say a word. Right, Jeff?"

"I'll take my payment in beer," Henderson called, climbing back into the hole.

Mick looked at Logan ashamed, but his boss and friend were reassuring and sympathetic. He hadn't even considered the impact of him vomiting might have had on his subordinates. "Now what?"

"Now you tie off that bag, place it in the trunk of the cruiser and dispose of it when we get back to town," Logan said. "Jeff, I think we should take a five-minute breather."

"I guess a good puke was just what I needed."

"Don't puke again, Mick; I'm all out of bags," Henderson laughed.

Logan smiled a bit. Black humor in what some might have thought inappropriate times often saw police officers through rough moments such as this.

Henderson climbed back out of the grave, wiped his dirty hands on the back of his pants and reached into his breast pocket. He produced a pack of cigarettes, pulled one out and prepared to light up.

"Let's do this over there." Logan pointed to the wood line. They all walked, looking to the ground, careful not to step on anything, and moved under the canopy of trees. "I'd say this is no man's land."

Logan lit up.

Mick heard himself say, "Can I have one of those?"

Logan looked surprised but didn't say anything. Smokers often welcome returning members with open arms. He was no different. Besides, if there ever was a day to start smoking again, this was it.

Henderson shook out a cigarette. Mick took it gratefully. His wife would give him hell for this, he knew – but she wasn't here. He lit up and took a deep draw off the cigarette as his two companions looked on. Strangely it did not taste the same as it had when he was a full-blown smoker. He took a second drag and let out a muffled cough. Just this once, he told himself.

"Kind of reminds you of the tough kid in school, doesn't he, Jeff?" Logan cracked.

"Yeah, Sluggo Collins," Henderson shot back, and at this, they all broke into a fit of giddy laughter. Thankfully, nobody was close enough to see the exchange, but a cop, a firefighter or even a soldier would have understood. They were not making light of their situation, but dealing with it. Laughing was merely a vent to let out the day's accumulated tension.

The laughter broke off into spaced hiccups and then faded altogether. They fell silent: smoking, not making eye contact, all their minds upon the grave and its inhabitant.

Just when it seemed one of them might speak up, Logan stifled that. "We better get back to work." He extinguished the cigar on his boot heel, then reached into his pocket and produced a large pill bottle. "All right, gents, put 'em out and drop your butts in here."

With that done, Logan screwed the lid back on and replaced the bottle in his pocket. He would dispose of its contents later.

Back inside the tent, Henderson climbed into the grave. Ten minutes later he'd uncovered most of the garbage bag as Logan documented it by taking more pictures. Below the body, Henderson had dug two trenches.

Mick watched as all this took place. He felt out of place, inadequate.

"Mick, I have a job for you to do," Henderson said.

"What," he asked, eager to redeem himself.

"Go to the wagon. In the back there's an old wooden box; inside you'll see some straps. Bring them back here, and then I want you to go back with Dave and get the mobile gurney. You're gonna have to help him with that, Dave."

As Mick set out to get the straps, Logan spotted a small hand protruding from the bag. A chill licked up his spine.

As if Henderson had read Logan's mind, he carefully reached up and tucked the hand back inside the bag and out of sight.

The shape of the body was easy to define beneath the black plastic cocoon. If there were any doubts, they had been expelled now: they had unearthed a child.

Logan did not know Tommy Parkins that well, but what he did know was that he was a boy who was very outgoing and friendly. Most of what he'd learned was on the fly as they searched and he was filled in by everyone who knew the boy. Thanks to his time in Homicide, he had developed a skill for building a relationship with victims. In the course of an investigation, you learned about them through family and friends. So he knew that Tommy Parkins loved baseball and fishing, that his favorite color was blue, his favorite meal was spaghetti and that he wanted to join the army when he grew up. It helped him keep perspective when he investigated a murder, and it also gave closure when he cleared a case – but not all cases got cleared. In Logan's mind, three names were unresolved, and they still haunted him.

Behind him, there was the 'schloosh schloosh' sound of Mick trudging back through the muck with the straps over his shoulder. He pushed into the tent, past Logan. "Here you go." He handed them down to Henderson. "What are you doing, Jeff?"

Henderson took the straps. "You boys go get the gurney, and I'll show you."

Mick and Logan went back to the car to remove the gurney. Considering the muddy ground, both of them knew that they would be carrying it rather than wheeling it. On top, there was a body-bag wrapped in cellophane ready for use. Henderson had readied this before leaving the mortuary. Each man picked up an end and carried it back to the tent where Henderson waited.

"Stop right there in the doorway, gents," he said, stepping up to the gurney. He unfolded, then unzipped the body bag as the two officers looked into the tent and studied what he had done. The garbage bag was unearthed entirely, and though they had kept most of the rain at bay, there were still puddles forming around its outer edges. The straps Mick had dropped off were now placed neatly under the bag in a parallel fashion and extended upward to the sides of the grave where they could be handled easily. They had been set at specific points on the body where it was unlikely to buckle.

"That's why you are digging those holes under there," Logan said.

"Yep." Henderson turned to Mick. "Now listen, are you going to be up to this?"

"I think I'll be okay," Mick replied.

"That's not good enough." His tone was stern. "If you're not up to it, tell me now. I don't want this body dropped."

"You have my word. Tell me what I have to do."

Henderson explained the chore they were about to carry out was a five-man procedure. One man was to be positioned on each strap, bringing up the slack as the fifth man steadied the body and removed it from the hole. As Henderson explained earlier, he had employed this exercise while unearthing the victims of a serial killer. The principle was similar to lowering a casket into the ground – though in reverse. In this case, Mick and Logan would be pulling double duty on the straps while Henderson steadied the body. The fact they were lifting the body of a small boy weighing approximately eighty-five pounds made the task at hand a little easier, at least physically.

Henderson jumped back into the hole, positioned himself at the head of the grave, and gave his first order. "Okay, now start taking up the slack: but slowly."

Mick and Logan stood with two straps each bundled into one hand and used their free hands to bring up the slack. They both fixated on the other's movements, trying to move in unison against the stick grasp of the muck. There was the sound of suction as the muddy ground struggled to hold its grip on the plastic bag and its contents, followed by a pop as the plastic pulled away from the vacuum.

It was working.

Logan and Mick continued holding each other's gaze, ensuring what they did was in total harmony. As the body was slowly raised, Henderson moved and adjusted himself to accommodate for any potential shifting. To add to the discomfort, Mick and Logan were both hunched over to keep from brushing against the canvas walls of the tent.

All around, the rain tapped on the canvas, beating like a funeral drum.

"Almost done, guys," Henderson assured as the body crested the edge of the grave. It was mere inches from each of their hands. The sickening feel of wet plastic grazed both man's knuckles, but they held the strapping firmly. Logan spied a protruding fingertip from the corner of his eye and silently prayed that Mick could not.

"Stand fast!" Henderson released his grip, checking the stability and getting ready to make his next move. Satisfied, he climbed out of the grave and adjusted the stretcher just outside the tent. "Okay, now carefully bring the body out of the doorway."

They moved gracefully, like two soldiers doing a slow march. Mick held his breath almost the entire way, not wanting to falter or stumble. When they reached their destination, he let out of sigh of relief. Simultaneously, Henderson adjusted the body bag intended to cocoon the remains and any potential crime scene evidence.

"Okay, put him down."

They lowered him onto the gurney and at Henderson's urging stepped away. As the coroner went about his business, Logan looked around perplexed. Something was different, but it couldn't put his finger on it.

"The rain stopped," Mick pointed out like some miracle had suddenly transpired unnoticed.

A nearby sparrow chirped. The world was starting to restore itself. Both Mick and Logan began to to feel a little better – but Henderson was quick to put a damper on that.

"Mick, you knew Tommy Parkins pretty well. Is that correct?" Henderson asked.

"Yes," Mick replied.

"Could you positively identify him?"

"Shouldn't that be done by the Parkins family?" Logan interjected.

"Normally yes, but I would like to get him cleaned up before the family has to view him," Henderson replied. "Those poor folks are going to have enough to deal with."

"I can identify him, Jeff," Mick said. "Go ahead."

Henderson reached in his pocket and pulled out a small jackknife, then sliced through the plastic. As he pulled back the thin membrane a wave of disbelief rippled through all of them.

His skin color was pale, blue. His eyes were still wide open, clouded and grey, holding onto the last moments of his life. His mouth was twisted into a grimace that evoked pain or surprise, and his now visible right hand was hooked into a claw. Even Henderson, who worked extensively with the dead, was taken aback.

"Is it him?"

Is this really him? Little Tommy, Mick wondered as he tried to marry this tortured face with the vibrant, outgoing kid he'd grown to know and like. This didn't look like a child at all, but a sculpted piece of wood without a soul. *Is this really John and Olivia's Tommy? Tommy, the leading pitcher for the Thomasville Coyotes? My God, his face. Little boys aren't supposed to look like that.* Mick brought his hand up to his mouth, his eyes wide.

"Mick," Logan said softly.

"It's him," he finally mumbled.

"Good enough." Henderson reached past him and zipped up the body bag.

A moment of silence passed between the three men. Ten seconds of respect to acknowledge the life of a boy who was struck down for some twisted reason. That was how Mick would remember it for the rest of his days.

In the chilly afternoon air, they looked upon one another, each understanding that the vigil must close.

Henderson spoke first. "Let's get him into the wagon and get out of here."

Logan placed a hand on Mick's shoulder and squeezed. "The tent stays in place. Have Westy seal the area off until we can finish a complete sweep tomorrow morning."

Perched on a branch, the black raven watched in stealth with great interest, while the men loaded into their vehicles and began the trip back to the main road. It had scrutinized them from the very beginning. Anger rippled through it: it had been deceived. When the vehicles rumbled to life, it spread its wings and took to the sky. It flew north, away from the farm to a place it often went.

They mounted the steps to John Parkins porch side by side without a single word passing between them. This was, by far, the worst part of a police officer's job. How many times had Logan come to somebody's home with bad news?

Too many.

Looming there in the doorway like the grim reaper he would ask if he could come in and the speech would always be the same. "I'm afraid I have some bad news," he'd always start. There were usually tears, and they always wanted to know something personal. *"Did they suffer? Did they speak to you or say anything?"* Or the ultimate question, the one Logan couldn't answer: *"Why did this happen?"*

There was no easy way to answer any of these questions, and in most cases, the most definitive reply he would give was, "I don't know."

Mick at his side, Logan knocked.

Constable Hardy opened the door, just behind her stood Olivia Parkins. She was a small woman, slightly overweight with a wholesome attractiveness. Yet none of that was apparent now. Her eyes were puffy and blue from the last three sleepless nights, and she had lost weight. When she saw them, her face knotted up. She knew instantly that her baby was never coming home.

She screamed, "No!" They stood there like Death incarnate, and she shrank away in a fit of spastic sobs. "No! No! No!"

John Parkins moved around his wife and into the doorway, looking like a man who had been sucker punched. He already knew the answer to the question he was going to ask, but he asked it anyway. "Please tell me my boy's alive."

"I'm so sorry, John," Mick answered, and there was a hitch in his throat.

Parkins smashed his massive fist against the door jamb, and his wife wailed even harder. A single tear spilled out of his right eye and tracked silently down his cheek.

"Where did you find him?"

"I think you better sit down, John," Logan said, placing a hand lightly on his shoulder.

Parkins walked over to the white wicker deck chair which had sat on his porch for the better part of eight years. Meanwhile, Hardy held Olivia Parkins in her arms and tried to console her.

"Tommy! No! Tommy! My baby! My baby!"

Logan began to explain as John sat there in a malaise of disbelief. Soon Olivia's cries quieted until they became only an echoing background of weeping. John just sat there nodding over and over, his world unraveling.

***

CHAPTER 5 - REVELATIONS

1

A headache that started out as a dull throb was now pounding fiercely behind Logan's eyes. The worst was in the left eye: it felt as if a tiny hand was alternately squeezing and releasing his optic nerve. The day had been long, and the autopsy of Tommy Parkins had been three hours of grueling anguish. He was ready for a stiff rye and coke. Unfortunately, he still had paperwork to deal with and there was Hopper.

At first, he thought of just leaving him in the cell for the night, but he couldn't do that. Right now Stephen Hopper was in a state of mind where he was ready to confess everything, and Kennedy had informed him that Hopper still didn't want a lawyer. With time his attitude might change so this would have to be dealt with tonight.

He dropped Mick off at home right after they delivered the bad news to the Parkins family. Poor Mick had had a rough day and looked thankful that he would not have to attend the autopsy. Security of the crime scene had been left to the senior corporal, and the investigation would resume in the morning.

The autopsy quickly determined that Tommy Parkins had died as a result of asphyxiation. Close examination revealed marks on his neck consistent with strangulation. Once the cause of death was determined, Logan called it a day. Henderson would investigate further and have more details, but some of the forensics would take time. In the meantime, he would focus on getting Hopper's confession.

When he got back to the station, eight of his officers waited patiently in the staff room for further orders. He went to the far side of the room and poured himself a cup of coffee. After a sip, he gave out orders and delegated shifts that would be staffed over the next twenty-four hours. For now, everything was off the cuff; there would be time to become more officially organized later.

Kennedy came up to him after the main bustle subsided and secretly Logan thought, I wonder what good news Peter Rabbit has got for me now?

Kennedy's nervousness made him an easy target for scrutiny.

"Chief?"

"What is it, Pete?" Logan rubbed his temples.

"It's Hopper. He wants to talk to you as soon as possible."

"What about?" Already Logan would bet his life that Hopper had done an about face and wanted a lawyer. Fuck him, we did everything by the numbers. He gets a lawyer, I can go home and get rid of this headache.

"He won't tell me anything. Just says he needs to talk to you."

"Where have you got him?"

"He's in a cell right now."

"Alright, put him in the main interview room." Logan reached into his desk drawer and pulled out a large bottle of aspirin. Popping four into his mouth he crunched them between his teeth, chased them with coffee, and mumbled over their vile bitterness.

Then I want you to do something for me."

"What's that, Chief?"

"Go home and get some rest. I want you back here tomorrow morning at six AM sharp. We're gonna have a long day ahead of us, and I want you well rested."

Logan got up and headed for the confection machine in the hall. He wasn't particularly hungry but wanted to get some food on top of the aspirin. Debating between a bag of corn chips and an apple fritter he considered what it was that Hopper wanted. He swallowed two more aspirin and decided on the fritter. He thumbed the button, slid the machine's plastic door open, removed his treat, peeled back the cellophane and bit into it, hoping it wouldn't taste as devoid of flavor as it looked. His hopes were instantly dashed.

He sat down chewing mechanically and considered how he was going to approach Hopper. There was already video equipment set up in the room, so he didn't have to worry about documenting the interview. Young Kennedy, for all his bumbling, took it upon himself to do that while the main arm of the investigation and body recovery were underway. Logan chastised himself privately for being irritated with the young officer. He was a good cop; just inexperienced and a little fidgety.

He popped the last of the apple fritter into his mouth. There was still a lot of work to be done.

As he walked down the corridor, his mind turned again to Hopper. He punched the combination on the cellblock door, opened it, and then proceeded down to the main interview room. Before opening the door, he peeked through the plate glass and saw the big man sitting there staring down at the table. Kennedy was behind him, standing guard.

He recited tonight's combination code for the interview room: 46921. When he opened the door, Hopper jumped a little, and then settled back in his chair when he saw it was Logan.

"Okay, Constable, I got this."

"Alright, Chief." Kennedy moved toward the exit. Logan caught him by the arm as he passed.

"Good work today, Pete. Thanks for the back-up. Before you leave, send Don Steel down here. Tell him to set up in observation."

"You got it, Chief." Kennedy gave him a smile and went on his way.

Logan watched the door close then turned to back toward the prisoner. "What's on your mind, Hopper?"

2

Perched in a tree, its bulbous eyes glazed over, resembling poached eggs. Often when it meditated, it would climb to a high place and melt in with its surroundings. To a passerby, it looked more like a grey ash statue carved into the tree than a living entity.

Below, a big buck grazed a nearby bush, oblivious to the danger lurking above.

Will he give in, it asked itself. Will the human give in? It was not so much a question as it was an observation. Humans were pitiful creatures that lacked discipline. The answer was obvious.

The man named Hopper would crumble – and then the hunter would come.

These thoughts infuriated it.

For the first time in years, it truly felt free, able to feed unrestrained and run in the night. This feeding ground was one of many, but this was where the food was delivered. Now that foolish human had ruined everything. It understood that this would not last forever, but that did not soothe its rage. When the hunter came, it would be forced to move on again. It did not like being a nomad, did not like running.

The hunter is relentless, his heart filled with revenge. He will not stop until one of us is dead.

It decided to stay, for a while at least, and see what the Hopper man would do. It had grown tired of running, and nothing would give it more satisfaction than tearing the hunter's beating heart from his chest and eating it before him. As for Hopper; his survival depended on how he conducted himself. If he kept quiet perhaps it would spare him.

The glaze melted from its bulbous eyes as its senses came back to life. The big buck had wandered away sometime in the intermittent period.

The creature blinked. Its deep black eyes reflected the forest landscape lit by a pale moon. It unfurled its talon fingers and pulled in the night air through the nostrils of its sunken nose. Not far away something moved through the underbrush.

Hunger clouded its reasoning, took control as its bones and muscles began to twitch and pulse in metamorphosis. It changed from its pure-form into a hybrid of predator that had never run in these woods. If left unfed the hunger would turn to pain and that would leave it irrational and vulnerable. It would think of the hunter later: it was time to feed.

The black bear was following the scent of the deer and never saw the predator coming from its right flank. It had hunted this area for over three years since leaving its mother's side and was threatened only by man. It was the master of this territory. It was also under its hunger's control, focused purely on feeding. So when it turned toward the sound of feet thumping along the forest floor, it was too late.

As it turned to look, a monster not of this place tore through its matted fur and opened its throat with one fell swoop. As the black bear lay on its side, lifeblood running out, the creature changed form and let out a bone-chilling shriek that drove a stake of fear right through the bear's heart.

Then, with razor precision, it tore open the bear's belly and began to feed.

"I want some things," Hopper said flatly, not making eye contact.

Logan sat down perplexed. "What?"

"I want them tonight." He was not asking but telling.

Logan felt his emotions take hold. The thumping behind his eye amplified, causing him to twitch. His initial plan to come off as an understanding figure to ease Hopper into a confession fizzled.

Hopper's eyes darted back and forth between the table and Logan's face. He was scared, and he had a right to be. Over the years Logan had developed a scowl meant to strike fear into the heart of anyone who might challenge his authority. To him it was theater, but it was convincing, and he had used it more than once. This was different though because Logan really was restraining himself from beating Hopper to a bloody pulp.

For better than two minutes they sat with their eyes locked until Hopper relented.

Logan continued to stare.

"I'll be right back."

He got up from the table and left the room.

Marching through the main staff room, he could feel Nero and Findlay stop abruptly and watch him as he entered his office. There he grabbed a directory and a remote phone. They must have seen it in his face because now everyone stood motionless gawking as he strutted back toward the interview room.

He stopped and wheeled around.

"What the hell is everyone looking at?" he roared. "Get back to work!"

Then there was a flurry of activity. Nero grabbed the phone to make an unintended call, another poked into a stack of files.

Logan punched the combination in for the second time that night and stormed into the interview room. The door hadn't quite closed behind him when he fired the phone book across the table. It thumped Hopper in the chest. Before he had a chance to respond Logan lunged forward and slammed the remote phone down hard enough to break it.

Hopper yelped.

"Call a lawyer," Logan spat.

"What?"

"I said call yourself a lawyer! If you can't afford one, I'll have the public defender here within the hour." Logan leaned in close now.

"What is this?"

"I'm doing you a favor. Now call," Logan thundered, bits of spittle and apple fritter dislodged from his teeth, spraying onto Hopper's face.

"I don't want to call a lawyer. I want to talk to you about —"

"Demands," Logan cut off. "Who in the name of sweet fuck are you to make demands? You've got some nerve, you. I just spent an afternoon digging up the body of a little boy you murdered!"

Hopper's voice was mechanical, low. "I don't want much."

Logan leaned in even closer, purposely aggressive. "I don't care what you want! Let me explain something to you. You nailed your ass to the floorboards when you gave up your right to remain silent and showed me where the body was. I have a witness who saw you bury the body. I've got another witness who you confessed to. I guess that the DNA evidence alone would be enough to convict you."

"I'll sign a confession." Hopper was shaking.

"I don't need your confession. You confessed the minute you showed me where the body was." He picked up the phone and offered it across the table. "Last chance."

Hopper shook his head.

"Fine, let's go."

"Where?"

"Back to your cell, Hopper."

Logan uncuffed him from the table and led him from the interview room. He remained quiet, only staring down at the rubberized floor. When they got to the cell, he went in without a word. Logan began to get a strange vibe off of him. Quietly he sat down on the bunk as the cell door slid shut and locked with an audible **shah-clink**.

Logan walked back up the corridor ready to push the buzzer when he heard Hopper murmur something. It took a second for him to process, and he stood frozen, turning the two words over in his mind, his finger an inch from the buzzer.

"There's more," Hopper had said.

Logan turned and walked back to the cell. "What did you say?"

"Right to remain silent." And Hopper looked up at him, smiling.

"Did you say there's more?"

Now Hopper had the upper hand, and he savored it.

The big burly cop held onto the bars, his knuckles whitening, a confused look of miscalculation on his face.

"Maybe I will call that lawyer."

Logan mentally chastised himself. Why had allowed his emotions to take over? What did this mean? More what? It could be almost anything. It could mean that he was involved in a kiddie porn ring. It could mean that he had more to confess – but Logan was worried about the other possibilities. Maybe he had an accomplice. Or worse! More bodies.

Logan relaxed his grip and tried to take control of the situation.

"Okay, Hopper, I was a bit hasty. What did you say?"

"Maybe it's time you shut your mouth and listened. I want some things, and until I get them, I am going to leave you in suspense." Logan opened his mouth to say something but Hopper cut him off. "You yell at me one more time, and I go mute."

4

They were back in the interview room sitting across from one another. Watching through the one-way glass was Corporal Steel. Logan had given him a brief overview of the situation after taking Hopper back to the room. From the corner the digital video camera blinked, recording everything.

"Ready to listen," Hopper asked.

"I'm all ears." Logan felt foolish, but he pushed that away. His bruised ego was the least of his worries now. It was game time.

"First thing I need is a smoke," Hopper said.

Logan looked at the [No Smoking Sign], then toward the two-way glass. "What kind of cigarettes do you smoke?"

"I'll need a carton of Pall Malls, but in the meantime, I'll take two of anything from one of your officers."

Steel bolted out into the staff room. "I need a couple cigarettes right now! And… shit, something to use as an ashtray." Only a few officers in the detachment smoked.

Constable Larson stepped up and pulled out a pack of home-rolled cigarettes. Steel took two and grabbed a soda can out of the recycle bin. No one had smoked in this building for over five years.

"Somebody head down to the store and buy a carton of Pall Malls, then bring them to me," he said and sprinted back toward the holding wing.

There was a knock at the door to the interview room. Logan opened it and took the cigarettes from Steel. He didn't bother to ask about the carton; he already knew that Steel was on it.

Hopper took a cigarette and put it between his teeth as Logan reached across and lit it for him. He inhaled, held it for a second, and then exhaled. "These taste like shit."

"Get on with it, Hopper." Logan was losing his patience.

"Alright." Hopper took another drag and exhaled. "I want four things."

"I'm listening."

"I want a bible, a crucifix, and unlimited cigarettes. I smoke about a pack and a half a day. I expect I'll be outdoors a lot so having a smoke shouldn't be an issue."

"You said four things."

"Yeah, that's right. The last thing is that I deal only with you. No one else."

"Little late to turn to God, isn't it?"

"Don't mock me, asshole," Hopper hissed. "I can always call a lawyer."

"Okay, I can get you those things, but how do I know you're not playing games to get special treatment? I'll need some kind of insurance."

"Give me those things, and I'll start talking tonight."

"I'll give you half tonight, and when I've verified you're not shooting me a line I'll give you the rest tomorrow." Logan had used this tactic on many other prisoners throughout his career. Something was chewing the fat man up, and he latched onto that vulnerability to regain the ground he had lost.

Hopper's eyes narrowed. He said, "Okay, the Bible and the crucifix. When they're delivered, I'll start talking."

Logan reached across the table and snatched up the cigarette. "Alright, I'll take this then. Your cigarettes will be delivered when I've determined you're not full of shit."

"Alright, the bible and the cigarettes."

"One other thing. You won't be able to smoke in here after tonight or in your cell. We will have to make other arrangements."

Ten minutes later there was a knock behind him, and he got up to meet Steel at the door. In his hand, he held a bible and on top of it a new carton of Pall Mall cigarettes. "Thanks, Don," he said and closed the door again.

Steel returned to his seat on the other side of the two-way mirror.

Constable Sandra Hardy came into the observation room. "How's it going?"

"You aren't going to believe this, Sandy," Steel said, "but I think this Hopper guy is a serial killer."

"Oh my God," Hardy whispered.

Hardy and Steel had been sleeping together for almost a year. No one in the detachment knew about it, except Steel's best friend, Jim West. They had kept it to themselves for professional reasons, and for fear that the Chief would separate them.

She absently placed a hand on his shoulder when another officer entered the observation room. It was Constable Larson. Everyone called him Oddball. Logan had coined the nickname after Donald Sutherland from the movie Kelly's Heroes. Strangely, Logan could not understand that his younger officers had no idea who Oddball was or that Clint Eastwood had once been a young, vibrant action movie star. Nevertheless, Oddball stuck, and no one in the detachment called him by his first name – which happened to be Keith.

"Hey, any progress?" Oddball asked.

Hardy slowly removed her hand from Steel's shoulder.

"Things are just warming up," Steel said.

5

Mick leaned over and knocked the phone off the night table. He had been dreaming about the day's events – except in his dream he had vomited all over the crime scene, and Logan fired him on the spot.

"Fuck," he cursed the darkness, reaching around blindly for the cordless phone. His hand touched the receiver, and he pushed the talk button as he brought it to his ear. "Hello?"

"Mick." It was Logan. "You gotta come back in."

"What's up?" he asked, sitting up and wiping his eyes.

"We've got more digging to do."

He sat there quietly trying to sort out what he had just heard.

More digging? Did we miss something?

"What are you saying, Dave?"

"There are more bodies. A lot more. Get in here as fast as you can and bring a change of clothes. We're gonna be at this a while." Logan's tone was uneasy, even rattled.

"I'll be there as quick as I can." He set the phone back in its cradle.

"What's going on, Hon," his wife, Nancy, murmured, half-asleep.

He leaned into her and ran his hands over the warmth of her shoulders beneath the covers. He kissed her temple. "I gotta go back to work. Do you want me to call and wake you up?"

"Okay, sweetheart."

Mick doubted she would even remember this. She slept like a log, and occasionally she snored.

He kissed her temple again, got up and went to the closet to grab a change of clothes and a fresh uniform.

More digging, his mind hammered. *More bodies? From where?*

***

CHAPTER 6 - HOPPER'S BASEMENT

1

The SPCA came that afternoon and cleared the small barn where Hopper kept a pig and a dozen chickens. The animals were in good health, exhibiting no signs of abuse or neglect. Following this, the small livestock barn was searched and sealed by Corporal West and Constable Findlay. The equipment Hopper used for harvesting his crop was stored off-site in a building rented from another farmer named Joel Hunt. The Thomasville Police intended on visiting this building, but Logan speculated there would not be much there in the way of evidence. A Co-op of farmers shared the large aluminum hut, which resembled an old airplane hangar. Among those farmers was Donald Wakeman.

Mick and Logan went out there alone that night to conduct a search of the house for anything that would help them with the investigation. Both were tired from the day's events, but this was only the beginning of many sleepless nights to come.

Mick carried a digital video camera, and as they walked through the house, he recorded everything. At first glance, it seemed a normal enough dwelling for a man in his mid-fifties. Dirty dishes sat in the sink, laundry was strewn about the single bedroom, and yellow stains surrounded the base of the toilet bowl. There was no evidence of murder or deviance in the main level of the house.

The cellar was another story altogether.

Mick tried to flip on the cellar light, but the old switch just clicked over, giving way to mute blackness. "Must be a breaker or a bulb out," he remarked. He tried to keep the uneasiness from his voice, but anxiety already pulsed through him.

He turned on the camera's LED and used it to light the way, and as they descended the narrow stairway, they were assaulted by a vile smell that caused the two of them to simultaneously gag. Covering their mouths and expecting the worst, they continued down the treacherous steps into the darkness. The combined white light from the camera and a big black mag-lite carried by Logan unveiled the inches of the dank underground room as they continued on toward the smell of death and decay.

"There's the source of the stink," Logan announced as the beam of his light illuminated the remains of a slaughtered pig laid out on a large blue tarp a few feet from the base of the staircase. It was gutted and left to spoil on the basement floor. Maggots squirmed within its eye sockets, and bluebottle flies buzzed about ready to deposit more offspring.

"Why would he leave it to rot?" Mick asked, simultaneously opening the freezer and praying it would not contain any surprises. Inside was a stew of blood, water, rotted vegetables, and decomposing meat. The smell that wafted out was worse than the pig; foul and acrid. "God, that's fucking ripe." He gagged and closed it quickly to seal off the stench.

Logan turned the light into the far corner of the basement, where he saw a glint of silver next to the hot water tank. He left Mick standing by the freezer swatting away the flies. As he stepped closer and the beam of light from his torch grew nearer, it became clear what it was. Using a pen, he lifted a three-foot length of chain that had been bolted to one of the legs of the hot water tank.

"I guess he had other things on his mind."

At the end of the chain was a set of cheap handcuffs. He wondered if the young victims had known then what their fate was going to be. Then he set the chain back on the cold floor. "Document this."

Mick moved away from the freezer and shot video of the chain and handcuff. He imagined poor Tommy hooked there like a dog at the mercy of the ghoul who lived here. It was almost more than he could take, but there was much more to come.

He followed Logan. His shoe grazed the chain. It clinked, and Mick felt sudden odd remorse. Strange as it might seem, he felt as though he had disturbed some artifact of the dead.

Logan spotted the big steel door at the other end of the basement and began moving toward it. It was slightly ajar, but it still blocked their line of sight to whatever dark secrets it confined. Both men wanted to know but sought the answers with gloomy trepidation as to the horrors of this modern-day dungeon.

Logan reached it first and pushed the big door with the butt of his flashlight. It swung open on rusty hinges.

What the two officers were faced with was a nightmare.

Formerly it had been a passage to a cold storage room built to keep preserves and vegetables in a time when freezers were a luxury. Now it had been used for something dark and ugly. Inside the room stood a metal table, once for welding and steelwork, now transformed by Hopper into a grisly tool of torture. The cold steel had a coat of battle grey paint and on the two front legs shackles had been welded.

Logan shone the light into the room as he stepped inside to examine the table. A second set of shackles, each attached to a foot of chain were welded to the far edge of the table, giving it the appearance of a 17th Century torture rack. There was just enough room to accommodate the table, the victim, and the torturer. Once inside, Hopper would have been able to close the door behind him. Logan presumed that is what he did because Hopper had doubled the insulation on the walls, making the compartment soundproof to stifle the screams of his victims.

"Oh man," Mick groaned, looking over Logan's shoulder. Set up on the shelves were stacks of duct tape and a bottle of clear liquid which they could only assume was a lubricant of some sort. "What kind of man does this to a kid?"

"We're not dealing with a man." Logan backed out of the room, careful not to touch anything. "We're dealing with a monster."

With the camera focused on Logan Mick observed vulnerabilities he had never seen before. Logan was doing some personal inventory and marrying it up to the madness in this basement. Mick watched his friend with guilty fascination. *He's blaming himself for this. He isn't saying it, but he doesn't have to.*

Feeling Mick's gaze, Logan said, "Go in there and document it."

He went into the room, leaving Logan there staring off into space. This whole thing, so surreal, was quickly taking its toll.

"How the hell could this have happened?" he muttered, unaware he'd said the words aloud, then added, "How did I let this happen?"

Hearing this, Mick finished documenting the cold storage room, placed the camera on pause and came back out into the main part of the basement. "We didn't know, Dave. How could we have? This guy Hopper is a ghost; he has no priors. Certainly, nothing that could link him to this."

Logan just looked through him, searching for some rhyme or reason to the mayhem that had taken place here. He was not just some hick cop: he had cut his teeth as a homicide detective and seen some pretty heinous things – but this had happened right under their noses. Even worse, they hadn't even begun the process of unearthing the dark secrets Hopper's cornfield held.

Caught in a malaise of self-deprecation, Logan stared into the abyss of 'what if?'

Mick had seen this look before, and it scared him.

Many years ago, under the command of Chief Spencer, a young patrol officer named Michael Sedgwick came upon the scene of an overturned car. Inside the car was a woman who was banged up, but conscious. Sedgwick had tried to free her, but the damage to the vehicle had locked her in tight. He called for emergency services and waited with her while the fire department was dispatched with the necessary tools to cut her out.

He saw the gasoline on the roadway and brought his fire extinguisher out, just in case. While they waited, they talked and joked, and it seemed that it was only a matter of time before she would be on our way to the emergency room in the back of an ambulance. Neither Sedgwick nor the trapped woman could see the hot wires that ran from the brake lights directly to the battery begin to short out and spark.

Sedgwick was just about to ask her if she had any kids when the vapors from the gasoline ignited. Within seconds, the car was engulfed. He desperately tried to free her as she screamed – but his fire extinguisher was no match for the fury of the gasoline fire.

When the fire department came on the scene, the overturned car was still burning. Only the mummified, charred remnants of the woman remained. Sedgwick had third-degree burns on his hands. His physical wounds would heal, but the internal ones never did.

He became introverted, and one day three months later he pulled his patrol car over onto a road that was just outside of town and wrote a suicide note. In it, he apologized to the family of the woman, to his girlfriend and to his parents. He then walked into a grain field and shot himself in the head.

Mick never forgot the look Sedgwick had on his face after the incident. It was a sad self-accusatory look. He was sure he saw a hint of that in Logan's eyes now. He would not say anything about this to anyone, but he would watch his friend carefully.

"How long," Logan whispered.

"How long what," Mick asked.

"How long did it go on before the bastard finally ended the misery?"

"Come on, Dave. Let's get out of here."

They left the basement and went back out to the front porch where Corporal West was standing guard. The big gangly corporal had already started losing his hair at twenty-eight, and towering six foot four he was a giant of a man, but his voice was soothing and thoughtful.

"All finished?" asked West.

Logan lit up a cigar staring gravely across Van Dyke Road.

"We're done for tonight, Jim," Mick replied and added, "What time does your relief get here?"

"We switch up after midnight, Sarge." He peered at the Chief, puzzled.

"Okay. I don't have to tell you how important security is, but if anyone goes back into that cornfield, I want you to call in." Mick patted the big officer on the shoulder. "Any questions?"

"Is it true? Is this guy a serial killer?"

"We haven't determined that yet, but it is looking quite possible."

Obviously West and Steel had been talking, but then most of the officers in the detachment were engrossed in speculation about the case. It was what cops did.

Logan took another puff on the cigar, walked down the steps toward the cruiser. Without looking back, he said, "Keep up the good work, Westy. Keep this place secure."

"Wilco that, Chief."

Logan crushed out the cigar, and just as Mick got into the driver seat, he turned and said, "This is bigger than us, Mick. We're going to need help from outside."

The next day Hopper confirmed their worst fears and led them to a burial site located at the west end of his cornfield. He was then ushered back to the cruiser while Logan, Mick, and Henderson unearthed another victim. This kid was older than the Parkins boy. Based on the bone structure, Henderson speculated that he was fifteen or sixteen. The body was horribly decomposed: DNA testing was the only way they'd be able to confirm his identity.

As the second victim was brought out of the cornfield, they got a call from a task force out of the city of Winnipeg. The chief investigator, Ron Pearson, asked a bunch of questions. How many victims were there? What was the sex and age of the victims? Logan wasn't sure yet, but a decision was made to have Hopper mark the grave sites.

His memory was outstanding as he led the officers of Thomasville from one location to another. They marked each position with a survey stake, photographed it and followed him to the next. Throughout this Hopper was without emotion, and by the end of the following day, all of his demands were met. Unlimited cigarettes, a bible, a crucifix and he spoke to no one but Logan.

By nightfall, Detective Pearson and his partner Kurt Cooper arrived at the Brandon Airport where they were met by Mick and Constable Frank Nero. Pearson and Cooper rented a vehicle and Mick rode along, bringing them up to speed as they drove.

"He's marked sixteen graves so far. We have unearthed two of the victims, but our coroner has requested help from the University's forensic department. They are dispatching a team that should be here by morning," Mick told them.

"This sounds like our guy," Cooper said.

"Yeah, it does," Pearson agreed.

"How many missing boys are we talking about?" Mick asked.

Pearson looked at his partner for a moment. "At present, we have eleven missing boys on our books, but the number could be much higher. These kids disappear off the map without anyone really knowing."

"Some have parents that aren't exactly model citizens. You know the type: drug addicts, abusers – not exactly candidates for Parent of the Year. Other kids come from long distances and when they arrive in the city many turn to prostitution or become a part of the homeless community," Cooper added.

"So chances are some of the victims might not be on your radar." Mick shook his head.

"Yeah, and looks like your perp didn't shit where he ate – up until recently, anyway." Pearson smiled. "A lucky break for us."

Mick didn't respond to this. Pearson knew immediately that his comment was not well-received. From that point, he remained quiet.

3

Logan was waiting for them at the front of the Police Station. He had stepped out front for a cigar, but the primary purpose was to meet the two Detectives and make them feel welcome.

"Dave Logan." He put out his hand.

"Hello, Dave. I'm Ron Pearson; this is my partner, Kurt Cooper."

"Everyone calls me Coop," The Detective shook Logan's hand.

Logan was leading them in now. "Alright, Ron, Coop, we are pretty relaxed around here. We've set you up in the corner of the detachment main squad room, and I'm having my officers bring in some dividers so that you guys can work with semi-privacy."

"You were saying on the phone that he won't talk to anyone but you. Would you mind if I took a crack at him?" Pearson asked.

This was a play Logan understood; Pearson didn't want his investigation taken over by some small-town cop. He really didn't feel one way or the other about it.

"Ron, if you want to take a shot at him, I have no issue whatsoever, but be assured that if that doesn't work my department will be forthcoming with everything you need."

"We're not in the business of stepping on people's dicks." Mick smiled, but there was a hint of sarcasm in his tone.

"Look, I apologize. I'm not here to try and push anyone around. I think we all want the same thing, so let me just say there will be no political maneuvering on our part. We want to work with you guys," Pearson said sincerely.

Logan looked from Pearson to Mick and wondered what had caused the friction. It didn't matter: they had to work together. "Alright. Let's go into my office, bring you guys up to speed – then we'll get started."

4

Spread out on the table were eleven photos of missing boys. Hopper did not look at them; nor did he look at Detective Pearson. Instead, he stared at the two-way mirror which he knew Logan was standing behind.

"Do you recognize any of these boys?" Pearson asked.

At first, Hopper said nothing – he just glared at the mirror. But then he broke his silence he spoke as if Pearson wasn't even in the room. "I know you're there, Chief Logan. We had a deal. If you want to break that deal, keep this fuckwad yapping at me, and I will start suffering memory loss."

"I'm right here," Pearson said.

"There is still a lot you can learn, Chief Logan, but my patience is wearing."

Pearson began gathering up the photos into a stack as he looked in the mirror and nodded. This investigation was too critical. If the fat man only wanted to talk to Logan so be it. The door buzzed, opened, and standing there was Logan. Pearson passed him the file folder of pictures and winked to show he wasn't tripping over his lip.

They swapped places: now Pearson watched from behind the glass while Logan laid out the photos on the table – but Hopper still wasn't looking at the pictures. Instead, he focused on Logan, waiting for their eyes to meet.

Satisfied that the pictures were easily viewed from Hopper's vantage point, Logan brought up his gaze to meet the prisoner. "Recognize any of them?"

"Listen to me, Chief Logan: we have a deal, and if you send anyone else through that door you will get no further cooperation from me." His face was red and flustered, drawing attention to the different liver spots on his forehead.

"Hopper, from this point on you, deal only with me, but whether you like it or not there are going to be other people involved. Judges, prosecutors, people from the medical community. Sooner or later you're going to have to open up to this idea."

"I don't trust anybody," Hopper spat. "Take me back to my cell!"

"Alright, Hopper. We're done for tonight, but tomorrow the digging starts."

Logan motioned to the mirror and began gathering up the photos. Sometimes it was better to not push. He'd flash some of the pictures during the excavation.

5

Three Weeks Later

The night air was filled with the sounds of men and equipment working. Overhead a full moon clung to the sky staring down on what now resembled a grisly archaeological dig. Generators rumbled, giving light to the darkness and unveiling some excavated graves. Vehicles were parked all over the land and men spoke loudly to each other as if the night air had suppressed their hearing.

Exactly three weeks after Hopper identified the site of Tommy Parkins body, they were now into the final stages of digging up the last grave. It didn't take long for word to travel, and the media had come to visit the sleepy little town of Thomasville. What had initially started out as a routine murder investigation had now turned into a complete media circus. Thanks to the internet, the story of mass murder in Thomasville had gone viral and was now being talked about across the continent, if not the world.

Trustees from the nearby Terrisdale Correctional Facility had been brought in to assist with the dig. The trustees from the prison were all minor offenders working off petty crimes such as possession of drugs or break and entry. Not one of them was serving anything more than two years. As an incentive, every day worked in the field meant five days off their original sentence. Many didn't have the stomach for it and returned to the prison. Logan really couldn't blame them: just because they were criminals didn't make them heartless.

Most of the bodies were in varying states of decay. Consequently, the workers had been fitted with environmental suits and masks to ward off the putrid stench. One body was so far gone that it had to be excavated with the ground that encased it and be cleaned up later at the makeshift lab. It was not an easy job, and certainly not one for the squeamish.

Pearson and Cooper had found their man. For them the hunt was over: twelve of the sixteen victims had been positively identified. Forensic specialists now worked in conjunction with Jeff Henderson, whose morgue was far too small to house the remains of so many victims. Federal Investigators purchased three double-wide mobile trailers which they converted into a makeshift lab until the bodies could be transported elsewhere.

Pearson and Cooper had integrated well with the Thomasville Department. The initial uncomfortable rub against Mick was now a vague memory. In fact, Pearson and he had spoken extensively about Mick's plan to pursue a career in drug enforcement.

Officers from nearby Brandon offered their assistance to Thomasville Police by filling in on local patrols and highway safety. Logan was eternally thankful; his detachment was now working around the clock on the case.

Defense Lawyers from all over the country were calling and offering their services to Hopper free of charge. The payment for them would be the celebrity his name afforded their practice. And all throughout, Hopper had remained steadfast in denying counsel and still would talk to no one but Logan.

Hopper was marched in front of Judge Paul Davio, and his case was remanded until such a time that the police had completed their investigation. Davio had cautioned Hopper and encouraged him to seek counsel, but Hopper ignored Judge Davio's recommendation. As a result, the judge ordered that once the investigators had finished with him, he would be sent to Artisan Institute, where he would undergo a thirty-day mental evaluation to see if he was fit to stand trial. In addition to the legal issues surrounding the case, there was still a trial venue to think of.

The Press dubbed him the Thomasville Stalker and sensationalized the tragedy that had befallen the small community. The people of Thomasville did not take lightly to the intervention of outsiders. The quiet little town had become a nightmare of cameras and reporters, all wanting profiles on Stephen Hopper or anyone who might have known him.

But it was the monster that they wanted to know about, as usual, not the victims.

To carry out the investigation, the police had to roadblock Van Dyke Road a mile away from Hopper's home at both ends. As this road was the main thoroughfare, an alternate detour had to be set up. Most of the press was respectful, but tabloid journalists and internet hacks didn't adhere to the same code of journalistic integrity. As a result, more than one overzealous reporter was caught sneaking across the bald ass Prairie to obtain footage of the dig. 'Field of Screams' was what one reporter dubbed the graveyard that had once been an inconspicuous cornfield.

In addition to blocking off Van Dyke road, they set up roving patrols in the wood line between the Wakeman and Hopper property. So far, they had caught two reporters and a posse of teenage boys trying to sneak through on a dare. Logan had jailed the reporters and turned the teenagers over to their parents.

Corporal West came up with the solution of putting the trespassers in the drunk tank. It was located on the other side of the building away from the cell block. Logan thought this was a brilliant idea. Thomasville's drunk tank was about the size of a small classroom. Concrete benches lined every wall and in the center of the room was a grated hole where a drunken inmate could urinate, defecate or vomit. Most drunks who ended up there were released in the morning after they sobered up. Following their departure, an officer would spray it down with disinfectant and hose the place out.

Most of the press was straight up, following the rules and showing consideration, but it was the cowboys who needed to be deterred. Considering this, he told the staff not to clean up the drunk tank and from this point on, anyone caught sneaking onto the site would do their time there.

Hopper stood uneasily at Logan's side as they uncovered the last body. Most of the remains were severely decomposed and appeared to be dismembered. Until Henderson and the forensic specialists would have a chance to clean the mud that clung to the skin and bone there really was no way to identify the cause of death. Hopper certainly wasn't giving them much.

This last body was Hopper's first victim and the only one planted in front of the house. Next to the grave was a dying maple tree, perhaps seventy years old. In the grave, a young trustee chipped away at the clay which ran a couple of feet into the earth before it turned to sand. As he did this, Hopper chain-smoked and fidgeted. The smoking was normal. The fidgeting wasn't. He had been at the site of every other dig, and not once had he acted like this.

Beyond identifying the location of the victims and matching photographs to the grave sites, Hopper did not talk about the actual murders. He stood there seemingly without remorse as they dug each of his victims and puffed away on the cigarettes purchased for him out of petty cash.

The trustee working in the hole now was about forty years old and was amongst the toughest of the bunch. He looked like a throwback from the seventies. His hair was shoulder length, he sported a ZZ Top beard, and every fifth word out of his mouth was, 'man.'

This last excavation was also the hardest. Due to its position at the base of the maple tree, they had to stop periodically to hack away the roots. Logan wondered why Hopper would bury this victim here. It didn't make sense. First of all, it was in front of the house and exposed to the main road. He could have easily been discovered in the process of digging the grave.

Secondly, the tree was nothing but a pain in the ass. They were not the only ones having to cut roots as they dug. Most of their cutting was fresh growth – but there was evidence that Hopper had cut out two very large roots when he dug the grave.

The final thing that puzzled Logan was the depth.

"Are you sure we're digging in the right place, man?" the trustee called up. He was asking this because they were seven feet down and still nothing.

"It's there," Hopper said to Logan, but he didn't look so sure.

"Keep digging," Logan ordered.

"Alright, man," the trustee grumbled and carried on digging.

Hopper lit one cigarette off another.

"It has to be there," Hopper whispered only loud enough for Logan to hear, but he wasn't talking to Logan. He was thinking out loud.

"Oh man, I just hit some… yeah, we're there. We're there, man," the trustee called excitedly.

Hopper closed his eyes, mumbled something. An inexplicable look of relief fell over him. He turned to Logan. "That's the last one. I'd like to go now, Chief Logan."

The trustee was climbing out of the hole, and one of the forensic specialists from the university came up to take over. Logan looked over the young woman. Her name was Andrea Chase. She was good looking and in her late twenties, dark hair tied back and eyes a deep brown. She was hardly what you would expect from someone who worked intimately with the dead.

"I got this," She donned a pair of safety glasses and a disposable mask before climbing into the grave to start prep.

Henderson had briefed Logan about her a week ago and said she was in the top of their field. She certainly didn't lack confidence.

"Alright, Hopper. Let's go." Logan led him away from the grave site and toward the cruiser. As they walked, he wondered what it was that had spooked the fat man. He had been detached at all the other digs. *But this one was different. Why? And what he'd said. It was as if he thought the body would not be there.*

Minutes later they drove down Van Dyke Road toward the roadblock. Hopper sat in the backseat of the cruiser, praying aloud.

"Our Father, who art in Heaven…"

Now that the last body had been removed from the ground Logan expected that the task force would be flying Hopper back to the city within a week or so. In a few days, a psychiatrist from Artisan Institute would be flying in.

The psychiatrist's name was Robert Kolchak. He had testified on behalf of the prosecution in over 150 cases in the last thirteen years. He was also a bestselling author with three books published about serial killers. Kolchak had cut his teeth at Quantico Virginia in behavioral sciences and was highly respected in his field. Logan was reading Kolchak's latest book: MANY FACES. The book examined known cases of serial murderers like Henry Lee Lucas and Jeffrey Dahmer, but Logan was not looking for insight into these minds. Instead, he was reading up on the man who would be interviewing him about the case.

What Logan surmised from Kolchak's book was that the author was arrogant and self-serving. There were a lot of (I's) and (me's) in the book where Kolchak often patted himself on the back for his brilliant insight into the minds of these social defects.

Testifying in these cases brought great monetary benefits, and drew media endeavors whenever expert panels on violent criminals made the national or international news. These panels paid handsomely and of course, propped up Kolchak's book sales.

Logan guessed the psychiatrist would be as he presented himself in his book, and that was good to know. If you are dealing with an asshole, it's always easier if you have a heads up beforehand.

The roadblock was illuminated by the cruiser's headlights. Beyond it stood Mick with scores of reporters waiting to catch a glimpse of the Thomasville Stalker. As the car drew closer, Hardy and Oddball did crowd control, and Mick moved the saw horse out of the way so they could get through.

A barrage of flashes, bright lights, and shouted questions came from all angles as they rolled through the gauntlet. Hopper peered out briefly, exposing himself to the cameras, but quickly pulled back. But not quickly enough: his photo was captured in a millisecond. It would headline the national news.

Logan had read and experienced how many of these ghouls enjoyed the notoriety, but Hopper seemed extremely uncomfortable with it. He glanced into his rearview mirror and watched the fat man continue to recite the Lord's prayer.

Keep praying, asshole. Even if there is an almighty God, I doubt He'll offer redemption to a monster like you. With that thought he pushed down on the gas pedal, leaving behind his officers to deal with the mob of reporters.

7

Daniel Blackbird was sitting in a truck stop, sipping a cup of hot tea and waiting for his breakfast. He had been doing odd jobs as he traveled: working in warehouses, loading trucks, even washing dishes. Getting work was a task in itself. Firstly, he had no fixed address, so he was forced to take jobs in the underground economy. Secondly, he was native. No matter what people might think, Daniel Blackbird still ran up against racism. It hindered his ability to find work, and now he was almost out of money.

His presence in the truck stop was also not appreciated. Politics and land claims had caused divisions between natives and whites. There used to be a time when people from his race were regarded as drunks and downtrodden. Now well-educated Natives were challenging broken treaties, and making land claims which spurred a whole new reason for dislike.

He had followed up six leads, and all had been fruitless. He felt defeated at this point. For all, he knew 'Skin' could be running around Europe or the Middle East while he continued running in circles.

The waitress set a plate of two eggs with a side of toast down in front of him. Gingerly he poked the fork into the yolk. Yellow fluid poured out and onto the plate. He rolled his eyes. He had ordered the eggs cooked over hard; the taste of an uncooked yolk disgusted him. For a second, he considered sending them back but then thought better of it. Whether it was paranoia or not, Blackbird thought that cook might spit on them.

In the booth to his right, a newspaper was strewn in segments. He reached over and picked a cluster of pages up for later. Maybe he could find some part-time work here. If he couldn't that meant going back to the Elders and asking for more money. This was something he did not want to do.

Grudgingly, he ate all of his breakfast, runny yolk and all. There was no point in starving, and with only $25 left in his pocket, he had to be as conservative as possible.

With breakfast gone, he asked the waitress to bring him some more hot water for his tea. As he waited, he skimmed the help wanted ads. The pickings were sparse, thanks to a worldwide recession.

The waitress refilled the mini steel teapot and asked, "Will there be anything else, sir?"

Blackbird shook his head.

She tore off a bill from the pad and laid it down on the table. He turned it over. Another $8 spent. As the waitress walked away he paid her no mind, nor did he pay attention to the two truck drivers who were making jokes at his expense.

It looked as though he was going to have to put a call into the Elders to send him money after all. This would mean giving a report on his progress and feeling the sting of scrutiny from his cousin Johnny Proudfoot. Maybe they'd even decline his request, thinking he was squandering their money.

It had been a long time since he'd felt the tug of the walker – now he wondered if he had lost the ability or if it was too far out of range. If only he had something to give them. Some assurance.

He folded the paper neatly, setting the classifieds down and sipped the last of his tea when something in the newspaper caught his eye.

MURDER PROBE WIDENS
By Curtis Johnson

Two days after his arrest for the alleged murder of an eleven-year-old boy, investigators allege Stephen Hopper has been connected to as many as seventeen murders. Police have confirmed seventeen victims, but are not commenting if there are more. All of the victims are young boys ranging between eleven and seventeen years old.

"The back field is littered with gravesites," Sgt. Mick Collins of the Thomasville Police Department said in a daily media briefing. "We have brought in additional investigators and forensic specialists to assist us with this grim task."

When asked how his officers are coping, Collins said, "Our officers are professionals and though there is an emotional attachment they are focused on evidence gathering."

Investigators from the city of Winnipeg have also been brought in and they have stated that there is a clear link between the situation in Thomasville and an ongoing investigation into the disappearance of teenage boys over the last two years. Detective Ron Pearson, who headed up a task force out of Winnipeg, has now joined the Thomasville authorities in the investigation. "It appears that the suspect was procuring these boys off the highways, but we are still piecing the evidence together."

One victim has been identified as ten-year-old Thomas Avery Parkins [of Thomasville]. An unnamed source is quoted as saying that he was the first victim uncovered and positively identified.

... continued on page 4

Blackbird picked up his tea, flipping the pages, but there was no page 4 to be found. The waitress was passing by, so he asked her for a refill. She picked up the stainless-steel pot and took it to the counter irritated. This deadbeat probably wouldn't leave a tip.

She was right; he could barely afford the meal.

He re-read the article touching the scar left by the walker, and he began to feel it. He did not know if it was telepathy or just a gut feeling, but when he was getting close, there was a sense that came over him. He could feel the walker's scent on this. There was some kind of a connection. Maybe this guy was procuring food for Skin?

He had stopped calling it 'the walker' a long time ago; instead, he called it 'Skin.'

Its handle harkened back to when they were children. "Skin's gonna get you, Daniel. Skin's gonna get you and eat your heart!" Johnny Proudfoot used to tease him. Back then 'Skin' had been a boy's fable – but as he would later find out, the Skinwalker, aka Skin, was no myth or legend.

He glanced at the dotted picture of Stephen Hopper and tried to see something in it, but the quality was poor. No matter. He trusted his instincts on this: the scar on his face tingled, and for the first time in more than two years he felt the same feeling as when he had stumbled upon the murder of that young prostitute in Chicago.

Outside he found a phone booth. There he punched in the number he knew by heart and waited for the operator to come on. It was all automated now, a frustrating part of technology. The computer asked who the collect call was for, and he answered, "Johnny Proudfoot." Then, as prompted, he gave his name. He traced his fingers over the stainless-steel pedestal as the phone began to ring. The tug was stronger now.

A woman picked up the phone. "Hello?"

"This is Bell Long Distance calling. I have collect call for 'Johnny Proudfoot' from 'Daniel Blackbird.' Please press one to accept the charges or two to –"

He heard the key pressed.

"Thank you, you are now connected. Go ahead please."

"Get me, Proudfoot," Blackbird said flatly.

"Just a minute." She placed a hand over the mouthpiece, but he could still hear her. "Uncle Johnny, it's Dan. Dan Blackbird!"

He folded the newspaper and began to reread it while he waited. The pull felt stronger now. He was confident that this was no blind alley.

The two truck drivers from inside the restaurant passed him, and one said, "How's it going, Chief?" and snorted.

Dickhead, he thought.

"Hello, Daniel," a voice greeted on the phone. "It's been quite a while."

"I've found him," Blackbird said.

"You're sure about this?" Proudfoot inquired.

"Johnny, I'm positive. I can feel him, just like in the city. It's unmistakable."

"Where?"

"A small town on the prairies called Thomasville. I think he's made contact this time, and I'm pretty sure he's still there, but I don't know for how long. I have to get there as soon as possible."

"How much money do you need?" There was a judgmental tone in Proudfoot's voice. Blackbird had heard it on more than one occasion.

He hadn't even thought about that. He tried doing some math, then gave up and said, "Stay by the phone. I have some calls to make. I'll get back to you within the hour."

He hung up and picked up the tattered phone book which was dangling between his knees on a steel cord. Flipping through the yellow pages, he found what he was looking for. He inserted two quarters and dialed the number. The phone rang twice, and a party answered.

"Greyhound, how can I help you?"

***

CHAPTER 7 - VISITATION AND PREPARATION

1

Hopper was opening his eyes when he saw something scuttling across the cell floor toward him. He hadn't even begun to realize what it was when black vapor began to plume upward from under his bunk and solidify. By then, all he had time to do was retreat to the corner of his mattress with his knees up to his chest. The Bible fell to the floor as he cowered. He reached for it, then thought better.

Dear God, no, he thought.

He opened his mouth to scream – but out shot a hooked claw from the smoke, which covered his mouth and contained his scream before it could escape. The smell of it ran up into his nose, and he almost vomited.

As he fought back the urge to spew, it continued changing to a chorus of pops of grinding bone and cartilage. From the black poisonous haze, it began to take form, and as it did the vapor became tar-like beads on its sickly grey skin, first settling like dew drops then absorbing inward.

Between the pop and grating bone, it greeted, "Stephen." The change was almost complete, and the ragged creature perched beside him in its true form. The cell was a chamber of wretched decay. The razor-sharp claws dug into the skin below each of Hopper's ears, just before the point they would puncture him. It could easily twist off his head or open both jugular veins from this position – it had done so many times before. Its black lips peeled back, exposing rotted teeth that had chewed up so much human flesh. Hopper could hold his breath no longer and inhaled the stink of its sour breath.

"If I uncover your mouth, are you going to be a good boy?" it hissed, and from one of its inflamed gums, black ick hemorrhaged, flooding over its lips and spilling down its chin.

He nodded: "Yes." In its reflective eyes, he could see his head bobbing up and down, enveloped by the vast claw.

The clamp loosened, then paused, waiting for him to screech. When he didn't, it removed its claw.

Hopper gasped, then quietly recited, "Our Father, who art –"

"That won't help you," it dismissed.

"–who art in heaven," he blubbered.

"Have you told them about me?"

Hopper shook his head.

"Doesn't matter. I'm going to make you pay for this."

"It wasn't my fault," he proclaimed.

"Shut up you, stupid man." It brought a claw up and absently pierced its inflamed gum. A stream of dark liquid squirted from its mouth out onto the bed but evaporated before the prison-issued blanket could absorb it. "My teeth hurt all the time. Do you know how bad that feels?"

"I'm sorry," Hopper replied.

It cackled. "You're sorry. We had a good thing going, Stephen, and you screwed it up. You'll be sorry for that. There just isn't enough time for the amount of pleasure I am going to take in dismantling you. I just wanted you to know that I am still here and it isn't over yet. What did I tell you?"

"Never take the locals." Hopper started crying.

"Exactly. Never take the locals. But you couldn't control yourself." Its lips drew back in a gruesome snarl. More vile black liquid leaked from between its teeth and gums. "I am going to pick you apart the same way a child pulls the wings off a fly, and I'm going to take my time." It laughed. "Oh yes, I will be savoring every moment of your agony."

"I never told them anything about you," he convulsed.

"Oh, but you will. Maybe not today, but one day when you're penned up somewhere, you'll talk. Humans always talk. It's their nature; it's your nature." A momentary pause. "Too late anyway; he's coming."

"Who? No, I won't! I promise I won't!"

"I've got to go now, Stephen. An old friend of mine is coming to town, and I've got people to see. I would kill you tonight, but there's so much to do." It let out a raspy laugh.

"Please, I'm begging you. Pleeease!" Tears gushed down onto his cheeks as he wailed. "Lord protect me, I have sinned. Please protect me." He balled his right hand up into a fist and bit down on it hard enough to break the skin. He dropped to the floor, clutched his knees to his chest.

Again it began to change. Droplets of tar seeped from its pores, and as its skin darkened, the black substance began to vaporize and swallow its body in a tiny storm of dirty smoke. There were pops intermingled with crackling, then an odd liquid sound as the black mist flowed down from Hopper's bunk and into the cracks where the concrete wall met the floor. The last of it vanishing out of sight, it let out a bone-chilling shriek that echoed through the walls.

Hopper opened his eyes ever so slowly, dumbly, scanning the confines of the cell. Once he had assured himself it was indeed gone, his composure crumbled.

Hopper started to scream.

2

Detective Pearson was at his desk tapping away on his laptop and chartering a flight for the entourage that would escort Hopper to Artisan Institute. The Institution was in a remote location where many violent criminals were evaluated before trial. It was also the residency of Dr. Robert Kolchak. Kolchak was scheduled to arrive tomorrow afternoon at the small airport in Brandon.

The doctor intended to spend a couple days in Thomasville. He wanted to look at the dig, go through Hopper's house, and meet with the Parkins family. This was, "All a part of the evaluation," he had said over the phone, but Pearson speculated the Good Doctor was already preparing a synopsis for a new bestseller. Not that he cared much either way. As long as Kolchak helped them get a guilty confession, his motives were of little relevance to Pearson.

They would be flying back to Artisan in a Dash 8. The twin-engine would more than meet their requirements when they left at the end of the week. Cooper, Kolchak, Hopper and himself would be the only passengers on board the craft. He missed the city and could not wait to get out of Thomasville. Chief Logan had been a decent enough host, and his 2I/C Collins turned out to be a good guy. The problem was, he hated these little communities where they rolled up the sidewalks at 8 PM.

Closing the laptop, he stood up to stretch his back. He was ready to call it a night – when suddenly he heard a distant moan which reminded him of wind whistling through the rafters of an old barn. There a second sound came. It sounded … jagged. Like a clanging metallic screech echoing through the walls again and again until it was gone.

"Did you hear that?" he asked the duty officer.

Hardy turned her head to listen, but she did not respond, deciding to wait and see if the sound would repeat itself. The two of them stood motionless, straining their ears. Hardy glanced toward the cell block, while Pearson gazed at her chest wondering how firm her breasts were.

Before he could visualize what they looked like beneath her uniform, his concentration was broken by the screaming of the only man they had locked up.

The two raced for the cell block.

Scott Masterson was the manager of the Thomasville Motor Inn for over fifteen years, and the small motel had been a landmark of the community for almost thirty. It was a cheap place to get a room, only $35 a night, but it was also run-down, and the air-conditioning in half the rooms didn't work.

Since the construction of the Holiday Inn just off the main highway, business at the motel suffered. Most travelers never ventured far enough into town. The recent influx of reporters had not even benefited the failing business.

Scott was not a particularly ambitious man. Masterson's father owned the place and gave Scott the management job when it became abundantly clear he had decided to do nothing else with his life.

Scott liked to smoke pot and gamble. Stud poker was his game of choice. He was a slave to the table, always looking for the turn of a friendly card, but rarely finding one. On his days off he dropped thousands of dollars in the casino in the city. As the lust consumed him, he began embezzling money from the Motel Maintenance fund, and when he drained that, he stopped paying bills. First, he rotated paying the utilities, always a month behind – and then after a weekend that cost $5000 Scott Masterson committed the equivalent of business suicide. He skipped paying the taxes.

There were two paying customers in his father's thirty-unit motel. In 7B there was a kid in his mid-twenties who had come in on his own dime to cover the murders. Scott had smoked a joint with him the other night. His name was Tim something-or-other, a wannabe reporter/blogger. In 11A was a married couple from town who used the room regularly for a bit of uninhibited sex. Masterson guessed they had kids and just wanted the privacy to cut loose and have a bit of fun.

Every day he waited for the end. He cringed when he thought about what his father would do when he found out about the taxes. On more than one occasion he contemplated going down to the basement and just hanging himself from the support beam. The old man was going to freak, and he really didn't want to face that. He didn't know if he really had the nerve to kill himself – but thought he would find out soon enough. Everything would come to a head sooner or later.

As he pondered this, the door chimed and in walked the answer to all of his problems. A tall man with broad shoulders, dressed all in black, strutted across the lobby, and without saying a word dropped two envelopes on the counter.

"What's this?" He drew back a little, thinking he was being served a summons or threat of foreclosure.

The tall man smiled and pushed the first envelope toward him with his index finger.

Scott reached down and picked up the large yellow envelope. It was bulky and overstuffed. Peeling back the seal, he glanced inside. There was an enormous wad of $100 bills. He tried to guess what the amount was, but the dark stranger answered for him.

"There are ten thousand dollars in that envelope," he said. "That is yours for the keeping if you can carry out one simple task."

He looked from the man, whom he now thought might be an Indian, and then back into the envelope. He was tempted, but then set it down on the counter. "I may not be the brightest guy, Mister, but I don't need trouble with the law, and you look like trouble."

He pushed the envelope back – but the stranger placed a hand over his and stopped him. The stranger's hand was icy cold and felt smooth, unreal.

"There will be no trouble or illegal dealings, Mr. Masterson. I simply want you to deliver this second envelope to a friend of mine. Inside this envelope is a message. That message is confidential which I do not want violated. Also, if my friend requires shelter, you will provide it free of charge for as long as he stays."

"A note? Ten thousand dollars to deliver a note?" Masterson sniffed.

"I represent a company that prides itself on anonymity. So what I expect is that you provide him with shelter, deliver this message, and take payment. If you feel my offer is too risky, I will find another courier for my harmless memorandum." He reached down and picked up the other envelope.

For two or three long seconds, Scott struggled with the idea. If this was illegal, he could end up dead. If it wasn't it might go a long way to solving some of his problems. He could pay down the taxes and skim a bit for the tables. What if it is illegal, though? This guy creeps me right out. Two or three days when they come for their blood money I'm screwed anyhow. Maybe God is cutting me a break.

So he reached out and said, "Okay, I'll deliver your message. What is the name of your company? What is your name?"

"None of your business. I will tell you the name of my associate, though. His name is Daniel Blackbird. He is aboriginal and may look a bit rough around the edges, but he poses no threat. When he arrives, you will have a room ready for him and give him that smaller envelope."

"Blackbird," Scott replied, taking the envelopes into his hands.

"This portion of our business is concluded, Mr. Masterson. Ensure that you take care of that note and make sure it is delivered unopened."

Scott knelt down to place the second envelope with the first. When he stood up the office was empty. The door chime had not sounded.

"What the?"

He ducked back down to see if the envelopes were still there. They were. "Okay, so I didn't hallucinate."

He touched the smaller envelope with his index finger and pondered what might be inside. He tried to remember the stranger's face – but he could only remember the eyes. They were large and dark, and there was a glint of silver in them, almost like chrome.

A chill rolled up his spine. He was not a superstitious man, but there was a side of him that told him that looking into that man's eyes could drive you completely insane.

4

The Walker strolled along the side of the highway, happy so far with its plan and confident that the man would not break the seal of the envelope it had given him. The man at the hotel was weak-minded and easily manipulated. It had gotten inside his head, made him see things that were not there. That was another one of its talents, one that had been used time and again to lure prey. A man's lust or greed was an open invitation to exploitation, and the Walker used these shortcomings expertly.

The hunter would be here within a day or two. When this was over, there would be much blood – and it would be free of pursuit at last. The hunter's days were drawing short: a new beginning was about to cycle.

It had not eaten properly for quite some time. Eating was, of course, necessary – but the taste of animal meat was not as pure or satisfying as that of man. But tonight it decided to make an exception and make a celebratory killing to endorse the new beginning.

The Walker changed form and flew southward, away from the town of Thomasville and the likes of Stephen Hopper. In the chilly autumn night, the raven flapped its great wings, leaving the prairie landscape behind.

But it would be back.

5

US Highway 83

South of Falkirk, ND

Four hours later on a deserted highway, a hitchhiker stuck out her thumb to an approaching car. The driver was a man in his mid-fifties heading home after an extended business trip in Bismarck. Typically he would not have even slowed down for the individual on the roadside, but this was not your average highway straggler out there on the shoulder. She had long dark brown hair, large breasts, and skin-tight jeans which hugged her slender legs. All of that was caught in his headlights, but he did not see her face. Truth be told, with a body like that she could have one eye and three teeth and he still would have pulled over.

When he pulled the car to the side of the road, he watched in the rearview mirror as she ran up through the crimson glow of his brake lights. "Looks good to me," he remarked, and lowered the passenger window.

"Hi, are you going to, Minot?" she asked.

He reached over, unlocked the car door and said, "Hop in! Minot is exactly where I'm going."

"That's great!" She climbed in, slammed the door, and the car pulled away.

As they drove, he stole an occasional glance at her. She appeared not to notice. She was beautiful, dark and raven, with high cheekbones and sultry eyes. The clothes clung tightly to her well-sculpted figure, and as he stole glance after glance, he found himself fantasizing about what it would be like to touch her.

One of her smooth and silky hands floated across the bench seat. It caressed his leg and moved upwards. This startled him at first, but he remained calm, keeping his eyes on the road. As it sank in, he held from letting out a bray of smug laughter. He still remembered all the Penthouse Forum letters he'd read as a teenager.

"Feel good?" she asked.

"Uh huh," That was all he could manage and thought, Dear Penthouse Forum: I never thought this would happen to me. I was driving down US 83, minding my own business when…

"Good," she interrupted, unzipped his pants and slid her hand inside. Finding what she was looking for, she clamped onto him and began to squeeze and release. "You're a big boy."

He wanted to look at her but knew if he took his eyes off the road he'd crash for sure. "Well, you're the cause of that, sweetheart."

She let out a seductive laugh and squeezed a couple more times, then leaned in closer, sliding her butt across the seat, her hip touching his. She whispered, "Wouldn't my tongue feel better?"

He felt a rush of excitement. She squeezed a little harder, moving her hand up and down and he said, "There's a motel about forty miles up."

"Oh no, baby," she whispered, hot breath in his ear. "I want it now. Pull in the next rest area, and I'll give you something that will last the rest of your life." She ran her tongue over his earlobe, continuing to squeeze and release.

Ahead a highway sign declared, 'Rest Area, 1 Mile ahead'.

When he rolled into the rest-stop, he took a cursory look around for other vehicles but saw none.

Thank you, God!

He barely had the car in park, and she was all over him. She pushed him against the driver's door, unbuttoned his already unzipped pants. In his excitement he did not see the shadow approaching from behind, or her reaching over to unlock the door.

One moment he was in his car and the next he was being pulled out onto the parking lot asphalt. A dreaded realization hit him: "Oh shit, I'm getting busted." Then the guy pulling him out kicked him square in the stomach.

"You like touching my old lady, asshole?" he barked and kicked him again. "Do yuh!"

He lay still, prone and whimpering. The girl searched through his pockets. When she found his wallet, she yanked it out. Inside were two twenty-dollar bills.

"This is all you have!" she screeched. "Forty dollars! I had to kiss this slob and touch his cock for forty bucks!"

He decided then that she was not the most beautiful creature he had ever seen.

"You better have more money there, fucker!"

The guy was just about to kick him again when something flashed overhead, and the driver was showered with a spray of warm sticky liquid.

Where did he go? Then, perversely: *I guess I'm not getting a blowjob.*

Something thudded down in front of him. Then pained amusement turned to terror when he realized it was the kicker's severed head. Even more horrifying: the head hadn't yet realized it should be still. The mouth opened, seemed to gasp for breath.

Behind him, the girl screamed and began to run. As he watched over his shoulder, he saw a blur of night air splash across the lot like oil across a canvas and come to a stop directly in front of her. It looked somewhat like a wingless grey gargoyle – then it grabbed hold of her and lifted her up off the ground.

"I didn't do anything!" she cried.

Wrapped around her fingers, the driver spied the twenty-dollar bills she had stolen. Even after what she had done he felt sorry for her – but not sorry enough to be a hero.

He still could not find his breath, but he wanted desperately to scream after what he saw next. As she begged, it let out a blood-curdling shriek, then disemboweled her with the razor toe on its left foot. As her entrails spilled onto the cold asphalt, he began to crawl toward his vehicle, desperately praying that his keys were still in the ignition. He slid along on his belly; the kick he'd taken in the guts seemed like a minor issue now, the prospect of highway sex and betrayal forgotten.

It only took seconds to get to the car.

Behind him the grey beast was feasting on her insides as he touched the key chain and slid into the car, trying not to make any noise. He turned the key, and the seatbelt alarm chimed.

Ding ding ding!

That was enough. The monster looked up from its feed. Its eyes locked onto him as he slumped in the driver seat, and it let out another blood-curdling shriek.

"No," the driver cried, then sat up and turned the key.

The ignition caught; the car rumbled to life. Jamming the gear selector in reverse, he punched the gas pedal all the way to the floor. As he did the monster gave chase, still holding a large handful of the girl's intestine in its clutch.

"No! No! No!" he screamed. "What in the name of fuck!"

The monster hurled its fistful of innards as it gained – they hit the hood with a vile wet slap. He screamed again, and in turn, the beast let out another high-pitched shriek. Then he rolled backward down the onramp he'd used minutes earlier, all the while transfixed on the unrelenting specter.

"This is a nightmare," he cried. "A fucking nightmare!"

6

Bobby Dulong had no intention of camping out for the night: he just wanted to make a quick stop, have a piss and draw a line in his log book. He exited onto the ramp a little fast. The need to piss clouded his judgment and he waited to down-shift a couple of gears on the relatively straight ramp. Behind his Freightliner were two Super-B train tankers full up with gasoline. Under any other circumstances, Dulong would have had no problem stopping the big rig, but this was not a typical set of circumstances. He never saw the monster chasing the car: he only saw the glow of backup lights coming the wrong way down the ramp and the explosion of plastic and steel when he collided with it.

He screamed, "Fuck!" But that was all he got out: the car's gas tank exploded, and his windshield became awash with liquid fire. Then the B train tankers, pushed by gravity, began to jackknife around and lose their balance. Dulong did not see them either, but he knew that his ticket had been punched. The tankers flipped, and the bladders inside them hemorrhaged. What ensued was what witnesses, if there were any, would have called two mushrooming explosions. First, the main tanker exploded, then the pup followed moments later.

From above the raven glided in a circular pattern as the fireballs lit up the night in a brilliant mixture of orange and yellow. When the second blast subsided, the raven landed on the paved lot where it had made its first kill. The two bodies were still steaming. The Walker wasted no time: it changed form, then resumed gorging.

7

Stomach swollen with fresh meat it sat lethargic, the fire reflecting in its eyes. The pain of hunger subsided for now. In the distance, it could hear sirens calling out.

It picked up the two disemboweled carcasses and dragged them to the fire which burned intensely. Heaving each body into the inferno, it watched with fascination and for a moment considered ambushing the rescuers when they arrived. Its hunger was satisfied, but the pull was still there – always there.

Better not, it thought, then changed form and flew into the abyss of night.

***

CHAPTER 8 - HOPPER TALKS

1

Pain! Oh my God, it hurts!

Logan massaged his chest after being jerked awake by a burning pain which tore through him. First, it was mild, just bringing him back from the realm of sleep, and then it erupted. It wasn't heartburn: he'd suffered acid reflux his whole life and knew this was different. The pain was center of the breastplate corkscrewing out across his barrel chest like splinters of glass burrowing into his bones and emitting agonizing fevered heat up into the surrounding muscle. *I have a heart attack!*

Then, as quickly as it had come, the eruption subsided. He couldn't see a thing through the pitch dark of the room, and for a brief instant, he wondered if he was destined to die here alone in the dark. The prospect of this terrified him in ways he could have never imagined. He lay there catching his breath, rubbing his chest making a mental note to go see the doctor tomorrow.

The phone suddenly rang, scaring him half to death. He fumbled for it and in his blindness knocked a whiskey tumbler off the nightstand. It dropped onto the hardwood floor, smashed, and sent splinters of glass everywhere. *Guess I'll be getting up on the other side of the bed.*

He picked up the phone through the dark, said, "Yeah," and realized the receiver was upside down. Turning it over, he repeated, "Yeah, what is it?"

"Hi, Chief." It was Hardy. "Sorry to wake you."

"Don't worry about it. What's up, Sandy?"

"I think you might want to come down to the station," she said. In the background, Logan could hear what sounded like muffled yelling.

"What's going on?"

"It's Hopper. He's freaking out, big time," she said and fell silent for a moment. "Can you hear that?"

Logan listened again. He strained to identify what he was yelling – but it was no use. "That's him?"

"That's him. Detective Pearson and I went to check on him, and he just kept screaming: 'Get me, Logan! Get me, Logan!'"

He swung out of bed forgetting about the glass. His toe brushed against its jagged edge, and he pulled his foot back. "Okay, hang tough. I'll be there in twenty-five minutes."

"Sorry, Chief; wasn't sure what else to do beyond gagging him."

"No problem, Sandy. Sleep is overrated anyhow."

He hung up the phone and rolled over to the other side of the bed. The pain which had cut through him earlier was now gone, but he popped a couple of antacids the doc had prescribed him for heartburn regardless.

Fuck! I can't wait to unload this fat pig, he thought while pulling on his trousers.

At first, it was okay. Everything was geared toward the investigation.

But now? Now he felt deep resentment at being the sounding board for this defect of nature.

Another stab of pain spiked in his chest as he dressed, but it subsided. Again, he reminded himself that he had to go to the doc tomorrow. He hated going for two reasons. The only doctor available to him was a woman, and she harped on him about his smoking and the extra thirty-five pounds he was carrying around.

Suck it up, Dave. Better to listen to a little of her bitching than dropping dead, he scolded, then aloud he mumbled, "Better than dying alone in the dark."

2

When he arrived at the station, the yelling had stopped, and the staff room was relatively calm. He hung up his coat and poured himself a cup of coffee. As he stirred, Hardy walked up to him and grabbed a Styrofoam cup.

"Seems awfully quiet in here, Sandy."

"He shut up about ten minutes ago," she replied. "We had to get him into the shower and change his jumpsuit."

"Why? Is he sick?" He tossed the plastic stir stick into the trash.

"He shit himself."

Logan laughed. "Better you than me, Sandy."

Thanks, Chief." She rolled her eyes. "I checked on him. He's okay. Well, okay as in not dangling from the ceiling from a homemade noose."

"As much as that prospect appeals to me, I don't need the paperwork."

"Detective Pearson is watching over him right now. He's in the moaning, whimpering stage of his temper tantrum and he won't talk to anyone but you. Pearson tried to ask him what's up and he told him to go fuck his mother." Hardy smiled, but for different reasons than Logan thought. She had felt Pearson's eyes crawling over her, examining her chest, and it made her uncomfortable. She usually didn't mind the attention, but Pearson was creepy.

Logan looked up, a mischievous smile on his lips and said, "Well, did he?"

"Huh?"

She didn't understand at first, then covered her mouth and giggled. She liked Logan. He was much older than her, but there was something about him that she found attractive. He was a thoughtful man, a little overweight, but he still had a charm about him, and he had a rugged, good-looking face. If not for love she felt for Don Steel, she might well have slept with Logan if the opportunity arose.

"Alright, I guess I better get this over with then."

Logan began to walk across the staff room. Halfway to the lockup, he sloshed coffee over his hand. He set the cup down on a desk and wiped it off on his uniform pants.

Behind him, Hardy laughed.

"Hilarious," he said, leaving the cup and winking at her.

Entering the cell block, he saw Pearson sitting in a chair watching over Hopper. He shot a glance Logan's way and got up to meet him.

"Ah, here comes the cavalry."

"Thanks. I was briefed by the Duty Officer. You mind hanging for a minute until I find out what's up?" Logan whispered.

"Not at all. You want to set him up in the interview room?"

"Let's see what's up first."

Logan patted him on the shoulder and walked down the corridor to Hopper's cell. When he peered through the bars Hopper was huddled in the corner, his knees pulled up to his chest, and the bible clutched tightly in both hands as he rocked back and forth. His hair was still wet from the shower he'd taken, but there was a faint ripe smell still lingering in the cell.

"You got a problem, Hopper?"

Hopper gaped at Logan awkwardly. Logan thought there was a minute hint of embarrassment on his face. His eyes were bloodshot and swollen, his nose runny and irritated: he'd been crying.

"I need to talk to you."

He wiped his nose with the back of his hand.

"You want to talk, Hopper? Okay, we'll talk. I'll give you an hour, but that's it. I need to get some sleep and thanks to you I haven't had much. So you have an hour."

"I'm sorry," Hopper whimpered, then sniffled.

Logan was bowled over. Sorry?

This from the man who had watched, lacking any emotion, while they dug up body after body. It had to be a ploy.

"I know you hate me, Chief Logan. Everyone hates me for what I've done, but this isn't over, and I have to tell someone because I'm damned and…" Hopper broke into a fresh bout of sobs and began to shudder uncontrollably.

Logan didn't feel any pity. Tommy Parkins and the sixteen other boys they'd dug up ensured that.

He looked over at Pearson and said, "Main interview room."

They cuffed and moved him to the room, then set up the video equipment. While Hardy stood guard, Pearson and Logan stepped out to discuss the approach and speculate. As they spoke, Logan poured them each a coffee.

"What do you make of this, Ron?"

"I don't know. Hopper knows he's going for a psych evaluation at the end of the week; maybe he's trying to work an insanity angle." Pearson took the coffee.

"Could be," Logan said, but he doubted it. The shaking, the tears – those had been too real, and he didn't think the fat man was that good of an actor. He speculated that whatever had him spooked was somehow tied into the uneasiness that Hopper displayed when they dug up the last grave.

He gave his watch a cursory glance; it was 1:33 AM. "Let's get this over with."

Pearson took his place, as he had done during all interviews since his arrival, behind the two-way mirror. Logan sat down across from Hopper at the table where he had first bartered for his cigarettes and bible.

"He's coming for me," Hopper said gravely.

"Who's coming for you?" Logan asked and shot a glance toward the mirror. The camera's red light blinked behind him.

"He calls himself Franklin, but that's not his real name. I don't want to die." He shuddered. "I'm afraid. Terrified, actually. I know I'm damned, but he's coming for me because I told."

Hopper looked like he wanted to be embraced, reassured, like a scared child. Logan shivered at the very thought of any human contact with this man and equated it to touching fecal matter.

"Hopper, slow down. What are you telling me here? Are you saying you had an accomplice? Who is Franklin?" *A second killer? It's possible, but all the evidence points towards one man. Then again, forensics had a lot of work to do in reconstruction and DNA,* he thought.

"You won't believe it, but it won't make any sense unless I start at the beginning," Hopper said, then asked. "Could I have a cigarette, Chief?"

"You can't smoke in this room," he answered. "I'll take you out for a smoke and then when we come back in here you better get at it. I don't want to be here all night and one more thing."

"What?" Hopper asked.

"After this, you are to give full cooperation to Detective Pearson. As of Friday, you will be leaving Thomasville and in his charge. We will be finished, Hopper, except for the trial. I'm assuming you will plead guilty and considering that I doubt there will be one. I want your word that from this point on you will allow Detective Pearson to take over and you will cooperate, especially in the department of identifying the other boys. Do we have a deal?"

Hopper's eyes flicked over to the two-way mirror. "Okay."

"Alright. Let's go have that smoke."

4

THOMASVILLE CITY POLICE

[INTERVIEW # 9]

SUBJECT: STEPHEN HOPPER

TIME: 2:15 AM-SEPTEMBER 18, 2009

It was the first boy. That is where it started. I picked him up on the highway about eight miles east of here. I asked him where he was going.

"I don't care," he said.

So, I took him home, not really sure what I would do when I got there. I'd never acted on my urges. I managed to keep that part of myself locked away for a long time, restricting myself to fantasy and self-gratification. I never intended to kill anyone; it wasn't that way at all, but living in solitaire out on that farm gave me too much time to think about the things I shouldn't be thinking about. Living out there then was like living in my cell now. The only difference is that I now have the companionship of police officers. There? I only had my corn.

Once the crop was in the urges intensified. I found myself driving my van up and down the highway, all the while lying to myself about what my true intentions were. I told myself this was a kind of therapy. That I wasn't out trolling for boys. I even passed over a couple of easy pickups, congratulating myself for doing so, but I knew in the back of my mind that once I saw the right boy, I would pull over and pick him up right away.

The right boy's name was Randy. I don't know what his last name was. I only know that he has haunted me every day and night since we crossed paths. I take full responsibility for this boy. Had I not picked him up I might still be sitting in the solitude of my corn.

I took him back to the farm and asked him if he needed a place to stay.

"No," he said. "I just took off for a while to scare my parents."

He was going to be a real badass when he grew up, and I used this as an excuse to talk myself into the idea of teaching him a lesson for being so disrespectful of his parents. Inside my head, the two voices argued.

Bad things happen to bad boys, and this boy is asking for it, the dark voice inside my head insisted. He's looking to be taught a lesson. He wants you to do it!

Does he, the other voice countered. Or are you just looking for excuses, you sick fuck? This is wrong! It's not too late to stop this. You can get him back into the van and drop him off where you found him – or better yet, you can take him home. You haven't done anything wrong! There's still a way out!

"Can I get a drink of water?" he interrupted.

"Huh?" I looked up from my internal argument. I had all but forgotten he was standing there.

"Water." And he mimicked holding a drinking glass.

"In the kitchen. The cupboard on the left side of the sink; that's where you'll find a clean glass."

I wondered if he could see the struggle on my face.

"Okay."

He turned and walked away.

I trained my eyes upon him. And the dark voice spoke again: *He's begging for it! Grab him now!*

When he rounded the corner, I went into the bathroom. I didn't need to go, but I wanted to be alone for a minute to try and decide what to do. In the bathroom mirror, I confronted myself, looked at the face of the man who held onto these devious thoughts.

Should I or shouldn't I?

No! There's no turning back from this!

If you don't do it today, you'll be back out on the highway tomorrow trolling again. You want to do it! It's inevitable. He wants you to do it.

Yes, he wants me.

I wanted it so badly. I could feel myself giving in. I can't explain the urges – they were intoxicating, stifling my thoughts and blinding me to the consequences. You might say that when this happened I would live in the moment of my desires and the voice of reason would withdraw.

I looked into the mirror, met my own eyes – and saw only descending darkness. That's when I knew there would be no further argument.

When I came out of that bathroom, my mind was made up. He was just coming back from the kitchen when I grabbed hold and dragged him into my bedroom. He pleaded, but I had passed the point of no return. I insisted it was what he wanted and that he deserved it. I repeated this over and over through all the begging, the cries, and I shut it all out.

When it was over, I felt ashamed of myself and tried to comfort him. I offered him $300 and said I would drive him home and that if he "didn't tell" I could give him more money. He held that money in his hand as he nodded and agreed with whatever I said, but I could see he was just looking for an escape plan.

"You go and get cleaned up." I sent him on to the washroom, and while the water ran, I began to deliberate on what I was to do with him.

He'll tell, and then you will go to prison. There you will be tortured and beaten and for what? The dark voice whispered to me. *He wanted it! You know he wanted it! You have to kill him! You have to!*

I stood and went out onto my porch. There was a short-handled shovel leaning against the handrail. I picked it and marched back into the house. As I crossed the living room, the screen door banged behind me, and I looked back, sure that someone would catch me. But there was no one. No one to stop me.

As I approached the bathroom, I could hear him pissing into the toilet. I stopped for a second, looked down at the shovel. The voice of reason was gone now. Why it wasn't there to stop me, as it had done so many times before? I waited for it to save me – but I had been abandoned, left to the dark side as it chanted, *Kill him! Kill Him!*

For reasons I will never know, he didn't latch the door. I wonder if I might have lost my nerve or if that other side of me would have returned to save the boy if he had just slid the mini deadbolt over.

I pushed the door open. His back was to me. I didn't want to kill him – I wanted to let him go no matter the circumstances.

Kill him now, Stephen! KILL HIM!

I swung the shovel in a tight arc, and it clipped the side of his head, sounding off in a metallic ping. A part of his scalp, the size of a folded piece of bread, tore away and both he and it began to fall in what seemed like slow motion. The silence of those few seconds felt like an eternity. I could not breathe, nor feel, or even hear what was happening. I was transfixed. His body turned as he collapsed, and he continued to urinate all over my floor. When he crashed onto his side, one of his eyes turned independent of the other and fell upon me.

"I wasn't going to tell, Mister," that single eye insisted, holding me in its gaze. "You didn't have to do this." The other eye rolled blindly upward in its socket.

I dropped the shovel. It clanged on the floor.

I could hear a continual banging. **Thump! Thump! Thump!**

It's done! **Thump!** *You had to do it!* **Thump!** *He would have told!*

He began to spasm, shooting jets of blood out from his head in great rhythmic spurts. My ears unsealed, and I realized the thumping noise was his foot kicking against the baseboard. It echoed inside my head, and I almost screamed. The pupil of his accusing eye widened, then contracted, and as it did he kicked the baseboard one final time – **Thump!** - later became still.

He was dead.

I stood over him, waiting for him to snap out of it. The blood spouting of his skull lessened without a pump pushing it anymore. Now only drawn by gravity, it spread out in a crimson pool across the linoleum.

My paralysis broke, and I ran for the kitchen.

There in the cupboard, I fumbled with a bottle of scotch and swallowed down three large gulps. It burned all the way down, and on the third gulp, it was ready to come back up. Without thinking, I began to run again for the bathroom to throw up, then pictured myself tripping over his body in an attempt to make the toilet. Instead, I pivoted and ran back to the kitchen sink. Hot burning vomit came out of my nose and mouth, spraying the wall and counter. I missed the sink entirely. Then I stood at the counter, my right hand immersed in a puddle of bile, waiting for a second wave that never came.

I do not know when I made it into the living room.

At some point, I had cleaned the puke from my hand, but I couldn't remember doing it – only that it was clean. I left the kitchen and fell into my recliner, slipping further into a state of numbness. I'm not even sure how long I sat there while his body lay still on the bathroom linoleum.

All the while I stared off into space and wondered what I would do next. I considered turning myself in. I thought about what would happen to me in jail. I have always been able to fight, but realistically I knew that the numbers would be against me. Somewhere in that train of thought, I also pondered suicide. It seemed the most valid solution to my problem. I had a couple of rifles in the house; it would be quick, painless and final.

Then, at last, the voice of reason came back. *You really did it! Oh my God! You really did it!*

"Where the fuck were you when I needed you?" I fired back, then fell silent.

It was hours before I came back to reality. At some point, I had pissed myself without realizing. It must have been quite a few hours ago because my crotch was cold and damp and it was also dark outside.

The power had gone out during my stupor. The clock on the stereo was blinking away. I picked up my cell phone, and it said 11:31 PM. I had been sitting there like that for over eight hours. I got up and grabbed the shovel from the hall and decided I better start digging.

5

Hopper stopped and looked over at the Logan. "I need another cigarette."

Logan rechecked his watch. This was going to be a sleepless night whether he liked it or not. He figured a break might do him some good.

"Alright, let's go."

He unlocked Hopper from the table and locked his handcuffs to the waist chain on the jumpsuit. Satisfied, he nodded at Pearson through the two-way mirror.

Hardy's shift was over. Her replacement was one of the graveyard officers, Ken Hill. Mick had also arrived, having come in to fill out paperwork and set up the following week's shifts. Before leaving, Hardy poked her head out the door where Logan and Hopper puffed away in the designated smoking area while Pearson watched.

"Hill's in, Chief. I'm off unless there's something else."

"No, that's it, Constable. Call it a night." Logan did not address his officers by first or last name in front of prisoners.

"Goodnight."

"Night, Constable," Pearson added.

She made a strange face at Pearson, then smiled at Logan. "Night, Chief."

Logan didn't say anything, but it was obvious.

6

[HOPPER INTERVIEW RESUMES]

I dug his grave under the anonymity of night, daring only to click on my flashlight when absolutely necessary. I didn't want to draw attention to what I was doing, even though the road rarely saw traffic at night. The only times I did turn the flashlight on was when I had to cut a couple of big tree roots with a branch saw. My van and the big maple tree shielded my activity from the roadway, but I have no idea what spurred me to bury him there.

I carried on for hours until it seemed I would not be able to climb from the hole. I was eight feet down at least and had to use the smaller roots to get up and out again.

When I got back to the surface, I was panting like a dog, and I collapsed on my side looking at the wheel of my van. I thought how ironic it would be if I suffered a coronary right here, only inches from the body of my victim hidden inside the van.

I took a deep breath, got up and opened the van doors. There he lay, wrapped in an old bed sheet, a dark stain marking the spot where I had hit him. I reached in and tried to grab the sheet and heave his body into the hole, but I knew immediately that it would tear under strain. Instead, I put my arms under him, like a father might carry a sleeping child, and picked him up.

As I stood holding his body over the grave, I couldn't help but think I should say or do something. The best I could come up with was, "Forgive me." Then I released him.

As he dropped, the sheet covering him caught on one of the amputated roots, and he unrolled from his shroud like a mummy, but that was not the worst. There was a crunch and a snap of bone when he bottomed out, and I could swear I heard a moan – but I reasoned later that it was just the last of the air escaping from his lungs.

The bed sheet was useless now, so I reached in, withdrew it and cast it aside. There was no point in tossing it into the hole, and I was sure it would just get hung up again.

Instead, I took one last look at the body. His neck had broken from the fall. His head was twisted to the right and was pulled back perversely. He looked more like a mutant than a boy. I shivered.

Behind me, the sun waited just below the horizon, threatening to rise. With that in mind, I scooped a shovelful of dirt and cast it into the hole. When the first scoop splashed across his broken carcass, my paralysis broke, and I refilled the hole with shovel after manic shovel fueled by my panic.

An hour and a half later, the sun beat against the back of the neck just as I was finishing up. With the grave filled and the body hidden deep within the ground, I felt my senses begin to sharpen.

Someone or something was watching me. I looked up and down Van Dyke Road then around my property, but there was nothing. But I could still feel it, the same way I felt when that neighbor kid was watching me.

Then I looked up at the old stone chimney on my house. That was the first time I saw the big Raven.

With the body buried I still had quite a few things to consider. I was intent on killing myself, but I struggled with the logistics. Shooting yourself is not as clean and straightforward as some think and I didn't want to end up with half a face in some hospital ward being fed liquids for the rest of my life.

So I did the next most enticing thing: I crawled into a bottle. I had a case of scotch in the cellar to add to my half-killed forty pounder. I went down and brought up four bottles, set them out neatly on my counter and began to binge.

Days passed as I drank heavily and slept intermittently. I was losing track of time, but I could feel the change inside me. It was around the second bottle when the transformation began.

How do I explain this?

I felt like I had fallen off the slimy edge of a submerged rock shelf into the abyss of darkness with nothing to hold onto. I was slowly sinking deeper and deeper and as I drowned in the dark crevasse the 'old me' died, and a monster took shape in my place. This new creature would be without remorse, without compassion, and it would crave more. As I slipped away, I could feel it taking over me.

Maybe I'll grab two boys next time, the dark half mused.

I had begun to abandon what was left of my conscience. I was changing and though you might argue that I was already a molester and a murderer, what I was becoming was even worse.

Then the paranoia started.

Something terrible was coming, of this I was sure.

The entire time I drank, I did nothing but watch the burial site through my front window. I poured drink after drink down my gullet, becoming delusional. My body would succumb, dragging me in and out of a comatose state. When I awoke, I began watching the grave again, looking for a change of some type. Anyone else might have thought the paranoia ridiculous, but 'anyone else' had not killed and buried a young boy under the maple tree in their front yard.

Something inside me demanded that I keep watch over that grave. Something powerful and frightening. All the while, I could feel that darker half picking at me. It was insisting that no police would be coming to ask questions about the missing boy. At first, I pushed the voice away, settling for the bottle – but with each passing hour, it continued to argue.

Come on, Stephen, what have you got to lose now? The voice asked. I'll tell you: nothing.

"Fuck you!" I barked drunkenly – but already it was enveloping me. It seemed that it was only a matter of time before I would go out cruising for a new victim.

In my semi-sober state, I decided that night that I would write a note, get the shotgun I kept around for coyotes and kill myself. With this decision, I poured another glass of scotch and decided to have one last blowout before I pulled the plug.

Numerous drinks later, a thunderstorm knocked out the power and the phone lines, so I decided to wait until morning. Then I would contact the police and tell them they had to come to the house. Once that was done, I would leave the note on the kitchen table and shoot myself in the head.

I took up my usual spot and opened the last bottle of scotch. By my second drink, the rain began to bead on the window outside as it became darker. With the recliner set right in front of the picture window, I stared at the gravesite and saw the raven again. It had flown down from a branch and was walking about upon the fresh sods. But this was much, much larger than your average bird.

I hated these fucking birds. They were always in my corn, wreaking havoc on my crop. I might have got my gun and taken a shot at it but reminded myself that very soon it would not matter.

It wandered atop the grave, pecking at the sods, then cast its gaze toward me. At first, I didn't believe it was looking at me. Dumb animals think about two things: sex and food. But it continued to gawk. I could not tear my eyes away, abruptly thinking that this big black bird knew my secret. Maybe it was a messenger from Hell coming to collect my soul?

"Come and get it or fuck off."

Then the bird took flight, leaving me to mock my own paranoia.

Jesus Christ, you're fucking losing it, Steve-O.

I settled back, took another sip, and another.

Soon I was pouring a new drink, and as I was on the edge of another stupor, I raised the glass defiantly. "Cheers." And I took another gulp.

"See you on my way to Hell, the kid."

Not long after, I blacked out.

7

Thunder crashed, startling me awake to the acrid stench of vomit. Brushing my hand against my shirt, I could feel the cold sticky bile peppered with tiny hard pebbles of whatever I had eaten during my blackout. I pulled my hand away in disgust and peered out into the darkness of the front yard as I wiped it on the armrest.

The sky was almost pitch black, and I could barely see the silhouette of the big maple. Then lightning flashed, imprinting a negative of the yard on my vision. At first, I thought it was a trick of the light or my mind playing games - then the lightning flashed again, timed with the rumble of thunder from the first strike. I jumped from the chair and pressed against the glass, gawking in disbelief.

Oh my God! Oh my God, no!

The grave had been unearthed, the sods askew and piles of dirt were haphazardly pushed outward. I backed away from the window, stupidly thinking it might be the police who had dug him up, but my mind was quick to dismiss that.

Maybe he isn't dead, my mind screamed, but that was impossible. I had left his body there to bleed out. Even if I had buried him alive, there was no way he could have dug his way free. I had covered him with at least seven or eight hundred pounds of dirt. Never mind that he had been underground for a couple days.

Nevertheless, I backed away from the window, yet unable to tear my eyes from it. I backed right into the coffee table. Empty scotch bottles clinked against each other, then fell to the floor. I pinwheeled and managed to catch myself before joining them.

I had one thing in mind now. *Get the gun!*

Using the wall as a guide, I continued to back up, and when I felt the door jamb, I turned to run for the bedroom and came face to face with what could only be conjured up from the mind of a terrified child.

I heard its labored breathing. In and out like an asthmatic horse. At first, I did not know who or what it was, just that it towered above me over seven feet high. Then I recognized tattered clothing and could see the thing's neck was twisted perversely to the right. That gave away its identity instantly.

It looked like a rotted corpse, huge and mutated.

"Steeeeeeeeeeeeeeeepheeeeeeeeeeeen," it hissed through a grin of clenched teeth. Its hair hung in wet braids, dripping plops of mud onto the floor. It was the boy, his spine and bones mutated and stretched, skin torn and rotted, malformed into this thing from hell.

My legs became rubbery.

It glared at me, with eyes ablaze a fiery white, like miniature fluorescent globes in its sockets. I could smell the stink of decay on its breath. I tried to back away, thinking I would die of a heart attack at any moment as the muscles in my chest contracted and wrung the breath from my body. That would have been a blessing.

"Where are you going?" it thundered. An oversized hand caught me by the scruff of my shirt. I tried to pull away, but it jerked me in and roared. "I said where are you going, Stephen?" Bits of dirt and spittle rained down on my face.

"Please," I begged, trying to wiggle free.

"Please! PLEASE!" It bellowed a loud echo of laughter that shook the whole house. Then it slapped something into my hand. I looked down to see it was the chunk of scalp.

"Nobody rides for free, Stephen, isn't that right? Not even you!"

That was a joke I had shared with him when I picked him up.

"God!" My heart almost stopped.

"God?" it parroted. "God will not help you."

It let out a high-pitched shriek that made the remaining upstanding scotch bottles tumble from the table with a series of hollow thuds. Then it pulled me even closer and lifted me off the ground so that I was inches from its face. A beetle crawled out of its nostril and up onto one of its eyes, where it cooked off in the searing heat.

"I'm sorry," I cried. "I didn't..."

"Sorry? You aren't sorry!" As it spoke it spat clods of dirt at me, and its grip tightened. My shirt twisted under its hand like a tourniquet crushing my windpipe.

I couldn't breathe. Thinking I would be killed at any moment, I closed my eyes, silently begging God's forgiveness. I would not look at it. I would only pray, and though I could hear the rush of its breath in and out, I clamped my eyes tightly closed.

Then it flung me against the door jamb, and I crashed to the floor. There at its feet, I prayed for a way out of this, pledging my soul to any God that would save me from this horrible fate. Its breathing became sluggish and muted. My ears sealed up, and I waited to be dealt the final indignity before it tore me apart.

Then there was only a vacuous silence.

I expected to open my eyes, and its face would be right there, just inches away. I waited for it to reach down and tear me apart limb from limb, but nothing. I could hear no panting, nor could I smell the dank stench of wet dirt: there was only the jackhammer in my chest pumping erratically, beating in my ears. It seemed a very long time I lay there, not daring to open my eyes.

Then I heard another voice.

"It's gone, Stephen."

This voice was calm and reassuring. I was paralyzed with fear, and sure this was a ruse.

"You can open your eyes, Stephen. It is gone." The voice was brittle and impatient, but added, "I promise."

I still didn't dare open my eyes. "Who are you?"

"I'm a friend. The only friend you have left in this world."

"I have no friends. I've gone mad. Dear God, please forgive me."

The voice sighed impatiently. "Open your eyes. Open them now, or I'll bring it back!"

And so, I squinted, the lashes on my eyelids still interlocked. I was ready to slam them shut at the first sign of the gruesome beast – but the voice spoke the truth. The monstrosity that had lifted me up was gone, and in the shadowy darkness of the living room, everything was back to normal, except for the dark figure who sat comfortably in my chair. That, and the fact that the room's temperature had dropped to below freezing.

"Feel better," he asked, but he really wasn't asking. Instead, he was implying that I should feel better.

I could not see his face; he sat in the shadows and spoke with the slow methodic voice of a man negotiating a business deal.

"Where did you come from?" I implored.

He reached over, picked up my pack of cigarettes and pulled out a smoke, tapping it on his thumbnail. "You beckoned me." Then he struck a match to light. It should have illuminated his face – but it didn't.

I don't think he had a face.

"Beckoned?"

He reached out and picked up the quarter full bottle of scotch, and the contents began to freeze almost instantly. Had I conjured up a demon, the devil himself?

A faint mist rose from his silhouette – though it was not so much a mist, but a gas like you might see rising from a slab of dry ice. He was the source of the cold in the room.

"I'm calling the police," I blurted suddenly, forgetting that the lines were down.

"Go ahead," he dared.

I picked the phone up off the floor.

He continued, "Do you want to know what they'll find?"

He was enjoying this exchange, almost as if we were engaged in a game of poker rather than a mad discussion of beckoning and the undead.

"What?"

"They'll find a man named Stephen Hopper, dead for no apparent reason. They won't know what horror or pain you will have suffered. They will not see you plead for death and believe me, Stephen; death will be an act of kindness. So go ahead; call the police."

He took a drag of the cigarette.

I set the receiver down on the table and stood before him a broken man. "Who are you?" I knew the word I meant to ask, but I didn't dare ask 'what.'

"I am either your friend or your worst nightmare. To defy me is the nastiest mistake you can make. I have powers that are unimaginable. You have seen some of those powers tonight, but they pale in comparison to what I am capable of. Perhaps we can delve deeper into that as we get to know each other – but for now, I am going to offer you a one-time deal."

"What is that?"

He raised his hand. Suddenly I was blinded and felt piercing red-hot needles behind my optic nerves. I fell to my knees in agony.

"Don't interrupt me, Stephen. Not only is it rude, but stupid."

My eyesight restored itself, the pain subsiding while he continued to speak as if nothing happened. "As I said, I am here to offer you a deal. I'm not going to patronize you, Stephen: you are damned, but I am giving you an option to prolong your stay here and keep doing what it is you like to do."

"Deal? I don't understand."

"Yes, you do. Don't act stupid. That is a quality I dislike, and it brings out a part of me you would rather not see. You can come with me now, and I will promise you an eternity of suffering, or you can simply carry on. If you act as my caretaker and do my bidding, I will allow you to stay here as long as there is air in your lungs."

"Carry on?" I didn't understand at first; or didn't want to.

He sighed then. "You humans can be so obtuse, needing everything spelled out for you. I have lived for centuries, and you don't know how irritating that is." He paused a second, gathering himself, or restraining the anger I had instilled in him. "You can do what it is that turns your fancy, but killing will not be a part of that equation."

"I can't do that," I protested, but it was weak and insincere.

He crushed out the cigarette on my coffee table and leaned forward, capturing me with his eyes. "I want you to bring back more boys, but you mustn't kill them. Once you are done with them, they will be mine."

He waved his hand, and the basement door swung slowly open – except it wasn't the opening to my basement anymore. Instantly, he was beside me, escorting me to the doorway. An eerie blue light emanated from the opening, cold fog billowed out and across the floor. A thousand voices cried and shrieked, and though I tried to cover my ears, I could not silence them.

I was convinced that I was staring into the chasm of hell. While the tormented souls continued their melody of pain, the cold vapor was lit up by strobes of light. There was something else moving down there in the void, something not suffering, but the inflictor of the anguish I heard. There were low guttural growls, followed by obscure words that could only be pleading. The door jamb cracked, splintering from the extreme cold, and I waited for him to push me down the stairwell into the depths of hell.

His voice, calm and business-like, overpowered the cries of the damned, and he gave his ultimatum. "What will it be, Stephen? Come now… or later?"

"Alright," I cried.

The door slammed shut with a crash, sealing the void and my fate.

"Good," he replied, leading me away. "I thought you'd see it my way. You'll be able to sleep now, but there are few more things we need to discuss before I go. Just some procedures, so you don't leave loose ends."

He told me never to take the locals. Taking the locals would raise eyebrows and bring suspicion, which would lead to the end of our contract and inevitably me. He also told me that I could bring them back and do whatever I wanted with them, but I was never to kill them.

"When you see a large raven perched at your window you will release them into the cornfield," he instructed.

I suddenly recalled the raven that had been watching when I buried the boy's body. I was not sure of its significance at the time but knew it was somehow attached to this man.

"I wouldn't recommend you watch what happens when you let them go. You might lose your nerve. Just do as I say, and everything will work out for both of us."

I listened intently as he gave a few more instructions and finally finished.

"Go to bed now, Stephen; get some rest. I will be back by the week's end. You have three days."

"What is your name?"

"You can call me Franklin."

"Franklin," I repeated turning my eyes to the floor. Did I just sign a pact with the Devil? Then, another voice: Goddamned right you did.

I looked back, and he was gone. I would have thought the whole event an alcohol-induced nightmare, or the beginnings of insanity if not for what he left behind. There, in the empty chair, was the frozen outline of where he'd been sitting.

I leaned across the table, daring to wave my hands through the area to make sure he was gone. I moaned, then covered my mouth, hushing the cries that wanted to get out, holding the madness in. I had just cut a deal with an agent of the devil, and like Faust, there would be no bartering when he came to collect me.

Terrified curiosity made me touch my index and middle finger to the frozen cloth on the chair, but I quickly pulled them away. The tips of my fingers were waxy white; frostbite set in instantly. I didn't dare put them in my mouth.

Suddenly, I was incredibly tired; the fatigue from the week's events and the more recent night terror had drained my strength completely. I went to my room and fell face down on my bed.

I did not dream.

I awoke late in the afternoon the next day. Initially, I thought it might have all been a horrible nightmare, but when I returned to the easy-chair, I saw the moisture that still clung to it. The crushed out cigarette on my coffee table also refuted any reasoning that the previous night's events were a hallucination.

I then went out and checked the boy's grave in front of the house. The sods, which I'd cut and laid so carefully, look disturbed somehow. I began to shake uncontrollably.

There would be no turning back. I did not want to face the consequences if this dark man returned, and I had nothing to offer. So I prepped my van and set out on the hunt.

Four days later a large black raven tapped at the picture window. I stood there frozen for a moment, and it stared at me - or into me. I knew what had to be done.

I went downstairs, unshackled the scared and confused boy from the water heater.

"It's okay, I'm letting you go." I led him upstairs and to the back door, speaking like his protector. "Go into the cornfield. On the other side of that wood line, there's a house. There you'll find safety."

He hesitated, unsure of my sincerity.

"Go," I urged.

He hesitated only a second more, then ran for his life down the back steps, through the maze of farm equipment, then into my corn. He disappeared from view, but the stalks marked his progress, shaking and shuddering as he grazed them. I watched for something to happen, wondering if Franklin was out there waiting.

He crossed three hundred yards with the speed of a gazelle. Strange as it sounds something inside of me wanted him to make it, even if it meant my demise - but that was instantly killed off.

I heard the flap of a giant bird taking flight from on top of my house. I should have turned away, but God help me, I didn't. My God, I saw it all.

The big raven flew across the field, climbing in altitude until it was right over top of him. For a second it seemed frozen in the sky - then it dived straight down, spinning as it did. When it entered the corn, there was the momentary cry of surprise, a bone-snapping crunch. Blood sprayed upward into the air, and then there were ripping, tearing sounds that could only be flesh. Before I tore my eyes away, I saw a few of the stalks swaying back and forth sporadically.

I could take no more and went back into the house.

Half an hour passed, maybe a little more.

"Stephen," a hollow voice called from outside.

I opened the back door and there he stood at the edge of the cornfield, completely naked, his eyes aglow, a glowing aura surrounding him, distorting him. I saw the black silken blood upon his gray semi-transparent skin. He was not a man at all. He looked more like a gargoyle or an alien.

"Clean it up," he commanded. "Leave no trace."

Then he turned his back to me and walked into the cornfield and out of sight. There was horrible sound, a shriek like nothing I'd heard before, and then a light flashed from between the corn stalks.

The raven flew up and into the night.

I must have stared up at the sky for better than twenty minutes before I finally snapped out of it. What I have done? I thought. What spawn of hell have I become?

I went out to my barn and gathered the things I would need. A shovel, a wheelbarrow, some plastic bags, and a few other things. Then I embarked on what would become my job description for the next year.

Gravedigger–caretaker–accomplice.

[INTERVIEW ENDS]

9

Hopper leaned back and let out a sigh of relief, his tale told. He doubted Logan believed him, but just the same it felt good to share. Sometimes confession is a good way of cleansing oneself, he thought.

"You know the rest, Logan. I don't think I have to go into detail. The events are pretty much the same, except in the case of that Parkins Boy." Hopper looked up at Logan for the first time. "I killed him and the first boy. The rest belong to Franklin."

Logan glanced at the two-way mirror, then to Hopper.

"Maybe if I hadn't been so stupid I wouldn't be sitting here right now," he added.

The video equipment let out a low whining alarm, then shut down. Logan and Hopper sat there facing each other for over five minutes as Logan tried to formulate a response.

Finally, he asked a question.

"Why did you take a local kid and break your pact?" He felt stupid asking this but wanted some insight into Tommy's demise. He imagined Pearson and anybody else watching must be questioning why he was entertaining such an outlandish tale.

"After the last boy, Franklin told me I had to lay off for a while. After that, he left and did not return. I guess I gave in to my own urges, thinking he wouldn't be coming back – and if he did, I would just keep the Parkins boy a secret. Franklin always gave me a schedule. First, he would show up at my house, usually at the oddest times. Sometimes I would walk into a room, and he'd be sitting there – but he didn't look like he had in the cornfield. He looked like a man. An Indian man dressed all in black. Occasionally he would want to talk; he'd ask me questions about things – but our conversations always ended the same way. He would tell me to start looking for a new boy. That he'd be back in a few days or a week. Then, like clockwork, the raven would appear."

"Are there any more bodies, Hopper?" Logan asked calmly. "Anything you haven't told me?"

Hopper shook his head. "I've told you everything. There are no more bodies, but Franklin is still out there."

"You're absolutely certain?"

"Yes."

"Okay. I am going to be straight with you, Hopper, because if I'm not, I will feel dirty for not doing so." As he spoke, he showed no emotion, as if instructing a wayward child. "We are finished, you and I. I am no longer your confidante, and from here in you deal exclusively with Detective Pearson.

To be quite honest, you sicken me. It is bad enough that you planted seventeen bodies in my county, but you humiliated them before doing so. You snuffed out seventeen kids and have damaged scores of others."

Hopper stared across the table, expecting the Chief to explode in anger and jump across at him – but Logan simply continued his lecture.

"In three days they will fly you to Artisan Institute for psychiatric evaluation. I imagine you can spin your tale for them as well to try and gain access to a mental health facility, but I will warn you that the people in this field will see you coming a mile away."

Then Logan looked to the two-way mirror and stood up.

10

Hopper sat in his cell, motionless. He had warned them, and now all he could do was hope to get out of this shithole before Franklin came back. Three days felt like three years. I'm fucked, he thought, then picked up his bible and began to read.

11

The sun was just coming up as Logan made his way out to the cruiser to finally head home. He told Pearson that he would meet for dinner later in the day after he picked up Doctor Kolchak from the airport. They would discuss things then: right now he was too tired to rationally discuss Hopper's crazy story. He could not wait to get this ghoul out of his county.

He had broken an old rule of police investigation. He had alienated the perpetrator. But he didn't care anymore: he was tired, and he wanted him gone.

It was going to be a long time before the people of this community healed, Logan among them.

***

CHAPTER 9 - JACKANOOB

1

Was he dreaming, or was it a vision? Blackbird did not know; he only knew he was bearing witness to something from the past. If this was a dream, it was surreal, almost a hallucination, lacking the disconnectedness he often felt when dreaming.

Inside a substantial shelter, he was surrounded by ten native people all standing in a circle. He was there, but invisible to their eyes. At the head of the ring stood an old man who looked somewhat like Grandfather, but much older. Outside the wind howled, blowing drifts of the snow against the sides of wooden and stone shelter. He could feel the cold in his bones, a cold that was akin to Spirit Woods.

As the natives spoke, he picked up the ancient language of his ancestors, and suddenly he understood it perfectly. It was the same dialect as his Grandfather, and the other members of the council shared.

This is amazing, he thought. *I understand it all.*

He remembered the story recounted by Grandfather embedded deep in Chocktee heritage. There was no food, and they were starving. Winters cold had cut them off, and the animals were scarce, hiding from the boney fingers of blizzard-kill. With starvation came sickness and disease. The temperatures outside were so cold that to venture out for a prolonged time was a death sentence. The Chief Elder, whose name was Jackanoob, gathered the Chocktee council to tell them of his decision.

"Go outside, take two bodies and prepare them. The children must not know. Tell them it is wild boar," Jackanoob ordered.

A stern looking man stepped forward; he was a warrior whose prime had almost passed. "It is a sin to eat of a man. We will summon evil spirits."

The others shuddered at the outburst. It was not customary to question the judgment of the Chief Elder. And to do so publically was unheard of. Such questioning was only to be done in confidence and with good judgment.

The warrior looked around at them all, then to the Chief Elder Jackanoob. "Forgive what you might think as disrespect, Chief Elder, but this is a decision which will affect everyone. You know I would follow you to the ends of the earth, I would sacrifice my life for Chocktee – it is only out of deep concern that I raise my voice now."

The others looked on in silence as the Chief Elder chose his words carefully. He knew it was a sin, but he feared for his people more than he dreaded the tales of evil. He could not let them fall victim to the cold. "We will die otherwise, Igasho! Do as I say."

"Elder Jackanoob is right," a younger member of the council, named Mongwau, agreed. "The spirits have forsaken us. We must survive the winter. We have a responsibility to our people."

Igasho turned his eyes upon Mongwau, sharp and angry, but he held his tongue.

Blackbird could hear Grandfather's words. "The biting cold of winter had come almost a month early, and they had not completely stocked their food supply. Early on, a fire tore through two of the shelters, burning up the dried fish and venison. With two months of winter still at their door, they knew that our people would not live to see the spring. So the Elders took counsel and determined that they had no choice but to consume the dead. There was little division, except for Igasho, but the ultimate decision rested with the Chief Elder, Jackanoob."

"I will bear the responsibility if the spirits are angered," Jackanoob said, interrupting Blackbird's memory. "I take it upon my shoulders."

There were grunts, but no one challenged the Chocktee Elder.

Blackbird turned left and right in awe of this piece of history unfolding before his eyes. As he did, not one of them looked his way. He was invisible.

The Chief Elder gazed upon his council one after another. They lowered their eyes in respect and to acknowledge his decision. All agreed until he reached Igasho, who stared back at him austerely.

The electricity between the two men was intense. Jackanoob and Igasho were locked in an argument without language. Words were not necessary. Igasho's eyes burned with the fire of disapproval. These two men were the titans of Chocktee history, spoke of in many talking circles and during what Grandfather called palaver. The great warrior Igasho understood the sin, but there was something more, something that Grandfather related to young Blackbird in the many stories. Something he might not know had Grandfather not told him and Johnny Proudfoot.

"Finally, with great trepidation, elder Igasho, the leader of the clan of five, lowered his eyes and when he did his heart broke for his people and his friend Jackanoob. For all his influence he could not stop the Chief Elder from making this decision, but at that moment he prayed to the Spirit Mother that she would make Jackanoob relent. They were like brothers – not unlike you, Young Daniel and Little Johnny," Grandfather told them. "Igasho was hard like stone, a fierce warrior, while his blood brother Jackanoob was a man of the people. Easy to approach, kind in words, and soft in the heart."

Grandfather made the comparison between him and Proudfoot, but Blackbird likened them more to Grandfather himself and that of Old Jake Toomey.

The atmosphere around him suddenly rippled, and there were clanging echoes as everything began to speed up. The people in the shelter moved in time lapse.

Time is shifting, he thought.

His surroundings rippled, darkened, then transitioned to the outside of another shelter somewhere else in the village. Snow blew on a forty-five-degree angle. Blackbird was impervious to the bitter cold of this vision, but he fully understood the discomfort it caused these men as they went about their work. They were taking the two bodies from where they had been laid amongst a group of 10 who had succumbed to winter's cruelty.

Time shifted again.

He was in another shelter, watching as they unsheathed their knives and began to butcher the now thawing dead, cutting long strips of meat. This was a secret activity, away from the eyes of the Chocktee people. Igasho, for all his objection, made the first cut, his face filled with angry determination.

Grandfather's voice was becoming clearer now, speaking inside Blackbird's head, narrating the vision as it unfolded. "Igasho did not agree with the Chief Elder's orders, but he carried them out. Young Mongwau vomited and fell backward, his eyes filled with fear, the weight of what they were doing too much for his shoulders to bear."

Igasho stopped his work, reached down and lifted Mongwau up with one mighty hand. He slapped the blade back into the Elder's hand. "It is too late now to have a weak heart! Get busy!"

Mongwau's eyes bulged with fear. Blackbird needed no narration from Grandfather, although he wondered what the Chocktee man was more afraid of. Butchering the dead and angering the spirits? Or the wrath of Chocktee's fiercest warrior?

Time was shifting again, but now he was accompanied by Grandfather's soothing voice. The images splashed by in liquid ripples, moving with comic speed while Grandfather whispered.

"Watch closely, Young Daniel: there is a lesson here."

He snapped his head right to look. This had not come from his memory. He could not see Grandfather, but he felt the old man beside him.

More darkness, fading, then light and colors converged into focus. Now Blackbird was in the Long House, surrounded by his ancestors, accompanied by the voice of Grandfather and bearing witness to the past. The Chocktee Elders were eating the meat from the two dead men they had butchered. They ate cautiously at first, with a heavy heart, but once committing it became easier. Their hunger was being sated. No matter the sin, their bodies took the much-needed nourishment.

"As they ate, beating away their hunger, smiles fell onto their faces, and the dread was swept away – but it was short-lived," Grandfather continued.

The Chocktee people smiled and laughed as they ate – all except those who knew what it was they were eating. The warrior Igasho looked from Jackanoob to the children of Chocktee and then back to the Chief Elder. His chiseled chin, which was strong and proud, trembled slightly.

He knows, and he is powerless to stop it, Blackbird mused.

"Yes, he knows," Grandfather echoed.

Another time shift.

"The Chocktee slept, their bellies full, their hunger is gone. All except the Elder Jackanoob and the warrior Igasho. The two stood vigil over the sleeping children of Chocktee and waited in the hope that the spirits would ignore their sins and that winter gales had blinded the guardians of Spirit Woods to the sins of the man. They would not be so fortunate."

A shriek cut through the village like shards of broken glass. Igasho was the first to stand up and look to the door that held the winter cold at bay. Blackbird recognized the shriek, even though it differed somewhat from the one he had heard.

The warrior muttered grimly, "Now we pay for our sins."

Igasho unsheathed his knife, ready to meet the beast.

A second shriek tore through the village waking the Chocktee, terrifying the children and a hush fell over them. "Move the children from the door!" Igasho commanded.

"What is it? Wendigo? Who goes there?" Mongwau shivered.

"The Spirits who have forsaken you! Now shut your mouth!" Igasho took a breath, then waved upon his Warrior Party of Five to move toward the door. The Chocktee people moved to the other end of the Long House, including Mongwau, who cowered with the women and children.

Jackanoob waited to see what evil they had awakened.

"Ready yourself!" Igasho commanded. His warriors moved into a half circle around the door, their knives at the ready.

He reached for the latch, slid it over. A child cried behind them.

Blackbird held his breath.

Reaching down with his left hand, Igasho pulled the door open. His teeth were clenched so tight that his jaw ached. The Chocktee warriors held their blades up high, ready to strike in unison. They were a single cell at this moment, and Igasho was their nucleus.

The unlatched door suddenly door blew open, and with it, another shriek came out of the blowing snow and into the shelter.

Igasho and his warriors were transfixed, waiting to do battle.

"Something, not of this world, had broken through the walls of time. It brought with it death," Grandfather narrated.

Then, from behind, Jackanoob called out, "Igasho!"

Mongwau suddenly shrieked, his eyes washing out – and with lightning speed, he was on one of the children with murderous rage. The child had no time to cry out before his life had been extinguished, then his belly was opened to dine.

Chaos. Screaming. Before Igasho or his warriors could react, a woman who had also been cowering in the corner let out a similar shriek, then tore out both her eyes and popped them into her mouth. As she chewed, she cackled madly.

Igasho jumped on Mongwau, set his blade against his throat. Pulling his head back Igasho slew him in a single cut. Blood spurted out across the Long House floor the as eyeless woman continued to laugh maniacally, clawing out at the others surrounding her.

"Some called it the fever. Others thought our people were possessed. It took hold in them and made them do things that no sane man or woman would do," Grandfather continued.

The warriors were ruthless in dispatching the woman.

Time raced and slowed down as fever took hold on Chocktee and began to spread. There were screams, madness, murder, and Igasho's warrior clan was saddled with killing the infected. Between each incident, Blackbird watched and listened as the landscape before him continued to morph into Grandfather's calm narrative.

"The Elder named Jackanoob listened to the shrieking accusations beyond the village in the Spirit Woods where the source of the madness resided in the blowing cold of the snow. They had awakened it. He was responsible."

Time shifted again. Darkness engulfed him.

The world slowly focused, the sounds of terror and mayhem gone, giving way to the solitude of spirit woods and a crackling fire. He was sitting on a log across from Jackanoob, happy to be away from the chaos of the longhouse. They were alone, the snow had stopped, but the biting cold still turned the old man's breath to ice.

He watched with fascination while Jackanoob spoke in the ancient Chocktee and realized that he could no longer understand the dialect. The village elder chanted as the liquid green glow in the sky above danced with the spirits of the dead. He was in a trance, calling to the spirits. That much Blackbird knew.

Overhead the aurora began to swirl and descend from the sky down into the woods. At first, it fell like raindrops solidifying, then evaporated into a green mist just beyond the fire.

He's making contact.

Blackbird reached across the fire and waved his hand, but the old man could not see him.

Behind the Elder, the mist glowed brighter, became dense and began to flow from the woods toward them. White lights shifted, moved to and fro just below its surface as it came. The old man increased the cadence of his chant and the mist pulsed and rippled as glowing green liquid began to drip upward like water droplets in reverse. As they did a sphere began to form just above the haze. It hovered four feet above the snow and a pulse of light emanating from its center. At first, it was about the size of a softball, but as each drop flowed upward, the sphere's volume tripled.

Then behind it, another began to form, then there were two, then four, then six. As they grew they spread, forming a semi-circle around the old man and the fire, each humming at different pitches, like tuning forks.

The fire itself became green, and Jackanoob's face was saturated by the afterglow as he continued to chant and rock rhythmically. Simultaneously each orb settled in front of him and hummed explicitly in its own tone. Blackbird understood that they were conversing.

"He is seeking their counsel," Grandfather whispered.

Blackbird was in awe. The old Indian could not see or hear him as he sat openly crying because he knew that the stories his Grandfather told of the Northern lights and how they held the souls of the dead were true.

The sixth orb before Jackanoob shone brightly and hummed loudly. Its exterior liquid washed over it, reflecting the snow and woods, but Daniel could not see himself in its reflective glaze. Jackanoob chanted louder, and the humming grew with him.

Together they counseled him on what to do about the madness.

Blackbird wondered if the old man could see the orbs or if he only heard their voices.

Each of the orbs began to grow brighter at once – then they dimmed and surrounded the old Indian and Blackbird. The green mist that clung low to the ground started to flicker electrically with light. As it did the orbs began to descend into the mist and melt away like so much gas.

The humming faded and then they were gone. The old man was statuesque and comatose as the mist began to roll back into the woods, taking with it the flickering lights. Only embers remained of the fire.

Still, Jackanoob sat motionless.

"Old man. Wake up," Blackbird said; though he knew the Elder could not hear him.

Time shifted again.

There was daylight, and the old Indian trudged through the snow deeper into the woods. Blackbird walked at his side. The snow had stopped, the sky was clearing, but the breath of the old man gave no illusion the biting cold had relented.

"Where are we going, old man?" There was no response. "Let me guess –"

Daniel stopped mid-sentence. He heard a sound, a sound that he recognized, a sound that had terrified and changed the course of his own life.

It was a high shriek.

"I don't think you want to go this way, old man," he called after the village Elder.

Jackanoob kept walking, his head hung low and determined.

The old man muttered something in Chocktee. Blackbird did not recognize this word, but he understood that the Elder was calling the creature out, summoning it. It was becoming clear what he intended to do.

In a blur the creature shot past him, sending up a flurry of snow. The Elder was no match for its speed or ferocity. Instead, he muttered that same beckoning call. The creature stopped suddenly, attached itself to a tree.

This creature was similar to Skin. Its eyes were also bulbous and reflective, but it was larger – almost nine feet tall, in fact. On its hands were four talon-like fingers, and its feet stretched out nearly ten inches. Its mouth was riddled with shards of broken teeth that fell back row after row, and between those rapturous shards were black-grey gums that bled an ooze of infection and disease. Its body was long and lanky, its skin tattered with sores that spread over its starved ribcage.

This was not a Skinwalker, but a wendigo brought on by the sins of the man.

Clinging to its perch, it stared down on him hungrily.

"What do you want of me, human?' It snarled. A gob of black saliva dripped from its large incisors.

The old Indian turned to look at the creature. Apparently, it did not like this as it shot past him, sending up another flurry of snow. This creature was much bigger and even more frightening than Skin.

It let out a shriek.

"I come with offerings," the Elder said.

"What could you possibly offer me?" It shot past him again, knocked him into the snow, and took hold on the same tree it had first faced him from. "Do not look at me or I will tear out your eyes and feed them to you!"

The old man stared down into the snow and kept talking. "I am here to atone for the sins of my people."

"I'm listening," the creature said.

"We have angered the spirits of this land by feasting upon the flesh of our dead. It was I, Jackanoob, who allowed my people to do so. I am the oldest and most respected member of my people, and I offer myself as a sacrifice if you lift the madness that now plagues them."

The creature swooped down from the tree, and for the first time, Jackanoob was standing face to face with the aberration of his peoples' sins. It towered over him, its hollow black sockets reflecting the sins of the Chocktee as they feasted on the dead.

"It is an interesting proposition, but hardly penance for bringing me forth." It let out another shriek. A thin runner of blood trickled from one of Jackanoob's ears: the cry burst one of his eardrums. "It is not enough, old man."

"We are a people who recognize when night and day are equal, and on that day in spring and fall, we celebrate the renewal and harvest of the earth. In addition to myself, I offer you these two days of sacrifice and service."

"I could take you now and then tear your people apart for summoning me. If I take you in exchange, what lesson will they have learned? What burden will they have carried?"

"I offer myself, and if you take me, you can set forth a curse on my people, that on those two days they will serve you. That the blood of animals will be left in the woods as a sacrifice."

The creature considered this, then: "I will take your offering, old man."

Then in a blur, it shot down, scooped him up with a single talon and pulled him in close, like a mother cradling a child.

"I will lift the sickness that plagues your people, and in return, you will give of yourself to me. In my world, you will serve me and on the two days a year when night are day are equal you'll roam these woods and feed."

Its hollow sockets became windows showing a future in which the people of Chocktee gathered in the woods. "They will be your caretaker on these two days."

"Oh my God," Blackbird muttered while the Elder named Jackanoob stared into the empty caverns and saw the ritual of the Equinox. He would be damning his people for generations to come.

"You will change, old man. You will have no love. You will only hunger, and you will kill anyone to feed that hunger. Do you understand?" the creature asked.

Jackanoob nodded.

"I could kill them all now, and it will be done. They will die but once," the creature offered.

The Elder shook his head. Then, in one swift, razor motion, the creature slashed Jackanoob's cheek open and spat black ick into the wound. The old Indian cried out. The wound began to glow blue – then sealed itself, becoming frostbitten and hard.

"Oh my God," Blackbird muttered again, realizing what he was really seeing.

The creature shot a glance toward Blackbird as if it had heard him and shrieked.

Jackanoob's eyes flooded with mercury as the black ick pulsed through his veins infected him. He shuddered in pain, a moan of agony escaping him while it worked into his marrow. All of this happened in seconds.

Then he began to come back.

"It is done. You may return to your people and prepare them. On the first day of Spring Equinox, you will return to these woods, and the cycle will begin."

The giant creature set him down.

It took a minute for the old man to come to his senses. He stared up at the wendigo understanding that it was different, more powerful and its kingdom not of this world.

The Elder reached up and gently, tentatively touched his fingers to the place his wound had been. Blackbird could see on his face that he now realized the extent of his sacrifice to spare his people the madness and mayhem which had forsaken them.

Jackanoob said nothing to the giant monster: he just turned and headed back for his village.

"Old man!" it called after him. He turned and looked back, and it was like staring at a carbon copy of himself. "We are one now, Jackanoob. When the snow is gone, I will be waiting. If you try to stay amongst your people, the hunger will overtake you, and you will slaughter them all."

The old man nodded.

He would keep his end of the bargain, although he had begun to think that death would have been a better alternative.

"Prepare them," it warned its voice and appearance a perfect mimic of the old man.

Then it shrieked again.

An orb, not unlike those Blackbird had seen earlier, coalesced in the air – but this was black, its haze blue, and Blackbird could feel the darkness coming off it in waves.

The orb punched through the air, spread out, opening a portal. Around it, the trees froze solid and bark cracked and split.

Jackanoob walked off. His head low, his heart drained, his soul damned.

Blackbird started to follow the old man, but the forest trembled. As the world about him began to twist and distort he watched the old man walk back toward his village to prepare his people for the burden he had brought them.

Time shifted again.

4

"Come to me, Daniel. The equinox has passed," his grandfather beckoned.

Blackbird was now watching himself in the Spirit Woods where this whole misadventure had begun. He had been sleeping; something had anesthetized him as he stood sentry in the ancient circle. This was his first involvement in the ritual since returning from college, and it was at his grandfather's insistence that he take part.

"Come now, sleepyhead. We will go back to your mother's house for blackberry tea and some much-needed rest."

Grandfather was inside the ancient circle where the Skinwalker roamed.

"You already know what is going to happen," Blackbird the witness said, and he felt the hot sting of tears forming in his eyes.

"What time is it, Grandfather?" Vision Daniel asked.

"My watch had stopped," Blackbird remembered. He started to cry.

The old man smiled, lines etched deep into his once brown skin, now weathered and grey. "It's time to go home. Come now; take my arm and help me; these old bones are brittle."

"Why must I watch this?" Blackbird cried, but he did not look away.

"There is a lesson in this," he heard again from inside his head.

Vision Daniel stepped forward and into the ancient circle to support the old man. He was ready to go home and spend time with his mother.

He had had enough rituals.

"Daniel! No!" The Daniel in the vision spun. His grandfather cried, "Jackanoob!" and then spat something in Chocktee.

Blackbird watched vision Daniel turn forward, back – and then the skinwalker was on him, knocking to the ground. He remembered its clutch was cold and breath stank of rotten meat, and from its lips dripped the black ick. For a moment it held him, and then it slit open his cheek, preparing to infect him with its curse.

Grandfather moved quickly, yelling in the ancient language, raising his diamond willow stick. He swung it with all his might. It connected with the creatures head – and snapped. First, the creature scowled, then it shrieked, before dropping Daniel and turning its attention on the old man.

They stood there, recognizing the other, exchanging words in the old language.

Grandfather dropped the broken diamond willow stick he had carried for as long as Daniel had known him. He looked to his grandson and smiled. "I will see you in the next world, Young Daniel."

The beast pounced on the old man and tore his weathered skin apart like tissue paper. Then, with one final swipe, its hooked toe ripped out the man's innards. In a millisecond the man, who Daniel Blackbird loved more than life itself, lay dead on the ground as the beast he called Jackanoob shot out of the ancient circle, free of the ritual which had held it captive for a century and a half.

Blackbird watched himself running to the old man's side as the lights of other Chocktee people began to close in. For a second the creature stopped to gobble down the old man's insides and locked eyes with Daniel. It smiled at him, its mouth smeared with blood.

Daniel sprang to give chase, and the creature darted off, scaling a large fir tree as the change began. It dropped its food and climbed, becoming a shadow in the night, contorting and changing into a giant raven. Then, the transformation complete, it shot upward into the darkness.

Vision Daniel looked up into the night and screamed. "I pledge my life to hunting you! I will not stop: I will track you until there is no breath in my body! Do you hear me! Do you hear me!"

Blood from the wound ran down his face, mixed with rain he didn't even realize had started. He looked crazed, his long slick black hair in tatters, his eyes filled with hate and every muscle and tendon on his body pulled tight. His knees buckled, and he began to sob.

"What have I done? Grandfather."

Blackbird could watch no more, having relived this night over and over enough in the waking world. Like the Daniel in his vision, he fell to his knees, overcome by the grief. He'd seen enough and broke into a fit of mournful sobs.

"Please. Let me wake up. I don't want to see this. Please," he begged. "Take me from this place."

There was a long and lonely silence then, filled only with sounds of Daniel Blackbird's despair. Time did not shift but faded, and with it, he hoped this would be the end. He no longer cared if this was a dream or a vision or if he had finally gone crazy. In real life, he had tortured himself every night with this for fifteen years. He did not want to relive this again. He just wanted it to be over.

But it wasn't.

And time shifted again.

There was a purring growl of something mechanical. Darkness gave way to grey, and suddenly he felt a hand on his shoulder and smelled the sweetness of Grandfather's skin splashed with Old Spice aftershave.

"We have much to discuss, Young Daniel." Grandfather removed his hand from his shoulder and smiled. "Come, let us palaver."

He almost fell over. They were in the Spirit Woods where he, Johnny and Grandfather had spent so much time. It was where the old man had counseled him on becoming a man, where he had heard so many stories.

Is this real?

In the center of a clearing, a fire burned brightly, and Grandfather took Daniel by the arm and led him toward it. The touch was reassuring, comforting.

He was no longer a witness to this vision, but a participant.

"That is the place, Young Daniel. We will go and make palaver and discuss what you will need to complete your quest."

"Is it really you?" Blackbird's voice cracked.

"Ah, Young Daniel, it is me, and you need to be strong. Follow me now, and we will have one last palaver." The old man smiled, the moon lighting his eyes and creating an aura about him that bled only kindness.

Blackbird walked to the fire with his grandfather and sat down across from him.

Carefully placed on an old blanket were the old man's things. A medicine bag, a long wooden pipe, a satchel of tobacco – but the diamond willow stick he had carried his whole life was not among these things.

Daniel used to joke with his grandfather that the tobacco was really devil weed and in turn, the old man used to reply often with a wink, "I've used it to seduce many squaws, Young Daniel, but that is our secret."

"I have missed you so much, Grandfather," Blackbird started.

The old man picked up the long wooden pipe and raised a finger to his lips. "There are things I must tell you. Things that you must know so that your judgment is not clouded." He was lighting his pipe, readying it for palaver.

Blackbird wept.

"You need not miss me, Young Daniel, I have been at your side all these years as you walked the soles off so many pairs of shoes. Do not weep for me, as we will again make palaver and watch the sun fall and rise in many worlds. Death is not the end: it is only the beginning. Do you understand?" Then the old man lit the pipe, puffed twice, then handed it across the fire to Blackbird.

Blackbird drew in the sweet tobacco, not wanting to take his eyes off the old man for fear he would fade, then exhaled out over the fire. It hung there magically above the flames as he handed the pipe back.

Grandfather took another deep draw and expelled the smoke out over the fire. As it intermingled with Blackbird's smoke, it began to swirl and reflect light.

"You have seen the orbs?" the old man started. "They are the guardians of this world and the next. They hold sentry in what the white man calls the Northern Lights or Borealis. That is but one portal, Young Daniel, from this world to the next."

The smoke that hung above the fire became a sphere and turned slowly between them, becoming semi-solid.

"The ones you saw Jackanoob consult have been here as long as the earth. Each is a living entity, and when it glows brightly, they share knowledge as they give us safe passage from this world to the next."

The old man took a long draw on the pipe and exhaled more smoke and handed it back across. Blackbird puffed again, then blew his smoke into the fire. As he did a second orb formed beside the other. But this orb was different: its surface was darker, and as it solidified it became bluish black.

"This is the black orb. It also is a guardian and a living entity, but it is the sentry for darker worlds where evil lurks. When our people ate of the man, they summoned the dark orb, and it opened the portal to a place where those with hearts that are black and cold lurk. Some call the creature that came forward Wendigo or Skinwalker – the white man has many variations on these creatures. Some are a fable, but not all. When Chocktee ate of the man, they brought with it madness. The Elder Jackanoob was a brave Chocktee, and though his bargain brought a curse upon our people, he paid a heavier price."

"He killed you," Blackbird said.

"The Elder named Jackanoob has been replaced by a predator that eats of man and holds captive the soul of an Elder who was set to take his place as a guardian. Jackanoob would not have passed into the next world; he was destined to be a guardian, and the only one of our people with the power to summon them. He sacrificed his being to save his people, and he had to do it of his own free will."

He reached out and ran his fingers through the smoke: the orbs collapsed.

"Is he still in there? Jackanoob?" Blackbird.

"He is." Grandfather blew a fresh rush of smoke. "Jackanoob resides within the creature's heart, forever witness to the horrors of its unending hunger. That is the punishment he suffers for making a pact with a creature from the black orb."

Blackbird considered this as he took the pipe from Grandfather and thought of when he was walking with the Elder. He too was a man of wisdom, not unlike his grandfather.

"Can the curse be lifted?"

"The cycle cannot be broken, only righted."

Grandfather waved his hand, and a new layer of smoke flickered in the firelight, taking on a life of its own. For a moment it shone radiantly – then it coalesced, forming a hologram which showed a burly man in a police uniform who looked out on over an excavated cornfield as men and equipment worked.

"This man will be of help. You will need to make contact, Young Daniel. You cannot be a lone wolf."

Blackbird recognized him from a newspaper clipping. "Logan."

"Yes, the man they call Logan. You must make contact with him. This time the skinwalker will stay to fight. There will be much blood, many deaths, but there is an opportunity at hand to stop it."

Once again Grandfather waved his hand, and the hologram swirled away.

"The arrows I used had no effect. How do I stop him without a weapon?"

The old man touched his face, then pointed.

"The feelings you get, that is from the mark it left on you. If you concentrate you will begin to see what it sees, feel what it feels – but be careful how deep you look into its soul, or you will find yourself lost in its blackness."

Blackbird stroked the scar with his index finger, felt the tingling and began to concentrate as he looked within. At first, he felt only madness coupled with need.

"The hunger is a pain," he said aloud.

"Yes, hunger drives it."

He felt its irrational side, the confusion, the hate, and the vulnerability of being tracked. Blackbird would have never thought the creature could feel insecure.

It fears me, he thought. *But why?*

"Your enduring drive consumes it with fear, and it is terrified at the prospect of going back to the void,"

Grandfather said. "This is a powerful tool, Young Daniel. You can confuse and intimidate it."

"I can't very well scare it to death, Grandfather."

"No. This man Logan; he is the key."

"I don't understand."

The old man took another draw on the pipe and began to explain. Blackbird listened intently as they continued their palaver. All the while, as he listened to his grandfather give counsel, he prayed that he would remember.

Then time shifted, began to distort their world. Daniel could feel himself pulling away from the blazing fire and falling backward through time as if he were an autumn leaf being tossed about in midnight storm.

"I will see you in the passage, Young Daniel," Grandfather called after him. "We will palaver again."

I must remember. Mustn't forget, he thought as the darkness enveloped him, the amber light and the distant voice of Grandfather fading out and being replaced by a steady vibrating purr and growl.

6

Blackbird opened his eyes his face pressed against the cold glass of the Greyhound bus window. It was over. He was back, and this was no vision.

Reaching into his pocket, he pulled out the ticket stub. In nine hours he would arrive in Thomasville, and then he would try and make contact with the man named Logan.

"He is the key," Grandfather had said.

Blackbird had no idea what that meant. All he knew was that he hoped this would provide an end to his long journey. He reached up and touched the scar on his face. It tingled a bit, and he pulled his hand away, afraid of what he might see or say aloud.

The pull of the walker was getting stronger as they closed the distance.

I'm coming for you, he thought, but there was no answer.

***

CHAPTER 10 - MISERY

1

John Parkins was killing time. It was Saturday, Ronny was delivering grain, so he was left here to mull over how utterly useless he felt. Inside the house, Olivia was milling about under the influence of her pills. He was resentful of this: she got to take off on her pill wagon vacation while he was expected to keep it all together.

Nothing makes sense anymore. What is the point, really?

To pass the time he decided to remove an old storage shelf from the workshop wall. He had meant to do it for some time, as it had become nothing more than a collection point for junk. Up until now, he'd been putting it off, but with nothing to do but brood and pick at his wounds, he thought it would be a good distraction.

Pulling a plastic garbage can across the workshop floor, he set it in front of his proposed project and began unloading the contents of the cabinet. There were empty plastic containers, stiff paint brushes and a bunch of other things. He reached in, taking an item and deciding whether to place it on the bench or turf it.

Empty jar? Garbage. Paint brush? Garbage. Old racing magazine? Garbage.

On it went. It seemed nothing would be salvaged: he dropped one item after another into the bin.

He was halfway done when he came across something that made him stop. Reaching into the cabinet, he felt something cold then hot drag across his middle and index finger.

"Fuck," he cussed and retracted his hand.

For a second there was no blood: just two perfect slices cut diagonally across the middle joint of the two digits. John stared at, wondering what caused the cut and pulling the skin back to inspect it. It was bad; almost to the bone.

Then blood began pouring out of the wound at a ferocious pace – but John Parkins was not alarmed. He didn't move: just watched the blood spill onto the bench.

I wonder how long it would take to bleed to death this way?

The pool of blood expanded to the size of a pie plate and still he was mesmerized.

I could just do nothing; let the poison flow out of me. Lose consciousness. Silence the voices.

He stood there, his first aid kit only a foot away, deciding what to do.

2

Olivia sat in Tommy's room staring at the mess. It was a typical little boy's room. Clothes hung sloppily out of the hamper and toys were secretly hidden under the bed and dresser in haste to get outside on another school-free day. She had told him to clean up his room, but he'd rushed out the door on his way to go fishing. She hadn't really looked at his room until now, but if she had, he wouldn't have gotten out.

Part of this was John's fault. He was far too soft with Tommy, always making her the heavy. Other boys had to help out with chores. Farm boys didn't even think about fishing until the work around the house was done. But John insisted that summer was a boy's time off and that he should be out catching frogs or fishing for brook trout, rather than becoming the workhorse of a parent.

"That's why I hired Ronny," John told her. "Tommy's too smart to be a hand like me. I want him as far away from farming as possible."

In her view, Tommy took full advantage of this, continually dodging chores. It went against how Olivia was raised. "There's no sin in hard work, John."

"This boy needs to be a boy, Olivia. When I grew up, I worked from the age of ten. I never got to be a boy really, and you know how it was with your dad. Trust me on this: he's going to be just fine," he reasoned.

And, as always, she succumbed to that reason. She didn't like being the authoritarian; she was a little jealous of the love they shared and often felt she was on the outside looking in. It wasn't often she put her foot down.

But that final day, enough was enough. She specifically told him to clean this room up before going out the door.

When he got home, she was going to have a talk with him.

Better yet, John would be the one to set him straight.

She sat on her son's bed and waited for John.

3

"I can't believe he'd be this irresponsible," Olivia exclaimed.

"What?" John was now standing in the doorway to their son's room.

Tap. Droplets of blood fell to the hardwood floor rhythmically from the two bandaged fingers on his right hand. The gauze was already soaked, sopping with claret, and every three or four seconds it released a new droplet.

Tap.

He couldn't hear the splash of blood: his focus was on his wife, who stared at him defiantly.

"Who are you talking to, Olivia?"

Tap.

"I specifically told him to clean up his room before he went out, John, and I have had enough of being ignored." She stared right at her husband – but she didn't see him.

Tap.

"Olivia."

"You've got to talk to him, John. Set him straight and..."

Tap.

"Olivia."

"… tell him that he can't cut corners …"

Tap.

"Olivia, Tommy is gone. We buried him two days ago," John croaked.

But she kept going. "…like this. He's been getting away with too much, John."

Tap.

He moved forward and took her by the shoulders. His right hand left a bloody mark on the shoulder of her robe.

"He's dead, Olivia! You were there! We buried him. Please stop this: I can't do this alone."

Tap.

She fell silent, his words finally breaking through, her face dawning with comprehension – and then she started to scream.

"Stop it!"

John drew up his hand, ready to slap her, an arc of blood spattering on the World Series Pennant that hung above Tommy's computer desk.

Then she said something that stopped him.

"He came out of me," she cried. "He always listened to you and loved you more, but he came out of me. I carried him all those months, Johnny. I loved him just as much as you, but he loved you more."

John Parkins stood frozen, his eyes welling up with tears. Then he dropped his hand in shame and pulled her toward him.

"He loved you too, sweetheart. Every boy loves his mom."

"I want my baby back, Johnny! I want him home!"

"He's gone, Olivia. I'm sorry. It's my fault! I should have taken the day off. It's all my fault!" he cried. "He'd be alive right now if I had been a good father!"

"He came out of me, he was my baby, and I want him back!"

They held each other in the emptiness of their son's room, drowning in despair. Surrounded by the memories of what was taken from them, little league pictures, baseball trophies, and from all sides pictures of their smiling little boy.

Gone forever.

4

"Hello?"

"Erin. It's John."

His hand was freshly bandaged now, and Olivia was in the other room, dozing in and out. He'd given her two of those God-forsaken pills this time.

"John, how are you?" his sister asked, then began to cry. "Oh, what a bloody stupid question, I'm sorry."

"I'm not doing so hot, Sis, but Olivia is even worse," he croaked. He almost lost control but caught himself.

"The poor girl. She looked so messed up at the funeral. Both of you guys have suffered such a tragedy. I don't know what to say, Johnny. I'm just a fucking airhead!" She cried even harder. "He was such a sweet little boy! Me and Rick just loved him so much."

John cut her off. "I need a favor, Sis."

"Anything, Johnny! You know that."

"I need some time to sort things out, and Olivia needs to get out of this house for a while. Everything in this place reminds her of Tommy. She just won't accept that he's gone. I try to talk to her, and she screams. She's stoned out of her head on pills, and I have a tough enough time keeping it together."

"I understand."

"Can she come to stay with you guys for a short while, at least until I get things sorted out?"

"Sure, Johnny. Maybe you should come too."

"No!" he blurted. "I need some time away from her. I'm so wrapped up in my own misery I just can't deal with hers right now. She needs someone to look out for her, Sis and someone to keep tabs on the God damned pills. I just can't help her right now. Could you come to get her tonight?"

"We'll be there after supper."

"Will Rick mind?"

"No! Of course not, Johnny; we're family. You hang on, and we'll be there around seven o'clock."

They ironed out the rest of the details over the phone then John went about redressing his hands after dousing them in peroxide. He then cleaned up the blood from Tommy's floor and packed a bag for Olivia.

5

They arrived just before 7 pm. The sun was still high, standing vigil over the grain and corn that was yet to be harvested.

Erin's husband, Rick, was a loan manager at a bank. They had a mansion on snob hill in Brandon, with no kids, so there was plenty of room. Erin and Rick had never had children. Instead, they spent their time traveling and focused their love on their only nephew. They might have been rich, but they both loved Tommy a great deal.

John dressed Olivia in a summer dress with a button sweater. As they came up the walk, he slipped another pill into her mouth. She swallowed it and said, "When is our boy coming home, Johnny?"

He just said, "Soon."

When they got to the door, he set the bag down, and Rick snatched it up while Erin took Olivia under the arm. He kept his hand low and hidden, not wanting to provoke questions and prolong the meeting.

Rick asked if he would like to come too and he declined.

Once Olivia was in the car they spoke briefly on the porch, and when the words became awkward and emotional, they turned and went to the car.

"Call me tomorrow, Johnny, just so I know you're okay," Erin called back.

"I will. Take care of her, Sis," he said and closed the door.

He watched through the window as Rick backed the Chrysler 300 out of the driveway. The big hulk of a car looked like a chariot of death as it whisked his wife away into the night.

"I'm sorry Olivia."

Then he left the window, no fight left in him, knowing he would never see his wife again.

***

CHAPTER 11- THE BIG BLIND

1

Blackbird stepped off the Greyhound bus just as the prairie sunset was giving way to the dark pastel blue of the dusk sky. He was the only one to get off. While he took in his surroundings, the driver reached into the compartment below the bus and handed him the weathered knapsack he had toted since leaving Chocktee for the last time. It was now a bit lighter: the bow he carried, along with the arrows, were confiscated in Chicago and never returned. Since then, he saw had no need for it and now he dismissed it altogether.

No one had considered the consequences of Skin breaking free from the ritual circle, not even Grandfather. There were no contingency plans, no weapons. The silver tipped arrows that the elders had given him were based strictly upon the assumption that Skin was a Wendigo. Now with the vision of Jackanoob burned into his mind's eye he really wasn't sure what it was or if it could be beaten.

Johnny Proudfoot recounted the story of Jack Fiddler and his brother Joseph who were said to have hunted and killed many wendigo. It was believed that if silver pierced a wendigo's heart, it would die instantly. Fiddler was a Shaman, Chief of Ojibwa Cree blood and well known for his power at defeating wendigo.

"The White Man brought him up on charges of murder in the early 1900s," Proudfoot said. "Fiddler took his own life, and they executed his brother Joseph." But Skin was not a run of the mill wendigo if one at all. The monster could metamorphose like a skinwalker: hence the name the Chocktee had given it.

Blackbird considered the variations on the mythology and the crossover to other creatures of lore. The Wendigo was not unlike the werewolf or the vampire – but then he thought that Jackanoob was not a wendigo or a skinwalker. He was, in fact, an offspring of the black orb.

In the back of his mind he could hear the children of Chocktee tittering and calling out to each other in the darkness: "Skin's going to get you!"

He abandoned these memories and thought about accommodations. Just in time, a taxi pulled up to the bus stop, and the driver rolled down his window asking, "You looking for a ride somewhere?"

"Yes, and a cheap motel. Can you recommend one?"

"There's only one available; reporters got everything else booked up. Thomasville Motor-Inn. Hop in. It'll cost you ten bucks for the ride." The driver reached over behind the passenger seat and the rear door.

Blackbird picked up his bag and tossed it on the bench seat, then climbed in.

The driver was an older man, and he sported an earring in one ear. The interior of the cab was clean, but had seen better days: the grey material on the seats was chafed. An old meter in the front looked like it had been busted for a few years.

"How far to the motel?"

"Five minutes," the driver replied and closed the sliding door. He got in and put the van in gear. "You're lucky you caught me. I used to roll by this stop anytime a bus came in, but since the murders, I can hardly keep up."

They were rolling down the road. Blackbird was amazed at the openness of the prairie landscape. It was a whole lot of nothing out here. In the distance, he could see the forest, but that was miles off.

Is Skin roaming those woods, he wondered.

"I read about that in the paper. Pretty bad stuff." Blackbird considered asking a few questions, then thought better of it. This was a one-horse town: if he asked a bunch of questions, it might draw unwanted interest.

"Bad is an understatement," the driver said. "This fiend was killing little boys, doing God knows what with them. He should be strung up by his balls."

Blackbird nodded.

The driver stole a glance in the rearview mirror. "So what brings you to town? You don't look much like a reporter, and we aren't exactly the epicenter of employment."

"Research," Blackbird lied. "I'm writing a book on the Métis Indian, and there are some old burial grounds in these parts I want to check out. I'll be in town for a few days."

The driver seemed to think this was a reasonable enough explanation. "Well then, welcome to Thomasville."

They turned the corner and pulled into the parking lot of an older motel. The cab parked out front and Blackbird reached into his wallet and pulled out a crisp twenty dollar bill.

"Do you have a card?" he asked. "I might need a guy with some knowledge of these parts to give me a lift." He pulled the knapsack onto his shoulder and leaned back inside the cab using a hand to steady himself.

"Absolutely." The driver smiled and pulled one off the clipboard Blackbird had seen on the dashboard while they drove. "Name's Bobby Morneau. I'm an independent here in Thomasville. There's a bigger cab company, but they charge by the click. You can call me anytime." He handed the card over, and ten dollars change.

Blackbird reached out, took the card and resisted the urge to snatch up the change. "You keep the extra ten. I'm not a rich guy, Mr. Morneau, but I might need a guy with a keen eye to show me around. My name's Dan Blackbird."

"You got it, Dan. The number on that card is my cell number. You need a ride I'll go out of my way." His smile broadened and revealed teeth stained brown with tobacco. They looked even worse under the orange glow of the Motel parking light. "Day or night," he winked.

"Thanks. Have a good night."

Blackbird stuck the card in the breast pocket of the jean jacket he was wearing and closed the door. He turned away from the cab and walked toward the lobby.

Behind the desk a guy in his mid-thirties, and he had stared Daniel down from the moment he stepped out of the cab. Blackbird could feel his stare, and he hoped that the guy wasn't going to blow him off because of his heritage.

A bell jingled as he pushed open the front door. The desk clerk never took his eyes off him.

"Hi," he said setting the knapsack down. "I need a room."

"I'll need some ID, sir," replied the clerk.

Blackbird pulled out his wallet and placed his identification on the counter.

"Daniel Blackbird," the clerk said. "I've been expecting you."

"Huh?"

"Yeah, prior arrangements were made for your arrival."

"Who made these arrangements?"

He expected to hear the name John Proudfoot but got an even more bizarre response.

"He didn't give his name; he said you were an associate of his and that I was to make arrangements for you." The clerk seemed jumpy, and quite possibly a little stoned. "Oh yeah, and he said to give you this." He put an envelope down on the counter.

Blackbird stared down at the plain white envelope. His scar tingled.

"What did this guy look like? Was he Indian like me?"

The clerk puzzled for a second and shook his head. "I don't remember his face; just his words. He said he represented a firm that wanted to remain anonymous and that you were to be given accommodations and that the envelope was to be delivered." He added, "He didn't look like you, Mister."

"What do you mean, like me?"

"You look like you've been on the road for quite a while, rough trade. No offense."

"None taken."

The clerk placed a key on the counter beside the envelope. Blackbird collected them both, then peered at the blue plastic chip on the key: 14A.

"I hope the upper level is okay. It's the best room I've got; the AC works, and the plumbing doesn't make too much noise." The clerk slid the registry forward. "Please sign here."

Blackbird signed his name and headed out of the office. As he reached the door, the clerk said one last thing.

"His eyes."

"What?"

"His eyes were like mirrors; kind of spooky." The clerk was looking past him into the night as if he recalled something on a witness stand. "Hope I never meet up with the guy again."

Hope you never do, Daniel thought. He waited to see if the clerk would say anything else, but he didn't. Instead, he stood there staring past him out into the lot where Blackbird assumed Skin had exited.

He left the motel office and found the room. He pushed the key into the door lock, and it clicked as he turned it. He looked left and then right, thinking Skin might ambush him as he pushed the door open – but no need. He would have known if Skin was there: his senses would have alerted him to its presence.

Flicking the light on, he noted that the room had two beds, a phone, and a television. The remote control for the tv was wired to the nightstand by the bed, to keep it from being stolen. He wondered what the odds a thief who stayed in a dive like this would have the same remote control requirements on his home television. Either way, he didn't think he would be watching much TV, so it really didn't matter. A small round table sat in the corner and on it was a microwave along with a small bar fridge. That would come in handy. He could grab some canned goods at the local grocery. He set the envelope on the nightstand then picked up the phone, which rang through to the front office. "Yes, Mr. Blackbird?"

"Can I make a long distance call on this phone?" he asked.

"Yes, you can. The phones are generally locked down, but I'll release the lock on yours. It will take about ten minutes while I program the system," the clerk said. "Will there be anything else?"

"No, that will be fine. Thank you."

He hung up and decided to take a shower while the clerk fixed the phone. He wanted to talk to Proudfoot about the envelope, the room, and of course the vision. This was the end of the road: he could feel it in his bones.

He stripped down naked and stood before the bathroom mirror, examining the lines on his face and how he had changed so drastically over the years. When did his smooth brown skin become pocked and marked by time? When did his jet black hair grow ashen and thin? He had once been a slim, handsome native man with features that snared more than his fair share of young ladies. Now he was weathered and beaten, and he wasn't even thirty-five yet. As he gazed at himself in the mirror, he saw a hybrid of his Mother and Grandfather – and the other who had never taken claim on his heart.

The stranger: his father.

"You will probably die in this place," he told the naked reflection looking back at him. "Are you prepared for that?"

He touched the scar, and it tingled a bit. Even after all these years, the skin was hard and raised.

"I will die if I have to," he said and climbed into the shower.

2

Two hours later Scott Masterson was on his way to the casino. The Indian was checked in, and Dennis, the weekend manager, took over an hour after he sorted out the phone. Dennis had asked about the phone and Scott said it was okay, that the Indian was welcome to make a few long distance calls and that his tab had been paid up in advance.

In a small bag beside him was a thousand dollars he'd skimmed from his take. He had put the rest into the night deposit so that he would not be tempted to take more. He had spent the day writing checks and mailing them, and it seemed almost fate that the Indian guy showed up when he did.

Masterson hadn't really expected the Indian would look like he did. He had expected some well-dressed chief in semi-formal attire. Not a guy who looked like he was out of seventies drive-in classic.

No matter: the debt was paid and his bacon had been pulled out of the fire. Tonight he was going to drop a G Note on the tables, and if the gods looked down on him, he might come home a little richer.

3

"I'm staying at the Thomasville Motor Inn, room 14A." Blackbird was sitting on the edge of the bed wearing only a towel. "He took care of everything, paid my bill and left an envelope."

"This is it then, Dan. He's waiting for you," Proudfoot said. "Have you opened the envelope?"

"I gotta be honest, Johnny: I'm kind of scared to." As he spoke, he turned the envelope this way and that in his hand. Something inside was sliding back and forth.

"Well, open it now, and maybe we can figure this out."

"Here goes."

He tore the end of the envelope off and out fell a small glass vial that contained what looked like black tar. Then he pulled out the letter.

"A vial of tar? Huh? If I didn't know better, I'd say he's trying to sell me some hash oil. There's a note in here, too."

"Read the note, Dan."

He unfolded it and set in on the nightstand, then readjusted himself so that he could hold the phone and read it allowed without touching it. Touching anything from the creature, even a letter, worried him. "You listening?"

"Go ahead. I have you on speaker so the others can hear." Proudfoot sounded tinny now, but audible.

"Alright, here goes." Blackbird cleared his throat.

Hello, Brave Hunter.

I trust your accommodations are acceptable. Consider this my gift to you, for all the years you have devoted to me.

Much has happened since we parted ways in the cityscape. I have learned many things of this world and eaten many as well. I want you to know that I respect your fortitude, but you have become a nuisance and to be honest I am tired of running. I have decided to stay here and wait for you. In doing so, I am offering you a choice. Make your decision carefully: I will not stop my course of action once it is set into motion.

I want you to leave, Brave Hunter. Go back to life and forget about me. Take a wife, have children, spend no more time on this pursuit of which you are doomed to fail. The world is a dirty place, and the forces of nature run their own course in cleaning up the soured parts with many things. Disease, war, fire – these are all methods of cleansing. And I, too, am one of those methods.

I could swoop down now and put out your eyes if I wanted to – but I will not. I know of the burning hatred that consumes you, and I know I am the source of that hatred.

With this letter, I have left you a liquid which will give you renewal. It is my blood, Brave Hunter, and if you take of it your heart will be healed, your scar removed and your age restored to that which it was before you set your sights upon me. That is the penance I will offer you for abandoning this pointless pursuit. You need only do two things: open the original wound and pour the contents of the vial into it. Then you will be free.

If you choose not to take my offer, I will tear this place and its people apart. For every day you stay, I will double my kill until the streets run red with blood.

I will kill them all, Brave Hunter. The men, the women, the children. Their blood and suffering will be your burden to carry, a heavier load upon your shoulders than that of a weak and dying old man.

Consider the consequences and my offer. You have two days, then the blood starts flowing.

F

Blackbird set down the letter and focused on the vial which contained the creature's blood, then thought of the black ick that had been spat into the open wound on Jackanoob's face.

"Are you there, Johnny?"

"Yes, Dan, we all heard. Give us a minute to consult on this."

"Take all the time you need," he said, trying not to sound sarcastic and thought, *I've got a whopping two days before the streets run red with blood.*

As he waited, he turned the vial over and over, watching the black ooze inside it. *Yeah, I'm really going to put that shit in an open wound on my face.*

4

Scott Masterson could feel the buzz from the moment he closed the door of his car and started across the parking lot. Just ahead he could see the track lighting to the entrance and picked up his pace a bit. His adrenaline was beginning to pump, and he could feel the pull of the tables.

He touched the leather bag he kept his cash in and smiled as he pushed the doorway open. Ahead a security guard stood post. This big gorilla was a regular: bald head, six two and given the opportunity he looked like he could turn a bowling ball inside out.

"Good evening, sir. Welcome to the Segway."

"How are you?" Masterson smiled and walked past him. That was part of the buzz: they made you feel like someone, even if you weren't.

He entered the main gaming room welcomed by the cacophonous chime of slot machine bells ringing. It was music when you thought about it.

He strutted past the nickel machines where scores of senior citizens dumped their money in a quest for the elusive progressive. One might think gamblers would not judge each other, but he detested the people who played the slots, especially the old folks.

He could picture them dumping their pension checks into these machines then going home and chowing down on cat food. How pathetic.

At the bar, he pulled a crisp twenty from his wallet and ordered a vodka and soda, then took his change and headed for the tables. He felt good tonight. The stars were on his side tonight – he was sure of it – and he would walk out with more than he walked in with.

Tonight we bet smart. No doubling up, and throw the bad cards out no matter what.

He found a $25 table with an open seat and sat down. On his right an Asian woman and on his left a very well-dressed old man. He watched the dealer lay down two cards and the deal out the remaining cards. In the circle where the ante was laid a slot was set up for each player to drop a dollar chip. This was to ensure that if a player hit a straight or royal flush, they would win the progressive. To the right of the dealer was a red digital counter that spun madly upward as each chip was deposited. A Royal Flush was worth $175,069.09 and counting upward with each hand. The odds of hitting a royal were incomprehensible, but Masterson figured he might someday, if not tonight.

The hand played out, the dealer won and collected up the chips and cards. The pit boss watched the dealer as he clapped his hands so that the eye in the sky could see he wasn't pilfering. Scott had arrived just as they were changing dealers: a female dealer came up to the table and began to get organized. "Good evening. My name is Jessica, and good luck, everyone."

Everyone was cordial, and Scott brought the small bag up and set it on the table. "I'd like to buy some chips before we start," he said, unzipping the bag.

"No problem, sir; just give me a second to get organized." Jessica loaded up three decks in the automatic shuffler. The mechanical shuffler began its job, and she ran a hand professionally across the green cloth to feel for any unseen issues that might tip a card. Happy with that, she turned to Scott and said, "Now, what can I get for you, sir?"

"Let's start with two hundred," Scott said and placed a stack on the table.

Her smile slipped away then as she looked to the stack then back at Scott. "Is this a joke?"

"What are you talking about?" Scott asked, then looked at his money. "I'd like two hundred in chips, please. Ten progressives, if you don't mind."

"Well that won't be a problem, sir, but I'll need to see some money first." She motioned the pit boss. A well-dressed guy with red hair made his way over.

"What the hell do you think this is?" Scott said and pushed the stack forward.

The older gentleman on his left said, "Mister, the pit boss is coming. Quit jacking around."

"Huh?" Scott's face twisted in confusion.

"Is there a problem here, sir?" the pit boss asked.

"What the hell is everyone's problem? I'd like a couple hundred bucks in chips, is that so hard?" He looked down at the stack of money. Its edges blurred.

"Sir, if you aren't going to play I'm going to have to ask you to vacate your seat." The pit boss spoke very slow and calm, but he meant business.

Everyone was looking now, even from the other tables.

"Look, I don't get what this issue is. I've played here hundreds of times. Why the fuck is everyone acting so goddamned crazy?" Scott was raising his voice now, becoming shrill.

"Sir, I am going to have to ask you to vacate your seat," the pit boss said, and that is when Scott stepped over the line.

"Look, Cock Jaws, all I wanted were some fucking chips so I could play a bit of poker!" He pushed to his feet, snatched up the stack of notes, turned to the pit boss and jabbed him in the chest. "I want to see your supervisor."

"No problem, sir."

Security was on him immediately. They grabbed him by each arm and began to walk him across the floor. One of them was the big bald gorilla that had greeted him at the door.

"Stay calm, sir," the gorilla said. "We are taking you over to the supervisor's office where we can discuss this rationally."

All eyes were on him as Scott was marched through the casino.

What in the fuck is going on here? Why are they treating me like this?

5

"Dan, this is Jake Toomey. The offer you were given is legitimate, and the blood would not infect you in the same way it did Jackanoob."

"How do you know this, Old Jake?" Blackbird asked.

"When Jackanoob met the creature of the black orb he did so after consulting with the guardians. As in your vision, it gave him a choice. No matter the magic or power that the creature holds it cannot pass onto you the curse without your permission."

"So if I cut open this scar and poured this blood into it, all that I have seen will be undone? That is what you're telling me?"

"No. What I am telling you is that the creature is offering you a way out, but you will be abandoning your providence. If you strike a deal with him, you will be destined to serve him if not in this world, the next. Jackanoob has escaped the clutches of the black orb and its world, but eventually, the portal will find him and take him back. It is about balance and struggle." Toomey sighed, then added, "That is why, during the spring and fall equinox, the powers of the guardians from both worlds are able to push through into this world. Our people used to celebrate, and it was a time of great joy, but Jackanoob bartered that away in his pact with the dark one. All I can tell you is that for there to be good there must be evil. There must always be a struggle. We are the fuel that feeds that struggle."

"You're starting to sound like a Catholic, Old Jake," Blackbird said.

"Perhaps, but this is not a Native rite, Dan; this runs across all belief systems. Even atheists believe that man is the nucleus of struggles between good and evil. One belief system might think the other preposterous, but that is only arrogance. There is only good and evil; everything else is man's arrogance. To us, the orbs are the guardians. To others, they are angels, to others they might be prophets or anomalies."

"So what do I do?" asked Blackbird.

"You have two days. Jackanoob has given you this time because something else is distracting him, some other dealing. Whatever it is, you need to take advantage of that and find a way to make contact with the chief of police and convince him to help."

Blackbird lay back on the bed with the phone to his ear.

"Easier said than done, Old Jake. You remember what happened in Chicago; the police aren't all that receptive to stories about shape changers and native lore."

"You'll just have to convince him. I guess that if you don't bring him around in the next day or two, there will be so much bloodshed he will seek you out." Then Jake Toomey said something then that caught Blackbird off-guard. "We are coming there, Dan. I will gather the council, and we will be on a flight by tomorrow."

Proudfoot came back on the phone. "You there, Dan."

"Yeah, I'm here." He was looking at the vial again, turning it over. "What the hell am I supposed to do, Johnny?"

"Reach out to this Logan. Start using the talent Grandfather told you about. Make contact and try to learn."

Proudfoot sounded anxious. "This may be our last chance, Dan. Old Jake has a ritual he wants you to perform. A kind of meditation. You will need to find a secluded area. Get a pen and paper."

He rummaged around in the nightstand and found some stationery and began to jot down Jake's instructions. At the top of the page, he wrote three words: Purification by Smoke.

6

Scott Masterson sat alone in the room. The stash of money kept tightly beside him. His face was beet red. He had been in this room for almost an hour, and he was completely and utterly confused. He looked down at the stack of bills and couldn't understand why they were acting this way.

The door opened and in walked a gentleman in a suit, a security guy at his side.

"Hello, Mr. Masterson. My name is Ken Hayford. I am the director of security here at the casino." He put out his hand. But Scott just looked at it, so he set it down at his side and continued. "I am here to help you. Hopefully, we can get past this and call it a night."

"Get past this," Scott stuttered. "I have been spending my money in this establishment for over three years. I've dropped thousands into this shithole, and suddenly I'm treated like some schmuck."

"Mr. Masterson, are you on some medication? Have you had some recent traumatic issue?" Hayford's voice aired concern.

"What are you implying?"

Hayford leaned over and picked up two of the $50 bills from Scott's stack. "This. It isn't money; it's paper. Plain paper." He waved the bills in front of his face. All at once the color ran out of the bills, and green became blank white.

Scott blinked then looked down at the stack which sat beside him. It too had become a stack of plain white paper. "What did you do? What did you do with my money?" he accused.

"I didn't do anything, Mr. Masterson. There never was any money. That is why the dealer called on the pit boss. That is why you're here now. Sir, I think you might need some help."

Hayford couldn't help but feel sorry for the guy. It was obvious he was a chronic. He'd seen people break down before, even saw a guy kill himself, but never this. He had no doubt this poor guy believed that the wads of paper were money – but at least now he was coming around.

Or so he thought.

"You motherfucking bastards, you stole my money," he growled. "Bad enough you fix the games, but now you're doing parlor tricks to steal from us. I want to see your supervisor, asshole!"

Any sympathy Hayford had for him melted away. "Okay, you have exhausted my patience." He looked to his security man. "Escort Mr. Masterson and his bag of paper to the door."

The big security guard walked over, and Scott immediately stood up, gathering the paper up in his hands. "This is evidence! There'll be fingerprints on this, you fuckers! I'm going to sue your asses off! This is un-fucking-believable!" he screamed.

Another security guard entered the room, and they clamped onto him. He began struggling, and they tightened their grip, pushing out of the security office and into the main area, Hayford trailing behind them as they manhandled him to the door. He was humiliated, and that set him on fire. When they passed the nickel slots, a little old lady stared at him, and it was more than he could take.

"What are you looking at, you dried up old cunt? Isn't it time you threw on another adult diaper and jammed your pension check into the slit?" he screamed. "This whole place sucks fucking ass!"

Then they pushed through the doors and outside. The doors swung shut behind them, and Hayford ordered his guards to let Scott go. He shook them off and turned on one heel.

"This isn't the end of this, fuck-face! Not by any stretch of the imagination!"

"Mister Masterson, I suggest you go to your car, or we will have the police remove you from the property."

"The police? What a great fucking idea there, cock fuck! Maybe I'll alert them to the bait and switch you pulled inside!" he screeched.

"Maybe they'll smell the marijuana on you and want to conduct a personal search," Hayford fired back. His patience had nearly worn out. "Get the fuck out of here. You're on the blacklist. I see you coming, and I'll have you arrested on the spot."

Scott suddenly stopped, the wind knocked out of his sails. Tucked in his shirt pocket were three joints of BC Bud. "This isn't the end of this."

"It is tonight, sir. Start walking or I'm calling the cops."

He turned and walked out toward his car as the security boss and his two goons watched. When he was about 100 yards away, he turned around holding up his middle finger and yelled, "Mother Fuckers!"

"Jesus Christ." The bigger security guard chuckled. "This guy just doesn't quit."

Scott walked another thirty steps and turned around again. "Fuck you! Thieving cock suckers!"

"Kevin, take out your cell phone," Hayford told the bald security guard.

Scott stood there a moment, his middle finger pointed up and into the air, and then he turned again and headed toward his car. When he got to it, he fumbled out the keys and unlocked the door. Before climbing inside, he yelled at them one last time: "Fuck you!"

"You want me to call the police, Ken?" the security guard asked.

"No, he's finished. Post his face in the security office and make sure all shifts know that Scott Masterson of Thomasville is banned permanently from these premises. The dickhead comes back he's leaving in a cop car."

Scott sped out of the parking lot. He was furious and had it not been for the pot he was carrying he would have waited for the cops. He couldn't believe this. After all the goddamned money he had dropped in this place – and they had the nerve to screw him over like this.

He ran a yellow light as he drove back toward the highway. Thomasville was an hour and a half away, and he decided that when he got back that the Indian in 14A had some questions to answer. Somebody had fucked him over, and he was going to get to the bottom of it. Then, when he hit the main highway, he suddenly thought about the night deposit, the checks written and mailed.

"Oh my God," he moaned. "Oh god, the checks, oh god."

His car hit the rumble strips on the side of the road, and he swerved the wheel. His anger was inhibiting his focus, and he thought it would be wise to pull over and take a deep breath before he smashed the car up.

Ten minutes later, he pulled the car onto the other side of a bridge that spanned the Red River. He got out. The fresh air awakened him, and he decided to smoke one of the three joints he'd earmarked for the night at the casino.

He lit it up and looked out over the river. He drew off the joint and felt himself begin to relax.

He'd sort this out.

He took another toke, held it, then exhaled.

"What a fucking bummer night," he said.

"What a bummer indeed."

Scott jerked around. At the end of the bridge stood the man who'd given him the money.

"Hello, Scott."

"You," he said. "How? You fucked me!"

The dark man stepped closer and plucked the joint out of his hand. He took a deep draw off it, then blew the smoke back in Scott's face. "Ah, devil weed."

"Who are you?"

"I am the one your mother warned you about." He waved a hand toward the far side of the bridge and said, "Do you know what day it is, Scott?"

A pack of coyotes lined up at the end of the bridge side by side, their eyes reflecting in the darkness.

"No." Scott's voice suddenly sounded hopeless.

"It is the tenth day by the old calendars. The tenth day is the day of the dog, and it is but one day in many as the autumn equinox approaches." He waved his hand again, and at the other end of the bridge another pack of coyotes set up and stood single file. "On this day I command the dog. Tomorrow I will command the monkey."

The man climbed upon the edge of the bridge and began to change.

Perched on the railing, not with feet but great talons, he handed the joint back to Scott. "Take another draw on that thing, Scott; you're going to need it."

He looked left, then right. The coyotes growled hungrily. He looked back upon the creature towering above. He whimpered.

"Go ahead and have a last draw." Scott Masterson took the last toke of his life and as he exhaled the creature before him said, "This is going to hurt like hell."

The talon tore upward and opened his belly, spilling his insides out. He wanted to scream at how it hurt – but the real pain was when the creature began to pull them out and feast on them. Scott fell weakly to his knees. The fire in his abdomen was all that kept him from collapsing.

The creature reached into his belly and pulled out a length of small intestine. As it gulped his insides down its eyes rolled, filming over, and Scott felt himself slipping away.

When it was done, it cracked his skull open on the railing and then said something in the ancient language to the waiting coyotes. They moved in to get their fill while it watched with satisfied interest. It was not the first time predatory animals shared in its kills, but it still studied their actions with amazement. The coyotes growled and bickered over the fresh meat while it meditated.

7

The police found Scott Masterson's body a few hours later. His stomach cavity was utterly emptied of all internal organs, and it appeared that one of the coyotes had taken his right eye, a good portion of his nose and upper lip. Holding Scott's body in the white glow of the police flashlight, two unnamed cops conversed.

"It looks like he pulled off to smoke a joint, and banged his head on the railing."

The older highway cop said, "He was probably dead when the coyotes got to him."

"Poor bastard."

The next day was spent retracing his steps and determining what brought him to the point of his demise. There was no indication to deem it as anything but an accident, and when investigators contacted Masterson's father, they would call it just that.

***

CHAPTER 12 - THE KOLCHAK FACTOR

1

Aboard the Dash 8 commuter jet, Doctor Robert Kolchak reviewed the digital video that had come via courier thanks to Detective Pearson. He took notes, as Hopper recounted the murder and resurrection of his first victim on the laptop's media player. This was his second time reviewing the video, and now he scribbled down questions for the upcoming interview.

Hopper was a curious creature: he had no history of pedophilia and had never been convicted of any type of violent crime. It was an intriguing case, and Kolchak was looking forward to having a sit down with the child killer. In addition to the interview, he planned on walking the crime scene and interviewing as many people involved with the case as possible.

The day after tomorrow they would be taking Hopper back to Artisan Institute where Kolchak hoped to probe deeper into his mind. At first glance, he appeared to be the classic sociopath: no remorse, and no emotional attachment to his victims. Yet the emergence of this other character, Franklin, was a curious development – one that led Kolchak to believe one of two things. One that Hopper was looking to manipulate the case and look for an insanity defense – or two, that he indeed was one of those rare specimens with multiple personality disorder.

If it were the former, Kolchak would know. He was a master at exposing individuals entering into fraudulent insanity pleas and had a track record with the prosecution. It had become his forte, and while some of his colleagues considered him a sell-out, he felt strongly that many mental health experts were far more interested in assigning blame to the illness rather than the individual.

For Kolchak, it came down to whether or not the individual knew what he was doing was wrong. If that could be proven, then blame could easily be assigned no matter the state of a killer's mental capacity.

What Kolchak found particularly interesting was Hopper's apparent fear of this Franklin character. He did not want to jump to conclusions, but he guessed that Franklin was a manifestation of Hopper's inability to assign culpability to himself. Secretly though, he hoped that Hopper was a multiple personality, and that further probing would lead to more discovery.

"I've told you everything. There are no more bodies, but Franklin is still out there," Hopper said on the video.

Kolchak wrote on the steno pad.

[Urgency- panic] Real or manufactured?

He was not sure but was excited at the prospect and opportunity it presented. Suddenly a voice over the intercom interrupted his thoughts.

"Ladies and Gentleman, this is your Captain speaking. We will be making our final approach to Brandon in about ten minutes. I would like to ask that you, please observe the seatbelt signs and shut down any electronic equipment that might interfere with our navigational system."

Kolchak looked up to see the attendant standing over him.

"I'm just finishing up, Miss." He smiled.

She nodded, smiled back and moved along.

He shut down the computer, yanked out the memory stick and replaced both in his laptop case. The aisle seat beside him was empty, but that was because he had purchased the second seat so that he would have relative privacy.

Shortly after he began to feel the bump and shake of turbulence as the aircraft started its descent. He glanced out the window, but still could not see land through the cloud cover. As they descended further the port window became moist and outside the atmosphere became white and misty. Kolchak tightened his belt a bit, always nervous of take-off and landings.

2

Pearson was standing beside Kurt Cooper in the Arrival section of the Brandon Airport. The airport was a small one compared to other city airports serving mostly the military and commuter craft.

It was raining. Miserable weather to be walking around in a cornfield, but that was where they would be once Kolchak had landed. He had sent an email to Pearson the day before outlining his plans upon arrival.

According to the Flight Monitor, OA127 was on schedule. Oasis Airlines was the same airline Pearson had booked for their departure to Artisan Institute. Pearson couldn't wait to get out of here, this place was anything but an oasis.

"I think that's our guy there." Cooper pointed to the light coming out of the clouds, and then the Dash 8 was in clear view. "You met him, Ron?"

"He testified at a murder trial I provided security on back in the day. He's kind of a tightwad, but he's our tightwad, so be nice."

Cooper chuckled. "Gotcha, be nice to the tightwad."

"You're a funny guy, Coop," Pearson snickered.

They watched the Dash 8 bump along, rocking back and forth a bit just as it was about to touch down. The small commuter plane set down, and as it rolled down the runway, it lurched a bit when its small jet engines reversed. They could not see Robert Kolchak tighten his grip on the armrest nor could they feel his anxiety. The Dash 8 was taxiing to the arrival gate as a ground crew came out with a self-propelled step to attach.

They waited for the psychiatrist to appear.

3

The seatbelt sign shut off and Kolchak stood up ready. The seats he had purchased were right behind the cabin which meant he would be the first to exit. There weren't that many people on the flight anyhow — maybe twenty-five — he wanted to get out ahead of everyone. He slung his laptop bag over his shoulder and stood there awkwardly while they connected the stairwell to the aircraft.

The flight attendant who had given him a nod earlier stood to the front of the walkway, alternately watching the door and Kolchak as they unloaded luggage from the belly of the craft. She had seen his type before: assholes ready to push everyone out of the way just to be first. What made this guy worse was that he looked like a constipated asshole. She smiled as she linked these two words and noticed that he was smiling at her.

Probably thinks I'm hitting on him, she thought. This broadened her smile even more, and consequently his. She almost laughed out loud.

"Ladies and gentlemen, thank you for flying Oasis Airlines. Enjoy your stay in Brandon, and we hope to see you again," the pilot said over the intercom, and then the pressurized door clunked and unlocked.

Kolchak stepped out into the aisle, ready to make his exit.

The flight attendant rolled her eyes.

"There he is." Pearson pointed at a slim, clumsy looking man working his way down the stairwell.

Kolchak had thick dark hair and what some called the quintessential seventies porno mustache. He looked a little like a very thin Geraldo Rivera, but unkempt and awkward.

He was picking over the baggage cart now, something that made Pearson happy.

No waiting for the luggage carousel with the rest of the sheep.

Kolchak pulled off a large canvas suitcase that doubled as a suit bag. Pearson hadn't seen that kind of thing in years. That done, he turned and walked across the tarmac toward the arrival gate.

"He doesn't look anything like him," Cooper said.

"Like who?" Pearson asked.

"Darrin McGavin."

"The Christmas Story guy?"

"Yeah, but the Night Stalker."

"What? What the hell are you talking about?"

"Carl Kolchak, the Night Stalker. Don't tell me you never heard of him."

"Nope."

"Did you even watch television as a kid?' Cooper sighed.

"Sure. I watched television."

"And yet you never heard of the Night Stalker?"

Pearson smiled and turned to his partner as Kolchak entered the building and began to look about for the two detectives. "I know about the Night Stalker, Coop; I'm just fucking with you. Besides, I never got into it."

"Well, what did you watch then?" Cooper asked.

"The Six Million Dollar Man."

"That is so fucking lame." Cooper laughed. "Gentlemen, we can rebuild him: make him better than he was before. We can make him jump and run in slow motion."

"Shut up. Here comes our tightwad."

Pearson stepped forward to meet the man. "Doctor Kolchak, welcome to Brandon. I'm Detective Ron Pearson, and this is my partner, Detective Kurt Cooper."

Cooper put out his hand. "Hello, Doctor. Can I get your bag for you?"

Kolchak shook his hand gingerly and smiled. "Why thank you." He handed over the bag and turned to Pearson. "Detective Pearson, I want to thank you for sending the updates. Your name and face is oddly familiar; have we met before?'

Pearson was impressed. "Yes: about fifteen years ago you resided over the Rosedale Murders. I was lead on security. I was also much younger and had a few more hair follicles."

"Oh yes, I thought I remembered you. Well for what you've lost in hair you've made up in career advancement, Detective." Kolchak's voice was patronizing.

"Would you like to go to your hotel? We've booked you at the Holiday Inn. We thought that you might like to clean up before getting started."

"Actually, no; if you don't mind I'd like to go directly to the crime scene. Along the way, you can brief me on specifics. I would also like to meet with Chief Logan."

"Alright," Pearson said. "We can do that. It's about a forty-five-minute drive out to Thomasville. There isn't a lot between here and there other than the odd tumbleweed, so I'd recommend you use the facilities. I'll buy us all a coffee in the meantime, and Detective Cooper can go grab the car."

"Sounds splendid," Kolchak said, then asked, "Where shall we meet?"

Cooper pointed toward the gate. "The car is already out front.

It's a dark blue Lincoln Navigator."

Kolchak handed his laptop case over to Cooper as if he were the hired help. "Take care of this, Detective. My whole life is in this thing." Then he bumbled away toward the washroom.

Once out of earshot, Cooper said, "He's not my tightwad, he's yours."

"Shut up, Coop!" Pearson chuckled and went to get the coffee.

5

"Sgt. Collins is overseeing of the crime scene. All the bodies have been removed, and forensics is at about 70%. The first victim recovered, Thomas Parkins, has been buried. He's the only native to Thomasville." Pearson paused and shifted uncomfortably in the front seat as he Cooper drove. "The majority of the victims were teens. Mostly throw-away kids, male prostitutes, homeless-types with a myriad of issues like drug addiction."

"So, the youngest was this Parkins boy?" Kolchak was taking notes.

"Yeah, him and the last kid we dug up whom we have yet to identify, but forensics has him at about fourteen or fifteen. Neither of them fit the profile of the other victims. According to Hopper, the second unidentified victim is the one connected to the Franklin business." Pearson sipped his coffee and narrowed his eyes.

"Sound like he's trying to cop an insanity plea, Doc?" Cooper interjected.

"It is a possibility," Kolchak replied. "Of course this is all subjective. Sociopaths are prone to blame others for their actions. An example would be someone like Ronald Kessel, who always had an excuse for the heinous acts he inflicted. Kessel had a penchant for killing prostitutes. In almost every recounting of murder, Kessel said that someone had spurred him to react. The prostitute laughed when she shouldn't have, bit him or tried to rob him. It was always their fault."

"Were you involved in the Kessel case?" Pearson asked.

"No, I wasn't, but I have studied the case extensively and wrote about it in my second book. Not straying too far from my train of thought I would say that our Mr. Hopper exhibits similar traits. He does not want to take responsibility. Although I must confess, I find the last interview rather puzzling."

"How so?" Cooper asked.

"Sociopaths don't usually show remorse unless it is to manipulate. Perhaps that is what Mr. Hopper is attempting here." Kolchak rubbed his nose absently.

"Do you think he's trying for a multiple personality thing?" Pearson asked.

"You are very astute, Detective. I think he is either trying or he is a multiple personality," Kolchak surmised. Pearson was quiet for a second and looked unhappy with this response, so Kolchak added, "Whether he is or isn't really is irrelevant to whether he understood that his crimes were wrong. From everything I have read and heard Mr. Hopper knows full well what he did was wrong, which makes him fit to stand trial."

"Either way, the end game for us is that he poses no further risk to society," Pearson said. "Whether he spends the rest of his days in a federal penitentiary or a high-security mental institution meets our requirements."

"Well he is most certainly what would be deemed a dangerous offender," Kolchak said. "If it makes you feel any better, I am positive it is highly unlikely that Stephen Hopper will ever be a free man again."

"It does."

They fell silent for a while as Cooper drove the car north-east toward Thomasville and Kolchak examined the mediocrity of the prairie landscape. There were few trees and little water: just small rolling hills peppered with low unassuming clusters of brush. Below him, the wheels hummed as the rubber met the pavement. Fall was upon them, and the crops were already harvested. Cornstalks, assaulted by thrashers, were now turning brown and rolls of hay that looked like oversized breakfast cereal littered the empty fields.

6

Mick was at the command post waiting for their guest to arrive. Dark clouds had gathered to the south-west and threatened rain, but so far, they had not made good on their threat. Just the same, he had several pairs of rubber galoshes standing by.

"This guy is a VIP, Mick," Logan had told him. "Make sure our officers are in top form and give him access to whatever he needs."

With all the bodies out of the ground and the evidence gathering winding down they would eventually be bringing in men and equipment to level the farmland and eventually demolish the house and small barn. Then the land would be sold if anyone would buy it. Mick doubted that, thinking this place would end up sitting a long time before anyone seriously looked at it.

Collins was not a religious man, but this place seethed of evil, and the moisture from the graveyard clay almost smelled like bile. He wondered how Donald Wakeman felt about having such a terrible chunk of real estate next to his home.

Once their field had been harvested, the Wakemans had taken a long overdue vacation. Word left with Logan was that Donald was taking Derek and his wife down to Rapid City for a two-week road trip. It was still undetermined whether his son would have to testify or not because no one knew if Hopper would just plead guilty. At any rate, a trial could be a few years off depending on how this played out.

Mick thought about the circumstances involving the crime and shuddered a little. If Wakeman had shot Hopper, they might never have known the extent of his crimes. Most of the graves were well covered, the vast majority of bodies so decomposed that they might never have been found. And even plowing probably would not have turned up anything: Hopper had buried the dead a minimum of five feet below the surface.

Mick was not the same man he once was. The case had taken a toll on him. He and his wife Nancy usually made love three or four times a week, but now not at all. It was not that he didn't find her attractive: she was a beautiful woman with natural blond hair, and she took care of herself. It was just this God damned horror show coupled with the prospect that he might get her pregnant and he didn't know if he could ever have kids after this. He had become very attached to Tommy Parkins through his friendship with John, thought of him as a nephew although they were not related.

"Mick, they're coming." Oddball was tapping him on the shoulder. "They just passed the Western checkpoint on VD."

Mick acknowledged him, overlooking his feeble attempt at humor by calling Van Dyke Road 'VD'. Hardy had already told him it wasn't funny, but Oddball sometimes needed to beat something to death before he realized no one was laughing.

Mick got onto the radio. "Attention all units on site, this is the CP. Our visitor has arrived. I will be accompanying him during a general walkthrough. I will alert all involved of our direction. In the meantime, keep all non-essential chatter to a minimum."

Sometimes when officers got bored unnecessary radio chatter would result. With the bulk of the work now behind them, an occasional nudge of authority was in order. Mick's style differed from Logan in that Dave would be far less diplomatic.

Mick got a round of responses, "Copy Sentry Echo." "Copy Sentry William." "Copy CS 1." "Copy CS 2." – before they all fell silent and awaited further orders.

The dark blue navigator rolled up to the police CP, and Mick got out to meet them even before they were out of the vehicle. Pearson gave him a smile, and when Kolchak climbed out of the back, Cooper brought his hand to his face and smiled.

Mick liked Cooper; he wasn't quite as stiff as Pearson – but he respected both and Pearson was definitely the star by which Coop navigated his career.

"Sgt. Mick Collins," he said and extended his hand. "I'll be your guide for this portion of your tour, Doctor Kolchak."

"You work for the local force? I was expecting Chief Logan," Kolchak replied.

"The Chief is bogged down with the Mayor at the moment. He's going to hook up with you later at the station when you interview Stephen Hopper." Mick smiled thinly as Coop rolled his eyes out of sight of both Kolchak and Pearson.

"Sgt. Collins can tell you anything you need to know about the crime scene," Pearson said. "His level of expertise here far exceeds anyone else, including myself or Chief Logan."

Kolchak looked at Mick for a second and smiled. "Please accept my apologies, Sergeant. I certainly was not questioning your credentials or professionalism."

"No apology necessary, Doctor. Are you ready to start?"

"Lead the way, Sergeant."

"Okay, probably best if we start with the house. That way we won't end up tracking anything from the cornfield in there. Just give me a second." He brought up his handheld. "CS 1, this CP we will commence with a walkthrough of your position in two minutes."

"Copy that CP," a static voice replied from Crime Scene 1.

"Alright, Doctor Kolchak, you can follow me. If you'd like to use any listening devices or have any questions, feel free to ask, and don't hesitate to stop me if you have any observations."

"Sounds good to me."

They walked from the CP, which was set up on Van Dyke Road, toward Stephen Hopper's house. On the porch, Corporal Steel stood waiting for the party of four as they embarked on a one hour tour of the house. Kolchak for all his self-importance was meticulous in detail as they walked the crime scene: he kept stopping to observe and scribble notes. More often than not he would murmur, "Interesting," and then scribble something down.

He bombarded Mick with questions about the state of the house. Not just the basement, either: he questioned the condition upstairs, too.

The house itself was not the same place Mick and Logan had initially walked through. The walls had been opened up, some floorboards removed in an attempt to find either trophies or possibly, more victims. If not for the clutter, the inside of the old farmhouse might look as though it were being renovated. The torture table had been removed and placed in a warehouse as future evidence.

7

"This was the last grave." Mick pointed into the hole beside the old maple tree.

"This is where he said the boy crawled out of?" Kolchak asked.

"Yeah."

Cooper laughed, but Pearson didn't. Nor did Mick.

"So, this was his first kill, the one he wanted to keep an eye on?"

"That's correct. It was also the last gravesite Hopper identified. When the Chief brought him out for this, he was pretty wound up."

"What was his demeanor at the other sites?"

Mick didn't look up. "Expressionless. No outward emotion at all."

They carried on from there into the cornfield where crows cawed with glee as the forgotten corn rotted on the stalks. Right now wasn't too bad, but there were times when the officers could not hear each other talk.

Mick took him to every grave, and at the edge of each hole, Doctor Kolchak asked different questions. When they reached Tommy's grave, Mick stood silently as Pearson took over answering questions, but that did not prevent the awkwardness.

"This boy was from here?" Kolchak asked Mick.

"Yes, he was. He was a nice kid," Mick answered.

"You knew him well?"

"Yes, very well. His father, John, and I grew up together; we used to play softball." Mick avoided looking into Kolchak's eyes, not wanting to be probed.

Kolchak scribbled something down on the pad and asked, "Can I see where the crime was uncovered?"

"Yes, this way."

Mick led him toward the tree, where Derek Wakeman witnessed Hopper's crime and pointed. "He was up there. Saw Hopper bury him and sat through the whole thing."

"Goodness." Kolchak shook his head and said, "Corrl."

"What?" Cooper questioned.

"During the early 1970s in Houston Texas, there was a trio of serial killers led by a homosexual sadist named Dean Corrl. His two accomplices procured boys for him, and in one instance when they were burying a body, they were happened upon by a hunter. The hunter had a rifle, but being safety conscious he had removed the bullets and placed them in his breast pocket. They overpowered, then killed the accidental witness and buried him in a grave beside the original victim. Later they would find the bullets in the pocket of the hunter's remains."

"This boy wasn't hunting. He was playing," Cooper said.

"He was fortunate that Hopper didn't catch him," Pearson said.

"And we'd be looking for two boys instead of one," Mick supposed.

"Well I rarely speculate, but in the end, it probably would have led you here." He asked, "Beyond that wood line, that is the neighbor child's farm?"

"Yes, the Wakeman farm. They took off for a few weeks," Mick answered.

"I may want to talk to that family in the future. Can I get a number?"

Mick hesitated at first. "I suppose, but as I said: they'll be gone for a few weeks. You may have to follow up later."

"I'm a patient man. I can wait." Kolchak reached out and shook Mick's hand. "Thank you for the tour, Sgt. Collins. To say it has been enlightening would be an understatement."

"You're very welcome, Doctor. If you need anything else, please feel free to contact Chief Logan or me."

Pearson led the way out of the cornfield with Cooper and Kolchak just ahead. It was a silent trek but for the occasional fallen stalk crunching beneath their feet. Mick unfolded a piece of paper Kolchak slipped him as they walked and read it.

> In addition to a Forensic Psychologist, I am also a Clinical Psychologist.
>
> Anytime you need to talk. I am available.
>
> RK

Was it that obvious? He supposed an outsider would see much more, especially one with a trained eye. He folded the slip of paper up and placed in his pocket. When they reached the front of the crime scene, everyone bade their farewells to the doctor. Then the trio headed off into town.

8

Logan sat with Detective Pearson behind the glass mirror that looked in on interview room one while Cooper went over to the Masonic Hall to hook up with Jeff Henderson. They would be transferring the remains of the victims to a Forensic Lab in Winnipeg where they would be undergoing a battery of tests. Due to the number of victims, they had to contract a local company to build airtight containers: a reefer trailer had been purchased specifically for this task.

Henderson wanted to ensure that each victim was transported individually. It wasn't just because it was SOP in forensics: it was also to respect the dead and treat them with dignity during transportation. While many consider people who work with the dead as dark or emotionless, there is a code among most who believe that they are doing the work of giving respect back to those who cannot command it.

With Cooper off on an errand, Pearson talked openly with Logan about his impressions of Kolchak. He really didn't want to slag the Doctor, especially in front of Coop. "He's a bit of a dick, Dave, but if you saw him at the crime scene… Man, he knows his shit."

"Mick called me on the phone," Logan responded. "I read his book. He seems to have quite a bit of insight into what makes these guys tick. I don't care if he's a dick as long as Hopper never walks free again."

They watched as the newcomer chipped away at Hopper. They had been in there for over two hours. At first, it went as expected: for the first hour, Kolchak did all the talking while Hopper sat across from him indifferently. He started with a few questions which were greeted by Hopper's expressionless stare.

Then Kolchak managed something none of them expected. He made his way around to Franklin – and as if he had flipped a switch, Hopper said, "You're all going to die."

Kolchak leaned forward. "Why do you say that?"

"Because he's the devil. He could kill everyone here." And Hopper started to shake.

As Kolchak continued to probe, Pearson and Logan watched from behind the glass, mesmerized.

"The devil? You mean like Satan?" Kolchak waited, then added, "Is he here with us now?"

Hopper let out a burst of laughter then began to blubber. "You don't understand."

"I want to understand, Stephen. Help me to understand."

"I spend day after day in that cell, waiting for him to come back! He's going to rip me to pieces, and there's not a thing anyone can do about it. He can be anything." Hopper looked up into the ceiling light as if he expected to see Franklin perched there.

"What do you mean 'he can be anything'?" Kolchak looked in the mirror hoping that the digital video was up and running.

"He can change shape. Oh, what's the fucking point? You don't believe me!"

"Where did he come from?"

"I don't know! He found me."

"Because of the boy, the first one?"

"I guess!" Hopper was vibrating. "I think he could smell the death, I don't know. He said he was going to make me suffer. Now I'm so fucked. The cops, they think this is some kind of insanity defense." Hopper turned toward the mirror and broke into hysterics. "It isn't! Do you hear me, Logan! He's real, and when he's done with me he might just tear this shithole town apart!"

"Calm down, Stephen," Kolchak said. "I want you to take some deep breaths for me."

But Hopper just continued to stare into the mirror. "I know you can hear me, Logan, and I want you to remember this moment. Franklin is coming back for me, and while you might not give a shit what happens to me, you remember this. I warned you! I gave you fair warning!"

Then Hopper fell back in his seat, crying and mumbling incoherently.

"Stephen, I am your friend. You can talk to me, and no one can hurt you here. This place is under guard, and the day after tomorrow we will be leaving Thomasville altogether." Kolchak got up out of his seat and walked around the table.

"What the fuck is he doing?" Logan grumbled, getting up.

Kolchak walked around behind Hopper and placed a hand upon his shoulder. Hopper shuddered at first and had his hands not been restrained in cuffs he might have wrapped his arms around the doctor. But instead, he leaned his head to the right and wept as Kolchak repeated, "There, there. Everything will be alright, Stephen."

Pearson was behind Logan as they made their way down the hall. "Dave, cool down," he warned.

"Bloody idiot," Logan cussed. He shook his head as he walked. "He's gonna get himself fucking killed."

The two of them stopped outside the interview room door and peered in. Logan's hand was on the keypad, ready to punch in. But through the wire mesh, they saw Kolchak was still behind the blubbering man. He had everything under control.

"Jesus Christ," Logan sighed. His heart raced in his chest. "When he comes out of there I am going to tear him a new asshole."

With Hopper returned to his cell, they went into the main conference room to discuss the case and interview. Logan had calmed down, thanks to Pearson, and Kolchak seemed oblivious to the chaos he had caused.

"Well, that went well." Kolchak smiled.

"Really? How so?" Logan asked.

"Trust, Chief. I have established a bridge of trust with Mr. Hopper which will make an in-road to my determining his state of mind." Kolchak smiled broadly.

"Can I ask you a question, Doctor?"

"Dave…" Pearson started, but Logan raised his hand and cut him off.

"By all means," Kolchak invited.

"When interviewing other murderers have you always been so reckless with your own safety?" Logan's voice was even, but it was obvious that he was angry.

"Ah yes, it was reckless, Chief, and I know I gave you a start – but it was a gamble worth taking." Kolchak never lowered his eyes, his confidence high.

"Gamble worth tak…"

He raised his hand now and stopped Logan mid-sentence. "Yes, there was a gamble to be made, and I took it. Up until now, Stephen Hopper has opened up to no one but you. Even as he went off into his tirade about the Devil and Franklin he wasn't addressing me; he was addressing you."

"Yes, I know that, but –"

"But in two days he will not have you as a confidante, and you have referred him over to Detective Pearson and myself. To be frank, Chief Logan, we couldn't very well fly you into Artisan every time we wanted to get him to open up. I saw an opportunity to establish trust, and that is what I have done."

Logan stared at Kolchak, wanted to chastise him, but what would be the point?

"Where do we go from here, Doctor," Pearson asked.

"Well, I would like to use some hypnosis to determine whether this Franklin is a manifestation of his mind or hallucinatory. I won't be able to do that here. It will have to wait until we get him into a clinical atmosphere. In the meantime, I will continue with a few more interviews that aren't as probing, but based on building rapport."

Logan ran his hand through his hair. "Okay, I'm fine with that, Doctor – but I do not want to see any harm come to you. So please, in the future keep your hands out of reach of the prisoner."

"I apologize, Chief. In the future, I'll try not to be so hasty."

"I would greatly appreciate that." Logan smiled. "What else do you require of us?"

"I would like to stop in on the Parkins family tomorrow. Background on their son could be helpful, and I will be far more delicate. I am well versed in counseling grief so I may be able to help them a bit with a recovery plan."

"I'll take you by tomorrow."

"I would prefer to go alone. These people have been through a lot, and the bulk of their anguish was delivered via men in uniforms. If you can point me in the right direction, I will make out just fine."

The comment irritated Logan – but he wasn't exactly charmed with the prospect of visiting the Parkins household, so he didn't argue. Besides, he had his doctor's appointment tomorrow morning.

"Anything else?"

"Yes, one last thing, and I hope you are not one who is easily offended." Kolchak looked him directly in the eye. His patronizing smile shifted slightly to his version of sincerity. "May I?"

"Go right ahead, Doctor. I'm a police officer; I have been called everything this side of next week."

"From this point on I would like you to make good on your promise to Stephen. I would prefer that he not see you again. This will avoid future distraction and provide a foundation for me to start to build on. If he knows that he cannot turn to you, he will feel compelled to find a new confidant. I want to bring Detective Pearson into this so that we can get on with identifying as many of the victims as possible, but your presence will be an unhealthy distraction." He paused and looked between both officers. "What do you think of that?"

"That suits me fine, and no offense taken."

Logan got up from the conference table, and both men followed his lead. The meeting was over, and as Doctor Kolchak gathered up his files, the two policemen stepped out into the hallway.

Halfway down, Logan said to Pearson, "You're right: he's a total dick."

Pearson laughed.

"Ron, make sure Doctor Tightwad doesn't get himself killed during interviews. I got enough paperwork to last me a lifetime as it is."

Logan glanced back down the hall to see Kolchak watching them. He didn't know if he'd heard or not and he really didn't care.

10

The next day Doctor Kolchak stepped out of the taxi as John Parkins' neighbor watched from the window across the street. In the driveway was a pickup truck, 'PARKINS FEED DELIVERY' emblazoned across the side. Yep: this was the place.

Kolchak looked up and down the street. It was deserted except for the prying eyes behind twitching curtains.

The night before he had called Mr. Parkins and requested the visit. When he told him who he was the man had been cordial and said he would be waiting.

As he walked up to the porch, he saw a softball sitting underneath a large shrub.

"We used to play ball together," Sgt. Collins had remarked.

When Kolchak looked up, he was startled to see a large man standing silently in the doorway and wondered how long he had been watching him. When their eyes met Kolchak asked, "John Parkins?"

"Yes," the big man replied.

"I'm Doctor Robert Kolchak. We spoke on the phone."

"Yes, I remember. Please come in."

***

CHAPTER 13 · NEKONEET

1

He was four miles into the woods north of Thomasville, where the trails and all signs of man faded into the serene silence of the forest. The trees here did not resemble those from the Spirit Woods: the spruces were weather beaten and sickly by comparison. Even so, branches poked down with demonic fingers threatening to pluck out an eye, and Blackbird had to duck his head occasionally weaving left or right.

As he moved through the heavier brush he could hear Old Jake Toomey's instructions in the back of his mind: "There must be an opening in the trees. Stone must protrude from the earth – the larger the better. There you will find the place to purify and make contact."

As he searched, Blackbird rehashed the events of his life. He understood that he could not change the past – but he tortured himself nonetheless. During the solitary moments of the last fifteen years, his mind was the only sounding board for such reflection. He could not share this with anyone. His dealings with man were often indifferent and related only to the need of the moment.

He marched forward, one foot in front of the other, as he had always done, ignoring the blisters, the raggedness of his shoes or the fear in his heart.

Even out here in the middle of nowhere he looked twenty years out of date. His hair, now threaded with grey, hung in a tight braid that was slung over his right shoulder. He dressed in blue jeans, both jacket and pants. Around his neck was the old medicine bag that Grandfather had given him years ago when he left Spirit Woods to go to college.

As he pushed on, his thoughts harkened back to the first time he departed Chocktee for college.

"Go to the big world, Young Daniel. The white squaws aren't as sweet ours, but snare as many as you can." Grandfather winked. Janice Blackbird slapped her father's arm lightly and he feigned pain, but no one was fooled by the old man's drama. He winked at Daniel again – then his face gave way to seriousness. "Gather knowledge, but remember your people are always here, and should you need a palaver the fire burns brightly in our hearts." The old man's eyes welled up over the smile he used to disguise his sadness and he fell quiet, succumbing to the ache in his heart. Before Blackbird could see more the old man pulled him into a grandfatherly hug.

He, too, almost broke down as they embraced. He would miss the warmth of his words, the sweet scent of burning tobacco and the love he offered so openly. As the old man held him as his cousin, Johnny Proudfoot stood there uncomfortably. There were no words necessary to express the bond they had.

After a moment, they pulled apart and Grandfather wiped his eyes.

Then Proudfoot stepped forward to address his cousin.

"I found this in the Spirit Woods." He handed over a dark black feather.

"Thank you, Johnny." Blackbird looked over the feather and ran his index finger down its edge. "I will keep it with me always."

"Remember where you came from, Dan."

Then Proudfoot turned and left the gathering without a goodbye. He never surrendered to his emotions: it was a trait he had developed after both his mother and father were killed by a rogue grizzly bear. He was only nine years old. Since the tragedy, he hardened himself, saving his outbursts for the solitude of the woods or the peace garden where they lay. Blackbird thought he was strong and unfeeling, but he was truly a tortured soul who kept his sentiment buried.

"His heart is only stone on the outside, Young Daniel," Grandfather whispered. "Your cousin loves you."

It was tough love, if love at all. Johnny was so serious about everything, and sometimes he could get rough.

When Daniel and his grandfather made palaver, Johnny would watch from his sleeping bag. It was obvious that the old man loved Daniel more than anyone else in the world, and no matter how much Johnny Proudfoot tried he would never be favored.

As adolescence gave in to young adulthood, Proudfoot took counsel from Old Jake Toomey, who taught him about being a warrior. In doing so he pledged himself to the Chocktee people and learned the lessons both Grandfather and Toomey taught.

Early on it was determined that both cousins would run separate paths. Blackbird would leave and go to college, while Proudfoot would stay in Chocktee and develop his leadership skills. Someday he would be Chief.

"And so, he is," Blackbird said aloud, and pushed on with his search.

2

Over a thousand miles away, Proudfoot also thought about his cousin as he packed a bag for the trip to the small Prairie community. He remembered the night that Grandfather was slain. He had been so infuriated that he thought he might kill Daniel.

He still heard the screams as the black rain fell down upon them and he saw the broken body of the old man.

A foot or two away sat the two pieces of diamond willow that had touched the earth so many times as Grandfather walked and talked and prayed. Reaching down he picked up one piece in each hand, inspecting the polished and carved wood.

No! This isn't supposed to happen!

His eyes shifted from the wood to Grandfather's body. The old man's eyes were closed, his mouth twisted into a grimace of pain that invoked a myriad of gut-wrenching images. In the blue-grey darkness of Spirit Woods, the old man's body looked more like a stone statue, frozen and unreal.

No, no, no…

Then Proudfoot turned his attention Blackbird.

"You damned fool! Do you know what you have done?" Daniel looked back him, no words to rebut, his eyes frozen with pain. "It wasn't just you who loved him, Daniel," Proudfoot yelled. "Damn you!" Their eyes were locked, as the others came running to see. "I hate you!"

Proudfoot turned his back on him and walked away into the solitude of the woods. As he stomped off into the darkness, he placed one of the broken pieces under his arm and removed the large hunting knife from his side praying to the Spirit Mother Earth that his cousin would follow him.

Thankfully, he never did.

He walked the woods aimlessly all night in the solitude of his own misery. Under the darkened canopy he wept.

Exhaustion finally overtook him sometime before dawn, and he collapsed upon the stone where Grandfather had built so many fires.

Hours passed. He was awakened by the continual solitary thump of a Chocktee drum, which was banged in mourning of his grandfather.

He watched from the rock outcropping as Daniel stood on the dock with Aunt Janice. He was leaving. Good! Then Daniel looked up and he felt caught off-guard. He stepped back into the tree line and waited.

As the aircraft climbed into the sky, he loosened his grip on the knife, sheathed it and walked back down to the village. He returned as the drum continued its farewell beat and the people of Chocktee looked on in silence, knowing no words could comfort him. All-consuming hatred showed in every muscle, every contour of his body.

Not a word was spoken, nor a child's whisper heard as he went to the center of the village and splashed water onto his face to clean away the grime and tears from the night before. Then, face clean, he stared down into the soft ripples at the man staring back.

What do we do now? Where do we go from here, he thought.

Malaise flowed over him like poison gas and he splashed his hand in the water, fearful he would break down in front of the onlookers.

We say goodbye, he thought, and headed for the Peace Garden.

Janice Blackbird started to follow her nephew, but Old Jake stopped her. "Let him alone, Janny," he said placing a soft hand on her shoulder. "Now is not the time."

For three days she followed at a distance when he visited the Peace Garden to stare morosely down upon Grandfather's grave.

The burial ground was a collage of markers that ranged from gatherings of stones to sticks bound by roots, each significant to the individual. Grandfather's marker was a jagged piece of jade that Daniel had brought back from the west coast.

This only deepened Proudfoot's resentment.

Toomey had engraved the marker with the old man's name using a coal chisel to chip into the green stone, before dabbing it with Indian ink.

Nekoneet, which meant **'One who leads'**, was inscribed into the stone, but no one, except the Elders and his mother, called him by his Chocktee name. He was called Grandfather or Old Blackbird by most, and to his mourning daughter he was simple 'Da'.

For the last three mornings, he felt her there behind him, waiting. The first two days she had said nothing; just waited in silence for him. He was tempted to yell at her, exact his anger on her for what Daniel had done. After all, she had brought him back to Chocktee. Her mongrel son whose blood was impure, his mind poisoned with white man doubt.

He could have lashed out at her, but he knew that she was in more pain than he, and he loved her too much. She had taken him in after his parents were killed, showing no favor over her own son, embracing him in the darkness as he wept secretly. He would no more yell at her than curse Grandfather for being a fool and trusting Daniel.

Still she waited, for risk that his words might turn venomous he did not speak. He simply looked down upon the marker and clenched his teeth, feeling his jaw muscles bunch up as he fought back the tears. He remained quiet and turned to pass her. He was bound for the woods where he could cry openly.

But then…

"You loved him a great deal," she said from behind him.

Proudfoot stopped.

"He spoke so highly of you, Johnny." She touched his shoulder. "He would not want you to live your life bound by hate."

"I can't forgive him, Aunt Janny." He kept his back to her.

"For today, Johnny, just forgive yourself." Her voice wavered slightly and she placed her frail hand upon the side of his head.

He lowered his head, and in series of shrugs his emotions uncorked and his tears began to fall.

"I miss him, Aunt Janny. I miss him so much. It hurts."

He turned and hugged her, and she held him against her frail body as best she could.

While Johnny Proudfoot wept she pushed away the dual loss she had been dealt and decided then that she would melt the ice which encased his heart. It was what her 'Da' would have wanted.

"I miss him too, Johnny." She cried with her nephew.

3

Blackbird walked on considering his past, realizing he hadn't thought about Johnny or how he felt. He did not see the jealousy or know that sometimes when he and Grandfather made palaver his cousin would watch from his sleeping bag. It was obvious that the old man loved him more than anyone else. He did not see any wrong in that. He was enveloped in his own rite of passage with the old man and he was also not of pure blood. His father had been a white man, and that was why he thought Grandfather had taken him tightly under his wing. In retrospect he understood the resentment, but could do nothing about it.

Aside from their claims on Grandfather's heart, Blackbird and Proudfoot were truly like brothers. Always fishing, always hunting and occasionally fighting – but whatever the quarrel neither Proudfoot nor Blackbird would turn their back if the other were in trouble.

Blackbird loved Proudfoot, just as any young man loves a tough older brother, and though he could not break through that rough exterior, he thought the feeling was mutual, at least back then.

"Now I am simply his ward," he said aloud.

He continued to push toward the clearing he had spotted, all the while hoping there would be a stone. On his back he carried the worn canvas knapsack and in it were the provisions he needed. Grandfather had left him a bit of Jimson in the medicine bag he carried, but the fallen bark from the surrounding trees would also help with the ritual.

"Grandfather's magic," he said and smiled, reflecting on his college days when he lay naked next to a cocoa brown girl he had met there. She was a philosophy major from Bellingham and her dark skin made his look pale by comparison. Always before having sex, he hung the leather medicine bag on the post.

"What's this?" she said, pointing toward the small leather pouch.

He reached up and brought it down, twirling it on the leather strap he normally wore around his neck. "That is Grandfather's magic." He smiled and ran his free hand over the curve of her naked thigh.

"What kind of magic?" she asked, her brown eyes meeting his.

"Secret magic. It keeps me safe." He kissed her and thought, *I have snared many a squaw with it*, and almost laughed.

"Don't be letting the world in on my secrets, Young Daniel," Grandfather echoed.

Never.

He replaced the bag on the post and took her in his arms. And they had another go at Grandfather's magic, below the dream catcher Daniel's mother had made.

He reached the clearing, and the smile on his face faded. He had business to attend to. He reached down and removed a knife, identical to the one that his cousin carried on the night they lost Grandfather.

"You must have a weapon to protect yourself." Toomey had told him.

"Why? I thought I had two days," he asked.

"You cannot trust him. There is something that is distracting him, but as the equinox approaches his strength grows. He can send others to try and hurt you while you are in this state," Toomey said.

Perfect. He didn't air this sarcasm aloud.

"Try and get the ritual done during daytime, Dan; his power isn't as strong in the day. He falls into a meditative state in daylight and especially after eating," came Toomey's voice from inside his head, while Blackbird kicked away at the autumn leaves and fallen spruce needles which littered the forest floor.

Dirt, moist and cold, exploded up into the air as he continued his search.

"The stone is 'wakanda' which means it possesses special power. You must sit upon it as you smudge and purify yourself."

On the other side of the clearing, he spotted it jutting out the ground. It was barely exposed, a hump of grey covered with a blanket of leaves and deadfall. Daniel crossed over to it and knelt down. Using the handle of his knife he tapped the ground: a returning click indicated the rest of the stone beneath the raised ground cover.

"It is better if the rock is exposed, but if you expose it to the light its power will come to life in the light of day. The Great Spirit that runs through the woods will awaken that power and it will protect you," Toomey told him.

"Let's just hope it's big enough, Old Jake," he said aloud as he cleared away more and more needles and ground cover.

While Jake Toomey rattled around in Blackbird's head, his mother inhabited the subconscious of John Proudfoot, who was now working in his woodshop away from the laughter of his children or the prying eyes of the others. This was the one place he lost himself. He loved the art of creation – though this was not creation, but repair.

"I was an outcast," she said. "I had broken the circle and left. I wanted more and when I came back, there were many who shunned me. Others who said I should be banished."

"We don't do that," Proudfoot argued. "Jake Toomey left to fight the white man's war and no one shunned him."

"Jake left with five others when the white man came calling, but they only went to fight in the war to protect Chocktee," Janice Blackbird had said. "We are of the old ways, and we only live now because of the sacrifice. With ancient ritual often comes outdated thinking. When I came back, I was in ill regard, my son considered a pariah, not because of his birthright, but because of my sin."

"Why? Because you had a child with a white man?" Proudfoot asked.

"No. I broke the ancient circle. Up until then no one left the Chocktee. We are a cursed people, Johnny. That's why we have not mixed with the other nations. It would have made no difference if I had mixed with a native man from the Ojibwa or any other people."

She was smoking a cigarette as they sipped blackberry tea. Her eyes were sunken and her skin stretched across her cheekbones like worn leather.

Proudfoot knew that Old Jake had gone off to fight in the war and though his aunt said it was to protect Chocktee he guessed that Jake's warrior blood had more to do with it.

The six men who left Chocktee enlisted in the Marine Corps and were deployed to Vietnam in 1969. Only Toomey returned. Three of the men had been killed during a bloody offensive and the other two were MIA. After the end of the Vietnam War the people of Chocktee waited for them to be released, but they never appeared. The three dead men were repatriated to the Peace Garden four months before Toomey came home, their bodies interred with the Chocktee warriors. The two missing men were never heard from again and they were honored with markers at the turn of the millennium after an official notice declared them killed in action.

"It was my father and Old Jake who had been the voices of reason when I returned and eventually made the council leaders surrender to their call for change." She coughed and set down her cup.

"Are you okay" he asked.

"No, Johnny. I am dying – but I will see my father soon. My heartache is here on earth."

"I am trying, Aunt Janice."

She lit another cigarette. "I know you are, Johnny, but you must try harder. Someday you will be a leader, likely an Elder. You must not burden your soul with what cannot be undone."

Over the short span of her remaining life, the two had many talks, and through them Janice slowly but surely chipped away at the hardness of Proudfoot's heart, until at last no anger was left.

In the last moments of her life he held her hand as the pain from the cancer consumed her. "You will take your place at the council soon, Johnny," she whispered to him from her death bed. "My only son, your blood brother, walks alone. I ask you to watch over him and be there. Do not leave him to walk alone." She waited for his answer, squeezing his hand tightly.

"I will not leave him, Aunt Janice," he promised. The weight lifted from his shoulders and was replaced by a solemn oath. "I will do everything in my power to help him."

Janice Blackbird smiled. Her commerce in this world now complete, the light in her eyes faded and her grip upon his hand loosened. He did not see the guardian waiting patiently to take her to the next world. She looked into the corner of the room and said, "Da…" then slipped peacefully away.

He set her hand upon her bosom and looked to the place where she had been staring. There was nothing.

And so, once again, Proudfoot was sad and alone – but she had left him with a purpose. He left the Blackbird house and went to mourn while the others prepared her for the peace garden.

Coming back from memory, he focused on the completed repair job. He wrapped it up in an old poncho and took a drum from the wall he had made a few months earlier. As he carried these two items back to his small house, he wondered if he would ever return to his workshop. The autumn air was fresh, a reminder of the coming equinox and the threat of bitter cold.

Later, after supper, he had a talking circle with the Elders.

From the window, his wife Joanne watched. When she caught his eye, she smiled, but it veiled her worry only thinly. He smiled back and then their two boys joined her at the window, lighting up his heart. He decided, after Toomey's talking circle, he would take them to the outcropping. There they would build a fire to roast marshmallows and hot dogs with the kids tonight. He would tell them the stories of his boyhood and about his blood brother, the brave hunter. Then, as they slept, he would make love to his wife under the canopy, possibly for the last time.

"Tomorrow we will fly away from this place and try and stop the evil our people have set upon the world," he whispered, just under his breath.

The bedrock was grey with veins of rusty ore running through it from one corner to the other. It spanned twenty-five by ten feet, and it took the better part of an hour to clear away the moss and overgrowth. As he worked, the sun peeked through the overcast sky, evaporating the dampness from its surface and causing its color to fade.

He could feel the energy in the rock and hear Old Jake's voice approval. "This will do nicely."

"Let's hope so," he said.

Blackbird began to gather firewood and stones from around the forest floor and set them in a circle to contain the flame. It was still early morning and he was not sure how long the ritual would take, but he wanted to be out of here before the darkness could disorient him.

Kneeling before the encircled kindling, he reached into his pack, pulled out a magnesium bar and scraped filings into the center of the circle using the dull side of his knife. Once that was done, he placed some twigs and dried leaves to start the fire. He dropped a match onto the pile of magnesium shavings. They flared up immediately. Daniel began to pile on the wood he had stacked beside him. Then, pleased with the fire, he rolled out the cloth poncho his mother had knitted and set it before him.

Some of the smaller twigs began to crackle and pop while he set out the items he had carried all these years: the pipe, the hunting knife, the tattered dream catcher, and the black feather.

He made a tripod of three long branches and lashed them together using a piece of cord from his pack. He hung the dream catcher from the tripod and set it behind the place where he would sit. As he did this, he prayed to the Mother Spirit that it would protect him.

Lifting the black feather up to the sky, he said, "Gather the forces of good, oh Mother Spirit: bring their energy and goodness to me in this time of withdrawal."

He laced its quill through the single braid of his hair.

The stone beneath him was warming to the heat of the flames that licked upward almost three feet. He added no more wood and heard Toomey's voice again giving counsel. "You must make an offering to the spirits, and in turn, they will purify you."

He removed the treasured medicine bag from around his neck and untied the leather which had bound its secrets for so many years. As he did this, he spoke aloud.

"Grandfather, I have worn this almost half my life and believe it was the thing that kept me safe all these years. I believe we will again make palaver."

Then he began to pray.

"I believe in the Spirit Mother Earth. I believe in the guardians of both worlds. Oh, Spirit Mother Earth, protect me."

He lay the contents of the medicine bag out and put some green branches atop the flames.

"I offer you the sweet tobacco of my ancestors," he said, sprinkling the small amount of dried powder over the flames. As it smoldered he bathed his hands in it and filled his pipe with jimson weed and bearberry, then said, "I offer you sweet the bark of these spruce woods, Spirit Mother." He puffed on the pipe, continued to smudge, and his words became a chant as the smoke swirled about and engulfed him. "Give me the strength to see that which should not be seen. Show me that which should not be shown as I pledge myself to right the wrong even if it means my life, oh Great Spirit Mother Earth."

He removed the vial of blood from his pocket and set it beside the other items as he picked up his knife and waved it through the smoke, washing away its negative energy.

"You must purify the mark," Toomey said.

Using the knife's jagged tip, Blackbird pierced the top of the fifteen-year-old scar on his cheek, and from it, blood flowed. Dormant nerves within the scar tissue came back to life, sending sparks of fresh hot pain up into his eye and down his jawline.

He set the tip of his knife in the coals of the fire. Then, using the fingers on both hands, he pried open the wound and ignoring the pain thrust his head into the swirling smoke, letting it filter into the gash. Droplets of blood fell and sizzled on the heated rocks as he put his index and middle finger into the wound, then pulled them back.

Using his own blood, he set two marks on either cheek, and as he bathed himself in the smoke, he continued his chant. "I offer you the magic of Nekoneet, my grandfather, wise man and teacher who stood firm against the evil of the black orb's abomination."

He tossed the leather pouch and the remaining contents into the fire. The flames flared, and the pouch turned to ash in the inferno. He felt the Jimson Weed anesthetizing him and kept his face bathing in the smoke. With his left hand he reached down and took the blade from the fire, its tip glowing white hot – and as he squeezed the scar together, he brought the tip down upon it and cauterized the wound.

He let a shrill cry and fell sideways. Burning agony expanded upward into his right eye socket and down into his mouth. The bleeding stopped instantly, and darkness swallowed him whole.

6

"Tonight, you will spend time with your loved ones," Old Jake said to them as they stood in the talking circle on the outcropping overlooking the ancient village. In his hand he held an eagle's feather, giving him dominion over the group. Not one of them was allowed to talk while he held the feather. The response was limited only to murmurs or nods of acknowledgment.

Distracted, Proudfoot stood silently, looking over the grounds of his people as he listened to Old Jake give his oration. He wondered if he would ever see this place again.

The others were also silent: Fortier, Michano, and Monias, all men twice his age who spoke little except to address the Chocktee law. Many times, they gathered in the council hut: a stone building built before the white man set out on his first Great War of the last century. There they would talk in the ancient language – not the one he or Daniel had learned, but an older dialect that would die with them.

"The Brave Hunter Blackbird has descended upon a village where the spirit of Jackanoob holds still. A struggle is imminent, my brothers, and after many years of walking alone it is time for us to take flight and assist our brother."

Toomey stood motionless as the others waited for him to continue. The Northern Wind blew his grey hair like spider webs about his weathered face. He stood statuesque, bringing his gaze upon each of them dramatically.

He continued, "Our people have lived out here for centuries. Their bloodline and fate were changed on the day Jackanoob bargained away our future. For over two hundred years we were guarded and kept this ritual secret, but that time has passed. What we do in the coming days will alter the future of our people. Some of you may ask: why are we concerned with one evil figure when the world is awash in the blood of immorality? It is a good question, but only one a fool would ask."

He paused and smiled.

Proudfoot laughed, as did the others.

"Go now: make peyak with your families, but tomorrow we are nîyânan."

Toomey stepped away from the talking circle and walked off down the path without another word, feather still poised in his grasp.

There was a confused silence as they watched him go. Rick Monias laughed first, then Fortier said, "Old Jake sure knows how to exit a talking circle."

The others joined in with the laughter. Then, laughter expelled, they scattered – all except Proudfoot, who stood at the outcropping a moment longer. He so loved this place, the tradition, and his people. His missed his talks with Aunt Janice, the soothing words of Grandfather, and now he missed Daniel.

They were truly blood brothers, Daniel and he. The large knife he carried was an exact copy of the one Blackbird had used to cut open and close the wound on his face.

They had performed the ritual of becoming blood brothers one day in the late eighties, at the height of summer. Other boys watched in fascination as the two cut their hands, clasped and bound them with a piece of cloth. For two hours they sat there, and all he said when it was over was, "It is done."

The rest of the world did not understand the significance of this place or that it was the last of its type. The Chocktee were not supposed to be here: they only existed because of the concordat that Jackanoob had made.

7

Blackbird opened his eyes and stood up, but his body was still, and it took him a second to realize he was no longer in it. For a moment he felt nauseous, but as he adapted he began to wonder, Is this astral travel, or lucid dreaming? Staring down upon himself he considered the possibility he might be dead, but then his body stirred as if to remind him not to abandon it.

Above him, the sky was black and without light. Around the rock, too, was only blackness. As his spirit-self moved along the edge of the lighted circle, he could see something swimming inside the darkness. He did not know what it was, but he did know one thing – it terrified him.

Then a voice he loved and trusted spoke.

"I will watch over you, my child," his mother promised.

He brought up his hand, waving it in front of the blackness, then dared to touch it with his fingertip. It rippled like liquid, and he asked, "How will I be able to breathe?"

"You were born in liquid, little one. Do not fear."

He took one last look at himself there on the rock as the fire flickered before him – and then he stepped off the rocky island and into the black abyss, feeling its shroud pull him into the darkness. His stomach fluttered as he began to fall, his heart thumped in his ears, mixed with the echoes of a language he could not understand.

He did not need to breathe or see: he was blind and could not physically feel his body. He was in the state of mind one feels as they travel through the world of dreams: disconnected and without control.

His heartbeat thumped louder. He began to understand some of what was being said. At first, he thought he heard, "Soiled feet." Then he felt its anger ripple through him as he fell ever deeper.

"Boompa Boompa Boompa," the pulse exclaimed.

"Soiled Feet," its distant voice said.

Is this a riddle? He couldn't understand.

The voice was muffled as if it came from the other side of a wall, and the heartbeat thumping in his ears did not help even as it receded.

"Gungry," it said – and suddenly he felt its madness as if it were his own. With madness came comprehension. Its ancient thoughts started to unravel, conjugate, and he began to understand.

"Hungry, so hungry."

He was falling toward a filtered light now.

"Spoiled meat," it lamented. "So hungry."

A shriek filled his ears, almost driving him insane. It echoed on and on to the thumping tempo of its black heart. Now he felt the ache of its hunger.

"Spoiled meat."

I'm inside its mind.

Then it said something he did understand.

"Unrelenting, never stop, must kill."

The creature was talking about him. He felt its fear and understood he was the source of that fear, but it gave him little reassurance.

The sensation of falling ceased. Now Blackbird felt himself hovering just beyond the filtered light, listening to the madness of its shriek mingling with the agony of its hunger.

"Spoiled meat!"

It was having a tantrum.

Why am I here? he thought. *What is it I am supposed to learn from this?*

The light behind the shroud shifted, and he drew closer, trying to see. As he did, he began to understand he was behind its eyes, staring outward.

"So hungry! The pain, the pain! So hungry!"

At first, it was unclear what he (it) was looking at, although he guessed that the creature was not so much searching, just lost in thought. From behind its eyes, he could barely see a wall, and on the wall, there was a picture with something on it. It was not clear; the veil blurred it – though this was not a veil at all. Its eyes were out of focus as it concentrated on the pain of hunger.

Focus, he thought, trying to decipher what was written there.

(eed delv) was all he could make out.

Then came flashes from above and below him, blocking out the view. He began to hear the shrill cries of terror. The mental picture before him shifted then and he felt himself pulling back away as the thumping of the creature's black heart grew louder.

"You must leave now," a voice said. "It will hear your thoughts."

He was falling again, back to the waking world while all around the synapses of the creature's mind sparked and its many memories of murder and mayhem were played out before him. There was desperation, there were cries, begging for forgiveness and horrible bone-crunching sounds.

"You have seen what you need to see," the voice said again, and Blackbird recognized it as the frail voice of the Elder Jackanoob.

But had he?

The last words echoed about him as he fell back to earth.

8

His eyes were sticky with sleep, and his head pounded as if from a hangover. He could smell the embers of the fire and feel the flash of pain from his cauterized wound.

eed delv, he thought. *That is what I did this for? What is it?*

The sun was still shining, and a mild breeze gently pushed his mother's dream catcher this way and that. His right arm had fallen asleep, and his knee ached from the laying on top of something. All around him there was silence.

Blackbird lay still. His bones ached. It seemed like a lot of work for nothing, the clearing of the rock, the fire, the sacrifice of his grandfather's offering. He could barely remember what he had seen and what he did remember were the creature's chaotic thoughts. Those he wished he could forget.

He forced himself to stand and pack the belongings that remained. He had trouble keeping his balance at first but steadied himself using the tripod. As he did this, he took down the dream catcher. Then he removed the tattered feather from his braid and wrapped it, along with his other treasures, in the oiled cloth he used to keep his knife free of rust. Then he folded the poncho.

Daniel glanced back down at the vial of black blood. The temptation was still there: he was so tired, and the road had been so long.

Why not, he thought.

"Because it is not your way." Grandfather echoed.

"I have lost my way," he said hopelessly.

Grandfather fell silent.

Guiltily Blackbird placed the vial into his pocket after wrapping it in Kleenex. He could only wonder how he must look after cutting open his face and smearing blood on it.

"My days of snaring squaws have passed, Grandfather," he laughed aloud.

After ensuring the fire was out, he set back down toward the town. Along the way, he stopped at a small stream and splashed cold water on his face and cleaned up. That helped, but still, he ached terribly and not just in his face. His whole body felt banged up and abused.

He had purchased a Pay-As-You-Go cell phone at the local convenience and pulled out the business card the cab driver had given him. He was still too deep in the woods to get a signal on the phone but knew a mile out there had been three bars. When he was closer, he would give the cab driver a call.

He tried to keep what he saw fresh in his mind so that when the others arrived, he would be able to consult them. Maybe they could make sense of it. As far as he was concerned, he was not sure he had done anything except poison himself with the creature's psychosis. He did not know if he could do that again without going stark raving mad. Unfortunately, Blackbird thought that this was just a test run of this new ability.

This afternoon he would call Chief Logan to arrange a meeting and somehow try to convince him of the danger that was coming.

"How the fuck am I going to do that, Toomey?" he said aloud and laughed. "Well you see, Chief, there's this monster I've been tracking and, well…" He broke up into giddy laughter, then, unknowingly, echoed Hopper: "I am so fucked."

The cell phone beeped: it had made communication with a tower.

He pulled out the card and punched the buttons.

"Morneau Taxi," the voice on the other end of the static answered.

"Hi Bobby, it's Dan. I'm finished my hike. Can you meet me at the same place you dropped me off?"

"Sure, Dan. How did it go and what time?"

"Forty minutes. I'll explain my hike when you pick me up," he said, already formulating a back-story to explain the fresh white burn mark on his cheek.

"Sounds good, Dan. I'll be there with bells."

9

"Geez, you sure you don't want me to take you over to Emergency?" Morneau's eyes widened. He looked confused, even a bit alarmed, but beyond the scar, Blackbird had no idea why. He added quickly, "You're lucky you didn't bleed to death out there."

"No, I'm fine. I hear you about lucky and the odds of ripping open an old scar. My past is coming back to haunt me." He tried to sound humble and embarrassed. Looking at the rearview mirror and into the cabby's eyes, he attempted to gauge whether or not he was buying the story. Not that it would matter, soon enough.

Morneau was putting the car into gear. "It's been a crazy day, Dan."

"Really? How so," Blackbird asked.

"Well, Scott Masterson was found dead on a bridge over the Red River, and they say it was some kind of freak accident." Morneau stepped on the gas a bit. "Old man Masterson got the word and dropped like a stone from a heart attack an hour after the cops visited him."

"What kind of freak accident?"

"Poor guy smacked his melon on a guardrail," Morneau said. "My sister is a dispatcher for the fire department – she heard them talking about it. Poor kid! Wasn't that bright, but he was okay. You know?"

"Yeah, he seemed like a nice guy." Blackbird leaned back in his seat, wondering if Skin had a hand in this. It could have been an accident, but he doubted it. "Do you think I'll have to vacate my room when I get back?"

"No; for now, Dennis is going to run the place until some of Masterson's family can come in from out of town – but when that happens I think it'll be the end of Thomasville's first motel."

Morneau fell silent then, and Blackbird was thankful. They were thirty minutes from the motel, and he needed to close his eyes.

***

CHAPTER 14 - EXIT STRATEGIES AND CONFESSIONS

1

September 22, 2009

"Sign right here and here," Logan said as Pearson autographed the paperwork that had been drawn up for prisoner transfer. He moved that sheet, set it aside. "And here."

"Great being in the computer age, isn't it?" Pearson remarked autographing another page. "Remember when they said it was going to be a paperless world?"

They were in Logan's office finishing the formalities that would release Hopper from the custody of the Thomasville Police Department and make him the ward of Artisan Institute under the secure supervision of Pearson and Cooper.

"Reporters are already tearing down," Cooper remarked.

Mick chimed, "Good riddance."

"Okay, Ron, last one." Logan handed two pages across the desk. Pearson signed them and then Logan placed each page in its respective stack. One was for Thomasville's files, and the other was accompany Pearson and Cooper. He sealed the paperwork in a manila envelope and handed it over to Pearson, who took it and placed it in his briefcase.

"Thanks, Dave." Pearson snapped the briefcase closed.

Logan said, "Mick, can you close the door and the blinds?"

Mick stepped inside and closed the door behind him, followed by the blind to the single window. Logan reached down and opened his bottom desk drawer and pulled out a bottle of Crown Royal and the four paper cups he had taken from the lunch room.

"I know this is kind of cliché, but I wanted to tell that this has been the worst detail I have ever had the displeasure of serving on," he said as he poured two fingers of whiskey in each cup and handed them to each officer. "I would also like to say that I hope I never deal with something like this again in my lifetime – but if I ever do, I can't think of three more professional men to work with. Ron, Coop, Mick, you have made this detail one that was bearable. I salute you. If I take anything away from this, it is the knowledge that I have been in the company of some of the country's most outstanding police officers."

The four tapped their paper cups together gently and sipped at the warm whiskey.

"Wow, not even noon yet and I'm having a drink," Pearson mused. "Dave, Mick, the feeling is mutual. Thank you for inviting us into your town and being such gracious hosts during this crummy detail. Often local cops get a bad rap, but you gentlemen have shown us big city types that expertise comes in many forms and venues. On behalf of my partner and department, I raise my cup to you." Pearson lifted the paper cup, and they repeated the process.

For a moment there was uncomfortable silence, then Cooper pulled out his business card and handed it over. "If there is anything we can ever do for you guys, feel free to call."

Logan took it.

Mick pulled out a pack of gum. "We should probably freshen up before talking to the detachment."

They all took a piece, and Logan replaced the bottle in his bottom drawer. He would take it home later. He wasn't a stereotypical cop, bottle stowed in his bottom drawer at all times: this he had purchased specially for the occasion. With it safely stowed they went out to address the detachment.

Pearson was very well spoken, thanking all officers for their part in the investigation and commending them for their courtesy and keen eye for detail. "I have had the pleasure of working among some of the best officers in the country, and all of you fall into that category." On that note, there was a bit of small talk and joking, and then they got down to business.

Mick read off the roster. "Corporal West, you will head to the airport with Constable Larson and secure the Airport thirty minutes before our jump off. Corporal Steel, you will retrieve Doctor Kolchak from his hotel and bring him here. Once here, Constable Hardy and I will mount the point car."

"Pardon me, Sarge, but how exactly will you and Hardy be mounting the point car?" Oddball cracked.

There was laughter.

"Larson, you really missed your calling," Cooper chuckled.

"Detectives –" Mick raised his voice – "Pearson and Cooper will ride in the Navigator behind Constables Kennedy and Jones, who will be driving the prisoner. Corporal Steel will bring up the rear with Doctor Kolchak. Any questions?"

There were none.

"Chief, anything to add?"

"I'll just say that up until this point you have demonstrated to everyone that you are top-notch professionals. I will just give you a warning. Do not, I repeat do not underestimate the ability or limitations of the prisoner. This man snuffed out the lives of seventeen boys, some of whom were almost men. While he has been somewhat lethargic, I want all of you to stay on your toes and handle him like you would a rattlesnake. Let's not fall asleep just because the show is winding down. You all know what you gotta do. Let's get it done." Logan looked at Mick and nodded.

"You heard the man! Let's go!" Mick ordered, and each officer set off to do their individual task.

2

Olivia Parkins was of clear mind as she sat in the guest room of her sister-in-law, Erin Grant. Erin was in the tub, and her husband was at work. Olivia sat alone on the daybed, her demeanor relaxed and serene. She had calmed down over the last few days, coming to a conclusion.

Reaching inside the small wad of Kleenex kept under the nightstand she unwrapped it to reveal the stash of pills she had been saving. There were thirty of them wadded up neatly for precisely this moment. She considered the stash momentarily, then placed them into her mouth one by one as she sipped the water that Erin left before going for her bath. Not once did she falter or second-guess herself. No longer able to stand the pain, or the emptiness brought to her on the day that Mick and the Chief showed up at their door. She could not stand to think of what terrible things her baby must have suffered at the hands of that swine.

Her only child was gone and behind he left a hole in her heart which could never be filled again. There would be no going home. She wanted to be with her son and could not bear another day knowing that he had been taken from her.

Each pill marked another step toward the silence, and with each, she relaxed just a little more. No more crying. No more screaming. No more longing. Only peace and Tommy.

She slipped the last pill into her mouth and waited.

That wasn't so hard, she thought.

She reached into her pocket and withdrew the short note she'd written to her sister-in-law. She unfolded it. Lying back on the bed she gave it one last glance, the tug of drowsiness already calling her away from this world. The words became to blur; it was too late to proofread, but she wanted to make sure that no one blamed themselves.

Erin: Please do not blame yourself. I am going to be with my son as I cannot bear to be without him. Tell my dearest love, John, that I am sorry I could not be stronger.

Please take care of him.

Olivia

Within minutes she was swimming in and out of consciousness. As Erin toweled herself dry, Olivia Parkins slipped peacefully away, her heartbeat slowing, her breathing becoming shallow, the world fading. She leaned back passively, her head resting on the pillow, her right hand clutching the handwritten note. Purposely, Olivia had gotten up, dressed, brushed her hair and readied herself for this moment. No longer was she a slave to the guilt or agony. The accusing voices that had tortured her now relented as the darkness welcomed her.

She exited this world with dignity and grace, something that had not been afforded to her only child.

3

Steel rolled up to the front of the Holiday Inn, and Kolchak was already standing out front with his bag and laptop slung over one shoulder. He stopped the car, got out and said, "Good Morning, Doctor. My name is Don Steel. I'll be escorting you back to the station."

"That will be perfect," Kolchak replied.

They stowed his luggage in the trunk of the cruiser.

For the most part, the drive was silent. Steel explained that they would be riding together and that they would fall into line with the convoy once they reached the station. It was strictly procedural. The doctor looked straight ahead, lost in thought about something, but Steel didn't feel much like pursuing small talk. In his opinion, they had about as much in common as a bowling ball and a banana.

4

Coroner Jeff Henderson loaded the last body into the reefer trailer himself. Not that anyone would know that the hand-made crate contained the remains of a body. It hardly seemed large enough. The refrigeration unit hummed away and kept the remains cold sufficient for transport. A mechanic had been brought in to ensure that unit was tip-top before they signed on to use it. After a minor overhaul, it had been given a clean bill of health.

Once the crate was set in place on the aluminum floor, he put a scissor load bar in front and behind it to keep it from shifting. Outside the trailer stood Andrea Chase, the forensic specialist who had assisted him throughout the dig. She was a beauty. Tall, blonde, and she always tied her hair back in a ponytail.

"That it?" she asked, but it was rhetorical. She knew this was the last and that Henderson wouldn't have come out until he was done.

"That's the last of them."

Henderson climbed out of the unit.

The bodies were being transported to the University Lab in Winnipeg where the Forensics and Entomology Departments would try to unravel the evidence that would lead to identifying who the remaining victims were and their estimated times of death.

They had their work cut out for them.

"What will you guys do with the reefer once you unload it?" Henderson asked as he closed the doors and Chase placed a bolt seal in each latch.

"It will be washed down with antiseptic, and then it's going directly to the scrap yard. The days of this wagon hauling food grade product are done."

"Amen to that," he said. "I sure appreciated your help on this, Andrea."

"Happy to be of service," she replied, and she really meant it. Her bold enthusiasm was that of an ambitious scientist. She had no shame about it, and Henderson admired her ability to compartmentalize.

"One thing left to do," he said.

They went back into the hall give a final address to their own team.

5

They gathered at the edge of the water where a Twin Otter waited for the party of five. The float plane was a regular, bringing medical supplies and acting as a taxi between civilizations. For those who worked in the Northern communities not accessible by road, this bush plane was the only mode of transport. This Otter jumped up and down the BC and Alaska Coast, transporting everything from students to oil workers. Today it would be heading south to the Vancouver Airport.

Old Jake Toomey stood before his people as the four waited behind for him to give his final summation. He was calm and collected, and he looked quite natural standing up there like some iconic prophet.

"Today is a good day for the people of this land," Toomey began. "We are the last of our kind. Unknown to man is our name and our culture. Much has happened to our people, and we have always stood tall against that what is wrong. We are the Chocktee Nation, the children of night and day. Up until this day we have been living on time borrowed by the sins of our ancestors, but today is the day that will all change." He smiled.

There were some grunts, but most of the people just watched the old man as he stood like a Sergeant Major addressing a parade square.

"Today I leave with your brothers, Proudfoot, Fortier, Michano and Monias. The Spirit Mother came to me in a vision and said to me, 'Take these boys and with them you will be nîyânan.'"

It did not occur to most of the onlookers to ask Toomey what 'We are nîyânan' meant or what language he was using because it was not Chocktee. Of those it did occur to, no one dared.

"Two wonderful things are going to happen today. One! We are setting out on a quest to set things right. Two! I get to ride in an airplane."

Toomey turned abruptly and walked away from his people, leaving the other four off-guard. "Let's go," he barked. "The pilot is waiting!"

The remaining nîyânan followed obediently.

6

The convoy left for Brandon at 2 PM sharp. Logan made himself scarce by shutting himself in his office as they ushered Hopper away. When they were gone, he went out into dispatch and listened on the radio to communications. He and his civilian dispatcher Sabrina shared a cup of coffee, quietly listening to the procedural chatter. It occurred to him, as he was sure it did her, that they had been first on base when this case broke. It seemed fitting that they would now sit together and see this through to the end.

"You look tired, Chief," Sabrina remarked.

"Do I?" Logan laughed a bit and sipped his coffee. He was tired, but there was still a great deal to do. Lots of loose ends to tie up, lots of wreckage and then there was the other thing. "Yeah, Sabrina, I'm pretty bushed."

"You need a vacation," she said, giving a look of disapproval for the answer she knew would be forthcoming.

Logan brought his hands up and rubbed his eyes then looked at her solemnly. "I'm dying, that's why I look so tired."

Then there was silence between them, except for muted horror in her face.

He hadn't told anyone, not even his ex-wife or the kids. That sit down was in the near future. He wasn't even sure why he told Sabrina, but he had been carrying this around since yesterday, and for some reason, he needed to say it out loud. Twice he almost told Mick but thought better.

But now the cat was out of the bag and having said it aloud, he felt a little less numb. He smiled awkwardly and said, "It's okay, Sabrina."

"It's not okay! Oh, my God." Tough though she was, there was a softer girl under the hard shell. She looked aghast. Tears welled up in her eyes. "Of what? Are you sure?"

"I have bone cancer." Logan sipped his coffee, an edge of desperation in his voice that she had never heard. "It started in my sternum. Since then it's spread to my left lung as well as my pancreas. The results came back yesterday."

"They can't do chemo? Radiation? My God, Dave, you're so young."

"I played a rough game, Sabrina: two packs of cigars a day, shitty food, booze. There is no treatment for what I have, and I will not spend my remaining days puking and shitting all over the place to try and extend it."

"I'm very sorry, Dave."

"Don't be: it's nobody's fault but mine." He gazed out over the vacant squad room searching for words. "I just don't know how I'm gonna tell my kids." His voice cracked, and he began to tremble.

Sabrina got up from her chair and wrapped her arms around him, something he had not felt since he and his wife split. He wanted to pull away and be strong but instead succumbed to her embrace. Her bosom was against his cheek, and he took comfort in it, sheltering himself like a little boy.

They stayed that way, without a single word for a few minutes, his arms around her waist and hers cradling his head against her chest to the tune of radio chatter. He did not cry: he just closed his eyes and accepted her warmth. After a while, he loosened his grip on her, and she him.

7

The twin Otter rumbled as it ascended into the clouds, leaving behind the ancient village of Chocktee and its people. Toomey looked out the window thrilled, while the others tried to hide the anxiety brought on by the bumpy ride. "I hope I come back to this world as an eagle. Flying around and eating salmon fresh from the river seems a grand way to live."

"I like the ground." Michano looked as though he might vomit.

"Adventure, my brothers: it is a gift; never refuse it," he advised them.

Toomey's face did not betray the bedlam they were headed for. His face was spread in an excited grin, like a child on Christmas morning, peering out of the windows as the clouds rolled by. This puzzled Proudfoot, but he didn't question it. While Old Jake could be a warm old man, not unlike his late grandfather, he was also imposing and tough. Respect in the inner circle was not only earned by warmth and wisdom.

They waited for the Chief Elder to draw his thoughts together and tell them how they were going to proceed once they reached Thomasville. When that would be none of them knew, but no one dared to prod or hurry Old Jake Toomey.

8

Blackbird was dreaming about home again, but this time about his mother. They were down at the dock where the bush plane bobbed gently on its floats as an Eastern wind pushed rippling waves across Jackneetow Lake. The pilot was unloading supplies and would be departing shortly. Beyond the lake on the mountain where his grandfather often took him, and Johnny was the rock outcropping. He saw his cousin standing there, watching him.

I'm sorry, Johnny, I'll make it right!

Then, as if his cousin had heard his thoughts, he turned and went back into the forest.

His mother stood by him, face contorted with sadness, guilt. "I am so afraid for you, Daniel."

"I will be okay, Mother. See to Johnny when he comes back. Tell him I am going to make this right. I promise to never stop." He felt a hitch in his throat, a hard ball that hurt and the only way to unseat it would be to cry. But he swallowed defiantly, keeping his composure. "I love you, Mother. I am so sorry to have hurt you this way."

"Oh, Daniel. My dear, sweet Daniel," she sobbed.

The pilot opened the door on the craft and looked his way.

"I will come back as soon as possible."

"Please hurry," she said reaching out to touch him one last time – and then a ringing sound came from his left, squelching her words, jerking him backward.

He opened his eyes. The digital clock on the nightstand glowed a bright red 1:30 PM. Letting out a long, bewildered sigh, he sat up on the bed.

"I'm sorry, Mother."

The dream had played out many times over the years, recurring and serving as a constant reminder that he had abandoned her. He tried, in vain to shake it off, then got up and went to the bathroom.

His urine came out as a dark yellow stream and turned the center toilet water green. *I'm a little on the dehydrated side*, he thought as he emptied his bladder. He reached down, flushed the toilet and turned to the sink to get a glass of water. When he looked up into the oversized vanity, he saw a stranger looking back at him.

"What the …"

He trailed off in shock. The reflection in the mirror mouthed the words, and he blinked to make sure he wasn't hallucinating. Absently, he brought up a hand to touch the scar on his face, but it was not the old wound that startled him.

"Is that really me?"

His hair was much greyer but even worse: his face had aged. By at least ten years. Now he looked twenty years older than he actually was. The scar which extended from his right cheekbone down to his lower jaw was white, and the burn mark from the heated knife looked as though it had been done years ago. *Yeah, but it still hurts like it happened today, doesn't it?* The ache he felt in his bones, and the strange look on the cabby's face all made sense now.

He ran the water cold and splashed his face, giving temporary relief to the pain, but thought he might pick up some Tylenol or Aspirin in the lobby if there was any to be had.

I'm like Moses after looking into the burning bush, he thought. *How many times could I do that? How many? Before it killed me?*

He dropped his underwear, climbed into the shower and muttered to himself, "Wait 'til they get a load of me."

The hot water beat against his naked body while he leaned against the porcelain tiles thinking about the dream and the guilt he carried for leaving his mother to die alone.

What a stupid, selfish bastard I am.

"You knew she was dying and you left anyway?" Hot water ran down over his face and into his mouth, tasting of sulfur and guilt. "You got Grandfather killed, and you left your mother to die alone."

He smashed his fist against the porcelain and let out a tortured cry.

"Enough," Grandfather scolded him. "You cannot undo the past."

So, he pushed away from the anger and self-hate, let it ebb away. He leaned back against the tiles, feeling the water wash over him, and he instead focused on Toomey and the others. By now they would be catching a connecting flight in Vancouver.

He grabbed a tiny bar of soap, rolled it in a face cloth to scrub away the grit and dirt from his trek in the woods.

Focus on the vision, he thought. Make that the source of your obsession. "eed delv," he said aloud, hoping that hearing the words might bring recognition. "What does it mean? It makes no sense."

"There is a lesson here," Grandfather had said. "There is always a lesson."

There were pieces to the puzzle which had not yet been set in place, and as a result, each lesson on its own did not make sense. Logan was part of it. 'eed delv' was another, and there was something else to consider. Tomorrow was September 23, the autumn equinox. Toomey had not said that it played a role in this, but he could only guess that it did, and by coincidence, Skin seemed adamant to finish its business with him by then once and for all.

"eed delv," he said once more and turned the shower knob off. Using his hands, he wrung water from his long grey hair and examined his naked body in the vanity mirror again.

"eed delv," the stranger in the mirror said.

9

A gathering of reporters were cordoned off in the eastern corner of the Brandon Airport, just close enough to snap a picture or shoot video of Hopper's departure. Logan had arranged everything with the local police and airport security. Hours had gone into planning this moment, and it could only last at most a minute. West and Larson liaised with the Brandon city police, who set up the cordon. West took control and coordinated with the senior officer.

All communication, except for convoy radio chatter, was done by cell phone for security reasons. Along with the media issue, there were numerous threats on Hopper's life, so it wasn't just about keeping reporters at bay.

West dialed into the lead car and Mick answered the phone. "Go ahead."

"We're secure here, Sarge. What's your ETA?" he asked.

"We are about ten minutes away. Have the main door open, and the departure room ready for our arrival," Mick ordered.

"Copy that."

"See you in ten, Westy."

West snapped the cell phone shut as he waved for Oddball and the two Brandon cops he was with. The three of them came over with Oddball leading. He said, "How long, Westy?"

"They're ten minutes out. When they get on scene, they are going to be coming in from the west end of the lot. The lead car will stop twenty feet past the door, then the Navigator will fall in beside the lead car. All officers will dismount and take up security positions around the prisoner car. That's when I need the main door open and you gentlemen to be waiting to take custody of Hopper."

"How long will the transfer take?" the bigger cop asked.

West said confidently, "Detectives Cooper and Pearson will do a sweep of the plane and touch base with the Captain and crew to go over protocol. It should be no more than thirty minutes, but likely less than that. At any rate, be ready for a quick rate of transfer. I would like your eyes roaming for any potential issues, and the prisoner is to be kept on a tight leash. Get him to sit in the assigned room. Once we get the all clear, Detectives Pearson and Cooper will take custody and board the plane." He was well-versed on his duties.

The convoy rolled in eight minutes later, and it went off as planned. Oddball and the two city cops took custody of Hopper and settled him in a waiting room while Pearson handed over the keys of the Navigator to Mick, who agreed to turn it into the rental agency.

"Mick, it has been a privilege working with you and Dave. If you are ever in the city, I would love to show you around or just have a drink." He shook his hand.

Mick smiled back. "Thanks, Ron, Coop, same goes here. Anyhow, you guys have your work cut out for you, so I will let you get at it."

Pearson and Cooper headed through the departure gate and across the tarmac to do their sweep as the plane sat idle on the tarmac. Simultaneously Corporal Steel escorted Doctor Kolchak up to Collins.

"What do we do now?" Kolchak asked.

"Well, Doctor, once the sweep is done and we get the thumbs up, you will follow the Detectives onboard and be on your way. In the meantime, you can enter the departure gate and hook up with Corporal West," Collins said, and he pointed in the gate's direction.

"Okay then. I will await your orders." Kolchak grabbed his bag and laptop and walked toward the rally point without looking back. "Good day, Officer Steel."

"Good day, Doctor," Steel replied.

Mick was on the phone. "Westy, I got Kolchak coming your way."

"Copy that, Sarge. I see him."

Mick looked everything over then gave the keys for the Navigator to Constable Hardy to take back to the rental agency. Ten minutes, later, Pearson and Cooper exited the Dash 8 and gave the thumbs up that they were ready to take Hopper on board. The two city officers escorted Hopper across the tarmac and to the stairwell. There Pearson and Cooper took over getting him up the stairs. The National news caught a glimpse of him in his orange jumpsuit being led onto the plane in cuffs, but no more. Once they were onboard, West escorted Kolchak to the stairwell and up into the waiting craft. A second later he came back down and was on his way back to the terminal.

Mick watched from the observation window as the ground crew pulled the stairwell away and began prepping the craft for departure. The props started turning then wound up, filling the small airport with a burr of high-intensity noise as Mick's officers fell in beside him. All felt the same mix of emotion. These officers were like a family. A family who had just worked through a crisis – and though they were not out of the woods, there was a sense that the storm was passing now that Hopper was leaving Thomasville.

"Good riddance," Steel said just under his breath.

"You said it, Don," West added.

"Fucking eh." Oddball spat.

Mick nodded. "Let's mount up."

10

"Denise," Logan said over the phone. "It's Dave."

"Hi, Dave," his ex-wife said. "The kids aren't here right now."

"Actually, I wanted to talk to you. Have you got time?"

"I was just going to grab some groceries, but I have a few minutes."

Logan looked up toward the ceiling. He inhaled. "Okay, well, I need to sit down with you about something, and I was wondering if I could buy you lunch. I could come into the city this weekend maybe?"

"Dave? Is this serious?" She sounded uneasy.

"Yeah, but I need to talk to you about it face to face." She would, of course, try to prod him for more information – but he didn't want that over the phone.

"What's going on, Dave? Is it about that case? Your face is all over the news."

"I really don't want to go into it over the phone, Denise. Could we meet in the city at the pub on 4th street?" Logan tried to keep his voice calm and level. He didn't want to fight with her – especially not now.

"The pub's gone, Dave. The recession pushed them under this year. Oh my God, this is serious! Are you ill?" Her voice rose.

"Okay, well then we can go to Kelsey's, or Boston Pizza," he cut her off. "I need to sit down with you and discuss some things, but I need to talk alone. Please don't say anything to Jamie and Howard until we've had a chance to talk. Please, Denny, do this for me."

A moment of silence passed.

She knew Dave was serious because he hadn't called her Denny since they separated.

"Okay," she surrendered. "Boston, noon Saturday. The one on Paramount Drive." "How are the kids?" Logan asked.

"Howard's looking at his college options for next year. He's going to graduate with honors. Jaimie is doing okay in school, but she's seventeen and driving me around the bend. She can be a little bitch sometimes." She laughed, but the strain was poorly masked.

"You were seventeen when we met," he reminded her.

"Yeah, and look where it got us, Dave," she snapped. Then, apologetically: "I just want more for them; I don't want to see them struggle like we did. You know?"

"Yeah. I know." He smiled a little, remembering what a firecracker she used to be. That seemed like a thousand fights and a hundred years ago. There was still a part of him that loved her, or what she once was. "You still seeing that school teacher, Brent?"

"Bruce? No," she sighed. "We broke up when he decided he was gay."

"Jesus Christ." Now he laughed. It was a good feeling: like unscrewing a valve and relieving some of the pressure that had been building since his biopsy results came back. "Okay, Denny, I'll buy you lunch on Saturday at noon."

"Uh, okay." The awkwardness came back to her voice. "Bye, Dave. See you on Saturday."

"See you Saturday."

He set the phone down and stared at it a moment. This was going to be tough, and Denise wouldn't be much help. She was a bundle of nerves and a bit of a drama queen when it came to stressful issues. How she would keep her head when he laid this on her was beyond him. He needed her, though: the kids were their permanent bond, and he needed her to be their mother when he broke the news.

The light on his phone lit up, and he answered it. "What is it, Sabrina?"

"I've got two calls, Chief. First is from Sgt. Collins and the second is from a Mr. Blackbird," she said.

Logan almost laughed. "Put Mick through, and I'll pick up the second call in a minute, or take his number, and I'll call him back."

"Okay, Chief."

The phone clicked over, and Logan waited a second. "Mick?"

"We're all done on this end, Dave. The plane has just left the ground," Mick said.

"Any problems?" Logan asked.

"No; everything went smooth as silk. As a footnote, Westy handled himself like a real pro. He took complete control of the airport, excellent oversight." Mick and Logan had discussed West as a possible replacement for when Mick left, and this was another evaluation of his leadership skills.

"Good deal. Okay, come back to base and let's get our reports filed by day's end."

"Copy that."

"Mick, have you got time for a beer after work?"

"Sure. Are we talking about a choir practice?"

"No, we'll do that later in the week. I just need a sit down with you."

"Yeah, sure. I should be wrapped up around five. Kennedy has volunteered to be duty officer tonight, so I think we should be able to put this together."

"Good enough."

11

Blackbird was sitting on his bed in the hotel room with the phone stuck against his ear, waiting for the call to go through. He still didn't know how or what he was going to say, but he had to get the cop to listen.

Then a voice on the other end of the phone broke through the silence: "Chief Logan. Hello?"

Blackbird tried to place it with the pictures he'd seen in the paper and the man from his vision.

"Hello, Chief Logan. My name is Dan Blackbird."

"Good day, Mr. Blackbird. How can I help you?"

"I was wondering if we could meet and talk about the situation you have here in Thomasville."

"Mr. Blackbird, if you're a reporter I can direct you to my communications officer, Sgt. Collins. I am not doing interviews." He moved to hang up.

"I am not a reporter, Chief Logan."

"Then what would be your interest in the case?"

Blackbird fell silent, trying to think of what he could say next.

"Hello, are you still there?"

"I have information on the case that you don't have yet. I would really like to sit down with you and discuss this."

"You're not a reporter?"

"No, sir, I am not."

"What kind of information?"

"I'd rather not say over the phone."

"Look, I have a hectic schedule and while I appreciate that you might have some information I would urge you to come into the station for an interview with one of our officers."

"I know who his accomplice is."

"What?"

"He had an accomplice, Chief. I know who he is, but I need to sit down with you and discuss this, and I'd prefer to do it in a neutral setting."

Logan was suddenly pissed. *Somebody leaked! A God damned leak!*

"Look, Mr. Blackbird, I don't know where you came by your information, but we don't have any other suspects in this case. Stephen Hopper acted alone."

For a moment Blackbird was silent. Then he took a gamble: "Franklin."

That caught his attention. "What did you say?"

"He calls himself Franklin."

Logan leaned forward in his chair and grabbed a pencil and a post note. "Where would you like to meet?"

"I was going to get a late lunch at the diner in town. Angela's?" Blackbird looked down at his watch. It was 2:25 PM. "I could be there in about twenty minutes."

"Okay, Mr. Blackbird, I'll meet you there. Can you give me a description of yourself so that I will know who you are when I get there?"

"I know who you are, Chief. When you come in, I will wave you over."

"Alright. See you in twenty minutes."

Blackbird hung up the phone and called his new chauffeur, Bobby Morneau.

12

Mick was sitting shotgun next to Hardy, who was driving back into town. His cell phone rang, and he flipped it open to see it was coming from the base. "Collins."

"Mick, it's Dave. What's your ETA back into town?"

"Thirty minutes, what's up?"

"Hardy is driving you, right?" Logan said.

"Yeah. What's going on?"

"I want you to have her jump in with one of the other cars and make your way over to Angela's Diner." Logan was thumping the pencil eraser off the desk, something he often did when he was trying to formulate a plan. "Once you've done that call me back on my cell."

"Okay."

Mick had no idea what was going on, but he trusted that it would not be long before he found out. He grabbed the handset and started giving orders. The convoy of police vehicles pulled over, and Mick got out and orders. He tried to be as casual as possible, not wanting to ring any alarms just yet.

He assigned Steel as duty officer and then jumped into the one unmarked car Thomasville Police had. It was a Chevy Impala that looked exactly like a police car without all the bells and whistles.

As he punched the accelerator, he pulled out his cell phone and called Logan back while the car climbed up in speed. Angela's Diner was on the west end of town.

"What's going on, Dave?"

Logan was getting into his cruiser now.

"I'm not sure yet. I just talked to a guy on the phone who wants to meet. He says he knows who Franklin is."

"You think we have a leak in the department?" Mick asked.

"That or something else."

"Like what? Wait a minute, Dave, you don't think Franklin is real, do you?"

Mick's heart began to race. He picked up the pace pushing the car to go faster.

"Well either this guy has credible information, or I'm going to meet Franklin. At any rate, I want you to meet me at Angela's, but come in incognito and set up behind me in case something goes sour."

Mick shut his cell phone and placed it in his breast pocket. He had a couple issues to deal with now. First, he would have to park a block away from Angela's. The second of course was how to enter a diner where everyone knew him in his police uniform without drawing any attention. He tightened his grip on the steering wheel and punched the accelerator to the floor.

***

CHAPTER 15 - MORE RITUALS AND INTERSECTIONS

1

Angela's Diner wasn't busy. On weekdays the lunch crowd was smaller, so only a few patrons populated the restaurant when Blackbird arrived. Bobby had dropped him off, and when he entered the place, everyone simultaneously stopped and looked. "Never seen an Injun before?" he almost said, but it wasn't that. He was an outsider. Outsiders stood out, especially in places like this where residents congregated.

He sat in a booth, sliding the knapsack in beside him, waiting for the Police Chief to arrive. He expected that his last words had rung a few alarm bells. He had no idea why the creature used the name Franklin, but he had picked it up during his previous encounters with the creature. He threw the dice that the child killer Hopper might have used, and apparently it paid off.

There was only one doorway to the diner and Blackbird made sure to face it so that he could wave the Chief down when he entered. I'm probably going to end up in the clink, he mused, but there was really nothing else he could do. The Police Chief played a part in this, so he had to try.

The big burly cop walked past the window, giving him a look, and it was suddenly apparent there would be no reason to wave him over. Logan walked in, nodded to the waitress, and headed straight to the booth Blackbird occupied.

He started to get up, and Logan motioned for him not to, so he settled back in the oversized booth and let the big cop take the lead. "You're Mr. Blackbird?"

"That's right," he answered, extending his hand.

"You sounded younger on the phone. Maybe mid-thirties." Logan shook his hand loosely, feeling for uneasiness or sweat, trying to determine his demeanor, but there came no warning signs from the handshake, so he released his grip, sat down, and continued sizing him up.

This guy is weathered and beaten. From what, Logan could only speculate. *Booze? Drugs?* He didn't think so. *I wonder where he got that scar.*

The waitress came over and made pleasantries. Logan ordered coffee while Blackbird got a cup of tea. As soon as she had returned with their order and departed Blackbird got right down to business.

"Stephen Hopper did not act alone. He had an accomplice. I would even say he was not the mastermind behind this."

As he spoke, he added milk to his tea and stirred, but he did not once lower his eyes.

"Franklin," Logan said, trying not to sound skeptical – but then again, after the story spun by Hopper, he was left to wonder how this Indian was connected. This man was confident and without nervousness, and Logan felt a temptation to divulge some of what he knew – but he shoved the impulse away.

"Yes, that is the name he goes by. I have some stuff in my bag I'd like to show you." Blackbird reached over and started to pull out the scrapbook when Logan tapped his leg under the table, stopping him.

"Look, Mr. Blackbird, I will talk and look at anything you would like to show me, but I am going to caution you now to move and act with great care." He had his right hand on the butt off his gun. "I don't know who you are or what your connection is to Stephen Hopper, so you leave me at a disadvantage. Remember this as you proceed." He unsnapped his holster.

Blackbird nodded, understanding. If he moved too fast, he might end up with a gun to his face – or worse, shot.

He did not waiver, instead of replying calmly to Logan's warning. "I'm going to remove a scrapbook from my bag. I want to show you some news clippings, and while you are looking at them, I am going to tell you some stuff that you probably won't believe. Okay?"

"Okay. Seeing that we are so honest here, I am going to tell you that my second-in-command should be here anytime. I alerted him to our meeting, and he will be coming in and watching us like a hawk." Logan didn't think Blackbird would miss Mick's entrance unless he came in the back way.

"That's fine. I didn't expect you to come alone. All I ask is that you hear me out." He reached over cautiously, brought up a binder that was about three inches thick and contained cellophane pages that encased the news clippings. The binder itself was cheap, dog-eared; it had endured a lot in that knapsack for a long time.

As Logan stared down at the binder, Mick entered the diner, and Blackbird acknowledged him with a nod.

So much for entering incognito, Mick thought, walked over and sat down at the table next to them, waiting for Logan to make his next move.

"Mr. Blackbird, this is Sgt. Collins."

"Hey," Blackbird greeted.

"Hey," Mick replied.

"Mr. Blackbird was just about to show me a scrapbook and fill me in on Franklin. He has also assured me there will be no issues." Logan looked to Mick as he spoke, his eyes warning him to be alert.

"Sounds good." Mick steadied himself just in case there were.

Blackbird pushed the binder across the table to Logan just as the waitress came over and interrupted to see if Mick wanted anything.

"We're good, Charlene." Mick smiled, and she wandered back to her station.

Logan opened the binder. Behind the first cellophane page was a newspaper clipping that was weathered and brown. The header was from the Chicago Sun-Times. The date was August 9th, 2001.

PROSTITUTES TARGET OF SERIAL KILLER?

By Ariel Clay

Police speculate as many as 20 women may have fallen victim to a serial killer in the city's red light district. The missing women all come from the sex trade and are extremely hard to track. Chicago Police Detective Sean Woodman stated that the missing women were not on their radar until prostitutes themselves started coming forward. "We have a lot of missing women and as of yet we still don't have a suspect, so we are urging all of these women to take extra precaution and alert us to anyone suspicious in nature."

One after another, page after page, Blackbird revealed more and more articles following the disappearances in Chicago. As he did this Logan remembered hearing something about this on a television newsmagazine, like 20/20 or 60 Minutes, but he couldn't recall which show it had been.

"He has a connection to multiple murders both north and south of the border," Blackbird said while Logan turned the pages, scanning the articles and Mick listened. "I have been tracking him for over fifteen years. Chicago was the closest I got."

Logan looked up briefly, then back down to the scrapbook. The last article referred to the take-down in the alley, and though it did not mention Blackbird by name, there was a dotted picture of him standing with a plainclothes police officer.

"He has likely killed in this general area." Now the pages Logan turned to held more recent articles, these about Hopper and Thomasville. "I know how this sounds, Chief, but we haven't got a lot of time."

Logan stopped and looked up. "What do you mean?"

Blackbird sighed. "Fuck it, you are going to think I'm nuts, but by tomorrow you won't so here goes. Did Hopper tell you anything unusual about Franklin? That he had strange powers? That he was a shape changer?"

Mick covered a smirk. Logan's face was grave. He had spent the night listening to the tale that was so far out there even a tabloid wouldn't touch it.

"You've got my attention, Mr. Blackbird. Carry on."

"Have you ever heard of a Wendigo or a Skinwalker, Chief Logan?"

"Indian legend? Kind of like a werewolf," Mick interjected.

"Franklin is something like that. I don't have time, nor do you, to recount all the mythology. I just need you to take what I am saying seriously because we have very little time."

"So you're telling me that we have another child-murdering monster in our midst that goes by the name of Franklin? That's what you're saying?" Logan closed the binder and sat back.

"I'm telling you that there is a creature out there that is drawn to evil like a magnet. That it sometimes goes by the alias Franklin, but his real name is Jackanoob. I'm telling you stuff you already know, but won't accept as it flies in the face of your belief system."

He was losing this: he could feel it.

"How do you know what my belief system is, Mr. Blackbird?" Logan asked.

Blackbird sighed again. This was getting him nowhere.

"Are you Franklin?" Mick asked.

Logan leaned forward on his elbows, waiting for an answer.

Blackbird laughed. "Why did I know you would ask that?"

"You have to look at it from our point of view, Mr. Blackbird," Logan said.

"I have looked at it from your point of view." It took a great deal of effort to keep from raising his voice. "I never believed any of this stuff, but fifteen years ago this creature killed my grandfather before my eyes, and I have been hunting it ever since. Think about this. How would I know?"

"You're going to have to give us something more substantial than some news clippings and a name. This is just too far out there."

Logan pushed the binder back across the table.

"It disembowels its victims and eats their organs."

Logan shot a sidelong glance at Mick, then said, "I probably shouldn't tell you this, but the hell with it. Both Sgt. Collins and I dug up the last victim. Cause of death was strangulation. All his organs were intact."

"Then that victim was not killed by Franklin."

The two cops looked at each other. Blackbird knew enough about this to be involved.

Mick leaned in. "Mr. Blackbird, I would like you to get up and accompany us out of here without a scene."

"Are you arresting me?"

"No, but some of what you said has hit a raw nerve, and that has compelled both Chief Logan and myself to insist that we discuss this in a private setting where the public at large won't be privy to information about the investigation."

Collins started to stand.

"You're arresting me." Blackbird shook his head.

Logan said, "Mr. Blackbird, we are not arresting you. But you have information that nobody should have and that has definitely caused curiosity. Come with us, and I promise we will be straight."

"You think I'm nuts then."

"I never said that. Mick, can you grab the bill?" Now Logan was getting up too.

Blackbird sat there a moment, trying to think. What could he do? He had to go with them. If he didn't, they would arrest him. If he bolted, they would arrest him. But how would he convince Logan that he wasn't crazy?

The clock was ticking.

"Okay, I'll go with you."

He stood and replaced the binder in his knapsack and then they walked out of the diner without argument or fanfare. When they got to Logan's cruiser, he waited for them to snap on the cuffs and place him in the back of the car. Instead, Logan opened the passenger door and said, "Please get in."

He sighed again and climbed into the cruiser.

2

Thomasville Police Department

3:30 PM

The three of them were in Logan's office. So far, Blackbird had not exhibited violent behavior. Therefore Logan wanted to keep it as cordial as possible. Mick stood in the corner watching, as Blackbird sat there looking around the office for something that might help leverage his argument. There was nothing.

"You have to understand how crazy this sounds," Logan said.

"I know how it sounds. And either way, it won't matter if you think I'm nuts or not: by tomorrow you'll be asking me what the hell is going on and what we can do to stop it. Chief, think about this for a second. If I was Franklin, why would I come forward?"

Logan stared at the Native man for a long time, trying to figure him out and what his connection was to all this. Ironically, he suddenly wished Hopper were still here. At the very least, they could march Blackbird up in front of him to draw some kind of reaction. Even though he thought Blackbird might sincere, he couldn't accept what he was saying.

"Mick, take Mr. Blackbird out to the coffee room while I make a couple calls," he said, looking at one of the Chicago Tribune articles in Blackbird's binder. A name popped out at him, one that might add a little light to the darkness surrounding this mystery. The name was Woodman. Detective Sean Woodman.

"Chief, you gotta listen to me. We are running out of time here." Blackbird was getting anxious. "He said there would be a massacre."

"I am listening, Mr. Blackbird; I am just following through. Give me a little time and talk to Mick over a coffee in our lunch room. So far, I am sure that you are not involved in this criminally, but your connection is troubling just the same."

"Well if you're checking something, check on the clerk from the motel who was killed. Check to see if his organs were there. Check that!"

He turned and was led to the lunch room by Mick. From the staff room, the other officers watched but were at a loss to what Logan and Collins were doing with this man.

3

The day before the creature had been sitting in the kitchen staring off in a state of meditation for quite some time. When it fell into this state, it would become almost petrified and intoxicated, but it was not completely vulnerable. It could still spring to life if it had to, and had in fact done so in the past many times.

Spoiled meat! What a waste of good food, it thought as it considered the rotten carcass in the other room. It had already eaten, but the waste and want still infuriated it.

There was something else banging around in its subconscious, clouding its thoughts and watching from within, something it could not explain. There was much to do, and it needed more energy. Its belly was full – but the pain would be back before long, and it always wanted to gorge. Something trying to see — pushing — faraway voices, distant. What was that? Was that the remaining phantom of its other? The one called Jackanoob?

Spoiled meat, it thought again and shifted drunkenly. The hunter will be coming. *Have to kill the hunter. Must draw strength.*

It began pulling itself together, finding motivation and coming back. It focused on the wall, and slowly it began to unfurl from its petrified state. Blowflies and maggots ravaged the spoiled meat in the other room – but this kill was still warm, still smelled of blood.

Must change, the creature thought and began to take the form it had held only hours before when the food had come knocking. Its skin pulsated, the black ick seething from its pores, rearranging its features, hiding the decay and rot, giving color to the flesh, the bulbous eyes shrinking inward and becoming cobalt blue.

It stood up and wavered, slightly disoriented, feeling the voyeur within.

Is that you? You still in there, Jackanoob? Still hiding from the truth?

There was no reply: only silence – and a faint pang of hunger – as it moved out of the kitchen and into the front room. Yes, I must eat more. I will need the energy.

It drew back the curtain, looked out the window at the house across the street and said, "Yes, must eat." The hunger called to it.

It opened the front door. The stench of death wafted out – and then the door was closed.

As it walked down the steps and into the road, eyes forward the whole time, it had one purpose. It could feel the presence inside the house watching it, not wanting to be seen, feeling the man inside and his voyeuristic uneasiness. Easy picking, it delighted, and rapped on the doorframe with its knuckle.

After a moment, the door lock clicked, and a man inside greeted him from behind a screen door. "Yes, hello, John."

"May I come in?"

"Please do," the man said and opened the door.

4

"Superintendent Woodman," the voice on the other end of the phone said.

"Hello, Superintendent, my name is Dave Logan. I'm the Chief of Police of Thomasville, and I was wondering if I could ask you a few questions?" Logan said.

"That where all those kids were murdered?" Woodman asked.

"Yeah, it's been a hell of a run."

"I have no doubt it has. Listen, Chief, my name is Sean. What I can do for you?"

"Okay, Sean, in that case, Dave will do just fine here."

"Good enough."

"I wanted to ask you about a case you were in charge of about eight years ago. The one with the murdered prostitutes."

"Sure. What would you like to know?" Woodman asked.

"Did you ever solve it?"

"No; it's a cold file. We've never closed it, we think that our guy took a hike, died, or is serving time for another crime."

"They never said in the papers how these girls were killed? How were they murdered?"

"I gotta stop you there, Dave. Why are you pumping me for info on an eight-year-old case?"

"There may be a connection to my case."

"Really? Okay, now you have my attention. Ask anything you want."

The conversation between Logan and Woodman carried on for almost a half hour as Woodman explained the number of victims and how they were being disposed of by use of the Chicago sewer system. "One of the working girls said she heard the last known victim, a Kerry McNeil, call the killer Franklin."

"Was Franklin an Indian?" Logan asked.

"Indian? Like North American? Or are we talking Kwicky-Mart Indian? We have both." Woodman snickered, and they both laughed at the Simpsons reference. "He might have been a North American Native, but something tells me you are barking up a different tree now."

"Daniel Blackbird."

"Wow, that's a name that brings up memories. We arrested him at the scene of the last murder, but he didn't do it. Is he there?"

"How do you know it wasn't him? And yes, he's here."

"Well, this is some crazy shit, Dave, but we had him under surveillance the night of the last murder, and a couple things just didn't jive for us."

"Like?"

"Timeline, for one. Blackbird would have never had time to do the things that were done to that girl in the short time we lost him off our radar. We had him under surveillance all evening, and he slipped out of our sights for about ten minutes. Anyway, the girl, this Kerry McNeil, she had been decapitated and eviscerated. Whoever killed her took most of her internal organs and then dumped her body down the sewer."

"Could the organs have been lost in the sewer?"

"Not a chance."

"How can you be sure?"

"We scoured those sewers for days and what we found was a jam of victims in one of the run-offs. All of them decapitated. All of them eviscerated. This was never released to the public, to help us separate the whackos and degenerates from the real suspects."

"So you let him go based on the timeline?"

"No. I might have been able to overlook the timeline if it wasn't for a witness corroborating his statement. God knows we liked him for every other reason."

"Who was the witness?"

"Just above the last murder scene was a low rent tenement housing complex – that's fancy talk for welfare apartments. Anyway, our killer was just about to drop this girl's body down the sewer when our witness opened her window and saw him. After that things got really bizarre."

"Bizarre?"

Woodman said, "Let me ask you a question, Dave."

"Go ahead."

"Is Blackbird still talking about monsters and Indian Shape-shifters?"

Logan hesitated, then said, "Something like that."

"Okay, well then this next bit won't come as a surprise. Our witness, a black woman in her mid-forties, grabs a gun she keeps around for burglars. Blackbird turns up in the alley carrying a bow and arrow." Woodman started to laugh. "I know how this fucking sounds, but next thing you know we got an Indian – oops, not PC – North American Native shooting arrows down the alleyway like he's Sitting Bull and the black woman shooting her gun off like Jesse James. Both are aiming at our perp."

Logan laughed. "Holy shit. You're kidding, right?"

"I shit you not. We got bows and arrows and gunplay, and when our officers hit the scene the perp was gone, Little Big Horn is over – but fear not: this story gets even more bizarre."

Logan had a pretty good idea he knew what was coming.

"Blackbird tells us he's been chasing an Indian shape-shifter, and that is what committed the murders. We were ready to lock him up just based on that, but then the black woman backs up his story independently. She didn't say shape-shifter, but she definitely said fucking monster."

"So how did you come to the conclusion that they weren't lying?"

"I didn't. My partner and I just sat down and added up the evidence then ruled both of them out as potential suspects. Neither of them knew each other. Blackbird was a twenty-something drifter; the woman was in her mid-forties, widowed, and worked as a short order in one of the local dives. Couple that with the timeline, and nothing minus our initial suspicion of Blackbird could keep him as a plausible suspect. The deeper we dug, the more bizarre it got. Our best guess is that Franklin – if that's his actual name – was taking the internal organs for food."

"Jesus."

"Yeah, well even JC would have raised his eyebrows at this one. In the end, we made a decision. We confiscated Blackbird's bow and her gun. Then we told them to keep their mouths shut and said if we read or heard anything in that grocery store rag the Weekly World News or on the Art Bell Show that they would find themselves named as prime suspects. After that, the case went cold."

"Did you buy any of what they were saying?"

"I'm a believe-it-if-I-see-it kind of guy. You tell me there's a Sasquatch running around in the mountains of Montana I'm skeptical. Show me the big hairy bastard, and that's a different story."

"So what did you make of their statements?"

"Me and my partner thought it might be some Whack-Job dressed up in a costume, but I'll be honest: that seemed highly implausible. I've come across some strange shit over the years, but there was something else... Just give me a second, Dave; I'm warming up my computer I'm going to pull the file for you."

"Alright."

"As I said, I've come across some strange shit over the years, but some of the stuff at the crime scene backed up the woman's claim. She said the monster was scaling the wall to her apartment and that it was digging its claws right into the bricks. We found holes and fresh tears in the brickwork that was consistent with her claim." Then, "Alright, here we go. Louise Weatherton, black, forty-five years old, widow. She was pretty fat and sassy as I recall. You got an email? I'll send over some pictures."

Logan gave him his email.

"So, what exactly makes you think that there may be a relation to your case?"

"The whole thing reared its head even before Blackbird came into town. Our guy, Hopper: he said he'd been feeding his victims to this Franklin. The MOs are completely different, and our last victim was strangled, but forensics of the other victims is still a work in progress. Most of the bodies were in the latter stages of decay."

"I'd be interested to know how this turns out, Dave, even if there isn't a connection. Can you keep in touch via email?"

"Sure, I can do that. Just one last thing, and it makes me think we're not talking about the same guy."

"What's that?"

"You said Blackbird was twenty-something. Can you clarify that? Early twenties or late twenties?"

"He was about twenty-five years old. Here, I'll send you the file now."

Computer keys clicked through the earpiece as Woodman set about sending Logan an email. "The one that says DCS589 is the picture of Blackbird. It should be in your inbox anytime now."

Logan opened his email and watched the send/receive prompt flash until it said completed. He opened the attachment, and there was a picture of a much younger Daniel Blackbird. The photo looked like it had been taken thirty years ago, not eight. The man in the other room could easily be his father, except for one thing: the scar on his right cheek. The guy in the coffee room was this man, Logan was sure of it.

"That's him. Except he looks thirty years older."

"Drugs maybe," Woodman suggested. "I've seen twenty-year-old crack heads that look fifty."

"This guy doesn't seem the drug using sort."

"I didn't think so then, either. Anyway, I could probably chew your ear off on this stuff, but I'm afraid they turned me into a bureaucrat here in the big wind. I got a meeting I'm late for. If you need anything else drop me a line and keep me up to date."

"Just one last thing before you go, Sean. You don't think this Blackbird was connected to your murders. I don't think he's connected to mine either. So what does that make him? Any ideas?"

"Your guess is as good as mine. Serial killer groupie? All kinds of freaks on the net these days you know. Our databases are under attack all the time by hackers. Some might be trying to expunge a speeding ticket, but others are just fishing for information. Maybe Blackbird is one of those freaks who latches on to other freaks?"

"You think that?"

"No… but I'm late for this meeting, and we're getting into the kind of conversation I'd prefer over a beer. I'm just speculating. Old habits die hard, even when they make you a bureaucrat."

Logan thanked Woodman for his help and assured him that he would keep him in the loop. He looked at his watch, surprised at how long they had talked and thought guiltily about poor Mick left to attend to Blackbird in the coffee room. And he still had to make one more phone call to Jeff Henderson to ask about the state of Scott Masterson's body.

"Hi, Dave, what's up?"

"Jeff, I'm going to get right to the point. The Masterson kid, from the motel, how did he die?" Logan said.

"Blunt trauma to the head. The object of his demise was a guardrail."

"So he wasn't eviscerated?"

"Huh? How did you know that?"

"Skip that for now. What eviscerated him?"

"My best guess would be coyotes after he was dead."

Logan asked a couple more questions about the other victims and if any of them had been eviscerated and Henderson was unable to give him an answer to either. "I can look into it tomorrow."

"Please do, Jeff, and get back to me as soon as possible. I got a couple of strange loose ends I need to tie up."

He hung the phone up and stood up. He had a fresh battery of questions for Blackbird, and he strode out of the office, ready to field them.

What he would find out was that they were already gone out of the building.

5

"Thomasville Police Department," Constable Kennedy answered.

"I need to talk to Mick Collins." It was a woman, and she was crying frantically.

"Miss, I'm afraid Sgt. Collins is busy at the moment. Is there something I can do for you?" Kennedy already had a steno pad and paper ready to take notes.

"Oh my God," she screeched. "Tell him it's Erin, Erin Grant. Oh fuck, Erin Parkins! Tell him it's an emergency!" She broke into a bout of hiccupping sobs.

"One moment please." Kennedy put her on hold, set down the phone, got up and walked down the hall to the coffee room and tapped on the door which was closed.

Mick opened it and peered through a small crack. "What's up, Pete?"

"I've got an Erin Parkins on the phone, and she says she needs to talk to you right away, that it's an emergency. I don't know if she's related to John Parkins or not, but –"

"Okay." Mick stopped him. "I'll take it at my desk." Mick turned to Blackbird, who was sipping on a soda, and said, "Come with me, I gotta take a call."

Blackbird got up and followed Collins out of the coffee room to his desk. This was situated in a cubicle at the head of the squad room, surrounded by gray dividers – the only kind of 'office' the small town budget could afford. They stepped into the cubicle, and there was a seat Mick kept in front of his desk when he wanted to go over a report with one of his subordinates. For more sensitive or personal issues, he used the interview room. Mick waved for Blackbird to sit down as he popped his head above the cubicle.

"Pete! What line is she on?"

"Line two, Sarge."

Mick sat down at the desk and punched the button on his phone while Blackbird looked about curiously at the cubicle and how Collins had decorated it. There were pictures of a good looking woman and a few Far Side photocopies. Then something caught his eye only a second after he took the phone call.

"Hi, Erin, this is Mick," he greeted.

"eed delv," Blackbird said.

"Mick, she's dead! She took a bunch of pills," Erin blurted.

It was all coming together now. Blackbird knew what he'd been looking at. "Spoiled meat," he muttered aloud.

"Who's dead, Erin?"

It wasn't "eed delv." It was this.

Blackbird stared, dumbfounded. He had only seen part of the puzzle. Hanging on Mick's cubicle was the same thing he had seen while looking through the walker's eyes. Except now it was much clearer, and he'd missed a letter.

"Olivia! She killed herself while I was taking a bath. Oh my God! It's all my fault!"

"John's Olivia?" Mick felt ill, the blood drained out of his face.

"Feed Delivery. Parkins Feed Delivery. I missed the I," Blackbird mumbled. A smile crossed his features – then vanished as he realized what it meant, and noticed the cop staring queerly at him.

"I can't get a hold of Johnny. My husband is coming to get me, but oh my God, Mick, what am I going to tell him? This is all my fault! I should have watched her closer! Why is this happening to us? First their little boy, now this!"

That was it. Erin broke down and began to cry.

"Erin, I am going to go see John. I want both you and your husband to sit tight. I will call you later once I've talked to John." Mick tried to keep his voice calm and level, but he was anything but. How was he going to face John a second time with another round of such devastating news?

"I gotta talk to him, Mick. Oh dear Lord," Erin whimpered.

"Look, I will drive him out there myself tonight, but you are in no shape to be out on that highway. Stay home, and I will get back to you."

It was a calendar that said PARKINS FEED DELIVERY that was hanging on the wall. The same calendar which hung in this cop's cubicle. Blackbird felt suddenly ill because he knew the name Parkins, knew that his child had been one of the victims. He was also quite aware that the cop had heard him.

Mick hung up the phone, ignoring Blackbird as he summoned Corporal Steel. "Don, get your gear: we're going to John Parkins' house."

Then Blackbird said something that stopped him cold.

"He's dead," Blackbird whispered.

"What?" Mick sat down in his seat and stared across at Blackbird. "What did you say?"

"He's dead. John Parkins is dead."

"How do you know this?"

"He's spoiled meat. Franklin didn't kill him." Blackbird stared off into space, his vision replaying in his head. He looked disconnected, almost hypnotized, but his words were clear and concise. "I think he killed himself."

Mick leaned across the desk and grabbed Blackbird by the shirt and dragged him forward. "I asked you a question! How you would know this?"

Steel walked into the exchange just as he was putting his jacket on.

"I saw it," Blackbird said. "In a vision."

"A vision?"

"What's going on, Sarge?"

Mick peered around the dividers. Logan was still on the phone. He wanted to bust in and interrupt but instead, he told Kennedy to fill him in once he was done.

"You're coming with us." Mick snapped a set of cuffs on Blackbird. "Get the God damned car, Don."

6

3:45 PM

The Dash 8 bumped along at 20,000 feet as the props let out a constant drone giving Pearson a mild headache. Across the aisle, Coop sat with Hopper as Kolchak was milling about at the front of the plane talking to the male flight attendant. Pearson wondered if Kolchak was gay.

Hopper's hands were shackled to the waistband on his orange jumpsuit. He was quiet, hadn't said a word to anyone except Pearson and Kolchak since the final interview yesterday. Either he was half-dozing or just pretended to be – whichever way, it suited Pearson just fine.

The flight had been uneventful to this point. The pilot had come on and informed them that they would be traveling along the US Canadian border for about fifteen minutes and then they would be head northward. On the ground, they were passed from one air traffic controller to the next as they changed flight corridors. The ATC that was now keeping them from getting tangled up with other aircraft was a veteran controller named Sidney Mayfield. Above, below and all around them, aircraft ran specific flight patterns and the people on the ground brought order to the chaos.

Pearson only cared about one thing: getting Hopper into a cell at Artisan and then calling an escort service so that he could get some much-needed attention. He had hoped he would get a crack at Hardy, but Cooper told him that she and Steel were carrying on after hours.

Lucky guy, that Steel; she had a great rack.

Pearson was married but spent at least four or five thousand on escorts every year. "The trick is to always carry cash," he told Coop, who was complicit about the whole thing. "A credit card statement will get you killed every time, Coop!"

Kolchak was embroiled deep in conversation. Pearson studied him. As Kolchak spoke, the attendant nodded. Maybe they were making plans for later as well.

"This is your Captain speaking. We are now moving along United States Airspace. If you look out your window in approximately five minutes, you will see Grand Rapids and the body of water to follow will be Lake Superior."

The attendant sat down in the seat provided for him behind the cabin as Kolchak began to make his way back to where they were seated. Pearson smiled at him, and he smiled back.

"Make a new friend?" Pearson asked.

Then all hell broke loose.

***

CHAPTER 16 - KAW SEU IGWHOT

1

3:47 PM

Sidney Mayfield was sitting at his monitor, tracking the progress of five call signs when he heard the distress call on his headset.

"Mayday! Mayday!" cried the voice, and there was a cracking sound in the background which he was sure was gunfire. "This is Oasis 182! We are under attack!"

Then more gunfire, followed by silence.

Mayfield covered his microphone, and feeling his chest tighten he uttered, "Oh Christ."

Others in control room suddenly fell silent. Everyone was aware of the possibilities. All transmission were muted, waiting for the desperate call from OA182's pilot – but none came. Terrorism was the first thing to pop into the minds of the air traffic controllers and pilots monitoring the channel. Mayfield had been in this flight service station for almost a year, and had he not taken particular interest in this plane he would have been of like mind. But he knew who was onboard, and this was no terrorist act. He had been following the investigation in Thomasville over the internet. Researching serial killers was a dark hobby of his, and when the story broke, Stephen Hopper had become his new pet project.

All eyes were upon him, and he snapped to it.

"OA182, this is Alpha Tango 411. State the nature of your emergency, over." No response. He was already sure the man who had issued the distress call was dead, but he repeated nonetheless: "OA182, this is Alpha Tango 411. Radio check, over." He turned his transmitter switch to mute, looked at the scope. "Fuck, this bird is going down."

Mayfield's supervisor, Cameron Howe, came to his side, placed a hand on his shoulder and leaned in to look at the scope. "What have we got, Sid?"

"OA182 issued a Mayday. Then I heard him say, 'We are under attack.' I'm sure I heard gunfire in the background, and now she's dropping like a stone."

"What's the altitude?" Howe's breath smelled of pepperoni.

"She's at 19,000 feet, down from 22,000."

"Alright! Listen up, people!" Howe yelled across the control room. "We have a bird dropping altitude at a significant rate which has drifted into US airspace. Get on your call signs, I want no overlap. Sid, send them the heading of your bird and coordinate keeping those corridors clear top to bottom." Howe grabbed the phone and contacted the switchboard. "I need a direct line to the command of 127 Wing on Selfridge Air Base!"

"Cam, it's not terrorism," Mayfield called from his post.

Howe held the phone against his chest. "How do you know?"

"It's a prisoner transfer plane, special charter."

"Who's onboard?"

"A serial killer named Stephen Hopper."

"Sid, I'm not even going to ask how you know this. I'm calling the Air Force for a look anyway. If this bird splashes down, we are going to need to coordinated emergency services." Howe put the phone back up to his ear and waited to be patched through. "Hello, who am I speaking to?"

Orders to scramble two F16s were given as the Dash 8, and its occupants continued to lose altitude at an alarming rate. While the call signs on his screen were being re-routed to other corridors, Mayfield watched with helpless dismay.

2

Minutes Earlier

"Make a new friend?" Pearson asked of Kolchak, and that was the last thing he saw or heard. He was dead the moment the words left his lips. A claw shot out over what seemed an impossible distance of four feet and impaled his eye sockets, popping his eyeballs like egg yolks and driving right through his brain. The third talon caught him under the chin, silencing any possibility of a scream, and before the creature had even taken form it twisted off his head.

The transformation made from a sloppily dressed 5' 9" psychiatrist to a seven-foot grotesque hairless monster happened in a blink of an eye and the only sound to indicate the change was a liquid noise somewhat like water boiling over onto a hot stove. What was once Dr. Robert Kolchak exploded into a black tar-like substance which then evaporated into a thick, toxic, caustic-smelling smoke. It hung in the air for a moment, then gravity dragged it to the flow. Pearson didn't even get to see the change take place.

As the dirty smoke dissipated the arm retracted and dropped, holding Pearson's head at its side like a bowling ball. The grey translucent skin over its chest cavity was riddled with spider veins which pushed the black ick through its body. The sound of its breathing was like fingernails on a chalkboard.

Pearson might not have seen the transformation, but Hopper and Cooper did. Hopper understood the danger. Cooper just stared dumbly.

"Now," it hissed, and for a moment both men thought it might be addressing them – but it was not.

At the front of the plane, the flight attendant stood up and knocked on the cockpit door. "It's Devon." When the lock released he swung it wide open, turned back to the creature, obediently chanting in the ancient language, "Kaw seu, Igwhot." This meant: 'For you, Master.'

Hopper's eyes darted right to see Pearson's headless body strapped into the seat. Great gluts of blood spurted upward onto the ceiling of the aircraft. Beside him, Cooper was fumbling out of his seat. Towering over them, the gigantic creature breathed in and out, and an out of place smile formed on its nightmarish face. Its eyes, reflecting the interior of the plane, were mirrors into the darkest places man dare not look. It let out a shriek that tore through the fuselage like a rusty chainsaw.

Hopper followed Cooper, and they crashed into the aisle much to its amusement. It loomed over them, its black lips peeled back, revealing jagged teeth that were weathered and petrified by time and bloodletting. They scrambled back down the aisle like crab men. It dropped Pearson's head on the carpet. There was a hollow thud.

Hopper, behind Cooper, used his elbows: he was still bound by chains.

Now the creature was almost ten feet away. Cooper pulled his gun out, but the creature paid him little mind. It reached over and disemboweled the headless corpse of Pearson, pulling out his small intestines like so much spaghetti pie. As it jerked more out, the lifeless body moved back and forth like some macabre puppet.

"What the? What the?" Cooper huffed and puffed almost dropping his gun.

"Oh no," Hopper moaned from behind him.

"Hello, Stephen."

The creature was chewing on Pearson's small intestine and gulping with a gleeful smile. Fresh blood ran down its face and onto its boney grey chest.

Cooper's hand shook madly as he trained the gun erratically on the monster. With his free hand, he pulled himself up onto the armrest of an empty passenger seat, staring back at Hopper. "What the fuck?"

The creature shrieked again, rattling the inside of the aircraft, wreaking havoc on Hopper's and Cooper's eardrums, making their ears ring intensely.

The creature dropped its clutch of intestines onto the carpet and began to work its way forward toward the cockpit. That was when Cooper knew that he had to try before it got to the cabin.

"Close the fucking door!" he screamed to the pilot and began squeezing off shots.

Behind him, Hopper backed away.

The flight attendant just held open the cabin door, chanting, "Kaw seu, Igwhot. Kaw seu, Igwhot Kaw seu, Igwhot."

The co-pilot looked back through the open doorway and at the flight attendant, not sure what had happened in the last five seconds. "What's going on, Devon," he got out –then the third bullet fired from Cooper's gun crashed through his head. He was killed instantly.

The pilot saw blood splash across the instrument panel and onto the windshield, and without another thought, he keyed his headset. "Mayday! Mayday!"

Three more bullets hit the creature – but they sailed right through and smashed into the console. Sparks flashed, and there was the mechanical sound of failure.

Devon only held the door. "Kaw seu, Igwhot. Kaw seu, Igwhot. Kaw seu, Igwhot."

The Dash 8 shuddered then and began a bumpy descent. The creature continued up the aisle, tearing down roof panels along the way, exposing wires and insulation.

"Devon! Close the fucking door!" the pilot screamed, but Devon wouldn't budge.

"Kaw seu, Igwhot."

His new master came forward to reward him.

Cooper's chamber ran empty. Thirty bullets and none had had any effect, just blowing right through the creature. He snapped the clip in, trying not to look at his partner's head lying in the aisle. *Fuck, Ron, what the hell happened?* To add to the madness, he was pretty sure he'd accidentally killed the co-pilot.

Devon looked up at the Master standing over him and then the illusion evaporated as the anesthesia it had used to fog his mind began to wear off. The goliath skinwalker towered above him, its mirrored eyes reflecting the carnage. The co-pilot was slumped over, the interior of the craft looked as though a hurricane had torn through it. Blood ran down from the creature's mouth over its grey papery skin, turning it a sickish ink. Devon was just about to scream when it slit open his belly with its incisor toe. His guts spilled out.

"This is Oasis 182! We are under attack!" the pilot yelled frantically.

Then the creature reached around, ripped out the pilot's windpipe. He slumped forward in his seat. From behind, Cooper fired again, and a bullet tore through the communications system. At the same time the craft's computer began sounding alarms, it was short circuiting and shutting down. The autopilot disengaged, and the circuitry controlling the fuel transfer shorted out.

The steady burr of the engine props cut out. First the left, then the right, and the Dash 8 shuddered. The aircraft continued to stay level, but it now was a doomed vessel. Oasis Airline 182 began its final descent into US airspace.

The creature looked through the cockpit window, listening to the warning bells, watching the clouds evaporate and become moisture as they hit the glass.

Such a large winged beast. So big, yet so fragile. It looked around, captivated.

Behind it, Cooper and Hopper were attuned to the stark reality that they were going to crash, but Hopper doubted they would live to see the ground. Oxygen masks swung uselessly above the seats, although the pressure in the craft was still holding.

That changed when the creature turned and made its way back toward them.

The first few steps it took were purposely slow, watching for its victims' reaction and craving the adrenaline that flowed through their veins. The sweet nectar of fear expanded inside both men as it dug its hooked claws into the ceiling and floor. It shrieked again and smashed out one of the port windows, creating a vacuum. Taking another step it tore a seat from the floor, tossing it over and behind it. The door which had been held open by the flight attendant now bumped back and forth between galley wall and body.

It smashed the second port window. A length of Pearson's severed small intestine danced about like a charmed snake drawn to the vacuum.

Cooper was staring right at it now, and he thought any moment he would wake up from this horrific nightmare. Behind him, he could hear Hopper screaming at him.

"Shoot me! Goddamn it! Shoot me!"

Shoot me? Doesn't he mean to shoot it? Cooper turned and looked at Hopper and yelled above the rush of oxygen whistling through the fuselage. "What is it?"

"Please, Detective! Shoot me, and if you're smart you'll shoot yourself!"

The creature was halfway to them now. Its lips peeled back in that devilish grin a mixture of black ick, and human blood spilled from its rotted mouth.

"What the fuck is that, Hopper?" Cooper screamed at him.

"That's Franklin!" Hopper screamed, backing into the lavatory, slamming the door shut and fumbling the lock over to the occupied position.

Cooper turned back toward it and took up a firing position. If he could hit its eyes, maybe he could blind it, but he knew they were finished no matter what the outcome.

He began squeezing off shots as he said aloud, "Yea, though I walk through the valley of the shadow of death."

Crack!

"I will fear no evil: for thou art with me!"

Crack!

"Thy rod and thy staff they –"

It came at him in a flurry of smoke.

Kurt Cooper looked down to where his forearm used to be and realized it had been torn off. The creature was right in front of him. He could smell its rotting breath, which stank of death.

"Aw, shit….."

It ripped out his beating heart and held it up as if to mock him.

The Dash 8 was not in a nosedive but looked as though it had been to Hell and back as it descended from the sky on its final voyage. Forty miles away two F16s were on their way to meet it.

Hopper gazed into the mirror over the stainless steel sink. He was as white as alabaster, his pudgy cheeks devoid of blood and his expression that of a man who has resigned himself to the inevitable. Behind him, a talon scraped along the textured surface of the carbon fiber door. Then it was ripped completely off.

"I know I deserve this," he said, not to the creature, but to himself.

"Hello, Stephen."

It yanked him from the lavatory, dragging him kicking and screaming up the aisle. The aircraft was at 8000 feet now. Beneath, the Michigan landscape passed peacefully, oblivious to the mayhem transpiring above.

Halfway up the aisle it stopped and hoisted Hopper up by one leg. From upside down, he saw the body of Detective

Cooper slung over the headrest of one of the seats. His back was broken, his right arm missing, and there was a gaping hole in his chest.

"Told you I'd be back," it hissed, then split a gash in his genitals with its incisor claw. He screamed, a bolt of searing pain rippling through his stomach and into his legs like ten thousand hot needles.

"Oh, that's nothing, Stephen."

It elevated him even further, and he felt the hot blood from his scrotum flowing down over his belly. Using both claws, it went to work on his foot, twisting it around, breaking the tendons and cartilage. It twisted and twisted, as the skin stretched and rippled into a macabre corkscrew until it ran out of elasticity and gave way.

Hopper bawled in agony.

"Like a fly, Stephen."

It tossed the foot onto a vacant seat and dragged him a little further up the aisle. A claw lifted him by his throat, ever careful not to crush his windpipe. "You should have controlled yourself, Stephen. You should have listened."

It plucked out his left eye.

Shock hit him. His brain started shutting down all the nerve pathways: the pain rolled away into the fog as he bled out – but that did not stop the creature from dismembering him.

Limb after limb fell onto the floor…

The aircraft was now at 6000 feet. Ahead Lake Superior was a beckoning watery grave. The creature dropped all that remained of Stephen Hopper on the spongy blood-soaked carpet and went to work on the window it had smashed out earlier. Digging a claw into the ceiling to anchor itself, it smashed a bigger hole in the side of the craft. As it did one of Hopper's severed arms was sucked out the hole and gone. The air was cold up here, freezing everything it enveloped.

Once it had torn through the last of the craft's outer skin with its free claw, nature did the rest. The gash in the side of the aircraft began to peel back and break away.

It ripped out two more seats and tossed them out the gaping hole. Then it exited the craft, just clearing the tail, falling to earth and twirling crazily like a life-sized ragdoll. Behind it, the airplane continued on toward its end, carrying with it the terrifying secrets of its deceased cargo.

It tumbled over and over, falling to the earth, and then it transformed, twisting, contorting, pulsing molecules rearranging themselves until it was complete. Black ick and smoke became like clay, and for a moment it was frozen.

Transformed, the black raven flew north-west to meet the hunter, and it's destiny.

3

4:35 PM

Daylight was giving way to grey clouds that threatened rain. Mick knocked on the door for the third time. Still, there was no answer. Steel was at his side, waiting, hoping that the Indian was wrong, but also thinking that life would be a lot simpler if John Parkins had pulled the pin. The Indian was in the back of the cruiser, waiting to be put into a jail cell.

Mick had grilled him along the way.

"What do you mean he's dead?" he yelled from the front seat as Steel tried to concentrate on driving to the Parkins house without getting in a wreck. Steel was a little pissed at Mick for this. He didn't think it was very professional dragging the Indian guy along. They should have secured him at the station and then come over here.

"I think he killed himself," Blackbird responded.

"Delay? Why is there a delay?" Toomey and the rest of his group were now standing in the Winnipeg Airport; they had overshot Brandon in the 757 and now had to catch a commuter back. "Did they say how long this delay will take?"

"No, Old Jake. This sort of thing happens from time to time," Proudfoot explained.

"How long would it take to rent a car and drive there?" Toomey sounded impatient.

"At least four hours," Fortier chimed.

"What do you think, Little John? Should we rent a car?" Toomey asked Proudfoot.

Proudfoot rubbed his chin and looked around to see all eyes were upon him. "Why don't we wait an hour? If by then we aren't boarding, I say we rent a car."

"Agreed," Toomey said. "Well I had hoped that we would be nikotwâsik, but it appears we will be nîyânan."

"Five and Six?" Proudfoot surmised. "Okay, Old Jake, what the hell language are you speaking, because it sure isn't Chocktee?"

"It's Swampy Cree," he replied. "My, Little Proudfoot, you really need to expand your mind to other cultures. Especially since it was you who bought me the book off the Amazon dot com."

The others laughed, and Proudfoot joined in.

"Come: let us go to a private corner of this place if there is one."

They gathered up their bags and found a relatively quiet area of the airport where some renovations were being done. Some of the fluorescents were down, and the maintenance men were nowhere to be found. Toomey pulled out an eagle's feather he regularly used in talking circles and addressed them. "I have told you what I know of Jackanoob, of his age and how he bargained away the future of our people with a creature of the black orb. Now I am going to pass the feather to each of you, and we will discuss the many things that need to be done when we reach this town of Thomasville. Each of you will pass me one question which I will try to answer. I had hoped that our brave hunter would be present in this talking circle, but I fear that time now works against us. There are some details we must talk out. For now, ask only one question."

He handed the feather to the Chief of the Chocktee people.

"How are we going to set this right, Old Jake?" Proudfoot asked and handed the feather back.

Toomey looked silently at each of the men in his charge. "Set your minds on fire, my brothers: this will be a day when none of us can falter or be weak. Young Daniel Blackbird will find a way, and we will be pillars upon which he stands when we do something not done since the days of Jackanoob."

He handed the feather to Michano.

"And what is that, Old Jake?" Michano asked handing it back.

"As all of you know, tomorrow is the fall equinox. The walls are thinning, my brothers. Tomorrow we are going to summon the Guardians."

5

Blackbird touched the scar on his face, feeling its tingle and looking through the windows into hell. While the two cops were up on the porch of the Parkins house, he was watching the mayhem taking place on Oasis Flight 182. He had found his way into the creature's mind just as it tore Kurt Cooper's heart from his chest.

The vision was much clearer this time. Daniel took care to keep his thoughts to himself because he guessed that in this state it might hear him.

He slumped back in the seat, his eyes rolling in his head. He could see its claw reach out and tear the bathroom door from the hinges. He could feel the physical toll it was taking on him. Blood splashed madly about as he watched from behind the two windows of the skinwalker's eyes. He tried to be strong and continue, but the vision was killing him, forcing him to pull away.

When he came to his nose was bleeding and looking through the car window was Chief David Logan.

6

Minutes before Logan arrived they forced the front door open to the Parkins house and were immediately overcome by a rancid smell. Steel looked to Mick, and for the moment they were equals in trepidation. Neither wanted to go forward: both knew what they would find.

He's dead, Mick thought and felt guilty relief that he would not have to deliver the terrible news of Olivia's death. This mingled with his anguish, threatening to make him freeze up – but he pushed on just the same.

He worked his way down the hallway toward the master bedroom while Steel headed across the living room toward the kitchen. The sour smell became worse the closer he got to the bedroom. His guts were filled with butterflies, compounding the dread. With one hand over his mouth, he turned the doorknob and pushed. It swung open soundlessly, and there he saw John's body sprawled out on the bed. He only recognized him by the shirt he wore and his giant hands. Beside him was the shotgun. It had tumbled from his dead hands and stood propped haphazardly against the dresser. Bluebottle flies buzzed about, depositing eggs on the decomposing corpse of John Parkins.

Mick stepped into the room and let out a low guttural moan.

Unknown to Mick, on the fateful night Olivia was ushered away by Erin Grant and her husband, John wasted no time. He went back to his room, removed the shotgun he kept in the closet and killed himself after writing a note to his wife. The note was sealed in an envelope and stood against Olivia's jewelry box on the dresser. It would never be opened.

Beyond the bed, blood mixed with pellets and gunpowder had long since coagulated, turning a reddish brown on the wall.

This is the end of the cycle, Mick thought, then corrected himself: the suffering would not end here. There was John's sister to think of, there were the friends who knew and loved them – including himself.

"I hope you guys are together, John," he whispered taking one last cursory look around, knowing the room would have to be sealed until it was documented. Then he backed out and closed the door. He wondered as he did whether or not he really wanted to be a cop anymore.

Steel was standing behind him in the hallway like a statue. Mick grabbed Steel by the shoulder. "John's dead, Don. He shot himself in the head."

Steel didn't respond. He was looking straight through Mick, leaving Mick to wonder if Steel was suffering from a form of post-traumatic stress.

"Come on."

Leading Steel toward the front door, he felt his sadness shift and make way for the anger.

"I got some questions for that Indian."

Someone would pay for this.

Once out on the porch, they saw a second cruiser parked on the street and Logan had Blackbird out of the car.

Mick came down the steps and across the walkway like a freight train, his eyes blurred with rage, his face radish ripe. He didn't notice Steel pull away and sit down, nor did he look at Logan, who undoubtedly had questions of his own. Instead, he marched straight up to Blackbird and grabbed him by the lapels of his jean jacket and shoved him onto the cruiser.

"How did you know?" he screamed and shoved harder.

"Mick!" Logan grabbed his shoulder.

"Were you here?" He used his forearm to heave Logan's hand off.

"Hopper is dead," Blackbird said, voice almost trancelike. "The plane is going down. There isn't much time."

"What in the name of fuck is going on? Who the hell are you?" Mick shook him like a ragdoll, ignoring the fact that he looked even older than when they first encountered him.

"I tried to tell you," he replied weakly.

"Mick!" Logan wrenched him off. "That is enough!"

He released his grip on Blackbird, let out an angry cry of frustration, and pounded his fist on top of the cruiser. Logan had never seen him like this. He looked on the verge of a nervous breakdown.

"What did you say about, Hopper?"

Logan noticed the aging as well. Blackbird's hair wasn't just streaked with grey, it had turned entirely white. He looked sick, like a man ready to expire.

"He's dead. Everyone on that plane is dead."

Logan keyed up his radio. "Base?"

"Go ahead, Chief," Sabrina answered.

"Dispatch Henderson to my location and call me on the cell."

There was a short pause and then as Logan was about to repeat himself Sabrina came back with, "Copy that."

His cell phone chimed up, and he answered immediately.

"Sabrina, have you heard anything about a downed plane?"

"Well CNN is reporting an aircraft in distress on the net. They're in full terror mode right now," she said, then added guiltily, "I was cruising the net on my break, Chief."

"Okay, if you hear anything more call me back." He hung up and leaned into Mick. "Sgt. Collins! Get your head on straight and fill me in on the situation!"

Blackbird slid down the door of the cruiser and parked himself on the curb. He was worn out from the vision on the plane, and in no position to fight off another attack by the big cop called Mick. His body felt frail, his mind in tatters: the projection he had done was killing him.

One or two more of those, Grandfather and we will be holding palaver before you can say, sweet squaw, he thought.

Mick turned around to face Logan. He was devastated; his eyes were swollen and bloodshot. "What do you know, Dave? It will save time."

"I know Olivia killed herself; I assume John did the same. I'm not sure what Blackbird is talking about."

"John killed himself with a shotgun in the bedroom. It looks like he did it a few days ago because the flies in the place are unreal." He wiped his nose. "That scumbag really fucked these people up."

"I know he did, Mick, but I need you to get a hold on yourself. I need you now more than ever to keep your cool."

Mick wiped his eyes with his forearm, collecting himself as Logan lifted Blackbird off the curb. "You okay, Mr. Blackbird? You don't look well."

"Yeah, I'm alright – but Chief Logan, please stop calling me Mr. Blackbird. Just call me Dan." He wiped the drip of blood from his nose then looked to the house across the street.

"Alright, Dan," Logan started, but felt something. "Give me a second."

Sitting on the step to the Parkins house Steel struggled with what he had seen. *Was it a hallucination? Am I going nuts,* he thought. *How can this be? None of this makes any sense.*

Logan turned his attention away from the others and looked at the house, Steel caught his eye. "Wait here," he told them and walked up the path to meet the befuddled officer who sat staring into space. "You okay, Don?"

"Can't be," Steel said, not looking up.

"What?"

Steel shook his head, then stood up and faced his boss. "Come with me, Chief, and tell me if I'm crazy." He turned and walked back up the porch steps, and Logan followed him into the house.

Blackbird and Mick stood uncomfortably beside each other.

"I'm sorry about your friend," Blackbird said.

Mick said nothing.

7

They were now in the kitchen and on the dining room table was the source of Steel's mental worry. At first, Logan thought it was Parkins – then he got a look at the corpse's face.

"Kolchak," Logan muttered.

"So I'm not nuts." Steel let out a sigh of relief.

"You saw him get on the plane?"

"We all saw him, Chief. I talked to him. We watched him go up the stairs and watched the plane take off." Steel paused. "What in the hell is going on, Chief?"

"I don't know, Don. Did Mick see this?"

"No; he gave me the bums rush when I went to get him."

Logan looked at the open and baron cavity of Kolchak's body.

Voices echoed inside his head.

"All of them eviscerated," Woodman said.

"My best guess would be coyotes after he was dead," Henderson had said.

"You're not nuts, Don. This is Kolchak." He placed a hand on his officer's shoulder to reassure him.

His cell rang. It was Sabrina.

"Chief, you're not going to believe this."

"Try me." He already knew the answer.

"The plane, the one they thought was a terror plane? They think it's the plane that Hopper was on. From what they're saying it strayed into US airspace and went down in Lake Superior. That's why they thought it was a terror plane, but now they're looking for survivors."

"Put in a call to Oasis and get a confirmation on the flight number. Not a word to anyone, Sabrina. I have a situation here so keep a line open for Mick." He closed the phone and shook his head.

"What is it?" Steel asked.

"It looks like Hopper's plane went down. It's all over the news. Maybe he's not so crazy after all," Logan mused aloud.

"Who?" Steel asked, but Logan couldn't hear him. He was remembering what Woodman had said about believing in what he saw. As mad as this was, it defied any other reasonable explanation.

Logan was starting to believe.

"Come on, Don. Let's get out of here for the time being."

When they got outside Henderson was just arriving.

Climbing out of his vehicle he already presumed that John Parkins was dead, even speculated that it was suicide, but had no idea about anything else.

Logan came down the steps with Steel, ignoring Henderson and walking straight up to Blackbird. "We are going to need to have a serious discussion, Dan."

"You might want to check the house across the street first," Blackbird replied.

Logan looked over his shoulder and whispered in his ear, "What is the name of fuck is going on here?" He pulled his face in close to Blackbird's, staring into his eyes, trying to assess what was going on behind them. "What have you brought into my town?"

"It isn't here right now, Chief, but it's coming back... And I didn't bring it," Blackbird whispered. "Please, we have very little time."

Logan released him and then led Mick away from everyone. "You gonna be okay?"

Mick was shaky. The man he had been was gone. "I'm going to be okay."

"I need you right now, Mick. More than anything I need you to act like a leader because we are in unknown waters here. You have to pull yourself together. I cannot do this alone." Logan hoped that the authority in his voice would bring his friend and 2IC back. If it didn't, he would have to turn to West and Steel to take over.

Mick shook for a second, took a couple of deep breaths, reached down inside himself, and wiped the tears from his face. "Okay, Dave, I won't let you down. What can I do?"

"For now I want you on the phone to the detachment, and I want you to rally the troops. Tell them to come without lights or sirens."

"How many, Dave?"

"All of them," he said and walked over to where Henderson stood.

Mick pulled out his cell phone, and once he had Kennedy on the line, he began giving orders. That helped steady him. The more orders he gave, the better he felt. This helped stave off the post-traumatic stress, at least for now. He felt ashamed for showing such weakness. The offensive nature of this had chipped away at the many protective layers he had managed to insulate himself with over the years. Now he felt raw, naked and vulnerable.

"Hello, Dave," Henderson greeted.

"Jeff, I don't even know where to begin, but I need you to sit tight until I get a handle on this." Logan reached down to his belt loop and brought up his keychain. "Dan, please come over here."

Blackbird stepped away from the car, uncertain at first, but Logan waved him over. Once in front of him, Logan opened the car door and motioned for him to get into the back.

Blackbird's face fell. "You're making a big mistake, Chief!"

"Don, I want you to take security on the scene. Have a command post set up and be ready for our people when they get on site." Then he looked to Mick and Henderson. "Me and Mick are going into that house, and I want you on standby, Jeff."

"What the hell is going on, Dave?" Henderson asked.

Logan pointed to the Sawyer house across the street. "Something isn't right. Frank Sawyer's car is in the driveway, and he is way too nosey to stay hunkered down inside that house. Be ready to come inside when I call for you."

9

Logan and Collins drew their guns and entered the house fully expecting to find a mirror image of the massacre across the street. The front door was unlocked, and they almost tripped over a cloth bag loaded with canned goods that had been dropped abruptly in the foyer.

At first, they saw nothing. The house seemed virtually undisturbed – but as they made their way further into the bungalow all hope for the Sawyers evaporated.

Logan spotted the first evidence of the horror which befell Frank Sawyer. It was a blood trail that started at the border between the doorway of the living room and kitchen. It was evident to both of them that he had been struck down in the living room while leading someone into the kitchen.

Unbeknownst to them, Frank Sawyer had muttered only one word as it dragged him to the counter and heaved him onto Kitchen Island: "Rhonda." Then he expired as it began to pull out his insides.

Now a shell of what was Sawyer lay on the counter, its interior hollow, the skin already starting to dry out. This kill was fresher: the acrid stench of rotting flesh had not yet taken hold.

The two officers stood transfixed over the body. Strangely, Logan was pondering whether or not to break the news about his cancer but then thought better of it.

"What in the name of God is going on here?" Mick groaned.

"Let's see if we can find Rhonda Sawyer," Logan said and thought, This is nothing, Mick. I've got a dead shrink across the street that you saw get on a plane. "Let's get this place secure before we start bogging ourselves down with questions we can't answer."

They walked through the house room by room, guns were drawn.

But Rhonda Sawyer's body wasn't there.

After checking the bathroom and the master bedroom they met in the hallway, gawking at each other. Then they glanced at the basement door.

Logan sighed and led the way.

10

They were all there, set up waiting for a call from inside the house. Steel was pretty tight-lipped, even with Hardy. He was still numb from what he had seen in John Parkins' house. He stared at the native guy in the car who had not torn his eyes from the Sawyer house since Logan and Mick had left.

"CP?" It was Logan hailing him on the radio.

Steel keyed the remote. "Go ahead."

"Scene is secure."

"Copy that," he replied, then to Henderson, "They want you inside, Jeff."

11

Nothing could have prepared Logan, Collins or even Henderson for what they found in the basement of the Sawyer house. In the center of the darkened chamber, hanging upside down from a support beam was the naked corpse of Rhonda Sawyer. Below her, an old steel wash tub, and in it, her lifeblood. Her throat had been opened up vertically, and she had been bled out like an animal in a slaughterhouse.

"Dear God, what is this?"

Henderson was looking beyond the slaughtered Mrs. Sawyer and to the symbols scrawled on the floors. The most distinctive was a large circle that looked somewhat like a wheel. In it were symbols which Blackbird would have recognized as numbers. At the center of the wheel were drawings, one of a bird, another of an orb. These were drawn with the precision of an artist. Surrounding them were more symbols and characters he did not recognize.

"I have no idea," Mick said, "But it looks like it was stenciled. The picture isn't drawn in blood, but the background is."

Henderson answered his own question: "I think it's a calendar."

"What makes you think that?"

Before he could answer, Logan's cell phone rang, scaring all three of them.

It was Sabrina again.

Logan took a deep breath and exhaled. "Yes, Sabrina?"

"Chief. I got confirmation on that flight. Oasis flight 182 chartered by Detective Pearson. According to the director of operations, Cindy Fowler, the flight experienced some sort of difficulty, but she wouldn't specify. They lost power then drifted into Michigan Airspace just over Lake Superior. They are looking for survivors at this time, but she sounded pretty grim about the prospects. I also flagged her number if you would like to contact her later."

"Thanks, Sabrina. I'll be in touch."

Logan shut his cell phone and turned back to Rhonda's body. "Hopper's plane is gone. Kolchak got on that plane, but his disemboweled body is across the street. This is fucking insane."

"What are you talking about? I didn't see another body. Just John's."

"Kolchak? The psychiatrist?" Henderson was still only halfway in the loop.

Logan ignored Henderson for a moment and focused on Mick. "You didn't get a chance; you dragged Steel out of there before he could show you. There's a second body in the kitchen – Robert Kolchak's body."

Henderson brought his hands up. "Somebody want to fill me in?"

"For now, Jeff, let's deal with this as a murder investigation. We are going to need forensics gathering, photos, and crime scene security. Hang on." He keyed the remote. "CP, we're coming out. We will give a full briefing on site and work out the logistics from there."

Mick stared into the floor. "How does the Indian figure into this, Dave?"

"I don't know, Mick. He's either has something to do with this or…"

"Or what?"

Logan shook his head. "I just don't know."

12

"What do you mean there are no rentals available?" Proudfoot sighed.

"I'm sorry, sir, but after the grounding of Oasis Airlines, we have had an overwhelming influx of people wanting to rent cars. Maybe one of the other agencies can help you," the woman said, but she knew better. Not only had Oasis been grounded, but the larger carriers had also stopped flying until they determined if there was a terror threat.

Proudfoot sighed. "We need a car really bad. Is there anything you can do?"

She tapped the keyboard, looked into her monitor, pursed her cheeks and clicked her mouse a couple times. "No, no, umm… I have a return coming in after midnight."

"That's like six and a half hours from now."

"That's the best I can do, sir. I would recommend you reserve it because if more airlines shut down, which may just happen, you won't be able to rent a donkey let alone a car." She glanced up from the monitor. "Would you like to reserve?"

Proudfoot said resignedly, "Yes, I'll reserve it." He put his credit card on the counter.

"Okay, Mr. Proudfoot. I do have some good news."

"Well, I can use some of that."

"It's a crossover."

"A what?"

"A crosser-over. It's kind of like a minivan, but also an SUV." She used her chin to acknowledge the group of native men waiting anxiously on the bench. "It should suit your needs."

13

When they emerged from the Sawyer house, all eyes were upon them, but neither Logan nor Collins were prepared to give a briefing to the waiting officers. But it didn't matter: their faces told a grim story, and all present were well aware that the dark chapter in their town's history had not concluded, but moved on to a new episode of police work to be conducted.

Logan and his 2IC walked down the steps side by side, Henderson bringing up the rear.

Logan looked to Don Steel. He had held everything back from the arriving officers until they emerged from the Sawyer place. "Get some tape and cordon off both houses, Don. Set up sentries and let's try and keep this as low key as possible." A stab of pain pulsed momentarily in his chest, and he winced, wishing for something to quiet it.

Not yet; we've still got business to conduct, he thought.

That business was two-fold. Logan wanted both himself and Mick to see the body of Kolchak so that there was no doubt in either of their minds. He was already second-guessing himself, wondering if the cancer was chewing away at his brain with the same lethal efficiency it was wreaking on his internal organs. Secretly, he had been taking half a Percocet to try and dull the pain, but all it did was lower the volume on an orchestra of intense agony. Making it through the day and managing the pain while on duty was a struggle, but he wanted a clear head, and even one Percocet made him sluggish. So he opted for a half a pill, which he had cut neatly on a plastic cutting board in his kitchen at home. After cutting the pills in half, he popped them into an aspirin bottle which he kept in his hip pocket. He'd take half a pill every four hours, and when he got home, he'd pop two and watch reality slip away.

"What about him?" Mick asked, pointing at Blackbird.

From the back of Logan's cruiser, Blackbird waited, looking haggard, but there was also a sense of urgency in his eyes as he stared them down. Logan tried not to connect with those eyes, knowing they would raise questions in himself that he couldn't answer right now. He had to stay focused.

"Have Westy take him back to the station house. We'll interview him when we're done here."

That was all Mick needed. "Westy!"

"Yes, Sarge."

"Jump in the Chief's cruiser and run Mr. Blackbird back into town. Keep him in cells until we get back."

"Sure thing," West replied.

Logan leaned over and placed his hand on West's arm. "Treat him with respect, Jim. We don't even know if he has a hand in this."

Mick shot Logan a glance of disapproval, but it faded quickly.

"Wouldn't do it any other way, Chief," West replied.

Steel was delegating officers, and Logan took a moment to look around, then said, "I knew you wouldn't, Westy, but we've been riding an emotional rollercoaster all summer. Sometimes I need my men to say it out loud to reinforce what I'm thinking."

Mick thought, *Is that directed at me?*

It seemed that since the excavation of Tommy Parkins he wasn't sure about anything anymore. His entire world felt like it was on shaky ground, his leadership, friendship. Even his marriage seemed uncertain. He hated feeling like this, but if he were to ask such a thing, it might further alienate him from Logan.

Something was going on with his boss: he sensed a negative vibe coming off him, but he couldn't quite put his finger on it. He had said he needed to talk. That was before all this Blackbird business. He speculated it might be his performance or lack of that warranted discussion.

Logan elbowed him. He jerked out of his thought. "Come on, Mick. Let's get this over with."

Mick nodded, and they started for the Parkins place.

"What about me?" Henderson asked.

"Come on, Jeff; you can follow along as we document the scene."

***

CHAPTER 17 - RED SKY IN MORNING

1

September 23rd Autumn Equinox

6:58 AM

Bobby Morneau wheeled his cab into Angela's Diner as the morning sun broke across the prairie horizon. He looked to the red sky and thought to himself that this was going to be a wet and miserable day. The morning crowd was in there, truckers, delivery folk, and Charlene.

Charlene had been waitressing in Angela's for over ten years, and Bobby was sweet on her. Of course, she just smiled and flirted for the buck he tossed her after his usual $4.99 breakfast, but he still fantasized about her saying yes to a night out at the drive-in.

Charlene Hampton was in her early forties, with a full head of bleach blond hair and a bust that gave the regular men a thrill every time she leaned over to set their plate. She reminded Bobby a bit of Marilyn Monroe or even Candy Clark: she had that sweet happy go lucky voice and she called everyone 'Hon' – except Bobby. She called him by his Christian name: Robert.

One day he might ask her out if he could muster the nerve, but for now, he'd just settle for ham and eggs with a glass of tomato juice and coffee.

He pushed the door open, and the bell chimed. For a moment the chatter muted somewhat, as heads peered around booths to see who had come in.

In the back was Norton Graves, who did water delivery for all of the cisterns in the area. Nort was a big guy, 6' 2", but as skinny as a rail. He raised his hand and waved Bobby over. They had breakfast together occasionally, talking town gossip and trading barbs about who was going to get on Charlene's sweet side first.

"What would she do with a bean pole like you?" Bobby would snipe.

"Listen, Morneau, by the time you work up the nerve she'll be collecting her social security. Be careful not to stand still too long, my friend. A dog might mistake you for a tree," Nort would fire back. But that was just friendly cajoling between two Thomasville old timers who would never have a bad word to say about each other.

Except, in person, that is.

Bobby motioned to Charlene. She flashed him her usual pearly smile. Bobby pointed to the back where Nort was sitting. She acknowledged the signal with a wink, and Bobby felt his heart flutter.

He worked his way down the aisle, which was somewhat like the inside of a rail car. Booths lined it on the left and right. Along the way on his right, he passed a young couple who looked like they hadn't been to bed yet. To his left were Craig Bronson and Herb Keele, the local real estate shysters, or so Bobby thought. They were the brains behind the Mayor's new land development on the west side. Usually, the Mayor could be found sitting with these two weasels laughing too loud and acting like some kind of big shot.

Across the street, Randy Maytum was opening Thomasville Hardware and putting out his daily displays with the help of his son Sidney. Maytum was a nice fellow who always kept to himself, and he ran a clean and organized store. Sidney was not a bad kid either, but he liked to hang out and smoke pot with a few of the local boys who had dropped out.

Overhead the red sky turned the street scarlet. The streetlights clicked off, and Maytum looked on to the morning sun which hadn't quite peeked over the horizon. He sighed. If the rain started, he would be dragging the displays back inside.

Just up the street sixteen-year-old Mary Rossi was jogging in the early morning. This was part of her vigorous daily training: she hoped that the school and Masonic hall would sponsor her to attend the Pan Am Games. Every morning she was up at 5 AM, stretching and prepping to get in shape. Up until today, it looked very promising.

Just as Bobby was about to sit down with his pal Nort and Randy Maytum was getting ready to send Sidney in for the wheelbarrow display, Mary Rossi saw the big black bird coming straight down the street.

It was huge, wings four feet across. Mary stayed her course, pumping her legs, thinking it would pull up and fly over the hardware store – but it didn't. It continued toward her, only thirty feet away. That was when she made the decision to cross the street and get out of its path.

"By the Jesus," one of the real estate agents muttered, staring out the window.

Bobby turned to look back at what the shyster was rambling on about.

Maytum also saw the big black bird coming, and it blew past him straight toward Mary Rossi, who was now crossing the street to escape it. The beating of its wings sounded like a bed sheet flapping in a crisp autumn wind, but that wasn't what startled Maytum. This thing was huge: two and a half feet tall, its wings spanning four, maybe four and a half feet. Worst of all it was flying toward Mary on her early morning jaunt.

Maytum picked up one of the garden hoes he had put on sale and began running up the street just as Sidney came out with the wheelbarrow.

"Dad," Sidney puzzled.

Bobby saw the bird from inside diner now and Charlene, carrying a fresh pot of coffee, also worked her way to the window. In fact, everyone was standing up, moving forward to watch the quiet drama unfold in the street.

Mary was halfway across the street when she saw the bird change course. She stopped, screamed, and began running the other way. From behind, Maytum was also running, trying to catch the bird, raising the garden hoe up to strike but he knew he wasn't going to make it.

"Oh my Lord," Charlene gasped and dropped the pot of coffee she had been holding onto the booth's red vinyl seat. It spilled over. No one noticed.

The bird dived. It crashed into Mary from behind, its talons tearing out a large part of her scalp and knocking her down. She stumbled forward, smacked hard into the asphalt. A terrified cry escaped her as she skidded across the pavement, skinning her right cheek and forearm.

From behind Maytum saw the bird knock her down and then arc straight upward, but what he saw next could not be described in his wildest nightmares. The bird seemed to stop four feet above the wounded Mary Rossi and explode in a mix of gas and black tar. Then, as the gas dissipated, Maytum took in the horror with a sense of fascination that completely blocked out the reality that he still was running toward it.

They all saw the transformation and the nine-foot monster which now stood over the body of the wounded Mary Rossi. Its breath turned to mist in the September air. It looked first left and right, then up the street. It blinked the grey and veined eyelids, unfurled its long arms that terminated in talons. A bit of drool like raw egg white dripped from its mouth.

Then it smiled and pushed one of its claws down into Mary Rossi's back, killing her instantly. The entire time it kept its eyes fixed on Maytum, who charged forward, hoe poised above his head.

"Dad!" Sidney screamed from behind him, but it was too late to turn back. Maytum swung the hoe as hard as he could – and the creature reached up and caught the handle in mid-air.

For a second they stood there, each holding one end of the hardwood, a sticker declaring '$5.98 Great Deal!' between them. Maytum might have had half a chance if he would have only released the garden hoe – but then the monster yanked him forward and in a blur pulled its claw free from Mary Rossi's back and disemboweled him right on the spot.

"Ooooooohhhhhhhhhh," Maytum groaned, the contents of his belly spilling out onto Mary's dead body. He fell to his knees, then keeled sideways while it reached down and grabbed a large helping of his intestines.

"Fresh meat."

"Daddy!" Sidney screamed again.

Then it let loose a shriek, blowing in the windows on both the hardware store and Angela's Diner. Morneau had just turned his head and – by sheer luck and coincidence – had grabbed Charlene's arm to pull her down from the window. The glass exploded inward, blinding the real estate agents and three other onlookers. Nort, who was still seated in the back, was spared the peppering.

"Come on!" Morneau yelled at Charlene. "We've gotta get out of here!"

He dragged her up the aisle as she screamed frantically. Shards of glass had embedded in her cheek and arm, but she had fared better than the others. Around them, the young couple seated by the window moaned and writhed in agony, and the two shysters held their hands to their bleeding faces. Another guy Bobby didn't know was standing there screaming and with good reason. A shard of glass the size of a matchbook had pierced his right eye.

"Nort! We gotta get the hell out of here," Bobby yelled back at his friend.

The creature rushed up the street in a blur, wrapped its talons around Sidney. "Are you scared?" it hissed, then tore him open like a wet grocery bag.

Bobby kept leading Charlene to the door, looking back and urging Nort to get moving. The moans and cries around them were enough to tear out his heart, but he knew they had to get to his cab before that thing – whatever the fuck it was – turned its sights on the diner.

"Nort! Let's go!"

They were at the front door. Nort was halfway up the aisle as Bobby fumbled for the keys to his cab.

"Move it, Nort!"

Charlene clutched his arm in a death grip, digging her nails into the skin, her lower lip quivering. She wanted to scream, but she did not dare.

The cab was five feet to the left of the entrance.

"Listen to me, Charlene. We are going to get in my cab. We're both going to get into on the driver's side. You scoot your arse over real fast so I can get us out of here, okay?"

She nodded. Her makeup ran down her face. Her lower lip continued to quiver.

Nort was almost up to the aisle. Then the air around him blurred crashing him right into a waiting booth, and a glut of his blood splashed up the wall.

Nort was no more.

Bobby didn't wait. He yanked Charlene out the entrance of the diner while whatever it was that had killed Mary, Randy and Sid went to work on Nort.

They ran for the car. He reached it first. He yanked open the door and shoved her in.

"Skooch over, girl," he ordered, abandoning his manners. She was fumbling around on the seat, her butt up in the air and he said, "Move your ass," – then placed a hand firmly on her buttock and shoved her headfirst into the passenger door.

In the back alley, Brad, the cook, was having a smoke when Angela's Diner broke into pandemonium. He had blocked the big steel door open with a piece of cardboard: there was no handle on the outside, for security reasons. More than once Brad had locked himself out and had to suffer the indignity of walking all the way around to the front of the building. He and Charlene didn't really get along, and she would put a dig into him every time.

He heard the shriek on the other side of the building, followed by the glass shattering inside the diner just as he was opening the door. It startled him: he released the handle. At the same time, the cardboard blocking the door open fell away.

The door clunked shut, locking him out.

"Fuck me," he cursed. "Fucking marvelous." He shook his head in frustration and shuffled down the alley preparing to fall victim to that cackling, balloon boob, bleach blond airhead. God, how he hated her!

Bobby put the key in the ignition and turned it – but the engine didn't start. Beside him, Charlene was looking into the smashed out windows of Angela's Diner when a girl appeared at the doorway screaming. It was the teenage girl sitting with her boyfriend. She was reaching out blindly, crying, "Help me! Please, someone, help me!"

Bobby turned the key again. The car still wouldn't start.

Suddenly the girl in the doorway was yanked back inside, and a bloodcurdling scream filled the morning air, followed by another horrific shriek. Charlene tapped at Bobby's leg frantically. "Hurry, hurry, hurry, hurry!"

"I'm trying!"

He was beginning to think they were going to have abandoned the car and go on foot, but he tried the key again. And …

Nothing!

More screams, this time a man. *One of the shysters?*

Then Bobby looked down and saw what the problem was. The car was not entirely in park. He grabbed the lever and pushed it all the way, then turned the key. The engine roared into life. He threw it into reverse and stepped on the gas, wheeling it around, almost taking out the fire hydrant across the street. Getting the car straight he took one last look at Angela's. The overhead lights inside were flashing on and off like strobe lights.

A body crashed out onto the street, entrails flapping behind him.

Shyster number two!

Bobby punched the accelerator.

At first, the car lunged and almost stalled, but the big 400 caught and began to move just as the creature came barreling out into the street behind them. Bobby stared into the rearview mirror. It came to a standstill behind them, its ragged grey flesh coated in the intermingled blood of its victims.

His eyes locked with the creature's – and it began to speak.

"Stop the car. Stop the car," the mirrored eyes insisted.

Dumbly, he realized it was hypnotizing him. He started to veer left and release his foot from the accelerator. Then Charlene screamed at him and knocked the rearview mirror right off the windshield. Bobby snapped out of it immediately. He regained control – but they were running up the sidewalk.

Brad came around the corner staring at what looked like two bodies lying on the roadway. He didn't even have a chance to say what he thought when Bobby Morneau's cab collided with him. In an instant, Brad was flat out on his back, and the front wheels decimated both his lower legs. Thankfully it had happened so fast that he hadn't yet time to process the pain being transmitted from the raw nerve endings in his broken shins.

"Bobby, look out!" Charlene screamed. Brad, in his white button-down cook's outfit, stepped out of the alleyway and then there was a thud and a bump. Charlene looked back, and the ghoul which stood watching now began to give chase. "Go go go!"

"I hit Brad! Jesus, I hit poor Brad!"

Brad tried to get up on one elbow. He had no idea why he was on the ground, why there were bodies to his left: he just knew he had to get up. Then he saw the thing coming at him in a flurry.

Through the back window, Charlene watched in horror as the creature pounced on Brad and tore him apart. "Don't stop!" she screamed. Her screaming became wails as the cab sped off, leaving the monster and bloodbath behind.

The monster pulled out Brad's heart and held it over its head, shrieking insanely like a football player who had just crossed the goal line to score a touchdown.

"Tell him I'm here! Tell the hunter I have arrived!" Blood and black spittle erupted from its mouth, and it laughed insanely as the fleeing vehicle disappeared over the hill. "I'm here!"

Bobby was driving like a maniac with no sense of direction, and he couldn't get the mental image of that thing tearing through the diner out of his head.

What in God's name was it? Some kind of animal I've never seen before? Beside him, Charlene was hyperventilating, and just as he was about to tell her to open the window, she barfed all over his dashboard.

"Aw, Christ," he groaned. "There's some napkins in the glove compartment."

"I'm sorry." She was a vision, her mouth laden with whatever she had for breakfast. The coat of make-up she had probably spent an hour putting on made her look like Alice Cooper wearing a blond wig.

She has better tits though.

"It's okay, Charlene. You're not the first one to barf in my cab." He reached behind him and grabbed a can of air freshener. She was wiping up now as he sprayed the air in the cab. "Man, what a crazy fucking morning,"

2

"What the hell?" Pete Kennedy was sitting at the corner of Bench Road and Yale East when the cab went by doing better than eighty. He didn't have his radar set up yet, but that didn't stop him from pulling out. It was Morneau. He usually drove too fast, but even for Bobby, this was much faster than usual. Kennedy fired up the lights and chirped the siren.

Just as he was closing on the cab, Morneau locked up the brakes. "Shit!"

The cruiser crashed right into the rear of Morneau's cab, pushing the trunk in and sending the back end up onto the push bar of the police car. Kennedy just sat in shock a moment – then he shook his head and got out of the car. Morneau was also getting out of his cab, and the passenger on the other side was getting out. They were okay, but this was a disaster. The Chief was going to have a field day with this.

"Thank God, Pete! I don't think I've ever been so happy to see your disco lights in my side view mirror," Morneau said, crossing over to him.

"Bobby, why did you slam on your brakes?"

"They're dead," Charlene started in. "They're all dead!"

Kennedy stopped and said. "Whaa? Who's dead?"

"Everyone, Pete. It just tore through Angela's Diner like the fucking Tasmanian devil. I've never seen anything like it in my life," Bobby blathered.

"Have you been drinking, Bobby?"

"He's telling the truth, Peter. It killed Randy Maytum and his son. It killed Brad, the cook." Charlene was almost frenzied. "And Nort and Mary Rossi and – fuck! A bunch of others! It's a fucking massacre!"

"Okay, everyone calm down. Let's get in my car and show me what you're talking about." Though Kennedy wasn't sure, he'd even be able to pull the cars apart if they did climb in.

"Not a fiddler's fucking chance in hell I'm going back there! In fact, I'm not even staying here. It could be coming this way." Morneau took Charlene's hand. "You coming?"

"Just hold on a minute there. You can't leave: we just had a crack up!"

"Look, Pete." Morneau turned, still holding Charlene by the hand. "We are the least of your problems today. The best advice I can give you is to call the cop shop and tell them to bring as much artillery as humanly possible. We are not staying." And he turned and hurried away.

"Damn it, Bobby! Stop," Kennedy yelled. Bobby complied and turned, but his face was restless, and Kennedy didn't think the pause would be for long. Kennedy keyed up his remote radio.

Base, come in."

"Go ahead, Pete." It was Jim West.

"Base, I have been involved in a minor collision." Kennedy raised his hand to Morneau, which essentially was asking him to wait.

"Anyone hurt, Pete?" West asked.

"Not at my location, but there is a secondary issue in which I request secure means."

"Copy that."

"Further to my last, I am sending two civilians down Yale Road East. Could you dispatch someone to pick them up and take them back to the station?"

"Will comply."

Kennedy gave Bobby and Charlene a hard look. "Okay, keep walking down Yale; they're dispatching a car to pick you up."

"Where are you going?"

"To Angela's Diner."

"Are you insane, Pete? Did you hear what we said?" Bobby protested.

"Yeah, I heard you, and I am calling for back up, but I don't just stop being a cop on the word of a Gypsy cab driver and his girlfriend. I gotta check it." Pete opened the door and started to climb into his broken cruiser, getting ready to see if he could unhook it from the smashed up cab.

"Pete, we're not drunk, and this isn't a joke."

"Okay, well I have to check it out no matter what, and I'm calling for backup – so you guys start walking and watch for a car to pick you up." He closed the door and started the cruiser as Bobby and Charlene looked on in disbelief. He put the car in reverse and revved it up: after a second the push bar ripped the rear bumper off Morneau's cab.

"Numbnuts," Morneau cussed, then turned and continued leading Charlene away.

In his breast pocket, Kennedy's phone started to vibrate. He withdrew it and flipped it open as he drove toward Angela's Diner.

3

"My name is John Proudfoot, and I am here to see my cousin Daniel Blackbird."

Proudfoot and the four other native fellows stood before Jim West at the counter. Jim dwarfed all five of them, who ranged in height from the shortest – Toomey – to the tallest – Proudfoot. They looked odd to West, like something out of an old spaghetti western.

Behind them, through the glass doors, the sun was making a brief appearance in a losing battle with the incoming thunderheads.

"Daniel Blackbird is indisposed at the moment."

Toomey stepped forward. "What is your name?"

"Corporal Jim West." His voice was soft and kind, like a gentle giant.

"Are you in charge here?"

"I'm the duty officer, so yeah, I am in charge. What would be your name, Sir?"

"My name is Jake Toomey. Most people just call me Jake or Old Jake, but you can call me Jake Toomey. Little Proudfoot here didn't make himself clear, so as the Elder of this band I am going to reinforce what he said. We must see Daniel now. It is vitally important, not just to us, but to you, Corporal Jim West."

West smiled. He instantly liked the little Indian guy, found it amusing that he was so small yet forceful. Like an aboriginal leprechaun with an attitude. "Jake Toomey, I appreciate your urgency, but Dan Blackbird is in an interview with Chief Logan and Sgt. Collins. As much as I don't want to impede the importance of you seeing him, I can't just bust in on them."

Toomey muttered something in Chocktee that West thought was a curse. Then Toomey turned to the others, and they began conversing in their language.

As they talked, the radio keyed up behind West.

"Base come in." It was Pete Kennedy.

He stepped away from the window and pushed the send button. "Go ahead, Pete."

4

Logan sat across from Blackbird in the same interview room he had spent endless hours in with Stephen Hopper. Mick stood in one corner. Spread out on the table were photos they had taken inside the Parkins and Sawyer households. They had been at it all night, and all three men looked exhausted. Logan didn't know which way was up anymore, and though he didn't think that Blackbird had killed the Sawyers or Kolchak, he still didn't buy the story he was selling.

"It's coming," Blackbird insisted.

At midnight they had watched the clock flip over and nothing.

"Apparently the Equinox shape-changer isn't happening in Thomasville." Mick slammed his fist down on the table. "Just admit your involvement!"

But Blackbird only repeated: "It's coming."

That was then, and now it was 7:10 and Daniel could barely keep his eyes open. He had given up speaking long ago. Every explanation he gave was being dissected and discredited. As the hours wore on, and as sleep deprivation took hold, he began to believe that maybe there was no Skinwalker. That perhaps he had gone crazy after all. Could this whole thing be a figment of my imagination, a chemical imbalance causing schizophrenia?

Get a grip, Dan: you're losing it!

He could feel the big cop, Mick, staring him down, wishing for him to confess. *I wonder if he'd beat me if I gave him his wish?* After all the sleepless hours, what he had seen through the monster's eyes in the aircraft, he was ready to believe or say anything. That was when a voice spoke up inside him, one that was not Grandfather's, his mother's or, even his own. *Keep your mouth shut. Don't tell them anything more.*

5

Kennedy crested the hill where Brad the cook had been struck down and devoured, and though the body was gone there was plenty of blood to mark the spot. He stopped the car and backed away from the crest. "Holy crap."

"I have an 11-99, multiple units required." So far, he'd seen only this bloody spot, but it gave credence to what that crazy Bobby Morneau had said.

His cell phone rang up, and he answered it. "Hello?"

"What's going on, Pete," West asked.

"I've got a lot of blood at the intersection of Bench Street and Yale Road East. There may be some validity to what Morneau was saying. Maybe a wild animal of some sort?"

"Okay, Pete, I'm sending two units your way. Steel and Hardy are en route. You just sit tight and wait for the cavalry. Report all observations over secure means only."

"Copy that, Jim."

Kennedy closed the flip phone and looked at the crest of the hill, wondering what else was beyond it. *Are they really all dead?* He drummed his fingers on the steering wheel and thought to himself, *I know what will happen when they get here. 'Pete, go do sentry,' or, 'Pete, head back and be duty officer.'*

Sometimes it sucked being the junior guy, and for this reason, he decided this time he wasn't going to sit tight. Slowly he got out of the cruiser and undid the snap on his weapon.

6

"Tell your officer to get out of there, Corporal Jim West," Toomey warned from behind. "Don't send anyone there!"

The little Indian man gave him a start, and had he not been such easygoing and thoughtful man, he might have scolded him. "Huh? What are you talking about?" But what West was thinking was: *How the hell did he know that?*

"The only thing waiting there is death. We must see Dan Blackbird right now! And Chief Logan too!" All at once the likeability was gone from the old man, and in its place was forcefulness.

At any rate, West had to alert the Chief to this new development at Angela's – and, of course, the party of five to see Blackbird.

Sabrina came in with a cup of coffee in her hand. Her shift still didn't start for another twenty minutes: her routine was to go to the lunch room and read the morning paper. She smiled at West and raised her eyebrows at the group of five. "Morning, James?"

"Hey, Sabrina, can you cover dispatch for a sec while I grab the Chief?"

"Sure," Sabrina nodded. Duty called. The paper would have to wait…

"Sit tight; I'll be right back," West said to Toomey.

He stepped away from the counter and started for the interview room. He was also tired, and maybe that was why this whole bizarre morning was easier to accept. Perhaps it was the nineteen hours he'd been up, but he felt that he should be moving a hell of a lot faster on the Kennedy situation and with that, he picked up his pace.

7

Kennedy was out of the car, gun drawn and working his way along the building next to Thomasville Hardware. The blood was in clear view now, but even worse he could see three bodies right off. Mary Rossi and Randy Maytum were slumped over each other. Blood seeped from all around them down the hill like a river. Maytum's son, Sid, was laid out on the sidewalk and it looked like someone took a shop-vac to his stomach.

He peered across the street at Angela's Diner. It was a bloodbath. Suddenly he didn't feel so secure or cocky.

Maybe waiting for the cavalry at the car wasn't such a bad idea after all.

He began to back up, using the building's brickwork as a guide. Adrenaline pumped through his body. His started to shake. He might be exhausted from pulling a double shift, but that did not muzzle the fear he suddenly felt, nor did it ease the tremors he felt run through his hands.

Gotta keep cool; backup's on the way.

Easier said than done.

When a liquid which felt like cold, raw egg white spilled down on his right shoulder, he almost fired into nothing. Then he looked up and saw it perched atop the hardware store, staring back down on him.

8

Blackbird was trying very hard to fight the lethargy, but sitting in this seat made doing so almost impossible. Logan and Collins also looked exhausted, but Logan looked worse: like he was gonna pass out.

Logan pushed the last photo across the table, and it was something that Blackbird immediately recognized. The picture was that of a drawing scrawled in blood on the Sawyer basement floor.

"Do you know what this is?"

"It's a calendar," he replied.

Collins, who had been leaning against the wall ready to pounce, stood up and walked over to the desk, steadying himself with his hands on the edge. He stared at the picture for a moment, then locked his eyes with Blackbird's. He was trying everything he could to intimidate him. "A calendar?"

"Yes; it is inscribed on the sentry posts in my village." He pointed to the writing at the top of the wheel: VᑕᐊꓶΛꓹ ⊃<Ꮟᗷꓶꓹ "This represents the vernal equinox." Then he pointed to the bottom ᏏꓹᏏꟼ⅃ ⊃<Ꮟᗷꓶꓹ "This is the autumn equinox. Today."

"This again," Mick sighed.

There was a knock at the door, and Mick went to get it while Logan looked at the photograph he had taken of the Sawyer basement floor. Rhonda's body, along with the other three, had been removed and were being examined by Henderson at the morgue. *This is a goddamned nightmare.*

"Do you want to hear this? Or not?"

"Go ahead." Logan rubbed his eyes, longing for a Percocet.

"The equinox is when night and day are equal, but it is also an alignment of worlds. I wish Jake Toomey were here; he could explain this far better than I." Blackbird sighed. "This calendar is a variation on a much older one, probably as old as the earth."

Mick interrupted, "Dave. We need to step outside for a minute." West was holding the door. The look of concern on their faces was enough to jolt Logan.

He stood up.

Blackbird stood up too. "It's here, isn't it?"

"Shut up and sit down," Collins barked.

"Sit down, Dan." Logan turned away and walked to the door. "What's going on?"

"In the hall," Mick motioned.

Logan looked from Blackbird to his officers and observed the raw emotion etched into their faces. This wasn't good. West's eyes widened. Logan quickened his step. "We'll be right back, Dan," he said without turning around and stepped out into the hallway with his officers.

9

Bobby Morneau saw the police cars coming and expected that they would stop to pick him and Charlene up – but they blew right by without slowing down, lights on, but no sirens. Guess they got confirmation from Pete.

"Let's get the hell out of here, Robert," Charlene said and nudged him.

"I'm with you on that," he agreed. They began walking again, hand in hand, up Yale Road toward town.

10

"Officer down! Officer needs assistance!" It was Hardy, and she sounded completely off-kilter. "Send all available units!"

"What is your situation?" Sabrina responded.

Logan, West, and Mick were all entering the staff room when the call came through, and they heard the distress in Hardy's voice.

So did Jake Toomey, who stood at the window. "Chief David Logan, I need to see Daniel Blackbird right now!"

Logan ignored the old man and went to the radio. "What have we got, Sabrina?"

"Constable Hardy, she's just sent an officer down, and officer needs assistance."

"Get everyone keyed up – and I mean everyone, Mick!"

Chief David Logan! Pull your people back! Do it now!" Toomey yelled. "If you care about your people pull them back now!"

"Calm down, Jake!" West barked now.

Logan to West: "Who the fuck is that?"

"Jake Toomey. They arrived just before I came and got you."

"Mr. Toomey, I have a situation here. Stay quiet for a minute." Logan reached over Sabrina and keyed the radio. "Sandy, this is Chief Logan, what is your status?"

The radio keyed up and then went silent. Logan was about to say something when Hardy's voice came on. "Chief, Kennedy is down, and Don is bleeding really bad."

"Pull your people back!" Toomey thundered.

"Shut him the fuck up!" Logan growled at Mick.

They were all standing at the window now, a band of Native men watching the chaos in the staff room. Toomey was muttering in Chocktee. Sabrina had her hand over her mouth and West hung like a great tree towering over the lot of them.

"Sandy, I want a straight up assessment."

11

The street looked like a war zone. Directly below the corner of the building where the creature was perched lay the body of Pete Kennedy, which looked like it had fallen into a giant trash compactor. Steel never saw the creature. Once he spotted Kennedy's body he was out of his car, gun drawn, screaming frantically at Hardy. "Call for backup. Officer down! Officer down!"

Oblivious to the danger lurking above, he sped toward Kennedy. Hardy was climbing out of her car, also drawing her weapon and reaching in through the open door to get the handset. That was when she saw the monster coming down the wall like an insect.

"Don!" she cried, but it was too late.

He never thought to look up, never considered that danger would come from above. He took a cursory look down the street, but his attention was on Pete, and he was already leaning over the young officer's mangled body when he heard Hardy call out.

Then something spun him around, yanked back his head hard enough to make his upper vertebrae pop, and slashed open his cheek. He sucked in a great gasp of breath, and he tasted decay, death. Before him the monster inhaled too, sucking fresh air over the rows of jagged teeth that seemed to stack up like tombstones in the landscape of speckled grey clay that was its gums.

Is this some kind of Halloween prank?

"Send the hunter," it hissed and spat something dark into the gash on his face.

Fire spread through his cheek, burning — then his face became numb as it swam through his veins. When it released him, he stumbled drunkenly backward.

Venom – I've been poisoned.

It moved away from him, an aura of grey-blue in its wake. He tried in vain to raise his gun, but lost the motor control in his hands and watched it tumble toward the ground in slow motion. It clicked when it hit the asphalt, and he thought about picking it up but abandoned the idea immediately. His feet felt swollen three times their original size. He tried to back up. Failed. He decided to move forward. Also failed.

I'm dying. This is how it feels to die after a monster spits venom into your face. Who would have thought? A morbid smile crossed his lips, like a kid overdosing on Novocain. Then he thought about Hardy, and that shook the drunken musings from his head.

She was fifteen feet in front of him, her gun drawn, staring wide-eyed at the building.

He was running out of energy, the poison taking control. *That's my sweetheart. Kill the fucker, Sandy: shoot it full of holes. Do it for me, baby.* His vision blurred and she became little more than a silhouette against the red morning sky.

Steel dragged one clown foot forward. Pins and needles moved up and down his legs, his arms became heavy, and as he tipped over he managed one word: "Sandy…" Then he hit the asphalt, thoughts swimming incoherently – and the darkness won.

Hardy dropped the handset, looked on in horror, a terrified moan escaping her like gas. She was sure he was dead and bit into her cheek to stifle a scream. As blood ran under her tongue, her eyes darted back and forth between Don and the creature above.

It came down the wall so fast, like a spider from its lair. What is it?

It wasn't moving, barely breathing, but she could smell it, and she knew that scent from the cornfield behind Hopper's house. It was the smell of rot and death. She was terrified but did not make the connection between this and the ranting of Stephen Hopper. Nor did she connect it to the murders at the Sawyer or Parkins residences: Hardy only knew that the creature which had killed Pete Kennedy sat thirty-five feet up on the corner of the building and she did not have time to debate what it was.

Don was ten feet away, but it felt like a mile. She loved Don Steel, was carrying his unborn child in fact, but could she muster the courage to retrieve him?

Then Don moved his arm just slightly, and she let out a whispered cry.

"Oh dear God."

And with that, she found the determination to go after him.

She stepped forward, watched the creature for a reaction – but none came. It was staring off into space, seemingly unmindful to its surroundings. This was little comfort to Hardy. She eased forward, gun at the ready, watching Steel from the corner of her eye. *Get in and get out, Sandy! Don't wait, don't assess, don't worry about anyone else but Don, she coached herself.*

Halfway now, and she moved in tight to the brick wall, following the same path Kennedy had taken before his end.

She could only see its bony knees and talons over the ledge of the masonry. If it moved an inch, Hardy would empty her clip into it. Carefully she got down on all fours and scrambled toward Don, keeping her gun trained on the ledge.

His eyes were open, but he wasn't responding, and the gash on his face bulged with infection. *He's breathing though,* Sandy. *That's something, but for how long? We've got to get him out of here!*

Don Steel was a short fellow, standing 5' 7" and he barely weighed 145 pounds, but right now he was dead weight. Adding to that, the street was littered with glass fragments, and she would not be able to fireman carry him. It was too risky with that thing looming overhead.

Ten feet, Hardy, she thought. *Ten feet, we get him in the car and call for help.*

She reached down with her left hand and hooked it into his belt and dragged him over so that she was spooning his body. With her right arm, she dug her elbow into the asphalt while running her index finger along the trigger guard of her weapon so as not to accidentally discharge it.

Okay, baby, hang on.

She heaved him back using her right elbow and legs. Broken glass cut through her uniform, dug into her hip and elbow. That's two feet; eight to go. She cast her eyes upward to see if the creature had moved from its perch, and for the moment it hadn't. Again, she dug in, feeling more fragments of glass grind deeper into her elbow and now into her buttock. *Fuck!* She heaved backward again, not daring to grunt or groan. *Four feet!* Stopping again, she looked up, then to the bumper of the first cruiser. It was so close – but not close enough.

Taking a couple of controlled breaths, she again checked the ledge. No movement.

Six feet to the car. Sweat ran down the small of her back and into the abrasion on her right bum cheek igniting a sting that felt like a hornet's kiss. But she ignored it and readied herself for another tug. This time she arched her back, using the strength in her legs to push backward – and she felt tiny pebbles of glass grind through the material in her shirt and embed into her left shoulder blade.

Heave!

They were beside the driver's door of Don's cruiser. She looked inside and saw the keys still hanging in the ignition. If the Chief had seen this, he would have gone ballistic, but for Hardy, it was a Godsend. She set him down, reached in, pulled the keys from the ignition and unlocked the shotgun from its security bracket.

Just in case!

She was exhausted and needed to prepare herself to lift him into the car. She pumped the shotgun as quietly as possible, chambering a shell and settled back against the wall with Don leaning on her. She watched to see if it would come.

Just give me a minute to catch my breath, Don.

Twenty seconds later she stood up and opened the rear door of the cruiser. Setting the shotgun on the roof, she reached down, lifted Don up, and pushed him into the backseat. He crumpled over, his face mashing against the front bench as she forced him into the car enough to close the rear door. She ignored the urge to straighten him and made her way around the front of the vehicle staring, eyes fixed all the while on the roof of the hardware store. In her right hand, she held her service pistol and in the left was the shotgun. On her index finger, the keys held tight.

She climbed in and set the shotgun on the bench seat – but held her pistol tightly and inserted the key into the ignition. She turned the key. The seatbelt warning chimed as she put the gear shift in neutral – and for a second she thought she would have to start it. But then the car began to roll backward, and the only sound was the crunching of shattered glass beneath the tires.

She looked back down Yale Road for any obstacles, holding the wheel straight so as not to hit anything, and then as the car rolled backward, she turned her eyes back to the creature on the building.

"Please don't move," She begged.

Thankfully, it didn't.

The car rolled 400 yards from where it had been left, and once they came to a stop she shuddered, and she reached for the radio handset.

12

"Sandy, what is your status?" Logan repeated again. The radio keyed up and then fell silent. The room was electric with anticipation. Everyone was waiting. No one spoke: not even from the window where Toomey stood.

Then, to their relief, she responded.

Their relief would be momentary.

"Pete Kennedy is down, no vitals. Don Steel is wounded, and I am okay; minor cuts and abrasions." Logan was about to ask what had happened, but she didn't release the switch on her handset. "Chief, we have a bunch of bodies between Angela's Diner and the hardware store, and you won't believe what –"

Logan glanced back at Toomey for a second, searching for a reaction. The man looked back at him, eyes wide, chin raised. That look was one of urgency and concern.

Then he turned his attention back to the radio. "Sandy, I'm listening."

"It came down the wall so fast, like a man-sized spider monkey. It cut Don… Steel's face and spat something into it. It's like something out of a nightmare. It was a monster, Chief. I know how crazy that sounds, but it's the only way I can describe it." There was a tremble in her voice. "I gotta get Steel to the hospital, I can't wait for backup."

He stole another look at Toomey, who was nodding his head.

"Get the hell out of there, Sandy, I'll dispatch EMS to Bench and Yale." He removed his hand from the button and looked about the room. "Mick, I want everyone mobile! Westy, open the weapons lock up, and Sabrina, I need you to call everyone in. Even off the crime scene at the Sawyer and Parkins place."

"What about us?" Toomey asked.

"Look, I don't know exactly who you are, but I'm guessing you have something to do with this. As you have probably noticed we have a situation. Once that is resolved I will give you my undivided attention."

"You need to listen," Proudfoot interrupted. "And we need Dan Blackbird."

"Stop!" Toomey interrupted. At the sound of the authority in his voice, everyone in the room stopped. "Your officer has been infected: he may pose a threat."

"Get Blackbird out of interview one and bring him out here," Logan told Mick then turned back to Toomey. "What threat? He's injured."

"Chief David Logan, up until now no one has listened to Dan Blackbird or us. Now you have dead in the street, your policeman killed and another infected! Do not send these people to slaughter! Now is the time to stop and listen!"

"Everyone get ready and do as I say; prepare to jump off in five minutes." Logan squared off with the old man. He could feel the indecision and chaos of the moment but resisted dropping his guard. "Get moving! We have two officers in need of assistance!"

"Send someone to retrieve your wounded, but no one to the site," Toomey whispered. "Please listen to me. I know you care about these people. I beg of you."

"Parking garage, five minutes! Sabrina, get the rest of our people in!"

Toomey barked, "Fools!" He threw his hands in the air and turned to his nîyânan. "Let them die. Stupid white devils never listen, always think they are smarter. Always have to touch the flame and feel the burn!" He locked eyes with Proudfoot, who looked confused. "You will come to see us, Chief Logan. You will ask for our help after more of your people are slaughtered. Go and learn your lesson, white devil!"

Then there was a pause, and those in the room exchanged glances between Toomey and Logan. Logan's face hardened like stone, and they thought he might explode with anger, but instead, he let out a breath and walked to the window.

"That was the worst case of acting I have ever seen." Logan didn't smile as he leaned over the counter, close enough to smell the tobacco on the old Indian's clothes. "Okay, Mr. Toomey, you have my attention."

Toomey turned around and whispered, "I know your secret."

"What secret would that be?" Logan whispered back.

Toomey inhaled through his nose, then trained his eyes on the burly cop. "You are in great pain, but you don't want to take anything, because you're scared it will cloud your judgment." Toomey took another whiff of the air.

Logan's mouth dropped.

"I can help you with this, Chief David Logan, but you have to listen. Bring us Dan Blackbird."

Before Logan could answer Bobby Morneau and Charlene Hampton burst through the door.

***

CHAPTER 18 - THE NEW HUNTERS [OMACHIW]

1

It was just a grey dot on the top corner of Thomasville Hardware, but once Mick got the tripod level that would all change. They were in the bell tower of Thomasville's First Alliance Church and from this vantage point their line of sight would be clear. The reconnaissance scope was an acquisition they had made two years earlier when they were watching the comings and goings of a suspected grow-op.

"Almost there, Dave." Mick was snapping the black scope on now as Logan scrutinized the grey figure. It was just too hard to tell if it was anything at all. To his right was Old Jake Toomey, who to this point had been quiet and unassuming. He too was fixated on the faraway building, waiting for the big cop to hurry up.

Mick leveled the bubble on the tripod and aimed it at the building. He peered through the eyepiece and then recoiled. "Jesus, what the hell is that?"

I guess this is going to be one fucked up day, Logan mused and then stepped in front of Mick to have a look for himself.

At first, it looked like some kind of wingless gargoyle perched on the corner of the building, and he might have pegged it for a statue, except for the telltale brown that caked its rough skin. He had been on enough crime scenes to recognize the discolored stain was coagulated blood. He released the swivel nut and swung the scope downward, to the street where the bodies lay. His heart sunk when he saw the khaki pants and powder grey uniform shirt of his junior officer.

"Pete," he whispered and pulled his eye away. Guilt tore through him. What would he tell Pete's fiancée, Monica?

He felt eyes on him. It was the old man, waiting for a decision.

The only reason they were up in this bell tower was because of what Bobby and Charlene had told them.

"By tomorrow you'll be begging me to help you," Blackbird had warned.

"Ah, shit!" Mick was back at the eyepiece, now sharing in Logan's sorrow and sudden guilt at not listening to Blackbird.

Poor Pete, lying out there in the street, no one at his side: like bloody road kill.

"It goes into states of reverie after it has gorged," Toomey told them. "It will stay that way for a few hours, but then it will be ready to gorge again."

"We gotta go get him, Dave," Mick cried. "We can't just leave him out there."

"You should do no such thing unless you want more dead," Toomey warned.

"Why can't we just go in and blow it to fucking Saturn while it's asleep?" Mick said.

"It's not sleeping, and it is still very dangerous. In my childhood, I saw a young warrior killed when he approached the Walker in this state. Most likely your infected officer is only alive because it wanted to leave him that way," Toomey wasn't looking at Logan, but at the big scope. "May I look?"

"Go ahead," Logan invited. "Just close your other eye."

Toomey surveyed the scene, murmuring in Chocktee as he did so. He trained the sight on the Walker and took the opportunity to really examine it. "You cannot kill this

Walker, Chief Logan. We can only try and send it back to where it came from."

"How can you be sure?" Collins asked.

"Why?" Logan added. "Why can't we kill it? It's a living thing, is it not?'

"It is an apparition, not of this world. What was once a living being was long ago consumed and discarded." He stepped away from the surveillance scope and rubbed his right eye.

Mick returned to the scope. "What then? What are we supposed to do?" His mind reeled. I know what I believe, and I believe what I see. I saw Kolchak get on the plane. I saw a man and woman butchered in their home and now I see poor Pete Kennedy and the rest killed in the street. He swung the scope back onto the creature. Any illusion it was a statue disappeared: it shifted. "Fuck! It just moved!"

"We don't have much time," Toomey said. "We should get out of this tower before it stirs."

Below they stood in a loose gaggle. West kept the three officers in check. In all, nine people were waiting for them. Two officers, Jack Nero and Roy Findlay, were still dressed in civilian attire. Ken Hill was still wearing the uniform he had worn the day before when called in to do detail on the Sawyer house. His uniform was a train wreck, wrinkled, and in dire need of dry cleaning. Oddball Larson had gone to escort the EMS to Steel and Hardy.

Blackbird, too weak to climb the tower, stayed with his cousin and the other three. While waiting, they talked back and forth in Chocktee.

2

Only half an hour before, the squabbling was muted by the distress call from Hardy. Testimonials from Bobby and Charlene reinforced that something, human or supernatural, had blasted through Angela's Diner. This, coupled with Hardy's distress call, was what finally softened the resistance from Logan and his officers. As a result, they brought Blackbird out of the interview room, where he gazed upon his people for the first time since standing in shame fifteen years before.

He looked almost as old as Toomey now. One of his eyes had fogged up in the pupil, and he was worn and beaten by the relentless pursuit. When they first encountered him at the police station, Toomey barely recognized him, and Proudfoot was aghast.

"Dan?" Proudfoot questioned.

"Hi, Johnny," he said, managing a weak smile that barely hid his exhaustion. Even his voice had aged, losing its wind between syllables. He bore a striking resemblance to Grandfather, and in his aging, the aboriginal side dominated his appearance.

"What happened to you? Oh, Dan, what did we do to you?" Proudfoot moaned. Was this man really his cousin? The young kid that once strutted about the Spirit Woods as his sidekick? He was always smiling, ready to follow him anywhere, sometimes falling victim to his jealous fits, and mean-spirited pranks – and now look at him. "My God, Dan, I'm so sorry."

"It's okay, Johnny. It's made me age."

"We do not have time for this," Toomey scolded, but even he was caught off-guard. Taking in the gaunt figure before him, he recalled that last meeting on the day he banished him, and for a second he searched for something to say. When he could not find the words he shifted his attention on Logan and asked, "Is there a place where we can watch without being seen?"

They were getting ready to load Steel into the ambulance when the first paramedic pulled back from the gurney. Hardy and Oddball were side by side, Oddball's arm slung around Hardy to offer some kind of comfort. As they watched the first paramedic pull away and put his hand to his mouth, Oddball spoke up. "Hey what the heck are you doing?"

Then the second paramedic got a look at what his partner had seen and also jumped back.

It was Steel's eyes: they had snapped open. Then they began to fill up. They did not bulge or increase in size but filled with what one of them would later describe as mercury. The whites and pupils seemed to wash out until they became mirrored, like polished ball bearings. The gurney moved just a bit, and Oddball almost jumped forward to stop it when Steel snapped straight up.

Hardy cried out.

Steel cocked his head back in the direction of the creature. "Kaw seu, Igwhot!"

"Don," she moaned.

"Kaw seu, Igwhot," Steel called out again beckoning the Master, and then he convulsed twice, a thin runner of blood trickling from his left nostril. A maniacal grin crossed his face, and Hardy knew then that this was not Don Steel, but something else.

It might have run amok at that moment and killed them – except for the belt they had secured across his waist and legs. Dumbly it looked about and fumbled with the straps – and then it began to speak. "Bring me the Hunter."

"Steel." Oddball was unlatching something from his belt. "What's the matter with you, Don?"

"I will kill everyone," he hissed turning his attention on Hardy. "Bring me the Hunter, and I will spare your child."

Oddball shot a glance toward Hardy, then back to Steel –
or, the thing he had become.

"You're pregnant?"

"What the hell is going on here?" the first paramedic
piped up.

Hardy didn't respond to Oddball's question. She stood
like a statue, caught in the deadly gaze of its chromium eyes.

"Shut up for now," Oddball barked at the paramedic.

"Kaw seu, Igwhot," Hardy suddenly whispered, never
breaking its stare. Then she reached down and unsnapped
the safety strap on her holster.

"Get down!" Oddball screamed at the paramedics. He
brought up his weapon and pulled the trigger. Steel fell back
on the gurney, letting out a horrific shriek that tore through
their ears. Simultaneously, Hardy collapsed, as if the trance
Steel had her in was all that had been holding her upright.

4

Blackbird knew his journey was almost over. His joints
ached, and his right eye had gone blurry in the night. He
supposed that the aging process came from leaving his body
for another and that the presence of his spirit was what
controlled the clock. He knew he looked terrible, but the
look on Johnny's face told him how bad off he really was.

"When they come down, Johnny, you should go up for a
look," he said.

"You can come with me, Dan; we'll look together."

"No. I can't climb those steps. Something tells me that
I'm going to need every ounce of energy I can find when
Old Jake comes down those stairs."

"I'm sorry, Dan. I should have come with you. You have
paid a high price, and I should have stood by you." He
choked back the tears that wanted to come, but it was hard.

"How do your kids like the Spirit Woods?"

His expression changed, the look of sadness replaced by the smile of a proud father. "My two boys love the Spirit Woods. They got a moose last year. They are very much like we were; fighting, but always together."

"What are their names?"

"John and Dan."

Blackbird laughed. "John and Dan. I wish I could meet them, Johnny."

"You can; when our business is done here, you are coming back with us."

"Yeah, okay."

But Blackbird doubted he would even see tomorrow, let alone walk the Spirit Woods again. He was not saddened by this: he longed for this journey to be over, to put the death and killing behind him. The fiery vengeance he carried in his heart was dwindling. He closed his eyes, exhausted, wanting nothing more than a few minutes of undisturbed sleep.

Monias and Fortier were at the base of the stairwell, waiting for them to return while Proudfoot and Blackbird conversed. Michano came back in from outside, a knitted wool blanket under his arm. Above the clunking of boots echoed through the church as each man took a turn peering through the surveillance scope.

"Johnny Proudfoot," Michano called. "Here is what you asked for."

Proudfoot stood, thanked Monias as he took the blanket and laid it on the lap of his cousin. Once he did, he sat back, watching as Blackbird slowly opened his eyes and looked down on the blanket. "What's this?"

"It's for you," Proudfoot said.

Blackbird slowly unfolded the blanket, unwrapping the enclosed artifact. At first, he thought it was a copy – but then he saw the hairline fracture and understood that he was holding the closest thing on this earth to his grandfather's memory.

"God, Johnny. You've had it all these years."

He traced his fingers down the crooked body of the diamond willow stick. There were seven knots, each shaped like a diamond and brown against the weathered grey wood. At the top, the nub worn by many walks was polished by Grandfather's grasp. It shone not from any lacquer or polish, but from the natural oils in the old man's hand.

Both Proudfoot and Blackbird had wanted that stick all through their adolescence, and on one day it became the source of argument.

When Grandfather caught the two boys fighting, he displayed a side of himself neither had known existed. He pulled them apart and shook each boy violently, yelling, "Stop this now!" Then the fire went out of his eyes, and he told them both to sit down while he did what he did best.

He taught.

"Respect is not measured by who carries a stick. It is measured by what you carry in your head and heart. If your head and heart are empty, no stick can hold you up in the eyes of your people. You both have a lot to learn; lucky for you the Spirit Mother has granted me the wisdom and patience to teach you."

Grandfather stepped out onto the great stone platform that overlooked the Spirit Woods. "I could throw this out there and bear it no mind, but my back is crooked, and my knees are boulders. Do you want me to ache into my dying days just so that you two will not fight over this piece of wood?"

The two cousins lowered their eyes in shame.

"No, Grandfather; it is your wisdom I seek. I am sorry," Proudfoot said first.

"Young Daniel?"

"I want you to walk straight and tell us all your stories. I will not fight over your walking stick again. I do not want it." This was a lie of course: both boys still wanted it, but they would never ask again.

Blackbird recalled the night Johnny stomped off holding the broken pieces, but he never thought about after that. The moment the old man expired the stick became inconsequential.

Now, it had gained new symbolic importance. Blackbird reached into his knapsack and produced the only three items left to his name: the knife, the tattered feather, and the broken dream catcher. Proudfoot glimpsed the feather, his eyes grew wide but he said nothing.

"I need you to do something for me."

"Anything, Dan."

"Do you still have your knife?"

"Yes." Proudfoot lifted his pullover to reveal the sheath that carried the knife.

"I may never get to see my young cousins, but I would be proud if you would pass mine and yours on to them." He handed all three items across to Proudfoot. "These are for you to take back to the Spirit Woods if I fall today. I would also ask that you bring my body home and bury it in the Peace Garden with my mother."

"You have my solemn promise," Proudfoot said, his teeth clenched as he fought to stave off tears. "You are more like him than I could ever be, Dan. I promise to do all these things if you will promise me the same and do one more."

"If I can." Blackbird reached out and touched his cousin's hand.

"If Old Jake doesn't get us all killed today…" He smiled momentarily and then turned serious. "I want you to come home to Spirit Woods and palaver with my sons and me. I want them to meet a true Chocktee. I want them to see that you are no tale told by a fire. That you are the hunter the people of our village speak of often."

"I left in disgrace, Johnny. Why would anyone speak about me other than to say I caused the death of so many people? Children, children have died because of me. I am no great hunter. I am a fool who was too arrogant and stupid to listen to the words of Grandfather."

"No, Dan, that is not true."

"But it is, Johnny." Blackbird wiped a tear from his eye. "If I had listened to you and Grandfather I would never have been fooled. Many people would not have died, including him. I have so much to be ashamed of; nothing about me should be celebrated."

"You have been on the hunt for many years. You have never stopped looking, holding firm to your promise. If not for that we would not be sitting here today. No man is without fault, Dan, and it was not you who cursed our people. Remember that when this is over." Proudfoot pulled his hand away from his cousin and sat back.

No, but I may have cursed these people, Blackbird thought, closing his eyes, then said, "I will return to Chocktee with you if the Spirit Mother permits it."

Beyond them, the three were coming down the cramped stairwell of the bell tower. Their boots clunked on the wooden steps as they made the final flight and Logan looked upon them, trying to think of what to say.

Toomey took care of that.

"We have to move very fast. We need to draw it away from that street and to a place where the earth is sour. There we will face it."

He was not talking to Logan or Mick, but to everyone.

5

"Oh my God, you killed him!" cried the paramedic.

Oddball was leaning over Hardy, desperately trying to bring her around while the other paramedic named Willy watched. He snapped his fingers in front of her face, ignoring the cries from behind for the time being.

"Sandy. Sandy." He shook her, now mindful that she was pregnant. Then he slapped her face gently trying to rouse her. "Sandy, can you hear me?"

"Is she dead?" Paramedic Willy asked.

"How 'bout a bloody hand?" Oddball snapped, and that got him going. "And you! Drama Queen! Get another strap on that man on the stretcher!"

"Why? You killed him."

"He's not dead, pantywaist, I zapped him with a taser! Now strap him in before he wakes up!"

Under his hands, Sandy shifted slightly, and his eyes jerked onto her. Her eyes fluttered beneath their lids. Jesus Christ, let her be normal. Please let her be normal. He unsnapped his gun just in case.

The paramedic quickly strapped Steel down and then cowered away from the gurney. His crotch was moist: he had pissed himself. There was not enough left in his bladder to cause a large stain but had there been it would have expelled it entirely.

Hardy opened her eyes. "Oddball?"

"You okay, Sandy?"

She blinked and looked to the gurney. "Don?"

"He's out like a light, kiddo. I had to taze him. He had you in some kind of a spell. I was afraid you were going to go postal on the lot of us." He smiled, showing off his crooked chompers and then started to help her up.

"The sky," she said, and they all gazed upward at the clouds as they churned and rolled. There was no wind, and yet they were rolling in from all sides. "What is going on, Oddball?"

"I have no idea!" He helped her to her feet with Paramedic Willy's assistance.

"We have to get to the Chief, Oddball! He needs us!"

6

People in Thomasville were beginning to fill the main street, cordoned off from the massacre at Angela's Diner only by a roadblock and a couple of saw horses. The mayhem that had occurred was just a part of the phenomena, and as the officers and natives gathered outside the church in a loose circle of conversation, people from all over town were looking to the skies and the anomalous churning clouds.

Above the thunderheads rolled not from one direction, but from east, west, north, and south. Where they collided they twisted into a great vortex, darkening the sky. Within the black vortex, distant rattles and far off thunderous collisions echoed behind the walls that separated worlds.

"Give me the vial of blood, Dan," Toomey ordered.

Blackbird reached into his bag and produced the vial of black fluid. Toomey took it from him and whispered something in his ear. Blackbird nodded and stepped back. The rest of them were looking to the skies, hypnotized by the majesty. Toomey knew he would lose them if he didn't move fast. He shouted: "Chief Logan, I am going to perform a ritual that will require all! We have very little time. If someone is afraid, send them off!"

He uncapped the vial with one hand and brought up an eagle feather with the other. "We must draw it to the sour earth." He dipped the tip of the feather into the vial and touched it to his own cheek while waving his four companions to come forward. "All of you, focus on me! Do not look to the skies or you will be lulled to sleep!"

That got their attention.

First Proudfoot stood before the old man as he muttered something in Chocktee and brushed the feather against his cheek, leaving a minute smear. It burned into his skin like dry ice, then subsided.

"You bear its mark. You are its keeper. Fear not, brave hunter. The Spirit Mother will guide you."

Then Fortier, Michano, and Monias took their turn. Blackbird did not come forward; he had already made the oath fifteen years before and wore its mark on his cheek. As Toomey performed the ritual, the others tried not to watch the skies and the turning of color while the electric storm silently exploded in flashes and pops overhead.

"Can you feel it?" Logan asked his officers. They all nodded.

There was no sound to be heard, but in their heads was a chorus of crashes and bangs, sounds of symbols and thunderclaps colliding as the fabric of time rippled and hemorrhaged. Logan could feel it pulling his eyes upward, just as the others, and he knew that the sounds he heard inside his head were simulcast with the atmospheric violence above.

Do not look up. It will lull you and steal your thoughts, Toomey was saying, and Logan realized that the words were in his head. He dropped his eyes up to meet the Chief Elder. Toomey nodded, and he heard, Come forward, brave hunter.

"God help us," Jim West said, and Logan realized that they were all looking at the old man and that he had been addressing everyone. The old Indian smiled, and that sent a wave of reassurance through the group.

All except one accepted the invitation.

Above them the apocalypse rolled and flashed, thinning the walls between this world and the next.

Logan did not know if what he was about to do was a sin or a slight of God, and under any other circumstances he might have sworn off the blood oath – but his people were watching. He had to do this.

Even in my darkest moment of uncertainty, they look to me for guidance, he thought, stealing a glimpse of the sky above, watching the black clouds roll a churn, electric flashes pulsing green and blue mutely. The air reeked of ozone and intermingled with unmitigated fear.

Then Logan considered his kids and brought his eyes back to meet the old Indian. Without another thought, he stepped forward. If it would shelter them from this, damn the consequences.

Toomey smiled and when he spoke Logan could smell sweet Indian tobacco pass between them carried by his words. "You are the Elder of this place, a wise protector who has sworn himself to stand against the darkness. Before I mark you now as its keeper and as a hunter, do you swear to do whatever it takes to protect the people of this village?"

"I do." Logan leaned forward.

Toomey brushed the feather across Logan's cheek, making a half-inch smear and he felt it freeze his skin. Even though pain erupted again in his chest, he did not speak. His head became light, and he did not see or hear anything but the words of the old Indian.

"You are a good Elder, David Logan. The spirits and the Guardians embrace and now call upon you. The mark bonds you with my people. You are now a Chocktee, as are all others who step forward from your band." Toomey placed a warm, smooth hand upon Logan's cheek. "When I am done with the others, come back. We must make palaver together, and I will give you something for the pain which plagues you."

Mick followed Logan, not because he was a team player, but because of his wife Nancy and the fear that she might fall victim to what had killed Pete Kennedy.

Toomey gave each man a choice, and each took the oath for their own reasons.

"I am a Christian, Jake Toomey. Am I damning my soul?" West asked after accepting the terms of the pact.

"You are a good man, Jim West, and I could not poison that goodness. Only you can do that." Toomey smiled his kind smile, touched the feather to West's cheek, then added, "Call me Old Jake. We are brothers now."

Nero and Findlay also stepped up. They could feel the change and knew that there was no turning back.

When it was over, they all bore a similar mark on their cheek. All but one. Ken Hill would not participate in the ritual.

"I can't do this," he protested, torn between his faith and the brotherhood of the police detachment. He shook his head look around guilty. "I… I just can't, Chief. Sarge, none of us should be doing this."

"It's okay, Ken. Nobody is forcing anybody to do anything," Mick reassured him.

"I'm sorry. It's the blood; I can't risk it. Risk my soul." He was shrill, defensive and then accusatory. "Quite frankly, Jim West I am surprised at you."

"Really?" West said.

"Have you forgotten about the church?" But his tone was already slipping. "This….. this is a sin against God!"

West said, "Ken, I understand your fear. I am scared too but look around. There are no passages in the bible about skinwalkers or native ritual. That leaves me questioning whether my faith is 100% accurate. From what I've seen today I can't say that anymore."

"Don't say that! You are the most decent man I know! Don't be taken in by this."

"Now just a bloody minute," Logan piped up. "Nobody is taking anyone in, and nobody is forcing anything on anybody!"

Hill dismissed Logan as if he weren't there. "Jim, we can still walk away from this!"

"Young man," Toomey interrupted. "You have seen the creature, what it has done."

"Those who take the mark of the beast are damned to serve him on earth and in hell. You are marking them with the blood of the beast. It has been prophesized."

Hill was backing away from them now.

"Go! We do not have time for a bible lesson. Go to your people; we don't need you," Toomey dismissed. "Time is short."

Hill gave West one last disapproving glance and headed for the police car. He walked on, waiting for them to stop him from leaving, but they didn't. Instead, they watched him go, some questioning their own judgment, the Chocktee dismissing him.

"Well, that was fun," Logan said. "Anyone else?" As soon as he had uttered it, he felt a twinge of remorse. Hill was a good man, a good husband, and father and it was unfair to judge him this way.

No one spoke. The sounds from the sky above echoed and clanked inside their heads as the walls continued to thin. It was a chorus of clattering, some mechanical, others explosive. Whatever it was that moved behind the membrane that rippled across the heavens was intensifying.

"We must draw it back to the sour ground," repeated Toomey, breaking their thoughts and silencing the chorus inside their heads.

"You keep saying that. Sour ground, what does that mean?" Collins asked. He brought his hand up to touch the mark, then thought better of it.

"A place where evil lingers; a place no man should care to step," Blackbird said without looking. "The only question is how."

"Hopper's cornfield," Logan said.

"Yes, that is the place where we must confront it," Toomey said. "Jim West, you will take my five brothers to this cornfield. There John Proudfoot will direct you." Toomey pointed to the members of his band. "You must go now."

7

Oddball and the paramedics lifted Steel into the ambulance as Hardy stood a safe distance away. He had told her not to get too close in case he awoke again. She held one hand protectively over her belly. She loved Don Steel, but whatever that thing had done to him could not be allowed to harm their unborn child.

"Alright, you're going to take him straight through to Thomasville General and no removing his straps under any circumstances," Oddball ordered.

"Are you two going to escort us?" Willy asked.

"No; we've got other business."

"What other business?"

Oddball shook his head impatiently, then pointed up toward the sky which was now turning dark ashen grey. He locked eyes with Willy and said, "You take care of my friend, but don't dare take those straps off."

The other paramedic aptly named Panty Waist was standing impatiently by the driver's door. "Come on, Willy, let's go!"

Willy climbed into the back of the ambulance and Oddball grabbed the door to close it. Just before shutting it he leaned in and handed the taser gun over. "No stops. He breaks loose you fucking zap him." Then he slammed the door, and the ambulance pulled away. He turned to Hardy, who watched the ambulance depart, regret radiated across her face. She had no choice. They had to join the Chief and the others because whatever that was on top of Randy Maytum's hardware store was going to be waking up very soon.

"Get in," Oddball said, and opened the driver's door of his cruiser. She climbed in, still watching as the ambulance rounded the corner with the father of her unborn child – and then it was out of sight.

Please don't let him die, she thought.

"Okay, they said they were heading to the old church, so that's where we're heading." Oddball picked up the radio handset. "Base, come in!"

"Go ahead, Keith." It was Sabrina; she was the only one on the force who called him that.

"Verify Chief and party are still at the old church?"

"Roger that. They are static at the moment."

"Copy that. Corporal Steel is on his way to Thomas Gen, and we are headed to Chief's location. Please notify me of any changes."

Oddball hung the handset up, his heart pumping now, the adrenaline making him shake a bit. Most people would be ready to break down, but Oddball Larson was wound up and lived for this type of excitement. A former member of the Airborne, Oddball, was what most considered a hair on the crazy side. He didn't look the part, but his gangly arms were wiry bands of steel beneath the Thomasville Police uniform, and he was deadly with numerous weapons. A marksman with both a pistol and rifle, Oddball was still an active reservist who had served in Afghanistan. When he came home, he was greeted by his friends and family, who looked upon his voluntary tour as a necessity of service.

Truth be known, he couldn't wait to go back.

"Oh my God," Hardy mumbled.

Scores of townspeople lined the streets as they moved down Yale Road East. They looked like they were getting ready for the Santa Claus parade, except for the fact that all of them were listening to the skies now and with good reason. It was turning from ashen grey to dark blue and black. The clouds which rolled and churned looked surreal, moving as though behind an enormous pane of glass. The sky appeared liquid. Drops and waves distorted the panoramic view, dancing to the dead silence uninterrupted by even a whisper of wind. In the darkness below the liquid sky were lights which moved chaotically. Any minute now she thought the four horsemen of the apocalypse would break out of the clouds and let loose the end times.

"Woe to you, oh earth and sea," Oddball whispered.

Hardy gave him a disapproving and frightened look.

"What?" He smiled his boneyard smile, then frowned. "Bad timing."

They rolled past the members of their community. None turned away from the sky to even consider the police car.

In their group was the coroner Jeff Henderson, standing there hypnotized, still wearing his lab smock and a pair of bloodied surgical gloves.

"No shit, Oddball. Get us to the Chief."

8

Mick tried to call Nancy, but she didn't answer. None of them were answering their phones, and this had all more than a little worried. "I can't raise her."

"Me either," Nero said, lowering the cell phone from his ear.

Each of them was becoming increasingly agitated and distracted. Logan was about to call his ex-wife on his cell, but Toomey placed a hand over his. He snapped the phone shut and put it in his pocket.

The calls were getting through, but no one was answering; they were all in the streets lining the roadways, standing on their porches and in their fields watching the skies, spellbound. Nancy Collins stood outside the veterinary clinic, holding a ringing cell phone absently. A block and a half down stood Jeff Henderson who had the blood of Frank Sawyer drying on the latex gloves he wore. The others, including Judy Nero, stood next to Bobby Morneau and Charlene Hampton, who had tried to make a getaway but were drawn to the crowds. All were transfixed, succumbing to the chorus of rattles and bangs, lulled into a state of waking sleep as the walls continued to thin.

Even Sabrina stepped out into the street when she saw the crowd gathering, and when she gazed upward she heard the sounds and felt herself being lulled into darkness.

She never got her call through to Logan.

"Your families are fine," Toomey soothed. "They are standing in awe of the coming storm, but our time is short. Mick Collins, I need you and Jim West to accompany my people to the sour ground. Daniel, you will wait for him there. Johnny Proudfoot will direct the rest of you what to do." Now Toomey was ordering them, taking charge. He knew that it was only a matter of time before the Walker awakened from its slumber – and then it would be too late. "Chief Logan, tell them."

"Mick, saddle up! Get these people moving!"

Mick came to life then, putting his trust in his friend and boss while praying he wouldn't live to regret it.

"Let's go," he barked. "You heard the Chief!"

They all began mounting cars. When Logan stepped forward to get in his, Toomey placed a hand on his arm.

"No, we are staying here. We still have business."

"Dave," Mick called after him.

"Go. We'll be along soon."

"You're sure?"

"Yeah, I'm sure. You take Blackbird and the others to Hopper's farm, and we'll join you when we're done here." Logan looked past Mick to see Oddball and Hardy rolling up and asked Toomey. "What about them?'

Overhead the sky darkened even more as the cruiser came to a stop. Oddball jumped out first and gave the Chief a queer look. "You got something on your face, Chief."

Logan touched the mark absently. "How's Don?"

"Headed for Thomasville General. Some spooky shit going on there, but then it looks as though you have had your fill, too." Oddball looked at Toomey. "Hey, he's got a mark on his face too."

"We all have, Oddball," Mick chimed in, then turned to Logan and Toomey. "What do we do now?"

"Come here," Toomey called to Oddball and Hardy, pulling out the feather and vial once more. He had been quick to mark them, no longer showing patience or offering warm words or wisdom. He was about as subtle as the preacher performing a wedding ceremony in a church that is on fire. "You are the keepers of the ritual and hunters. You are all brothers and sisters bound by the oath of blood," he said, dabbed them both, and then ordered: "Now go with them."

***

CHAPTER 19 - BLOOD AND SMOKE

1

The convoy pushed south-east, away from town and toward the sour ground of Hopper's farm. As they drove, scores of men and women stood like scarecrows by the road, staring toward the sky as it continued its dance of light and liquid.

"Holy shit," Mick gasped to Blackbird. "Is this real?"

"It's real," Blackbird replied, and Mick could see he was crying. He didn't ask why; he just watched the police vehicles behind him and the SUV filled with native men who looked to be from a different time.

Then on the side of the road, facing in the same direction as they, was a car he recognized. Standing in front of it were three figures: a husband, wife, and son. On the back bumper, a sticker proclaimed: We visited the Devil's Tower! Beside that, another sticker said: Jesus is coming! Are you ready? That and the luggage Donald Wakeman had tied firmly to the roof of his car was a dead giveaway. *Guess you might get to meet the Messiah today, Wakeman – or maybe the Anti-Christ.* He glanced at them through the rearview mirror as they passed. They stood as stiff as mannequins.

"You know them?" Blackbird asked.

"Yeah. The boy is the one who saw Hopper burying Tommy Parkins."

"I see." Blackbird gripped the diamond willow stick in both hands. "When we get there you will need to help me to the center of that field."

"Why?"

"Because I'm the bait."

2

Lighting a cigar, Logan watched his people go and wondered if he would ever see them again. The pain which he had kept so well hidden dragged over the center of his chest like jagged fingernails.

Toomey was looking up at him: the old man wanted one of his cigars. Logan reached into his breast pocket and pulled one out.

"Did anyone ever tell you," Toomey said, puffing on the cigar after lighting up with an old Zippo, "that you look kind of like Lee Marvin, but fatter?" On the lighter was a weathered logo. Just above Toomey's thumb, he read the worn lettering: Recon 101 and below that: Shock Force.

Logan chuckled, forgetting the lighter. "Well, you're too short for Chief Dan George."

Toomey blew out a smoke ring and smiled. "Ah yes, Little Big Man. White Devil's being taught lessons. Again." He smiled and lifted a thumb to show his approval, but there really was no malice in the statement. There were many layers to Old Jake Toomey. He was a leader, an Elder, a warrior, a mind reader and now it appeared he was also a comedian. Logan felt at ease with this old Indian.

"What now, Old Jake?" he asked.

"How long will it take them to get to the farm?"

"Twenty minutes."

Logan had an idea they would not be following them.

"That should be enough time."

Toomey reached under his shirt and produced a leather satchel the size of a clutch purse and set it on the hood of the cruiser. From it, he pulled four smaller bags, each decorated with their own colored beads. He then pulled out a small pipe, approximately six inches long and fashioned from a piece of jade. It was a beautiful work of craftsmanship, polished green and round in its neck where the cup had been carved out. It was solid jade: not a vein of any other rock or mineral tainted its purity. Toomey placed this, too, on the hood. Then he set down the vial of blood.

"I promised you that I would help you with your pain, and I always keep my word, Chief David Logan."

Logan considered the pipe, the urge to resist smoking something that could quite possibly be illegal. This tugged at his conscience. Even as the scourge of death ran through his body, the skies overhead churned and flashed and in the center of town the street looked like a war zone. Even now he was thinking like a cop. And why not? That was who he was.

But the jagged fingernails dug into his sternum again, reminding him that the agony would only get worse – so he decided to accept the old Indian's magic.

"Alright, Old Jake. I'll smoke some of that stuff, but from here on call me Dave or Chief."

"The smoking of the pipe has been a ritual with my people longer than I can even begin to tell you." He was stuffing bits of tobacco from each satchel into the cup, not looking up, concentrating on the amounts. "This pipe has been passed from one Elder to the next and will leave my hand for the next in line when it is my time to join my brothers and sisters in the passage."

"The passage?"

He was lifting the pipe now, pressing the contents down into the cup with his index finger. "Yes. When the Spirit Mother calls, I will be beckoned to the passage, where my brothers and sisters will guide me to the Guardians. The passage is very beautiful. It is a portico between this world and the next."

Logan watched the old man lift the pipe up and flip open the Zippo lighter. He snapped the flint wheel as he had done thousands of times before. The contents glowed blood orange, and the sweet smell was inviting to even the most hardcore anti-smoker.

"Is this going to dope me up, Old Jake?"

"No. It will open your mind and release you from any pain or anxiety." Toomey smiled and took a deep draw, filling his lungs to capacity. He then handed it across to his new friend as he expelled the smoke. "Draw deeply… Dave."

Taking the artifact in his hand, he was amazed at its weight and feel. When he raised it to his lips, he felt the moisture left behind from Toomey's draw. He checked the time. His watch read 11:45. Then he drew on the pipe. He expected he would cough at first, but it was smooth, non–intrusive, and a wave rolled over him that was reminiscent of the days when he and his high school friends blasted hash in the garage of his teenage pal Brian Burke.

Goddamn, I'm smoking up.

He felt a buzz, but it was not at all disconnected. His mind had become completely clear except for the fact that he'd forgotten to exhale. Toomey loomed there in front of him as the sky danced psychedelically above in splashes of emerald and blue, rippling ethereal.

"Let it out and pass me the pipe, Dave." Toomey was smiling mischievously like they were two teenagers smoking up in the woods.

Or Burke's garage, he thought and laughed aloud. Toomey had already taken another draw and was handing it back. How long has the old guy been standing there smiling? I wonder if he can read my thoughts. *Boy, Old Jake, my pal Burkee would have thought you were one mystical dude.*

He once again took the cool stone into his grasp, understanding that it had been passed on for centuries and its bowl filled and refilled. He wondered what this pipe had gone through to travel to this place.

A relaxed feeling washed over him. His pain subsided with it.

"It's the Jimson Weed," said Toomey and motioned with his hand. "Take another; it will clear your mind."

Logan took another deep draw and passed it back across while Toomey fumbled with something from his bag.

This stuff is great! I feel focused and, Jesus, where are my aches and pains?

Toomey had the vial open. He was heating the last of the black tar. "You feel better, Dave. Yes?"

"Great stuff, Old Jake. I gotta get some of this off you when we're done saving the world from Indian shape-changers." He laughed a bit and decided that maybe he was just a little high.

"Skinwalker," Jake said, holding the pipe below the vial as he poured the last of its black contents into the bowl. The glowing embers sizzled as the blood smothered them, and then a smell not unlike burning hair rose up. "He is a skinwalker, the servant of the black orb. A bastard child of Wendigo. His name was Jackanoob once, but now he is only darkness and pain."

"That stinks. What are you up to with that?"

"We are going to draw from its blood and gather the knowledge we need to beat it." Now he stuffed more tobacco into the pipe, burying the tar beneath it.

"What I am about to show you will come hard and fast. Do you trust me?"

Logan considered the question. Overhead the sky pulsed and rippled, a mile off, a monster was perched atop a building digesting its breakfast, and he was waiting to die from a killer he could only feel moving through him, eating his insides.

Do I trust you? A good question.

"Is your pain gone?" asked Toomey.

"Yes, it is." Logan raised his thumb to mimic Toomey's Little Big Horn seal of approval. "Can you give this white devil some for later?"

Laughing, Toomey said, "You are no longer a white devil; I cured you of that when I made you a Chocktee Hunter. To answer your question: yes, I will give you all my magic, but this next part must be of your own free will. One draw and we will know what it knows, see what it sees – and then we will be ready. So I ask again: do you trust me?"

Logan decided he had no choice. If they didn't die today, he would wind up in a hospice probably doped out of his mind as the plague inside him converted his cells to dark matter. So he said, "I trust you, Old Jake."

Toomey handed the pipe over. "You will draw first. Do not be afraid; I will guide you."

"I never smoke alone."

"I will take a draw as well, Dave, and be at your side; a guide as we walk through passages. Together we will gather strength and knowledge."

Logan stared deep into the old man's eyes. There was no deception in them – and he knew the same was true of Toomey's heart.

Time was short. He brought the pipe up to his lips and waited as Toomey rolled the round stone over the flint. The flame licked upward, an amber tongue with a rim of black. The odor of butane filled the air.

"Come let us palaver."

And with that Logan abandoned all caution and drew on the pipe as the flame was pulled downward and ignited the mixture of blood and herb. At first, it was warm and sweet, the last of the resin from the first mixture burning off – then came the bitter blood of the creature's dark heart. It tasted like copper pennies, old and caustic, and with it came a cold that felt like dry ice burning the roof of his mouth.

Poisoning me. Infected.

The smoke rolled across his tongue, down his throat, and into his lungs. He could feel his core temperature begin to drop at an alarming rate. Had he seen what the old Indian was seeing he never would've drawn from the pipe. The veins that were visible on his neck and hands turned dark almost instantaneously, but it was eyes that were the worst. Like Steel, they seemed to wash out, at first becoming clear marbles – then liquid mercury rolled into them, and they turned to chrome.

"Mamiswin," Logan said in the old language, which was universal for trust.

Toomey took the pipe gently from Logan and brought it to his own lips.

It was like watching an old television blink out. One moment Toomey was standing before him. Next, there was a crash of white noise and the light which stimulated the cones and rods in his optic nerve closed off and drifted away. Logan cried out, and for a moment thought he might be dying, when all around him he saw the specter off in the distance. He could hear something: water dripping, a drum, voices, shrieks: a symphony of thousands of sounds all fighting for dominance.

This is the sound of madness, he thought.

Toomey was suddenly beside him.

"We must walk," Toomey said, and suddenly they were moving forward through the void. The dripping sounds grew louder about them as they went. "This world is just one among many; a staging ground where the light and the darkness try to seize ownership of our hearts."

"Where are we going?" Logan asked. Below his feet, he could see water, and beneath its skin things moved. Some green with life, others black with death.

"Look into the passage, Dave," Toomey urged, and he watched a glowing green orb pass directly under him. It was stunning, and the light was blinding as it pushed past the skin. The water rippled as the droplets of rain from above plopped downward. "That is a Guardian. There is no evil in it, just love. It is the vessel which guides us between worlds. When a man dies, a Guardian carries him on, and if you accept it, they will stand vigil as you breathe your last breath."

Logan wanted to turn to Toomey, to ask him questions: but Toomey was not really there; not in body anyway. So he turned back and watched the Guardian move off its light dimming.

Is that what will come for me?

"Yes. Now we must walk."

And so they did – but as they moved on, the warmth of the Guardian was gone, and Logan felt something else. Something colder.

3

They parked the cars on the road and dismounted in front of Hopper's house. John Proudfoot walked over to Collins' cruiser as they got out. The three Elders stayed in the SUV, waiting for him to return. This was the last meeting they would have before this was over. Or before or they were all dead, Proudfoot thought.

Drawing up to the car, he said, "Do you have the map of the area?"

"Yeah." Mick reached into the cruiser and pulled out the topographical map they had been using to unearth Hopper's graveyard. He spread it out on the police car's hood and pointed. "We are here."

Proudfoot examined the map, the perimeter road that ran around the Wakeman and Hopper Farm and the woods that stretched through it and to the north. "Here is where Dan must be," he said, pointing to the center of the graveyard where the ground swelled above the rest of the terrain. Using his finger, he drew an imaginary circle around where

Blackbird would be waiting. "Here is where you will place all your people."

"Where are you guys going?" Mick asked.

"We will set up outside the circle, one to the north, south, east, and west. When it comes, stay out of sight until you hear the drums: then close the circle."

"Drums?" Mick asked.

"The drums of Chocktee," Blackbird said. "When the drums start the circle must be closed and not broken under any circumstances."

"Do you hear that?" Proudfoot called to all of them. "The circle must not be broken! If it breaks out, we will not be able to get it back."

"No matter what – even if it kills – the circle must not be broken," Blackbird added.

They all nodded.

"How do we know it will come?" Oddball chimed in.

"Jake Toomey will see to that," Proudfoot said and turned to his cousin. "We will palaver in the Spirit Wood, cousin. I only wish I could stand with you, but my duty is with the drums."

"I hope to meet your children, but I am glad to see you, no matter the outcome." Blackbird reached out, setting his free hand on Proudfoot's shoulder, steadying himself on the diamond willow stick with his other.

"Grandfather's magic." Proudfoot placed a hand over his and hugged him. "I love you, Dan. I always have," he said, and before Blackbird could respond, he turned to others, raising his voice again. "When the circle closes, all of you chant 'Kihci-manitow' over and over. One after another around the circle, use the drums for cadence. Do not stop and do not break the circle!"

Proudfoot let go of his cousin and left him standing there. He walked over to West, and they spoke briefly. The officer handed Proudfoot something, and he turned and marched to the SUV.

"Kihci-manitow," Blackbird said absently.

"What does that mean?" Hardy asked. She pronounced it phonetically: "Kee-kee-man-ee-towe?"

"Great Spirit God," Blackbird said, then called after his cousin as he mounted the vehicle. "Johnny!"

Proudfoot stuck his head out the window.

"Grandfather's magic!" He raised the diamond willow high above his head like a Chocktee Warrior about to go into battle. It was a sight to see, his long gray hair hanging about his weathered face as the spirits tossed and turned in the clouds above. "Spirit Woods."

Proudfoot smiled at his cousin, then pulled his head back into the SUV and peeled off down Van Dyke Road. For a moment they watched the dust cloud kicked up by the SUV, then it fell flat as the air became thick and still from the impending storm.

"Let's get these vehicles out of sight," Mick barked.

4

Logan felt like he was moving through a dream, but he was lucid. From beside him, in his right ear, the affable Toomey narrated the purpose of their quest. Much as Blackbird walked with his grandfather and watched the fall of Jackanoob, Logan also absorbed the knowledge of the creature and its origin.

"It is always hungry," Toomey told him. "A curse for eating of the man."

Logan watched the Elder Jackanoob bargain with the Wendigo. Like a 360-degree movie he watched as the beast stood before the old man, its grey skin pulled against its ribs, tattered and malignant with sores. Watched it pull the old man up and cut open his cheek with its razor claw then spit into the wound, understanding this was a pact. He thought of the scar on Blackbird's cheek.

"Our destiny was sold," Toomey said.

Now the vision changed and he watched the men of Chocktee preparing for the coming equinox. They moved fast, marking spots in the woods, carving out the calendar he had seen scrawled out on the basement floor in Rhonda Sawyer's blood.

All the while he watched Jackanoob standing with another younger Native as they oversaw the preparation, and even without Toomey's words he understood that the old man was doing what the creature had told him.

"Prepare them," the Wendigo said.

Time shifted.

Then the poison began to take him. As time marched forward, the Chief Elder would stop and slip into states of waking sleep as his people watched in dismay. In these states he would chant; other times he would stare blankly, drool flowing from his mouth.

Something terrible is coming, Logan thought.

"He knew he would not be able to stay among his people," Toomey schooled.

The sun rose and fell over Spirit Woods in the panoramic vision before them, and a double exposure of the Chocktee calendar turned and clicked over.

"Goodbye," Jackanoob said to the high council in the Chocktee tongue, and Logan understood. Sadness settled into his heart as he realized that the old man was going off to martyr himself.

They watched the old man walk away to the tune of a single drum tap-tapping as the sun crested the morning sky. The snow was gone, and the vernal equinox was in full bloom. He did not look back at his people for fear he would lose his nerve.

"He's going to die," Logan said.

"Worse," Toomey replied.

Out there in the woods, it was waiting for him. With each step, he could hear its call, feel its infection moving inside him. As he walked his skin became yellow with jaundice, the muscles in his face began to melt away, and the whites of his eyes darkened. He stripped off his clothes, dropping them to the ground, never to be worn again, and the madness ate into him like a horde of earwigs.

The pain, the pain of hunger; it hurts so badly.

Logan shuddered, feeling Jackanoob's tortured thoughts. As did Toomey, and for the moment they felt nothing but sympathy as he transformed from man to skinwalker.

His marrow became hot. His bones twisted and warped, and his arms became long and skeletal, bands of muscle twisting around the underneath the grey translucent skin. His head began to swell, his eye sockets doubling, and while his jaw started to fall unhinged, the agony he felt was horrible. Tendons stretched and snapped, then crawled under his skin like tapeworms eating their way through and reattaching themselves in unnatural places.

The old man carried on forward, no longer his former self, but a hybrid. Then he stumbled, falling on all fours, and as he did the small and ring fingers on both hands shriveled and rotted off. His remaining appendages began to twist and hook into deadly talons.

He held up one claw, looked at it through the new bulbous eyes that swam with mercury and let out a shriek of pain and angst that could be heard by every man, woman, and child in the Chocktee Nation.

Jackanoob was gone, but it wasn't over.

In the woods, the beckoning of his Master Wendigo called.

He hissed. "Kaw seu Igwhot."

This was answered by a higher pitched shriek. The thing that had been Jackanoob tensed up, still on all fours, black yolky drool spilling from its mouth as the vertebrae on its back pushed against the thin rotted skin. Turning its head once more Logan caught the creature's mirrored eyes, for a moment thinking he saw the tortured Elder's reflection.

It shrieked again and looked to the woods where its Master waited.

For a second it hesitated, turning back toward the village, wanting to sate the new unbearable hunger which plagued it – but then the commanding shriek called once more, and it tore up a clump of the forest floor in frustration and shrieked aloud.

From behind its eyes, they watched as it shot forward. Branches whipped by, animals in proximity bolted left and right as it tore through the forest with unimaginable speed. Neither Toomey nor Logan spoke as it drew closer to its Master. Anxiety rippled through it.

It entered the clearing where the bargain was struck. There the Master waited, clutching a tree. It was not unlike the creature that was once Jackanoob, but much larger. Below it lay the carcass of a moose, its belly torn open, killed only an hour before, the warmth of life force still clutched the forest floor.

The wendigo spoke in a language that was not Chocktee, but a series of hisses and shrieks that only the former Jackanoob could begin to comprehend. It was demanding something. Jackanoob cowered at first, then crawled on his belly toward the Master.

It reached down and snatched him up, holding him there in its clutch, studying. From behind them, the air seemed to change and swell and undulate just as the sky in the waking world was doing. Blue fog rolled into the clearing, seemingly from nowhere, while lights moved within its haze. The bigger creature could only be seen from the waist up, but it was twice the size of Jackanoob, and as it held him there, the mist began to pulse with light.

What is it doing? Logan thought.

Toomey answered: "It's taking him back to the void."

A sphere began to rise from the haze behind them. As it rose blue light flashed within the sphere and it hovered ominously, dwarfing them. The orb was approximately twenty-five feet in circumference and semi-transparent. It hummed as it waited for its occupants.

"Some Guardians serve the light and the dark. This is a Guardian of the dark world," Toomey said, but there was no need. Logan understood.

As the light within the orb began to grow brighter, the fascia started to tear open, revealing its true interior.

Jackanoob began to squeal, struggling to pull from the Master's embrace. Inside the sphere was blue mist – and beyond that, another world altogether. One with bare rocky hills and darkened skies. Upon the peaks of stone, things not of this world moved and twisted, painfully, hungrily waiting for the sentry to bring forth the new meat.

"Oh my God," Logan said aloud now.

Jackanoob clawed at the air. No longer able to formulate words, his shrieks were cries of terror and remorse. Then they entered the black orb. The humming and pulsing blue light intensified – then Logan and Toomey were moving again, pulling away from the scene before them.

Logan was thankful.

5

Paralyzed! Can't move! In front of him, Jake Toomey, also frozen, his eyes locked and unblinking.

The vision had been so surreal, but it was fading. There had been more, after the exit of the creature from this world, visions of murder and mayhem, anguish. It was too overwhelming, so much information. Trying to stuff all of this into their minds might kill them, Logan guessed.

Toomey blinked, and Logan wiggled his big toe. The paralysis was easing. Toomey managed a smile, a bit of drool pooling in the corner of his mouth.

Two toes now, and a finger. Logan wondered, How long were we out? Is the creature still there? Up there on the hardware store? Or!

Terror swept through him.

Oh no! What if it's standing over us!

He struggled to bring his arm and get a look at his watch. Dread fueled anxiety, and he started working the tendons in his legs while his mind hammered away: *Gotta get up! Gotta get the fuck up!*

Stay calm, Toomey's eyes said, but he still couldn't manage the words necessary to ease Logan's panic. The old man moved his mouth and swallowed. His throat clicked dryly. He was even more sluggish than Logan.

Using all his strength, Logan pulled his arm up, an invisible 100-pound weight attached to it. Overhead the sky still rolled and churned, but it had darkened. He was sure they had been gone for hours, even days. Turning his wrist he tried to focus on the face of his watch, but the light from the sky reflected across the plastic cover, making it impossible to read.

God damn it!

He freed his other arm, which was trapped under his body, a chunk of useless meat plagued with pins and needles. So he used his good arm to climb up. He sucked in a great breath of air and was instantly impacted with a thudding migraine.

Logan looked around to make sure they were alone, feeling for his sidearm. They were – at least for the moment – although it hardly eased his anxiety. He desperately wanted to bound back up the church steps and into the bell tower to check the scope but knew it would be a while before he could walk normally, let alone run.

Toomey groaned and rolled on his side.

Poor Old Jake. This must be hurting him twice as much as me.

He wiped off the face of his watch and pushed the button to light it.

Eleven forty-eight, he thought. A bit of saliva ran down his cheek. "That can't be." The watch flipped over to 11:49 AM. *So it hadn't stopped.*

"Time moves faster over there," croaked Toomey. "That is why young Daniel Blackbird has aged." His back was to him, leaving Logan to wonder how Old Jake had known he was looking at his watch.

Logan tried to stand up, stumbling at first, then using the bush guard on the car to support himself. Toomey stayed on his butt, leaning back on his hands, waiting for his body to forgive him.

"What do we do now, Old Jake?" He rubbed his temples.

"Standing up would be a good start," Toomey replied. He tried to push up but stumbled backward. Logan caught him and helped him to his feet, then brushed dirt from the road off of Toomey's shoulder.

"My head feels like I went on a two-day bender, but according to my watch we were only out a couple minutes." Logan was looking at his watch again. *Still 11:49 AM?*

"There are no clocks where we were; that is why you feel burned out." Toomey had the pipe in his hand again but was using a knife to clean the contaminated contents from the bowl. "If we had stayed longer you would have aged, and I would have died."

"I don't think I can do that again. Shouldn't we get going? Join the others?"

"Shortly; we have one piece of business left." He was burning the contents out of the bowl with his Zippo, blackening the jade pipe as he burned off the last of the creature's blood.

Logan wished he had a couple aspirin to chew on. "What would that be?"

Toomey looked up from his work and took a deep breath. "I am going to give you my pipe. You will give it to Daniel when you reach the sour ground."

"Where are you going?"

"I am going to meet Jackanoob and lure him to the sour ground."

"How the hell do you intend to do that?"

"The devil is in the details," Toomey laughed, looking up at his newfound brother. "I am going to invite him."

6

They were driving on Bench Road toward the massacre at Angela's Diner and passed more people standing motionless on each side of the road. Logan wondered if they could see what was happening in the sky if the anomaly was showing up everywhere.

It stretches from horizon to horizon. Is this happening around the world?

"It is," Toomey answered. "But only we can see it."

"This happens every year, but we don't see it."

"Twice, and yes, but do not feel bad Dave; none of my people except the chosen ones have had this type of vision. The walls have thinned, and the struggle is at a standstill: the light and the dark are equal." Toomey was reaching into his jacket now, pulling out a smaller pipe and the sachets containing the herbs and tobacco. "You know something I have come to love in this life, Dave."

"What?"

"Movies. That is the one good thing you white devils brought to this land. Last year Johnny Proudfoot saw that my VHS tape machine died and bought me a DVD player and about forty movies."

"What kind of movies?" Logan was thinking about the Little Big Horn reference.

"All kinds: war, comedy, a couple of good Westerns – but the Indians always get the shaft. Did you ever see the movie Prime Cut?"

"No, can't say I have."

"It's a crime movie where an evil cattle rancher grinds his competition up in a sausage making machine. Lee Marvin was the leading man, and Gene Hackman plays the bad guy. You look a lot like Lee Marvin in that movie Dave, but…"

"Yeah, I know. Fatter."

"Well that too, but I was going to say you are a man of many layers. Marvin always looks angry or doubtful. That is the real difference between you two. You look like a thinker. I can tell from your people that you are a good Elder."

"Elder? I never thought about myself that way."

They were three blocks away.

"This will be good. Pull the car over. I must walk from here."

Logan pulled the car to the curb, put it in the park and looked up the road. He wanted to go and see. He felt a hand touch his and turned to see that Toomey was handing him the satchel. "I don't feel right about you going up there alone, Old Jake."

"This is a walk I must take alone. I have my business, you have yours." He placed the leather satchel in his hand. "Before you get to the sour ground smoke a bit of the herb in the satchel. It should see you through your end of this business."

"I'm not going to see you again." Logan placed his own hand over the old man's.

"Yes, you will; just not in this world." And with that Toomey released his hand, opened the car door and got out. "I am an old man whose friends have left this earth to run through the passage into the next world. It is my time." There was no fear on the old Indian's face: his eyes were bright, his demeanor cheerful. His hand settled onto Logan's right shoulder. "It has been my pleasure to have known you in this world, and I will promise you one thing before I go."

"What is that?" Logan asked.

"When your time comes, I will meet you in the passage and lead you to the next world. There we will make palaver."

Toomey released his shoulder then. "Give the pipe to Daniel Blackbird. He is the Chief Elder of our people now. He will lead the council until the breath is gone from his body."

And Toomey closed the door.

Watching the old man walk up the hill, Logan felt a bit like crying. Old Jake raised his hand over his head, palm open, but did not look back. Logan put the car in drive but held the brake as he continued to watch Toomey depart. The old Indian kept moving, and though Logan wanted to see him disappear he knew the time was short, and he had other people who needed him.

"Goodbye, Old Jake," he said and started for the sour ground.

***

CHAPTER 20 - THE DRUMS OF CHOCKTEE

1

"Oh Spirit Mother, be my eyes, be my ears, be my strength as I walk forth toward the darkness," Toomey chanted in Chocktee, cresting the hill where Hardy and Steel had arrived a few hours earlier. Both Steel and Kennedy's cruisers were still sitting on the hill, silent witnesses to the events of that morning. Toomey did not feel fear; he already knew the outcome. "Protect my brothers and sisters as they stand strong before the darkness Show them the way and the light."

"Igasho," the creature hissed from above.

Toomey looked up to see it peering down at him from the perch it had taken on the hardware store. "Igasho was my great-grandfather; my name is Jake Toomey, Jackanoob."

"Jackanoob is dead. You look like Igasho, but he would not be so stupid to walk here alone." The walker seemed serene, in the mood for conversation. "What would possess you to come into my midst unarmed?"

"I come with a message for you and a call to challenge."

It scrambled down the wall in a blur, blowing past him and perching atop Kennedy's police car. "A challenge? You must think me stupid."

"The hunter calls you to the sour ground where you killed those boys between the stalks of corn. There he will face you." Toomey would not look directly into its eyes, instead focusing on the creature's cavernous mouth.

"Why would I go there when there is so much to eat here? I gave the hunter a chance to walk away; he chose to ignore it. I will be eating the prey of this world long after his bones turn to dust." It wiped the spittle from its chin and smiled.

"No, Jackanoob. You will go."

The creature cackled a piercing shriek that spun out in a ripple of octaves.

2

Logan was two miles away from Hopper's farm when he felt the pain erupt in his chest. It was back, and it had come with a furious vengeance that almost made him crash the car.

This is how it will feel in the end, he thought. *An assault of agonizing torture until I either have to be so doped up that I'm in diapers or crying like a baby.*

He hated not being able to control this, at its mercy whenever to reared its ugly head. He pulled the car over and leaned back in the seat. To his right on the bench seat, laid the satchel of herbs Toomey had left him. The second pipe was lashed onto the satchel with a piece of cord made from animal hide.

Gotta be quick about this.

He filled the pipe.

3

The party at Hopper's farm spread out into a circle. Daniel Blackbird stood in the center, holding his grandfather's walking stick and waiting for death to come calling. The abandoned farm looked like a battlefield scored by tire tracks and gravesites that could have passed for abandoned trenches. The smell of death had definitely soured the earth here, and all around him and beneath his feet he could feel evil.

He was surrounded by them, secretly lurking in the shadows, forming an inner cordon, while Proudfoot set up an outer cordon with the other three members of the Chocktee council. He was the nucleus of this mad plan, hoping to draw it into the circle so they would trap it – but this was not the Spirit Woods of Chocktee. Even with the magic in the sky and whatever plan Toomey had hatched he wondered if they would be able to send it back.

He fully expected to die on this day and that his journey would come to an end. Like Old Jake Toomey, he had little trouble with this idea but hoped that he would right the wrong.

Above them, the sky churned and rolled, green light dancing with blue, sentries of white moving dangerously like vessels in a fog bank. The struggle between dark and light had reached equal, and – for the moment at least – it halted.

In the wood line where Derek Wakeman had first seen Hopper burying his secrets stood Jim West. Twenty-five feet to his right was Hardy, and so it went as they surrounded him. Blackbird guessed the creature would come by flight, so the men behind him who did not have the overhead cover of woods were hidden in every place imaginable. Oddball was standing in the grave of the fourteenth boy, an old tarpaulin bundled up over him. To some, this prospect might have seemed unthinkable, but for Oddball it was the most logical place for an ambush.

The sky overhead was darkening. A fork of lightning flashed, and rain began to fall. Mercifully it came slowly at first, pattering against his jacket and the ground, breaking the intense.

West had two things on his mind while they waited.

First, he was worried about Don Steel. They had been friends for years, always taking potshots at each other, but he was his best friend. West had known about the romance with Hardy long before anyone else. He was surprised to see Hardy show up with Oddball when they did. If he had not known better, he would have judged her as being cold, but Hardy was the best thing to happen to Don.

The second was whether he had taken a leap of fate without really thinking through what he was getting himself into. Kenny Hill's judgment dug into him. They had both attended church every Sunday and held onto the idea that Christ was the son of God. Nobody comes to the Father except through me, he thought. Have I abandoned my savior? Am I being duped by false prophets? God, give me guidance in these unchartered waters.

Though West pondered heavy questions, Hardy did not. She only hoped they had gotten Steel into the emergency, wanted desperately to go with him – but the mother had insisted she come. At the moment she fainted she had been told by a woman that she must come here for the sake of her child and the people. That was why she had insisted they leave Don with the ambulance attendants and get to the Chief and the others.

"You are the key," said the mother. "You must be there."

She did not speak about this, only telling Oddball that they had to come and nothing more.

"For your child and mine," the mother had urged. She did not know what she meant by 'mine' until she saw Blackbird standing there when they rolled up. The resemblance was there in the eyes, and even though one of his had fogged over, she immediately recognized the shape of his face and understood this was her son. If she had not been so wrought with fear and confusion, she might have said something, but now was not the time.

Mick was positioned between a front end loader and a bulldozer that was going to be used to level the ground once the police department completed its tasks here. After witnessing the carnage at Angela's, Mick wondered if this place would become another killing ground and if he and the rest of them would be collected as evidence after the foreseeable confrontation was over. All of this was so alien to him. He was trying to come to terms with it but didn't think he ever would. He worried about Nancy and hoped she was still indoors. He puzzled over Logan's seeming acceptance of this madness.

What the hell was with him anyway?

He had seen the grey thing move, but this was just all too crazy. Now as the rain tapped away at the earth and the sky churned and pulsed he began to question whether his hold onto sanity had faltered somewhere along the line.

"Wait until it is in the circle," Proudfoot had said.

"You will find a cadence, a whisper that is in unison with those to the left and the right. Great Spirit God," Blackbird told them. "No matter what you see or hear, friend or foe, do not break the circle! It is a master of manipulation."

"What if someone is attacked or injured?" Mick asked.

"That is how it will try and betray our circle. No matter what, stand firm."

"Even if someone dies?" Hardy inquired.

"Yes, even if I am killed, or you, or you!" He pointed a finger indiscriminately at the members of his audience. "No matter what, we cannot let it escape."

Where the fuck are you, Dave? You should be here with us, showing leadership instead of leaving your people in the trust of strangers. Mick felt guilty for thinking this way but thought so just the same.

After that they took up their positions, arranging into a circle at Mick's direction from Blackbird's side. It was easy until Oddball climbed into the grave. That caught Mick off-guard: but there was nowhere else to hide.

Blackbird reached and touched his arm. "When it comes it will be fast and furious. It may appear as Old Jake or Chief

Logan. Do not be fooled. Once in the circle, it can only influence us; we must not break the circle."

Mick nodded and made his way over to the front end loader.

"Now what?" Findlay called from his spot.

"Now we wait."

4

Logan slumped across the steering wheel, a wave of relief flowing over him. The herbs pushed the mutating cells and their pain back.

Where have you been all my life?

The clarity he felt was astounding. With the Percocet, his skin itched, and he felt out of control. This was heaven sent: no drowsiness or impaired judgment; just a switch that shut down the pain. Toomey was in the wrong business: he could make a mint from this stuff. He thought about the old man walking away, open hand raised and again felt like crying.

He's going to his death, and I let him.

Get to your people, Dave, Toomey's voice commanded.

Logan jumped, spilling the contents of the satchel onto the seat and knocking the pipe onto the floor. He reached down over the seat, feeling the shotgun bracket dig into his side as he cleaned up his clumsiness. "I'm going, Old Jake."

5

"You will go, Jackanoob."

"Why?" It shifted slightly, still lethargic from the morning feed. "Why would I go?"

"Because you want him to stop."

"He'll be dead in no time."

"But the others won't."

"I'm not one to be bluffed, Jake Toomey. I could remove the top of your head and let out all the lies."

"I do not lie, Jackanoob." Toomey brought a finger up to the mark on his face. "Ten hunters, ready to follow you to all ends of the world."

"You are one of those hunters, a broken down old man?" It grinned, more drool spilling from the corner of its mouth, but there was insecurity in its retort.

"Yes, I am but an old Chocktee Warrior – but the men who have been marked are young and strong. They will not relent. They will follow you day and night. You will have to feed on animal meat because wherever you go, they will be watching."

"You're lying," it growled.

"I have already scattered them to the wind. You will not see them, but they will smell you; they already have the scent of your blood. The same pull that has drawn the hunter now leads the hearts of ten hunters." Toomey could feel it trying to probe him, but he would not succumb to its pull. He was succeeding: he could feel its uncertainty.

"You are a long way from your people to be spinning such tales."

"I don't spin tales, Jackanoob. I am the eldest and wisest Chocktee of my nation, and just as you once were, I am bound by truth. You will go and meet the hunter on the sour ground, or we will let loose the hunters, and you will spend your days in this world feasting on raccoons and squirrels." Toomey's voice was high and confident.

"I don't believe you," it lied.

"Always hungry, never daring to eat anything bigger than a rodent. What a pitiful existence you will have." He was pushing harder now, maybe a little too hard, but time was short.

The Walker shrieked and dug its lower claws into the roof of the police cruiser, driving great holes into the metal. It felt vulnerable, even afraid, but worse: it could feel the disease that plagued it. The agonizing emptiness of hunger was returning. "Don't push me, Jake Toomey: I could open you in the heartbeat of a shrew."

"You will meet the hunter on the sour ground," Toomey snapped.

"What then?" it snapped right back.

"You will fight! His magic against yours."

"What magic could that be?"

"The magic of Nekoneet, the Great Chocktee Elder you struck down."

It cackled once more, a chalkboard echo of scrapings and feedback. "It will be a short event. What are the terms of this challenge?"

"If you win, the hunters will relent."

"I will win."

"Arrogance is a trait that is unbecoming, even for a beast such as you."

The creature laughed. "You have a lot of nerve, Jake Toomey. Your grandfather Igasho would approve of the steel in your bones."

It pounced from the car, pulling him in, their faces close enough to touch. Toomey could smell the stink of rot coming off it. He fought the urge to gag.

Look into my eyes.

It was trying to lull him but Jake would not be quieted. He instead focused on the papery skin that clung to the creature's bones. "You really should wash, Jackanoob. You smell like a salmon five days after its final spawn."

"What will be your prize should the hunter prevail?" its voice patronized.

"You return to Spirit Woods."

It laughed aloud at the prospect.

"Laugh if you like, but that is the provisos."

It released him. In a flash it was back on top of the car, towering above, sniffing the air for the scent of fear – but it detected none. "So I am supposed to let you go so that you can bring the message to the hunter of my coming?"

Jake Toomey grinned, readying himself as he undid the sheath which held his bone handled knife. "I would expect nothing of the sort."

The Walker watched in amazement as the old man brought out a knife. The glint of steel hardened and pocked from years of use caught what little light remained in the darkening sky. It was awestruck at the steadiness in the old man.

The creature remembered something Igasho had said in its other life: "Now we pay for our sins."

Igasho, the Chocktee Warrior, whose only wish was to be forever young and unrestrained by politics or time. Igasho's blood ran deep through this brave old man's veins, and it admired his courage, foolhardy or not.

"You are going to fight me, with that?"

"Let's get busy, Jackanoob! I have business with my ancestors and friends." Toomey flicked the knife threateningly through the air. "Maybe I will spare the hunter his challenge and send you back to the void myself."

The Walker changed, fading into the dark man that solicited prostitutes from the streets of Chicago. "You have heart, old man. The warrior Igasho runs rampant even through your dried up bones, but I will not engage you in battle."

Toomey was motionless, confused by the Walker's reaction.

"You go back to the hunter and tell him I'm coming. The Guardians are likely following you every time you take a step, waiting for your heart to seize. Get out of my sight. You are not a warrior any longer: just a messenger." It waved him off like a nuisance. "Tell him I'm coming."

Toomey did not move. "Are you afraid of me, Jackanoob?"

"Afraid?" It snorted. "Have you looked into the gleam of the blade you would try and slay me with? No, of course not, so I will tell you what I see. I see spoiled meat. Death lurks so closely. You would not feed my hunger if you were the last man on earth. Your time is almost done, old man. I will not cheat you of what little you have left. Go now, or I will leave this place and leave you and your hunters to the chase."

So Toomey turned and began to amble away, the knife at his side, thinking that it might jump him from behind – yet when he glanced back to see, it hadn't moved.

Now what?

Walking down the hill, angry with the outcome, he tried to formulate a plan that included him. It would take too long to reach the sour ground.

Then from behind, he heard the flap of wings. A shadow passed over him, and Toomey's hairs stood up on the back of his neck with the chill of death. Ten feet ahead it waited, half-man, half-creature, its long hair hung over its dark eyes as it unfurled its deadly talons, spreading its elongated arms.

"Nôtinew!"

Toomey froze, recognizing the ancient language and the word which meant battle. Fire flared in his heart, and his warrior blood again boiled with anticipation. His eyes darkened, steeling himself for one last battle. Bringing the old knife up, a vicious scowl fell from his eyes across the weathered landscape of his face. "Nôtinew!"

Then Toomey ran headlong to his destiny.

To the creature's surprise, the old man was grinning ear to ear.

6

Logan pulled his car in next to the others around the same time that Toomey locked into his skirmish with Jackanoob. They had parked all the vehicles closer to Donald Wakeman's place. He noted that Mick had seen to camouflaging them before they walked the last 400 yards to the Hopper farm. He grabbed the satchel and the pipes, placing the one Toomey had asked him to pass to Blackbird in his breast pocket and snapping the button closed over it to keep it from falling out. After getting out of the car, he grabbed some brush and threw it onto the police cruiser. There might have been a moment of insecurity, a second to rethink how insane the world had become, but he was well beyond that now.

I wonder if this is how a madman feels before he goes on a shooting spree?

The comparison was ludicrous. The world might have changed, but Logan was no less sane than he had been yesterday. His actions were for the good of his people. Of this, he was absolute, and though the world had suddenly become a mad place with monsters and spirits, David Logan steeled himself to see it through. Reaching down, he checked his weapon, chambering a round, but did not set the safety before holstering it. Placing the satchel on his neck, he began walking. Droplets of rain began to fall around him as he went.

Maybe Toomey will not be able to convince the shape-changer to come. Perhaps it would kill him and flee. One could selfishly hope, but knowing what he knew now gave him pause to consider that the death and destruction would only compound if it did escape. He felt guilty for thinking such thoughts, mainly because he knew that Toomey was looking death in the face. If he wasn't already dead.

What balls the old guy had. He didn't even bat an eye when he got out of the car; just raised his hand without a word. Logan squeezed the satchel feeling the contents inside, a silent acknowledgment.

He would have liked to know him better. He looked forward to meeting him again and was now sure he would. He'd seen so much during their meditation of blood and smoke. And not just of the creature, either. Now he understood that this indeed was not the end.

The rain pattered on him a little harder. There was no sun: the swollen clouds saw to that, blotting it out. The vortex above, now almost black, swirled violently as flashes of amber and blue clashed silently within, while the inverted funnel sucked all sanity from the world. He kept his eyes fixed upon the ground, knowing it would lull him and steal his thoughts.

The walls are thinning.

He crossed the field behind the Wakeman place at a faster pace now. Overhead, the sky cast an all-encompassing shadow as though there was an eclipse underway. Silhouettes crossed the prairie landscape, turning the afternoon charcoal grey and stealing the light as they went. The air was ripe with electricity, reminding Logan of the smell the toy train transformer he had bought his son Howard over a decade ago.

He was not aware that he was taking almost the exact path that Derek Wakeman had on that fateful day before everything went wrong. Before that day there had been no bodies, no Hopper, no skinwalker, and no cancer.

Let this be happening in Thomasville only.

He was worried about his kids and Denise. He prayed that they were going about their afternoons oblivious to what was happening in the skies and here on earth.

Up ahead, Logan saw the trees that separated the two properties. He had to give the pipe to Blackbird: that was Toomey's last wish, and he intended on doing just that. Whether Blackbird or any of them would live beyond today was another matter altogether, yet agonizing over it was pointless.

The woods were only twenty feet away. There was no movement in them.

"God help us," he murmured, and that's when he heard Westy.

"Chief," West whispered.

"Jim? That you?" Logan called back. Happy to hear a familiar voice, his spirits lifted, bringing a grin to his face. Scanning the woods, he saw Westy's silhouette waving his arm. Looking over his shoulder, he half-expected something to run him down the same way it had Pete Kennedy – but nothing was there. So he bolted into the trees, forgetting for a moment why they were all there.

"Chief, it's sure good to see you." West grinned.

"I'm happy to see you too, Jim." Logan pumped his hand as if they hadn't seen each other in weeks. "Where's Mick?"

West pointed to the front end loader. "He's over there, Chief."

"Where's Old Jake?"

Logan gazed over at Westy and frowned. No words were necessary. West didn't ask about the old guy again; he guessed Logan would let him know if he felt it was appropriate.

Logan saw Blackbird standing alone in the field and then scanned the area for his officers. He picked up Hardy right away and thought he saw Nero and Findlay, but Mick and Oddball were out of sight. "Okay, Jim; you grab Mick for me. I gotta talk to Blackbird. We are on limited time here, so make it snappy."

"We can't break the circle, Chief. We are in it for the long haul now," West said. "You're going to have to stay here and wait with us until we see this through."

Logan looked about, scolding himself for pulling over to smoke the herbs Toomey had given him. It was out of his control: he little more than a spectator now, and it appeared that Blackbird was the ringmaster. "What do I do, Jim? How can I help?"

"We wait, Chief. We wait for it to come," West replied.

And so they did.

7

It came like rolling thunder, blasting through the woods uncaring of who or what got in its way. It did not see the danger nor did it really care. In its claws, it carried a trophy for the hunter, something to show it had no fear of him or the new band of men. It had already reduced their numbers by one, and very soon it would be more. It had only one thing on its mind.

Kill the hunter and be done with this stale place.

It scrambled on all fours like a cougar, ready to pounce and kill whatever got in its way. Ahead it could see something flicker, and it moved in for the strike.

Fortier readied his drum. Proudfoot dropped him at the crossroad to the south of the killing ground. He was in his late fifties, and next to Toomey the oldest on the council. Monias and Machino came after him, and they were only years apart. They were the last living members of the council.

Each council Elder had picked a successor if they were to die or be killed. On the day they set out for Thomasville a new council was put in place. Now five new men oversaw the good of the Chocktee people.

He tightened the lashes on the big drum, tapping it and testing the sound. He did not see the Walker coming from behind, nor did he hear it, but in the last moment of his life he could smell it and reached for his knife.

But it was too late.

8

"Westy, hit the deck!" Logan screamed.

He hit the dirt without even looking – and luckily so. The thing, a mere blur, blew over him, generating an explosion of branches that rained down. If he had been standing it would have mowed him down or worse, cut him in half. West hadn't even turned over when he heard its horrible shriek, and all he could think was, There's no stopping this now.

It didn't see or care about the man it had almost killed: it only saw the Hunter and felt the feverish hunger. It smashed through the trees and stopped directly in front of the unflinching Blackbird. Then it shrieked, and the blast of air was strong enough to blow the hair away from his face. Towering above him, almost seven and a half feet, long arms dangling at its sides, it sniffed the air and looked about.

Then it spoke.

"For you," it said, dropping the gift at his feet.

What it had been holding were the heads of Toomey and Fortier, but even more horrific that it had used their spinal cords as a lanyard to carry them. The two heads thumped to the ground, mad renditions of a prisoner's ball and chain.

Hardy covered her mouth to avoid crying out; the others watched and waited.

Blackbird stared up at the creature, his heart once filled with hate now hastened to empathy. He had never been this close, not seen the starvation or the confusion brought on by hunger.

"Well, I have come at your request. Where is this magic you are supposed to carry with you?" it hissed. In one swift movement, it snatched the diamond willow stick from Blackbird's hand and examined it. "Is this the source of your magic?"

West was turning over now, watching Blackbird, waiting for the signal.

The creature stepped down on Blackbird's foot and pierced it with its incisor toe. Agony pulsed through him as tendons and bone crunched and snapped. Blackbird balled up his fists, clenched his jaw, holding on. The others began to show themselves. Yet the creature was unaware, and it throttled him with its right claw and hooked his shoulder just below the collarbone.

Blackbird moaned but still said nothing.

"Have you lost the ability to speak?" it asked, clubbing him with the stick. If he had not staked to the ground by its claws, he would fallen. Fresh blood spilled from a gash on the side of his head "Where is your magic, hunter?"

Why the hell doesn't he do something? Logan thought.

And then Daniel Blackbird did do something.

Through the pain, he managed a smirk and said, "It's all around you."

"What?" It did not understand.

"Kihci-manitow!" Blackbird called.

From behind it, West raised the radio and repeated. "Kihci-manitow!"

A voice on the radio responded: "Kihci-manitow!"

Then in the distance, the drums of Chocktee began.

Thump! Thump! Pause – **crash!**

Around them, the new hunters began their chant clumsily one after another: "Kihci-manitow! Kihci-manitow! Kihci-manitow! Kihci-manitow! Kihci-manitow! Kihci-manitow! Kihci-manitow!"

The creature shrieked and dropped Blackbird, panic running through it.

Trapped! No... trapped! The old man lied!

The members of the ritual circle stepped forward as the drums of Chocktee called to the Guardians – with the absence of Fortier. Monias, Machino, and Proudfoot all understood after that first pause that Fortier was no longer at his post and closed the cadence. They knew the answer to the silent drum.

Thump!

"Kihci-manitow!"

Thump!

"Kihci-manitow!"

Crash!

"Kihci-manitow!"

Forgotten, Blackbird lay bleeding on the ground. The creature paced back and forth, staring at each of them, sizing each up as it frantically looked for an exit.

"Let me out," It growled.

"Kihci-manitow!"

Thump!

It screeched at Blackbird: "Tell them to release me!"

"Kihci-manitow!" He smiled. "You're finished!"

It shrieked again and then traced its claw in the lower part of his belly. Daniel looked beyond the creature. Drifting down from the sky in all directions fell raindrops of glowing color. They spattered onto the earth, where they turned to mist, spreading all around them. "The Guardians are coming."

"No!" it shrieked.

It drew Blackbird up and threw him across the ritual circle, where he hit the dirt – hard. It began to dart around madly and ran at West, screeching, demanding its release. But they were protected by an invisible barrier. No matter its angst or strength it could not break the circle.

Blackbird, barely able to breathe, could see them watching from beyond the circle. They waited: Grandfather, his mother, Toomey and Fortier, all aglow in the luminous green that lit the hearts of the Guardian. He wanted to die and be with them, a spectator to this madness instead of a participant.

"Be strong, Young Daniel," Grandfather said.

"Do not look into its eyes," Blackbird warned. "If it catches you in its gaze it can influence you and cause you to hallucinate."

West stared through it, chanting to God, waiting for rhythmic thump and crash of the drums.

Look at me, the Walker beckoned. *I will give you everything. Feel me!*

"Kihci-manitow."

It moved to Logan, and he suddenly heard Toomey calling him.

"Let me out, Dave! I will die in this circle. Let me free before I am dragged to the dark world!" Then it was his son, Howard. "Dad, we need you!" – and then his daughter, Jamie. "Daddy, they're everywhere, we need you!" But Logan stared down, would not meet its eyes.

It shrieked again and moved to Nero.

As the Walker moved from one to the next, the mist in the woods thickened and in it, lights began to pulse and move. From the sky, a fork of lightning cracked, splitting spruce and sending a tremor of thunder crashing across the farm.

The walls are thinning. The time is short, Toomey echoed inside Logan's head.

The drums beat.

The new hunters of the Chocktee continued their chant.

"Kihci-manitow."

The dull silence of the day had been replaced with echoes, crashes, drumbeats and the thunder of muted voices from the skies. West looked first to Blackbird, whom he thought had succumbed to his injuries, then at the dense fog that solidified inside the forest landscape outside the circle. He saw the lights pulsing, coming together and realized that the pulse was following the cadence of the drums.

Thump! Thump! Crash!

9

Beyond the ritual circle, the three drummers of Chocktee were each locked in a spotlight of brilliant green illumination as they set about their task. Each man continued to pound their drum as they bathed in its life and warmth. Outside the glowing light, only blackness presided, wanting to engulf them and steal the life from their lungs, but they were each under the protection of a separate Guardian, each hovering a thousand feet above.

"Kihci-manitow!" Monias chanted and beat his drum. Thump!

"Kihci-manitow!" Machino added and thumped.

"Kihci-manitow!" Proudfoot cried out and crashed the big bass drum.

In the light swam smaller creatures that rose and fell, while outside in the dark reaches of the void something else watched and waited. They could not see or hear the drama unfolding on the sour earth of Hopper's farm: they only saw the shining light and felt the cadence of the drums and their hearts.

10

Probing, reaching inside them, looking for a way out and finding the flaw in their magic. It settled in front of Hardy and stood motionless as the others continued their chant.

Its body stiffened and its eyes began to glow fiery white, but the specter in the woods to the north of the farm was a frightening distraction as well. It started to rise out of the fog, humming as it did and emitting electrical flashes from inside. The creature saw it and let out a disheveled murmur that Logan thought was reminiscent of what he had seen in the vision he shared with Toomey.

It's scared now. The Master is returning; coming to claim it.

The orb glowed bluish black, a light inside pulsing like a heartbeat. It was just outside the circle, behind Mick and Oddball, and from the mist, light and blue liquid seemed to draw to it magnetically.

It's drawing power. Logan hoped the creature inside it was only there to claim its property and take it back. He hoped it wasn't hungry.

"Don't stop," Blackbird called weakly.

And with that, they continued to chant as the drums beat, and the walls between the worlds thinned. The vessel known as the black orb pulsed in and out, its skin rippling, its circumference growing as the mist and dark matter drew to it.

It shrieked turning its attention on the flaw in their circle.

Hardy could feel it tugging at her mind, probing deeper into her, and she tried to push it off as she chanted. "Kihci-manitow! "Kihci-manitow!" "Kihci-manitow…"

Come to me, the Walker soothed.

"Kihci-manitow!"

I will not hurt you. I am your friend.

"Kihci-manitow." She could not hear the drums or the voices of the others anymore, and suddenly she felt alone. She began to feel the anesthesia running through her, the loss of fear and the impulse of abandon.

I love you, the voice inside her assured. This belonged not to the creature, but Don Steel. Just let go, Sand. It's okay to let go. I love you, and I love our child. Look into my eyes. Look into my eyes.

She felt her eyes rising upward, and she saw Steel standing in front of her, a smile on his face – and when her eyes met his, she felt herself let go.

"Sandy, no," Logan cried out, but it was too late: it had taken hold of her.

"Kaw seu, Igwhot," she hissed and stepped into the circle.

"Close the circle!" Blackbird wheezed.

Logan and West continued their chant, shortening the distance between them. The creature had been distracted by Blackbird, and now rage-filled it at its missed opportunity. It scowled and shot over to where he lay, lifting him. It shrieked again and again as it shook him like a ragdoll, then threw him to the ground.

The drums continued, and thunder clapped above in acknowledgment to their calling while the black orb continued to draw energy, gaining the power it needed to break through the thinning walls.

Logan looked at the slumped body of Blackbird, sure he was dead now. Then called between chants to the others, "We cannot let it go! It is running out of time! Keep the cadence! Kihci-manitow!"

Now it was not just drizzling, but pouring, and the lightning flashed strobe-like. The mist swirled, and the black orb pulsed, growing to an enormous size and cracking the tree branches around it.

The creature was losing its focus, feeling the pull of the Master, not wanting to go back to the void. Then it heard the new hunter giving orders and turned its attention on him, scooping Hardy into its clutch.

"Sandy!" Oddball yelled, and almost broke ranks.

"Don't move!" Mick ordered.

"That's what it wants," Nero chimed in.

"Kihci-manitow!"

Thump! Thump! Crash!

"Let me go," it hissed, holding Hardy before him.

"Kaw seu, Igwhot," Hardy mumbled, her eyes shiny mirrors.

"No," Logan said. "I will not break the circle."

"Let me go or I will kill her!" it demanded.

"Fuck you! You are going back! You have killed enough! We will not free you!"

It shrieked and dug a talon into Hardy's shoulder. She screamed.

"Chief, no, we can't let it kill her!" Findlay shouted.

"Chief!" Oddball cried.

"Kihci-manitow!"

The chant continued, and the drums beat mercilessly. Logan felt panic but knew they couldn't let it go. The orb beyond the circle was gaining strength; it could be only a matter of minutes.

Then Hardy said something, fracturing his resolve.

"My baby," she whimpered. "Please, Chief! Don't let it kill my baby."

The hum from the orb grew louder and pulsed electrically. It seemed to be surrounded by a thin membrane of skin, and something beneath moved about wanting to break free. The drums were almost muted by the hum, and Logan suddenly was unsure what to do.

"Baby?"

"Chief! She's got Steel's kid in her!" Oddball cried out.

"Chief!" Findlay was stepping forward.

"Don't fucking move! Stand still!" Mick screamed at both of them.

"Kihci-manitow!"

Thump! Thump! Crash!

The rain was pummeling them. Trees froze around the orb then cracked from the intense cold. They popped between the humming, the drums, the thunder and chants as Logan tried desperately to buy time.

"I will disembowel her before your eyes!" It drew up its claw and scraped it over her belly. "I will eat her child, and it will be your burden to carry!"

"Please, Chief, please don't let it hurt my baby," she begged, but her eyes were still shiny mirrors. "Please, just let me die then."

It cackled then and tore open her shirt, exposing her belly. Scraping a claw across the milky skin which was ready to give way to the jagged edge, a small cut opened up. Black drool ran from its mouth.

Behind it, the orb hummed louder.

"Time's up," it growled, baring its jagged network of teeth.

"Wait!" Logan called. "We will not break the circle, but I will give you what you want!"

"Break the circle," it demanded.

"No! But I will make a trade with you!"

The orb was beginning to hemorrhage, black ick bleeding from the outer skin. The thing within it continued to move, wanting to get out.

"You for them? Hardly a fair trade," it snarled. "If I must go back I will enjoy one last taste of this world's innocence."

You are the key, Toomey whispered, and suddenly Logan knew.

"I will offer you your freedom, but only if I can take your place."

The creature stopped and snapped its head. "What are you offering, hunter?"

"I will make the same pledge you made for your people,"

"Dave, no," Mick called.

"You will be free. I will take your burden. No chance of returning to the void, and once I take your place you can walk out of here. Grow old, unburdened by the hunger or the pain that plagues you."

Logan kept his eyes on Hardy, hoping that it wasn't too late to save her.

The Walker contemplated the bargain, but did so quickly: the skin on the black orb was rupturing, and the blue lights began to shoot from the lacerations. Time was running out. It set Hardy down and hissed at her in the ancient language, but they all knew what it was telling her.

"Kaw seu, Igwhot," she whimpered, standing beneath it like a cowering pet.

"Klay gor orum gaw!" it thundered at her, and she fled toward Mick and Oddball. Then it turned back toward Logan and said, "Come to me now!"

"First release her from your spell," Logan demanded.

"Don't test me, hunter. I will not be tested!"

"Release her or I'll leave you to the punishment of your Master."

At once, Hardy fell to the ground, unconscious. The creature turned back to Logan and beckoned with its long talons. Its venom spilled from between its weathered, broken teeth. It would waste no time.

Logan reached into his breast pocket, removing the pipe Toomey had given him. He tossed it over to West. "Give that to Blackbird when this is over. Tell him that Toomey wanted the Chief Elder of the Chocktee people to have that."

"Chief, what in God's name are you doing?"

"Mick," Logan yelled across to his friend. "Take care of my kids! Tell them I did my best."

"Dave, stop this! God damn it! Stop," Mick yelled back.

"Mick, promise me!"

"No! Dave! This is madness!"

"Please, Mick, take care of my kids. Tell them!"

Their eyes met, and in that instant, Mick knew that he could not stop Logan. So he nodded, every muscle in his face contorting. He croaked, "I will! I promise, Dave, I will!"

The drums of Chocktee were but a distant muted thumping. The hum of the black orb was deafening, like that of an overheating subwoofer. Logan glanced at his people, saw the heartbreak in their eyes and was content that what he was about to do was right.

The rain stopped abruptly.

"Get her out," Logan yelled, stepping into the circle.

Oddball stepped in and pulled Hardy clear.

The need to chant had passed: now everything had been set into motion and could not be stopped by prayer or curse.

Blackbird peered at the burly cop, barely conscious, well aware of the sacrifice Logan was about to make. "He is the key," Grandfather had told him, but he had no idea that it would come to this.

Logan walked toward the creature and as he did his people stood motionless. Hardy started to come around, but she was unaware of what was happening, and for that he was thankful.

"I know you all think I've lost my mind and if I had time to explain I would, but Sabrina will be able to tell you.

You are all my friends, and our journey together has been a pleasure. I love my children, my ex-wife and all of you." He was standing before the Walker.

His wet grey hair clung to his wrinkled brow.

"Are you finished?" the creature asked.

"I'm finished," Logan said, raising his arms.

It snatched him up in a cradling position, the stink of death, sour and malignant, rolling off it. Then it slashed his cheek open, blood spurting from the wound, but Logan didn't wince.

"Fuck me!" Mick was crying.

The orb was opening now. Light poured from it, flooding the ground like gas. Oddball and Mick moved aside, afraid to be touched by the poison that spilled from it. Across from them, West and Findlay caught a glimpse through the portal and saw the other world.

The Walker readied itself to spit into the gaping wound on Logan's face when it saw him staring outward at something it could not see. He was smiling at something or someone – but not someone who was part of the ritual circle.

"I'm coming, Old Jake," he said.

Then there was a crack, the smell of gunpowder, and his head snapped and fell over awkwardly against the creature's chest plate. Slumped lifelessly in its arms, the service pistol tumbled from his hand and onto the muddy ground.

At first, it didn't understand, its eyes narrowing in confusion – and then the comprehension that it had been bested replaced the confusion with fury. It shrieked, tossing Logan aside, and went to finish off Blackbird. Scrambling across the ritual circle, it prepared to tear out his heart and eat it before them, even if the hunter was already dead.

Collins could not believe what had just happened.

Is Dave really gone?

Blackbird lay bloody and broken as he watched Logan in those last moments reaching down, removing the gun from the holster as it cut open his face, understanding what

Grandfather had meant. In the distance, he could see them waiting to take him home. They were in the woods, and beyond them was the passage.

Now the creature was shrieking, casting the lifeless body of Logan aside, and then it came toward him to invoke its vengeance.

Blackbird welcomed it as it bore down on him: it would mean the end. One of his eyes was now completely blind, a number of his ribs were broken and digging into the muscles of his right side. Beyond the imminent death, he could see the blurry figures moving outside the ritual circle. Grandfather, Toomey, Mother, and he smiled as he began to lose consciousness.

Come and get me, Skin!

The others watched Logan take his own life with equal horror. Numb disconnect melted over all of them as the creature shrieked in anger, discarded him and went in to finish Blackbird.

All except West, who saw the orb cast forth the contents of its world. As the Walker scrambled across the circle toward Blackbird, it did not see the Master step through the portal or what looked to be numerous smaller carbon copies hanging about its long and weathered frame. The Master unfurled itself and looked, unblinking, at all of them. It was humongous: twice that of the creature that had wrought havoc in this world. As it peered about, the smaller minions that clung to its body dropped to the ground and spread out defensively.

Kill you, kill you!

And then, from behind it felt an icy chill and the breathing of its own master. It froze only feet from Blackbird, standing motionless, no longer the dominant aggressor, and the rage in its eyes turned to fear.

"Jeg Lo, Igwhot," the Master snarled.

The Walker fell to its knees and shrieked in frustration.

"Kaw mau," the Master ordered, its heavy voice undulating.

Shrieking again, the creature stared beyond the circle, wanting to be free, angry at the trickery the new hunters had bested it with.

Its eyes swirled with liquid mercury, and for a brief moment, Nero thought he saw the reflection of an old Indian in them. "Kaw seu, Igwhot."

The Master lumbered forward and snatched the shoulder of its wayward child, then dragged it along the ground. The smaller minions abandoned their defensive posture, swarming the Walker, biting it and tearing at its papery flesh as the orb began to hum and the world beyond it beckoned. The mist now flowed back into the sphere, being vacuumed from this world as they continued to bite and claw the creature. It cried out in agony, but the Master was oblivious as it dragged it back toward the portal.

Instead, it looked right and left upon Collins and Oddball.

"Kihci-manitow," Oddball said.

"Kihci-manitow." Mick wiped his tears.

"Dear God," West gasped as the Master flung its ward through the portal. They heard one final shriek, and then it was tumbling away into the void.

The orb hummed louder, lightning flashed, the last of the mist flowed back, and the creature leaned down and stared into Mick's eyes. He tried to look away but could not: the giant towered above him at twelve feet, its head the size of a 100 lb potato sack. Its breath stunk of rot, and he thought it might reach through their flimsy ritual circle and drag him away to the void.

"Kihci-manitow," he said weakly.

Prepare them, he heard a voice inside his head hissed.

The Master grinned.

"Kihci-manitow."

It cackled then, hoarse and baritone, then withdrew to the waiting orb as they looked on in terror. Once inside, the hum intensified, the skin began to crawl back over the orb. Inside, the agonizing shriek of Jackanoob echoed on and on.

They could hear the drums of Chocktee, which had never stopped, begin to rise in domination of the darkness. The dense blue fog which had brought forth the black orb now enveloped it, and it started to melt away like liquid. Above, the clouds rolled backward, revealing a jet black night sky. To the north, south and west beams of green shot up like searchlights from the remaining three drummers.

Then they saw them.

From the heavens the Guardians descended, humming as they did.

"Do you see them?" Mick called.

"Yes," West called back. "They're beautiful; like angels."

"Spirit God," Oddball marveled.

Blackbird saw the single green orb floating in the woods. He saw it open, saw the ghosts watching and waiting to welcome the fallen. He did not see Logan meet Toomey in the passage, nor did he hear them calling to him.

He began to lose consciousness, feeling hands upon him and something cold and hard being placed into his hand.

It was over.

***

EPILOGUE - THE SPIRIT WALK

1

Four months after the Fall Equinox

They were in the Spirit Woods, just the four of them. A fire crackled as the boys looked on in wonderment, having taken palaver with their Father and the Chief Elder Blackbird. He had healed from his wounds after three months in the Thomasville Hospital, and his brothers and sisters both from the Chocktee of Spirit Woods and Thomasville stood vigil as the doctors put him back together. But though his wounds were healed, the aging had not reversed. His hair now hung loosely like cobwebs about the deeply etched lines in his face.

He had not been awake when they placed the body of David Logan or the others who had been massacred on that day, into the ground. He slipped in and out of consciousness, wandering the corridors of his mind as he underwent numerous operations. They fused and pinned his broken bones, stitched his foot and shoulder. For all their trying, they had not been able to correct his blind eye. He had trouble with this as his depth perception was gone, but he found the strength to carry on and adjust.

Once, when he awoke, he saw the woman sitting there staring at him intently. She was pregnant. Her belly had swelled, along with her bosom. She looked beautiful, but the worry on her face wore lines into the corners of her eyes.

He did not say anything to her, feeling the dull throb of pain, trying to adjust as his good eye overcompensated and became sore. He was about to slip away into the corridors again when she spoke up.

"Your mother is very beautiful," she said and wiped a tear from her right eye using the sleeve of her shirt. "I'm sorry, it's the baby. My emotions sometimes overtake me."

"Where did you…" he started and almost choked: his throat was dry. He motioned to her for the water jug sitting on the nightstand. She poured him a Dixie cup of water. It was near lukewarm, but the moisture lubricated the back of his throat. He began again: "My mother, where did you see my mother?"

"In the passage."

"You were in the passage?"

"Yes, for a short while. She made me go back. I wanted to stay, but she said I could not. She gave me a message for you." Tears streamed down her face.

Blackbird sat up, the pins in his broken bones grating against the healing tissue between his ribs. Yet he welcomed the pain: it served as a reminder that he was alive and not floating in some purgatory between this world and the next.

"What did she tell you?"

"She said: 'Tell him I love him. Tell him that he will be able to go home now. Tell him I will be waiting in the Peace Garden with Da.'" Her voice cracked. "She is so beautiful."

Blackbird did not speak then. He just gaped at her with his one good eye and began to cry. No words would come to explain the myriad of emotions that ran through him: the bottled up anger, guilt, and anguish he had carried all these years, becoming heavier with each step. That was why he wanted to die, to be done with this.

Hardy got up from the chair awkwardly balancing her belly, as pregnant women often do when they rise. She placed a hand in his. It was warm and comforting. She gently touched his head. "Dan, please tell me my baby will be okay."

He squeezed her hand tightly but could not find the reassuring words she desperately wanted. He did not think that the skinwalker could have inhabited her child, but he really did not know.

2

"Dan," Proudfoot said from across the fire. "It's time to get the boys to ground."

"No, Papa, we aren't tired. Uncle, tell us another story," Young Daniel Proudfoot asked.

"Please, one more story," his brother Johnny begged.

"I am out of stories, but if you listen to your father, I will give both of you something." Blackbird looked to his cousin and nodded. Proudfoot smiled and went to the pack he had brought on the spirit walk. He reached into it and pulled out leather roll that held the objects. He and Blackbird had placed this there earlier for this moment.

"Johnny, Daniel, stand before the Chief Elder and prepare to receive counsel," the father ordered with love and admiration in his voice. He was so proud of them and so happy that he was able to bring Dan home to Spirit Woods.

He stood beside his cousin, and his two children lined up in front of them. The difference in appearance between him and Blackbird was so drastic that they could have passed for father and son.

"Thank you, cousin," Blackbird said taking the leather roll.

Proudfoot could hear a hint of Grandfather in the pleasantry. He scanned the campsite to see if the old man had joined them, but found nothing. It was all Daniel. They had been out here for three days and three nights, and not far off was the burial ground known as the Peace Garden.

"This was given to us, when we were just boys, by the bravest man both your father and I have ever known. He was a descendant of a great Warrior Chief named Igasho. His name was Jake Toomey, and he is the bravest, fiercest warrior the Chocktee people have ever known." Blackbird spread the roll, revealing the two bone handled knives Toomey had crafted for them in their adolescence.

The boys gasped in awe as Blackbird held a knife in each weathered hand. Upon each of the polished and oiled blades, the flames of the fire flickered. Blackbird held the first knife up to his young cousin Johnny.

"This is your father's knife. He has carried it with him his whole life, and I pass it to you with his permission as you are moving toward becoming a man. Use this knife to hunt and aid you in your travels, but never use it in anger. Can you do this, Little John?"

Little John nodded his eyes wide with excitement and pride. "Yes, Uncle."

"Then it is yours to carry," he said and handed the knife across.

John took it, his eyes filled with awe.

"This is my knife," Blackbird said. "I carried it in my travels, and it is the bond that holds me to this place and your father. I give this knife to you to carry as you walk toward manhood. Never use this knife in anger. Can you do this as well, Young Daniel?"

"Yes, Uncle."

Blackbird handed the knife to his young cousin. "It is yours to carry."

They kneeled there, wide-eyed, the crackling fire shining upon their silken black hair, holding the presents with what little amount of discipline young boys can muster when excited and want steal away to enjoy their treasure.

"Kihci-manitow," Blackbird said. They responded in turn.

"Hold on," Proudfoot laughed at the excitement of his sons. "I have something for you as well." They looked to one another even more excitedly. He stepped forward, and in his hand, he held two medicine bags. "These were made and blessed by the wisest elder of our people. His name was Nekoneet, but no one except his mother called him that. He, too, was one of the bravest men we knew and loved, and I give you the last two satchels he made on the day he went to the passage."

First Little John stepped forward and then Daniel as their father placed the medicine bag around their necks. "This will protect you in your travels. It is powerful because it was made with love and magic."

Young Daniel gasped. He clutched the medicine bag tightly.

"What kind of magic?" Little John asked.

"Grandfather's Magic."

Blackbird grinned at the boys, and in this light, he looked like the old man more than ever.

"Grandfather's Magic," Proudfoot said and wiped a tear from his eye.

3

The boys were fast asleep, nestled into the hooch. Blackbird sat quietly across from his cousin, watching the embers in the fire crackle and pop. The last flames licked the charred pieces of wood, their fuel almost expended. The forest smelled of cedar and the snow blanketing the ground cast light up onto their faces. He removed the pipe that West had tucked into his hand and filled the bowl with herbs and bearberry. Above the trees, aurora borealis ran like watercolor paint across an infinite canvas.

"When do you leave?" Blackbird asked.

"The end of the week," Proudfoot replied.

"They are awakening?"

"Yes, the amnesia seems to be wearing off. Mick said the townspeople are starting to become aware. There have been dreams, waking visions. First the relatives of the hunters, then the others. Mick said that his wife knows everything, and she has accepted it."

"You will need to prepare them."

"Yes, I know."

"You will be the Chief Elder."

"I suppose."

"Your boys will learn many things, Johnny. Things they would have never learned here." Blackbird lit the pipe, passed it across to his cousin, and then exhaled.

"What will become of our people?"

"They will move with the time. Grandfather and Toomey knew this day was coming."

"I will miss this place very much." Proudfoot drew and passed the pipe back.

Blackbird felt drowsy. He considered the hooch they had set up where the boys were now nestled in their sleeping bags. He wanted to go up there and sleep a while: but there was business still at hand. The air was cold tonight, barely repelled by the massive fire they had started to keep warm.

"What did Mick say about the family that lived on the other side of Hopper's farm?"

"He said the town has purchased the land and the family has moved out. Mick had to twist a few arms to get that done, but as more of them start to awaken the easier it has become."

Proudfoot also looked tired.

"This year only the hunters will take up the ritual, but with time as the people come to terms with the responsibility, there must be teachers and counsel. Machino and Monias can see to that." He had taken on this new authority a lot easier than he thought. "The woman, Sandra, and her husband Don must not partake until her child is born. They may pose a threat."

"Yes, I was going to suggest that." Proudfoot suppressed a yawn.

"You know what to do, Johnny. Get some sleep, and I will be up shortly."

Blackbird looked very much like Grandfather, old and weathered, but serene and thoughtful. He looked to be almost seventy now; it was difficult for him to walk and the scars, though healed, still ached.

Proudfoot stood up. "Are you okay, Dan?"

Blackbird was tapping the contents from the pipe. "My bones are aching, but in my head, I am a happy man. I just need a bit of time to collect my thoughts. Can you take this for me?"

Proudfoot took the pipe from his cousin and yawned again. Overhead the northern lights danced green and yellow. A knot in the fire popped; an owl screeched. "I can stay with you."

"No, you go to ground. The pipe is yours now, Johnny. Use it in palaver as you teach the people of the town our ways." In his foggy eye, the reflected lights of the Spirit Woods danced. "I will be up shortly."

"Goodnight, Dan." Proudfoot did not argue. To do so would be disrespectful of Chocktee tradition.

As he wandered up the path leading to the hooch, he felt another pang of guilt, but could not undo what had been done. Just beyond the hooch was the cliff and rock outcropping on which Grandfather had spent so many nights with them.

4

The light glowed dimly, and that was what caught his good eye as he passed the pipe to his cousin. He waited until he could hear Johnny snoring. Then he stood and began to walk through the snow. Blackbird felt better. The ache in his bones was subsiding with every step he took. The snow was soft beneath his feet, the trees welcoming, the sky lighting the way. The light moved between the trunks, watching him, calling to him. The cold relented, his vision cleared, and the weight fell from his shoulders.

A silhouette appeared beside a tree in the darkness just outside the warmth of green light. Just beyond loomed other figures that stood in wait.

The old man stepped from the shadows and into the green light.

"Hello, Young Daniel."

Heart racing, he reached out his hand.

"Come, let us palaver."

The Beginning

ᒥᒋᐸᔭᐃᐧᑐ

ACKNOWLEDGMENT

Writing a novel is a massive undertaking, and while it is the author's name on the cover, there are scores of people responsible for the finished product. From beta readers to research consultants, I would like to thank the following people who volunteered to help me with this project:

Author R James (Jim) Steel: Without the numerous readings and following suggestions by my dear friend Jim, I don't know how I would have gotten this book written. Jim accepted and reviewed draft after draft without complaint. That is until I told him I was done, in which he hinted that if I sent him another draft he would likely be getting a restraining order.

Ohgwá:ih Steele & Elizabeth Niish Wawashkeshshi: Schooled me on the fascinating lore surrounding North America's aboriginal peoples. So as not to offend or bastardize the religion or tradition of real native people, I opted to create the fictional Nation of Chocktee. Variations or error regarding existing lore or legend rests solely with the author.

Kelly Allen Bouchard MS, BBA: It was her expertise in psychology, behavioral sciences and review that helped mold my character traits and interaction. I am indebted to her for volunteering her time and appreciate the insight she contributed.

Keith Parker and Paul Rutledge: Both these men acted as beta readers and offered feedback that was instrumental in getting the book finished and ready for publication.

Marc A Roy: My friend and webmaster, the architect who developed my website and breathed life into what I envisioned as a hub to promote Equinox, not only as a book but through the medium of Art and Video.

Tony Preston and Michael Hillaby: For the expertise, they offered in aircraft structural capabilities and limitations.

Chapter 1 - Infamous

1

7 May 2000

Syracuse, NY

The time was 1:00 a.m., Wednesday night, and the bar was dead. Wendy Birrell had been tending bar at Murphy's for three years. Her wage was eight bucks an hour, plus tips. That was on weekends; on weeknights, the place was a tomb except for the odd barfly, so tips were scarce. Tonight, like most, she wore tight, low rider jeans that hugged her slim figure, and a plaid button-down shirt that draped neatly across her ample breasts. Her hair flowed in straight, dirty blonde cascades over her shoulders and onto the swell of her breasts. This was done purposely to arouse the male patrons. Aside from her figure, it was Wendy's eyes that turned a man's head. They were deep glacial blue, a color found in arctic waters lapping against icebergs.

Wendy Birrell was twenty-eight, she had a high school education and only one motivation in life. His name was Patrick. He was four, had his mother's eyes, and curly, corn silk hair. Patrick's father, also blond, had been a marine. Had, because he'd been killed in Iraq when Patrick was only four months old. He and Wendy were never a couple. He had been a fling, nothing more, but had he lived, she would have included him in her son's life; had he known. He hadn't and Wendy didn't have a lot of options, so she tended bar, lived paycheck to paycheck and, for now, that was enough.

Most of the regulars were gone at this hour. Shuffling out after a few too many, slurring their words as they put on a coat or slung a purse like awkward preschoolers dressing to go outside and play. All gone. Except for one young man sitting at the corner of the bar sipping a Rolling Rock and stealing glances at her. He couldn't have been more than twenty-one. He'd been in a couple of times this week, sitting unremarkably on the corner stool. She would have carded him, but then that would have chewed up any chance at a tip, and he'd left her a ten spot every time he was in. No one at Murphy's left a ten spot. She figured him for a college kid, or maybe he'd been working at one of the vineyards during the spring plant. Tonight, just like every night he'd been in, he sat alone, glancing her way and checking her out. When she looked over, he would avert his contemplation to the beer bottle he held. No doubt perusing the alcohol content or maybe the origin of the brewery. Men were such predictable animals. She was checking him out as well, but it wasn't as obvious. Eventually, she worked her way to that corner of the bar, and he began to chat her up.

"You from around here?" He was looking directly at her.

"I live in Westvale." She polished the bar with the rag as she spoke.

"You go to SU when you're not working?" he asked.

She laughed, shook her head. "No, I'm not exactly what you would call university material."

Silence then, hanging between them uncomfortably.

"I just thought..."

"What? That I was working my way through college." She smiled scathingly. "Isn't that what half the strippers say over at The Chub?" The Chub, aka Chubby's, was what some might call a gentleman's club. "Why aren't you there?"

"Sorry, I guess I was mistaken."

She stopped then, furrowed her brow and the cynical smile fell away. Why had she spoken to this guy like that? He wasn't anything but nice, and he had slipped her a ten every night he's been in. "Aw, shit. That didn't come out right. I'm sorry, I didn't mean that."

"It's okay. I shouldn't have been nosy."

"No, I shouldn't have been a bitch. Let's start over."

"Okay."

"My name's Wendy. What's yours?"

He looked up from the beer and grinned. "Devon."

She dropped the cloth on the bar, stuck out her hand and said, "It's nice to meet you, Devon. Are you from around here?"

He took her hand, his skin warm, smooth, and without callous. "I'm going to the university."

She pulled her hand back, placed it over her mouth, giggled and then broke into laughter. He shook his head and smiled. When the laughter subsided, she grabbed him another beer. He reached for his wallet, and she said, "This is on the house."

It was an hour before closing, and at that moment, she really didn't think that she would end up sleeping with him. She hadn't been with anyone for some months. But when she got home that evening and squared Patrick away, well... The idea of a warm body next to hers seemed appealing. This idea hadn't begun to brew in the beginning, but as he sipped his beer, talked a bit about what he was taking at Syracuse University, the word "maybe" began to echo in the back of her subconscious.

Fifteen minutes later, she set another Rolling Rock on the bar at his request, and she said, "You're not driving are you, Devon?"

"No, I walked. I'll probably grab a cab back to the university."

And then she decided. "I'm off in half hour. I can drive you to the university if you like."

"Aw, that's okay. I don't wanna be any trouble."

"No trouble. Besides, you'll never get a cab at this hour. I can drive you back to the university if you like, or maybe we can go somewhere for coffee." His eyes brightened at this, became charmingly boyish. She imagined a lean, young man beneath those clothes. Virile young man too. He would probably only last thirty seconds after getting into bed, but he'd be quick on the rebound.

"I don't have any classes until tomorrow afternoon."

"That settles it then," Wendy said, and as he finished his beer, she went about the business of closing down. She moved around the bar collecting glasses, wiping things down, and eventually squaring up the cash. He sipped the last of his beer, watching her every move.

This was going to be easy.

She had him step out and wait on the front walk while she put away the evening deposit and set the alarm. Devon was the consummate young gentleman. He'd only had three beers, and if she made an offer to bring him back to her place, she guessed it wouldn't affect his performance in the least. When she slid the deadbolt over and removed her key, she made her final decision. He was cute.

"Let's go." She led him to her car, a beat-up Chrysler Cirrus sitting curbside. She unlocked the car. They climbed in. She turned the key in the ignition, and the engine came alive. She reached over, placed a hand on his, and said, "You want me to take you back to the university, or would you rather come home with me?"

He smiled. "What do you think?"

She slid her hand up his leg and held it there, a finger teasing his manhood. "I think you want to come home with me." Then she kissed him. Wendy was not promiscuous— this was definitely out of the norm for her—but she was a single mom, and that was a lonely business. She pulled back from the kiss, put the gearshift into drive, and pulled away from the curb.

The ride to her house consisted of touching and feeling, but very few words. There was no need for discussion. It had been established: they were going to have sex. As she steered the car with her left hand, the right reached down between his legs, rubbing and massaging. He answered by caressing her breasts, causing her nipples to harden and stirring something inside her. This anticipation was almost too much and Wendy considered pulling the Cirrus over and jumping into the back seat with him.

No, she couldn't do that. Patrick was at home, and... oh shit, she'd almost forgotten about her mother. She pushed him off gently. "Devon, I need you to do something when we get to my house."

"Okay. What?"

"My mom, she's watching my son. You'll have to stay outside until she leaves."

Devon laughed, "You want me to hide in the bushes or something?"

She turned left up another street and said, "How about you just duck down in the car until I give you a signal."

"I could do that, but what if she catches me and..."

He was going to say *calls the cops*. But Wendy cut him off.

"I park my car in the front of the house, on the street. There's only one parking spot out front, so my mom parks in the back alley. She won't be coming out the front. She won't catch you if you duck down low. I'm sorry about all the cloak and dagger stuff, but I just don't feel like explaining to my mother that I'm bringing a stranger home for the night.

"How long will I have to wait?"

"Probably not too long, my mom sometimes falls asleep in front of the TV. So I may have to wake her up. I don't know, five maybe ten minutes."

"Alright. I don't generally do this on first dates, so I hope you'll appreciate all the effort."

She grinned. "I do, and it'll be worth your while."

2

They rolled up to the curb five minutes later. About a hundred feet before coming to a stop, she told him to get down and lay his head on her lap. And with that, she parked and cut the engine. He could feel the heat coming off of her. It was a subterranean heat. Brought on by the petting and groping.

She shut off the ignition and whispered, "Ten minutes and I'll come get you."

"Okay, ten minutes," he agreed.

She slid out from underneath him, leaving his head to rest on the cloth seat. She closed the car door, and he heard her footsteps as she made her way up the walk. He heard the clicking of steps as she climbed the porch, then the screen door creaked, a door handle clicked over, or maybe it was a deadbolt. He couldn't be sure. He couldn't see anything above the orange bleaching of the dashboard from the arc sodium street lamps.

Ten minutes, he thought.

He wondered if the mother would come out and catch him hiding in the car. Or maybe a local patrol notified by a nosy neighbor. What if she were to deny his presence? "Oh no, officer, I don't know him. I have no idea why he was hiding in my car." The game would have ended right there. He'd be carted off to jail. He was sure shit like that happened from time to time. What would his father say to that? The old man would be royally pissed.

This made him grin.

3

None of those things happened. As promised, in less than ten minutes, she came down the steps to the car and whispered, "Come on, the coast is clear." He sat upright, and she opened the car door.

"You're sure it's safe?"

She smiled, took his hand, and led him up the path.

When she closed the front door behind them and turned the bolt, she reached over, pulled him in and gave him a long kiss, running her tongue over his. Then she drew back and said, "I have some beer in the fridge."

She kissed him again.

He said, "Maybe later" and began touching her all over. She ran her hands down to his nether regions, feeling his hardness. He did the same, feeling her heat. They kissed, an intertwining mess of fumbled gropes that were desperate and blurry with sexual need. All the while, they worked their way toward the bedroom, once almost tripping and falling down. She laughed and pulled off his shirt. He tugged off hers. She stroked his chest, barren of even a single hair. He unsnapped her bra. By the time they were at the bedroom door, she was in her panties, he in his briefs. Behind them a debris trail of clothing. She dropped her undies and tugged at his briefs. When they dropped, she cupped him, and suddenly stopped and looked down. Then she looked up at him.

"My last girl didn't like hair."

She looked down again. She held onto him. Not even a single hair. "Why?" she asked. "What was her problem with hair?" She brought her eyes up to his, still holding his manhood tightly.

"She said, 'It ruined the mood if you had to lick the pillow.'" He started to grin.

Wendy giggled and worked her hand.

They fell onto the bed side by side. No more talk, just touching.

But then...

"I gotta get something out of my jeans," he said.

"I have condoms in the nightstand," she whispered, and she reached over with one hand and pulled the drawer clumsily open. She brought a strip of condoms up and held it before him. He bit down on the corner with his teeth, and she removed it and went to work. It rolled on with ease, she supposed the smoothness of his clean-shaven skin helped in that regard.

Then they got busy.

He lasted longer than she initially thought. Over two minutes. Then she went to work on him and got him back into the game in under four. Young men bounced back so quickly. With the old condom tied off and discarded, she rolled a second one on and they found their rhythm. This time, he lasted almost twenty-five minutes. When it was over, she was spent.

"Thank you," she said.

He didn't say anything, he just lay there watching her, a thin smile on his face.

"I gotta check on my son. Do you want that beer now?"

"I'd love one," he said.

He sat up against the headboard, watching her naked form disappear through the doorway, fading in the dim light of the hall. She was wraith-like, melting in and out of reality. A little while later, she returned with a can of Budweiser and handed it to him. It was ice cold.

"Thank you," he said and sipped. Then added, "That was fun."

"More fun than a college girl?"

He turned his head and said, "Way more fun than a college girl."

"And no pillow licking." She giggled.

"Yeah."

She wrapped herself around him. Using his bare chest as a headrest and he listened to her breathing. In no time, she was falling asleep. He counted down the space between each inhalation and exhalation, the gap was widening. He'd been afraid he wouldn't be able to perform, but he'd come through. She was, and he meant it, way better than any college girl. Most of the girls at SU were fucking airheads, but moreover, they were dead fucks. Not her. She wrapped her legs around him, then literally squeezed from inside as he thrust. That was talent. Definitely a sign of experience. He hadn't expected this to happen: he was planning on a couple beers and fully intended on heading back to the dorm.

He grinned. Fate was a strange thing.

Half an hour later, cossetted in sleep, she rolled off him, turning her back and pressing her buttocks against his leg. He lay still, fully alert, considering the situation as he ran a hand over her shoulder and into the hourglass of her waist. She had a nice body for a woman who had a child. He guessed you made it your business to look good, especially when you were raising a kid alone. He wondered where the father might be. Guessed that he wouldn't be too happy if he were to walk in now.

Somehow, he doubted this scenario was likely. Daddy was long gone. He looked at the two spent condoms sitting on the nightstand.

Then slid quietly from the bed.

There was much to do.

4

She hadn't known what woke her. Dream or premonition, but she had come up out of the sleep into a sitting position even before her senses were roused. Her mind pricked, pins and needles, her eyesight still unfocused. She had heard her name. Not urgent, but calling in a whisper.

"Wendy, wake up. Wendy, wake up."

Slowly, she pulled focus adjusting to the dark of the room. She saw a naked silhouette standing in the bedroom doorway. It was him. Devon.

"What are you doing?" she asked.

"Are you awake now?"

"Come back to bed."

He said nothing, stepping through the doorway, moving closer. He was holding something in his right hand. She couldn't quite see.

He took another step.

It didn't register at first. Or wouldn't register.

Something in his hand, something in his right hand. What was it?

He took yet another step.

"Wendy?"

"What are you holding?"

He took another step.

Then it began to register.

No. Oh dear God, no. No! Oh my...

"It's okay. He never felt a thing."

Never felt a thing? No!

She felt the scream building, expanding inside her, a hard, jagged ball in her throat, cutting her oxygen. It wanted to escape, but she couldn't find her voice.

Or wouldn't.

To do so was to acknowledge the unthinkable.

He took another step.

The small, round object hung from his right hand. Like the head of a doll.

No, not a doll: bigger.

It was...

She knew then.

Oh my god!

"Patrick," she moaned and then the scream began to rise like a whistling tea kettle.

Why?

He closed in then, his pace quick and deliberate. His other hand rising—moonlight gleaming off steel—before she could scream, he severed her windpipe. She felt an initial sting, and then there was a pop, but no actual pain. He hovered, watching intently as the darkness turned the black to blue, light to gray. Her life was spilling out, like a river running into the sea, swallowed by the abyss.

Her eyes closed.

Opened.

It was better this way. At least she would be with him.

Then nothing.

5

He showered. Massaging the water over his skin, pushing into the contour of each muscle and rubbing away the blood. There had been a lot of blood. Some had already congealed on his naked form, and when he touched it, it flecked away.

He worked his way to the shower, using a towel to pull back the curtain and stepped in. The water had been cold at first, causing his limp penis to contract even further. At his feet, the water puddled in swirls of diluted crimson before being pulled to the drain in tendrils. He followed the drops as they fell into the pool.

Plop... Plop... Plop...

It was a lot of blood.

A lot of DNA, he told himself.

He shouldn't have had sex with her. But then, he hadn't planned on killing her. No, that wasn't quite right. He was thinking about killing her. She was the one who had initiated the sex. He had been thinking about killing her from the first time he saw her, but he thought about killing people all the time. It wasn't unique to her. He could have easily taken the ride back to the dorm and continued his fantasy.

He rubbed the back of his neck, the hot water beating away even more blood.

How did that get back there?

Correction. He hadn't planned on killing them. Yes, them, but he needed to be thinking about other things. "DNA," he said aloud. How much DNA had he dropped here? "A lot of DNA." He rubbed the back of his neck and considered his penis. He'd used a condom, but there would be drops left on the bed. And what of his skin? The bump and grind they'd performed would have rubbed off dead skin. He'd shaved down there for that reason, but there was still the short, cropped cut on his head. His eyebrows.

"Fucking DNA."

He wasn't in a database anywhere. He had no record.

But your DNA will be now and if you're ever picked up?

"Fucking DNA!" He smashed a fist against the tiling.

He inventoried his body. Every nook visible to the naked eye and thought he was clean. He then took a cloth and used the shower head to rinse the tub in swirling gyrations. Why? He wasn't sure. He'd probably left enough fiber and

DNA lying around for an easy conviction. He needed to get dressed, clean up, and consider his options.

He climbed from the shower onto the bath mat and toweled off. Once dry, he dressed and stared into the small vanity. Was it how he thought it would be? This being his first. No, but then was it ever going to be? The act had been deliberate and mechanical. He didn't think it was the act that he sought for gratification anyway. No, the act was just a means to an end. He thought of all the others he read about. The killers who'd risen through the ranks to stardom. Ted Bundy, John Wayne Gacy, whose names were as household in modern culture as Van Gogh or da Vinci. Perhaps even more.

He wiped the tub with the towel.

"Notoriety," he said. That's what they had in common. But that wasn't exactly right either. Then the word came to him. He wandered back to the bedroom. Looked in on them. The clock on the nightstand read 3:34 a.m.

"Fucking DNA." He glanced out the window into the back yard. There was a small aluminum gardening shed back there. On either side of the yard, tall hedges offered relative privacy.

Better get to it, he thought.

He went out the back door as quietly as possible and found the shed unlocked. He slid the door over, the aluminum scraping against the track in weak protest. He had rubber gloves on now. The yellow ones used for washing dishes. Condoms for the hands. Glancing around he saw a tricycle, presumably Patrick's, lying on its side. There was an old lawnmower. Beside that, a five-gallon jerry can, much too big for the likes of a lawnmower. He could see Wendy struggling with that jerry can, splashing gas all over the lawn mower.

Not anymore, he thought and smiled.

Neither she nor Patrick would be visiting this shed again.

He lifted the jerry can; it was half full.

It'll have to do.

Inside the house, he retraced his path, as best he could remember, splashing the gas in places where he thought he might have left evidence. He doused the bodies, the condoms, the towels he'd used. He gave the bed where they'd had sex a good soaking. The kid's crib also got a good soaking. When he emptied it, he placed the can at the foot of her bed.

He then went back to the kitchen and opened the stove. It was an electric job. He turned the oven on and watched the burners. They immediately began to glow. He switched it off and searched the cupboards. He needed more accelerant. This place had to burn. The DNA had to be destroyed.

"Fucking DNA," he grunted again and pulled out a bottle of vegetable oil. He unscrewed the cap and soaked the counter. That wouldn't burn as fast, but it would still burn. Then he grabbed a bag of sugar and spread the granules into the oil. He'd seen sugar burn, had tossed it into a fire once, it flared and left a sweet scent in the air. He wandered into the living room, careful not to step on the trail of gas he'd left on the carpet. The vapors that hung in the air were intoxicating, and he was getting the beginnings of a headache. He'd been very careful not to get any on him, but he would probably still smell of it. He'd have to get his clothes into the wash as soon as he got back to SU.

He found a stack of newspapers and magazines by the couch and brought them back to the kitchen. He arranged them on the oven rack and considered. It looked plausible. Stove ignites papers, papers ignite the gas and soon enough the house would be on fire and...

"No more fucking DNA," he said.

How long would it take? Five minutes? Ten?

He wasn't sure. Arson wasn't his strength.

He'd have to move fast.

He gazed at the body of the woman and that of her decapitated son, burning the images into his mind.

This is like painting a masterpiece and setting it on fire, he thought.

He took one last glance around the house. Then the word came to him. He turned on the oven and tossed the rubber gloves onto the counter. Tore off a roll of paper towel and used it to wipe the doorknob as he exited the house. *Infamous,* he thought. *That was the word I was looking for. Infamous, and I just did something that would be remembered for a long time.*

"And I just burned it all up," he muttered in a low, angry grunt.

Lighting fire to a masterpiece.

Not yet; it was only art at this point. He had to hone his craft. Polish his work, and if he didn't get caught for this, he would be well on his way. He made it four blocks and disappeared around the corner when the paper flared up.

By the time he was a mile away, fire snaked down the halls into the adjacent room to the main sources of gasoline. The smoke detectors in Patrick and Wendy's room cried out, but only briefly, falling victim to the intense heat.

He walked all the way back to SU, drawing the attention of a slumbering homeless man, but only for a second and it rose no alarm.

When he reached the dorm, he stripped and put his clothes in the wash. An hour had elapsed, and miles away, the little, post-war bungalow was burning savagely. He was stepping into the shower when the fire department arrived. They turned on the water, sprayed it on all sides, but it was already too far gone, burning out of control. The volunteer fire captain had no illusions; there wouldn't be anyone in the furnace left alive to save. The chief was on his way. All they could do was try and protect the neighboring houses.

Showered, Lance, not Devon, dressed in sweat pants and a Syracuse University tee. "Infamous," he said and lay back on the bed. He hoped that he'd gotten everything. He'd heard the sirens calling in the night, at first far off. Then, another set of sirens awoke, and he knew they were on their way to help. He considered going online, to see if there was something about it on one of the local media sites, then thought better of it. Too dangerous. The Internet was like a strand of DNA, maybe even worse; he didn't want to leave a trail. But that would all change, because he was learning about the Web, and soon he'd be learning about the Deep Web, and in those murky waters, a predator could hide in plain sight.

"Next time," he said. "Next time, I will be prepared." He thought about Bundy, about Gacy, as if he were aspiring to their greatness, their infamy. No, he would be better. He had no intention of being caged, electrocuted or injected. His achievements would be greater, would shock and horrify. He shut his mind down then, falling off to sleep, sliding in the shade of dreamlessness.

***

Chapter 2 - Out of the Ashes

1

8 May 2000

Westvale, NY — Crime Scene

A morose collectiveness hung over the scene, infecting all involved, painted on the faces of rescue workers, the uniformed cops. With it, a pungent aroma of septic water, slag, and cooked flesh hung in the air. The house was gone except for the framework of charred wall studs that looked like black toothpicks spiking out of the floor plan. The scene smoldered beneath the thousands of gallons of water that had been poured upon it. Crime scene tape surrounded the property, twisting in the morning breeze. The tape had been put up by a uniformed cop after the fire chief told him to do it. The chief called the Syracuse PD asking for a homicide detective.

Hayward had caught the case and was waiting on the fire chief to fill him in. The lawn below his feet had been scorched by the intense blaze. Blades of grass, now coarse straw, crunched beneath his shoes as he drifted just outside the perimeter.

What am I looking at? he wondered.

"I'll be right with you, Detective." The man calling to him was Westvale Fire Chief Ronny Bush. Hayward knew Bush; they were related through marriage. Bush's daughter had married Hayward's nephew. Though they didn't fish or drink together, they had eaten an occasional meal at an outdoor barbeque or three. He thought Bush was a decent guy.

Hayward raised his hand, acknowledging the fire chief, running over the unknowns in his head. Even the uniformed cop, he'd shown his shield upon arrival, had been tight-lipped about the victims. Hayward didn't push the kid, figured he probably didn't have much anyway. As he waited, he considered the scene. He'd been to plenty of fires and those that involved homicide were usually murder-suicide. Some mutt, who's on the cusp of divorce, decides to off his family, then kill himself. It wasn't always a man, women could be equally selfish. Maybe that's what this was, individual kills lover or perhaps kid, then lights the place up and checks out.

Makes sense, he thought, *but after an inferno like this, how would first responders know? The bodies or body would be burned beyond recognition, and the body snatchers weren't even here to transport the victims back to the morgue. So how does everyone know it's a crime scene?*

Hayward knew he was going to find out. In fact, it was down to minutes—but he was a creature of inquisition—not all that good at waiting. Speculation was the mental game he played at crime scenes in anticipation of the facts. It was his way of staving off impatience and prepping to compartmentalize emotion. For him, emotion was the enemy when investigating a murder. Not that he was a heartless bastard, he wasn't. Becoming attached to a victim, no matter what the mystery novels said, was never what led to closing a case. He'd seen his share of fellow detectives become attached, usually as a case grew colder and solving it became less likely. He had a case that he was close to, that had never been solved, probably never would be, but he knew if he were going to continue to be a homicide detective, he had to jettison his emotions. Not completely, but as much as possible.

Bush was at his left, drawing him out of the mental game. He'd finished with his own detail and giving out orders to his own people. "We have two victims. One adult and one child."

"Okay, Ron, and I am here because?"

"You're here because the victims didn't start the fire. They were murdered before the fire was started."

Hayward turned towards the chief, an intrusive smile tugging at the edges of his mouth. "You say this fire was started by someone else, okay. What makes you think it was a murder?"

Bush's face transformed then, his complexion graying, his demeanor softening, even empathetic. Ronny Bush looked Hayward straight in the eyes and said, "Because we found a skull in the adult victim's bedroom. It was a child's skull, and it should've been attached to the body, which we found in another bedroom."

"Fuck." Hayward heard himself say, then, "Go on."

"I don't know what could be left for evidence. The place is a mess. We really soaked it down. It'll be really muddy in there. Shit, some of it is still smoldering, and my guys have tromped all over it. We found a molten gas can, we think that's the accelerant. Right next to it, we found the skull at the foot of what used to be the adult victim's bed. When we found the kid's skull, we backed off." Bush took a deep breath. "I've seen a lot of horrible shit as a firefighter, but this takes the fucking cake. It's not just horrible. It's fucking abominable. The worst part, Brad. Worst fucking part is we might have assisted this animal in destroying whatever evidence you might need to catch him." Bush sat down on the hood of Hayward's car. He was knocked over by this.

"Take it easy, Ron." Hayward patted him on the shoulder, then he was on the phone. Calling for more backup and crime scene techs, more uniforms to canvas for witnesses. As he did this, he was assessing. The street would have to be cordoned off better than this. Sooner or later, there'd be a lot more press.

He looked past Bush and waved over the uniform who had let him on to the scene. When the kid came up, he told him to gather everyone who worked the scene and have them meet at his car.

"Ron, we need to keep a lid on this."

"Keep a lid on it?"

"The murder will get out, but the details... The kid's head being cut off. Can you get your people to dummy up on the details? It's important. I need to hold stuff back. There'll be wackos confessing to this."

"Yeah, I think so."

"Good, let's gather 'em up and have us a chat." His cell rang and he answered. "Hayward." This was followed by "Yeah." And "ETA?" and "Whatever you can give me."

Bush was listening, rubbing his pug nose and collecting himself at the same time. He felt weak, ashamed, and he wondered if his own people had seen that weakness. He stiffened, let out a brooding sigh, one of a man who is waiting for an unpleasant situation to end.

2

9 May 2000

Syracuse University

The police showed a full twenty-four hours after the murders. Almost to the exact time. The call came on his cell. The ringtone, an Animals' tune, "House of the Rising Sun," woke him. When he picked it up, the caller ID read Unknown Caller. He pushed the answer button and said, "Hello?"

"Hello, is this Lance Belanger?" said a man's voice.

He sat up, wiped his eyes. "Yes."

"Lance, my name is Detective Brad Hayward. I need to speak to you. I am parked outside your dormitory. Can I confirm your room number and come up?"

Panic cut through him. He gave his head a shake, trying to jar the sleepiness. "I was sleeping."

"Yes, I understand and I apologize, but I need to talk to you."

"Um, okay? But what is this about?"

"Son, I would prefer to come up and speak to a person."

"Okay, I'm in room 341."

"You have a roommate, Lance?"

His stomach churned.

He's here to arrest me! They know about the killings, something I left behind. Something I missed! He swallowed— his throat clicked—he needed water. He croaked, "No... I have my own room."

Did that sound desperate, afraid?

He thought so.

"Alright, I'll be up in a minute." The detective's voice had the sound of regret. Or maybe it was disappointment. Yes, disappointment at having to arrest a young man with his whole future in front of him. Lance began to panic. What was he going to do?

Calm down, he thought. *There's no way the cops would call me if they were coming to arrest me. It has to be something else.*

Maybe, but why take a chance?

He stood, the blood in his veins diluted with adrenaline, and went over to his desk. He yanked the drawer open, rummaged through it until he found the pocket knife. *If he's here to arrest me, I'll have to kill him and run. They will freeze everything within hours. I'll need to empty my bank account.* Which wasn't much, maybe nine hundred dollars. He didn't want to go to jail. He'd do whatever he had to. That included killing a cop. He pulled on his sweats, opened the blade and carefully placed it into the pocket.

Then he waited.

There was a knock. A courtesy, he supposed, extended to the other students in the dorm. No point in ruining everyone's night. He took in a breath, wrapped his hand around the knife and opened the door. The man on the other side was an inch shorter than him, roughly fifty years old, and balding. The crown of his head shone under the hall fluorescents. His face was pudgy, much like his stomach. He held an expression of deep concern. "Lance?"

"Yes."

"Can I please come in?"

There was no SWAT team behind him.

"Sure." Lance stepped back and opened the door wider with his left hand, while his right was gently touching the blade in his pocket. He wondered if the anxiety he felt showed on his face. "What's this all about?"

The detective stepped inside, looked around, pulled out the computer chair and said, "I think you better sit down, son."

Lance placed both hands into his pockets, his right tightening around the handle of the knife. "I don't want to sit down, I want to know what this is about."

The second he says anything about the murders I'll cut his throat.

"There's been a fire," Hayward said and sighed.

Lance tightened his grip, readying himself.

"I don't know how to tell you this, son, so I'm just gonna come right out and say it." He stared directly into Lance's eyes and his voice seemed far off. "There was a fire..."

I knew it! I don't have a choice.

"I am afraid I have some really bad news for you."

"Bad news?"

"There was a fire, son. Your parents, they died in a house fire." The detective studied him, waiting for a reaction. They were still investigating the fire, but he doubted this kid had anything to do with it, but still, he waited. He'd seen a few rich kids murder their parents. But he didn't think that was the case here. Then again, he was getting a weird vibe off this kid.

"A fire?" Lance was computing what he'd said. *My parents? I never killed my parents? Was this some sort of cop ruse? Some misdirect?*

Hayward reached out and placed a hand on Lance's shoulder. He stared directly at him, trying to get a bead on what the kid was thinking.

Lance thought that if he knew, Hayward would be reaching for his gun.

Hayward didn't think the kid was guilty. He'd been waiting for a sign, and thus far, there had been none. "I am very sorry, Lance."

Lance lowered his head, unknown to Detective Hayward, he was suppressing a smile.

They're dead, he thought. *A fire.* He wanted to laugh out loud, but he couldn't. There was the knife to think about. He had to say something. "They're dead? Both of them?"

"I'm afraid so."

Safe, he thought. But his reaction. *Was it authentic?*

He sat down on the edge of his bed, and in turn, Detective Hayward took a seat in the computer chair. It creaked under his girth. Hayward was eyeing him, and Lance suddenly realized he was going to be free.

Not if you smile and spook this fat, pig detective. But a smile was coming, completely involuntary, and he wasn't sure if he would be able to stop it. He took evasive action. "I'm sorry, but I think I'm going to vomit." He popped up and pushed passed the detective, opening the door and running down the hall.

Hayward was completely caught off guard. Lance was out the door and halfway to the shared bathroom before Hayward thought of following. The return spring on the door closed behind him, and that was enough time to pull out the knife and dump it into the garbage can as he ran by. When he reached the bathroom, the detective was opening the door and following.

I have to do this fast, he thought. Then he pushed into the toilet stall open and dropped to his knees. Simultaneously, he thrust two fingers, the middle and index, into his throat— accidentally scraping the nail of his index against his uvula. He did not hold back and a second later, the contents of his stomach came up, splashing down over his hand and into the waiting bowl. By the time Hayward got to the stall, he was unspooling the toilet paper to wipe his mouth.

Lance stared into the bowl. A slick of yellow bile, peppered with half-digested food, floated in the center of the toilet water. Like an acidic iceberg, it held its molecular form. A sour stench permeated from the stall. Tears welled up in his eyes, not from remorse, but from the forced discharge of stomach content. *This is good,* he thought and was pulling a large wad of the roll just as the detective entered the stall. He did not wipe the tears, he instead let them track down his face.

"They're dead," he moaned. "I'm... I'm sorry."

"It's okay, son," Hayward said running his hand between his shoulder blades. "This is a perfectly natural reaction."

"I'm alright," Lance said. "Shit, it stinks in here."

"I understand completely." Hayward removed his hand and stepped back as Lance stood up and wiped his mouth.

"I'm not gonna throw up again, Detective," Lance said. "We can go back to my room." He tossed the toilet paper into the bowl but didn't bother to flush. Then he led the detective back to his room.

When they got there, Hayward filled Lance in on what he could. He still didn't know what had caused the fire. The detective was sympathetic and compassionate considering what he'd seen that day. Lance had no idea that Hayward had been on the scene of two fires. The first being set by Lance and the second being coincidence. Hayward only attended the second fire thinking there might be a connection. Normally, a uniformed officer would have been dispatched to deliver the news. Hayward was doing this as a courtesy; he was pretty sure the second fire had nothing to do with the individual he sought. Or with this young man who sat across from him.

"For now, it has been deemed a fire of unknown origin. It's under investigation. Once the fire investigator is done, we'll know more." He patted Lance on the knee. "I'm sorry, Lance. There is no easy way to deliver news like this. Is there someone who can come down and stay with you? A relative maybe?"

Lance nodded. "I have a few friends here. And an uncle in Clarence."

"Would you like me to contact them?"

"No, Detective. I can do that."

Hayward felt guilty relief. As much as he felt sorry for this kid, he was on the hunt. There was a killer out there. A monster that had taken the life of a young woman and her child. He wasn't up for babysitting the bereaved. That might sound insensitive, but he had to get back to his case.

http://wbp.bz/highwaymana

ONE

Sitting upon a bough, the raven watched.

In the dying of the light the little boy swung slowly from the tree, his body broken, a noose around his neck. And at the edge of the forest a car burned and the raven watched as flame rose from the heat like hate rising from the heart of the sun.

The raven and the boy were together as the fire burned and burned and began to fade in the last of the day but still the raven did not move. It stayed upon the bough and did not leave the boy alone until the sun had descended and was gone.

The raven watched as the boy was claimed by the darkness of the night. It watched as the fire smoldered and the smoke vanished in the evening gray that overcame the day. It watched and it watched and it watched and it watched until something else had begun to burn in the dying of the light …

Fire rose in the raven's eyes.

* * *

Joe Mac felt the gray November cold more completely than he'd ever felt it before because he could no longer see the leaves fade from rust to gold or gaze upon the skeletal silhouettes of trees etched against the gray November sky.

Now he lived in the world of the blind, so feeling the cold was all that remained. The rest was darkness and he would inhabit this darkness until the day he died and they buried him in the dirt and this darkness.

The raven came as it always came; it descended with the sound of enormous wings to land with a thunderclap on the home Joe Mac had built for it.

Three years ago they met as Joe Mac was first learning to live in the world of the blind. The raven had come to him every day as he sat alone in the back of the barn, and Joe Mac named him "Poe" after the old poem. And every evening they would sit together in the back of the barn in Joe Mac's eternal night.

Poe did not rise or even seem to notice the familiar Mrs. Clemens as she approached, but then Poe rarely flew away when someone came close. Rather, he seemed to know the exact distance for danger and ignored anything else.

Mrs. Clemens brought Joe Mac his supper – an act Joe Mac reckoned to her uncommon human kindness – and spent a moment to inquire about his health. But Joe Mac sensed something different in Mrs. Clemens tonight. Her steps were halting and seemed to wander before she laid a hand on his shoulder.

Lifting his face, Joe Mac asked, "What is it, Mrs. Clemens?"

Mrs. Clemens shuffled, and Joe Mac felt the strength lessen in the hand; it was not much of a change, it was true, but a hand with little strength is even more revealing when what little strength it possesses is diminished ever more.

Joe Mac repeated more sternly, "What is it, Mrs. Clemens?"

"Oh," moaned Mrs. Clemens, "it's horrible, Mr. Joe Mac. Just horrible. Oh, god, I don't know how to tell you."

"Just say it."

She faltered, "It's about your grandson, Mr. Joe Mac. It's about Aaron. The poor thing disappeared from daycare today."

Joe Mac's left hand tightened on the arm of the chair. "How could they lose a four-year-old boy? Have they called the police?"

"Your poor daughter has called everyone! We're all scared to death something terrible has happened!"

With a shrill cry Poe erupted into the night sky as Joe Mac stood pulling his wool coat more tightly across his chest; he snapped his cane to length. "Why didn't someone tell me about this earlier?" he demanded.

"They've been too busy searching for him, Mr. Joe Mac! They've looked everywhere! And you can't even …"

She let the sentence die.

"Take me to my daughter," said Joe Mac. "And compose yourself, Mrs. Clemens. We don't know that anything terrible has happened. Compose yourself! Stay calm. And take me to my daughter."

TWO

"Here's the case file on that little kid."

Jodi Strong raised her eyes as the file was laid upon her desk. The veteran New York City detective, Thomas Grimes, who delivered the file pulled up a chair and leaned back, folding hands on his chest.

"What do you want with this thing, Jodi?" Grimes asked and didn't attempt to conceal either his curiosity or confusion. "There's already a million cops on this, and we got twenty cases of our own to work."

"I took the original call last week when I was in uniform," said Jodi. "I interviewed the daycare workers, the mother, the father. And then they found the little kid but he was already dead. Just like the others."

Grimes spoke in a weary monotone, "Jodi, it was your case when you were in uniform. It was your case when you took the missing person report. But you got promoted to detective three days ago, and it ain't your case no more. It belongs to the task force and you ain't on the task force, neither. So what are you doing?"

Jodi shook her head, "Grimes, I know it's always a mistake to get personally involved in a case but —"

"Then don't."

"But that scene at the house really shook me up," Jodi continued. "I saw the little boy's room. I saw his picture. I felt like I knew him. And then he ends up … like he ended up." She slapped the file. "I'm tired of this psycho!"

Grimes sighed, "Jodi, the FBI has a thousand people on this. We've got about a million. One more cop ain't gonna make no difference in this. And we need you *here*."

Jodi made a slight sound as she sucked breath through her teeth. Then she said, "He's made a mistake, Grimes. They're just not finding it. Nobody's perfect."

"Well, this psycho is pretty close to perfect because right now the task force guys tell me they don't have a clue. One of 'em told me they're no closer to catching him now than they were four years ago."

Jodi opened the file and leaned back; "Aaron Roberts. Four years old. Abducted from the playground of his daycare. His body was found one hour after sunset –"

"Same as the rest of 'em."

Jodi continued reading as Grimes stood and leaned over her desk.

"Jodi," he began in a patient tone, "listen to me; I'm glad you made detective. I think you're a natural. But you're wasting your time. Whatever mistake this guy made ain't gonna be in no file. There's no fibers, no hairs, no prints, no DNA. There's no witnesses, no video, no tracks." He pointed toward the door. "This guy has killed twenty-four people, and he could walk through that door right now and confess to everything we've got and we wouldn't be able to pin him to a single thing. He doesn't take anything. He doesn't leave anything. He has no motive. He has no face. He has no name. *He's a ghost.*"

"Excuse me."

Jodi lifted her face to see an exceeding large man standing on the far side of her desk at the same moment she realized he was blind.

The man was slightly less than six feet but built like a brick. His body seemed one uniform size from his linebacker shoulders down through his barrel chest to his waist and weightlifter legs. His head was a square granite block set on a short neck. His white hair was standard military high-and-tight. His arms were heavy and the hand holding the cane was thick with strong-looking fingers although he held the shaft with a fisherman's touch.

Jodi was instantly curious why the man's presence gave her a palpitation of alarm. There was certainly nothing obviously threatening about him. And yet an aura of doom seemed to cloak him even more than the knee-length undertaker coat or the impenetrable black glasses; it occurred to Jodi that his appearance could not have been more unsettling if he'd been wearing a black funeral veil over his face. In all he reminded Jodi of a Texas tombstone she'd once seen that read, "*As you are, I once was. As I am, you will be…*"

Jodi whispered, "Good god …"

Grimes turned, gaped, and grabbed one of the man's blacksmith arms. "Joe Mac Blake! I haven't seen you in years, Joe! How ya been, man?"

"You're lookin' at it," said Joe Mac. "They still got you in robbery, Grimes?"

"Same 'ol same." Grimes theatrically lifted a hand toward Jodi as she rolled her eyes; *he's blind, you dolt*. "Jodi, this is ex-homicide detective Joe Mac Blake. Joe is a legend! Joe, this is Detective Jodi Strong. She's the newest member of the team." A laugh. "Well, this is a blast from the past, buddy. What are you doing downtown, man?"

Joe Mac lightly tapped the desk with his cane. "Got a seat for me?"

"Sure." Grimes pulled up a rolling chair. "Sit down."

Joe Mac felt, found the chair, and sat. He turned his face toward Jodi, "Nice to meet you, Jodi. Grimes is a good man. He'll help you get the lay of the land around here, but it won't take you too long." He paused. "Can one of you tell me who's handling the Aaron Roberts case? He was the little boy that got killed last week."

"Officially that case belongs to the task force," said Jodi. "He's another victim of a serial killer we've been trying to catch for a long time."

"The Hangman?"

Jodi stared, then, "We've been ordered from on-high not to use that phrase, but, yeah, it was 'The Hangman.'" She glanced at the file. "But as it happens, Joe, I've got a copy of the file right here."

Joe Mac lifted his face. "Have you had a chance to look at it?"

"No. I just got it. What can I do for you, Joe?"

"Aaron was my grandson." Joe Mac's face was stone. "I know I can't contribute to the forensics, but if you have any personal questions about Aaron, maybe I could help you out a little bit."

Jodi stared. "I'm sorry for your loss, Joe."

"Appreciate it."

After expelling a long breath Jodi said, "Look, Joe, they've got a task force briefing in about twenty minutes. Why don't you come with me? The FBI will be there along with Captain Brightbarton. He's in charge."

"I don't have a badge anymore."

"You're with me. You'll be okay."

Joe Mac rose, his hand moving his cane.

"Let's go."

* * *

Joe Mac knew he was seated in the third row from the back, the second chair from the right side of the room. He'd been here many times during his thirty-five-year career as a New York City uniform patrol officer and then as a gold shield homicide investigator, and he knew every line of this place.

He also knew that the front few rows would be filled with investigators and uniform patrol supervisors. The next rows would contain FBI personnel. And the last few rows would be filled with forensics experts, psychologists, and people like himself.

Captain Steve Brightbarton announced, "All right, gentlemen, you've all had a chance to review the forensics on four-year-old Aaron Roberts. As of this moment we can confirm that Aaron was killed inside that warehouse. The suspect used blunt force trauma to break all his bones – the same thing he did to the other victims – and then he hung him by a noose around his neck. Same as the rest. Forensics says the tool used in the attack was a club coated in bronze, so keep your eyes open for a plain-view search. Crime Scene didn't recover any DNA. No hairs. No fibers. No prints. Not even any touch-DNA. We don't have him on video. We have no witnesses. The car was stolen from a police impound lot, and that's all we got. At this time I'll turn it over to FBI Special Agent Jack Rollins."

There was little to hear besides the rustling of clothing as Jack Rollins stood and Brightbarton took a chair.

"Afternoon," Rollins began, "you all know me. But for the uninitiated my name is Jack Rollins, and I am the Special Agent in charge of the FBI task force. Everything Captain Brightbarton just told you is accurate. I'll only add that the murder of Aaron Roberts is consistent with the twenty-three murders preceding this, so confidence is high that we're dealing with the same suspect. As usual, the suspect left nothing behind. The rope he used was standard clothesline that you can purchase at any hardware store. He torched the vehicle with a half-gallon of gasoline inside a one gallon milk jug armed with a two-dollar, off-the-shelf egg timer so we have no prints, no fibers, and no DNA.

"We have nothing further on a description. We know he uses disguises, and we have him on traffic cameras as an old man, a young man, a poor man, a rich man. The only thing we know for sure is that it's a man. We have isolated no salient physical characteristics that would make him easier to identify. He could be me. He could be you. All we can tell you is that we believe he's a white male in his mid-thirties. He's about six foot, 180 pounds. He very, very strong physically, and we believe he has a superior IQ. So our strategy is for the NYPD to continue their stop and frisk strategy of any and every person of interest. We want you to continue priority patrols and stakeouts of secular daycares, church daycares, schools, malls, playgrounds, parks. Meanwhile, we at the FBI will continue to work forensics and continue our enhanced surveillance of every name the computer spits out. Now, we do not know if this psychopath is armed but, of course, you know to approach him as if he is." He paused. "I know I certainly will. And now I'll turn this over to Dr. Marvin Mason. He's assistant senior anthropologist for New York's American Museum of Natural History. He also has a doctorate in archeology, and he is continuing to work with our Division of Behavioral Science to keep an up-to-date profile on this guy. So, Dr. Mason? Would you, please?"

The chamber was subdued, which allowed Joe Mac to hear Dr. Mason's soft steps and then the microphone was turned, apparently to accommodate his height.

"Thank you," said Mason.

Imperceptibly Joe Mac nodded; yeah, from the depth of his voice Mason wasn't big, but he wasn't a lightweight, either. Joe Mac estimated him at a few inches less than six feet, about 170 pounds. His accent was native Long Island.

"All I can tell you is what I've already told you," Dr. Mason began. "As you know, this subject takes the time to break every bone in a victim's body, and then he hangs them by the neck from a tree. We've done extensive research, and we have found this manner of human sacrifice, or punishment, to be so prevalent in ancient cultures that we can't isolate any specific cult or religion or sect or civilization as the primary instigator. He could have taken it from the Jews or the Gaelic tribes or the Vikings or various Asiatic cultures. All we can say is that we believe you're looking for an individual who kills in this highly methodical manner because he is motivated by some kind of pathological religious psychosis." He paused. "We know you guys are working hard, and all of us at the museum want to help. But that's all we've been able to come up with. There's just nothing exotic enough about what's he doing to narrow it down to any one culture or religion. It's barbaric and savage. But it's not exotic. Throughout recorded history it's something that's been done by almost everybody."

Jodi said, "Dr. Mason?"

Mason paused. "Yes?"

Beside Joe Mac, Jodi stood; she was leaning on the chair before them. "Doctor, how long is he going to keep this up?"

"We believe he's going to keep it up until you catch him or kill him."

"Why do you say that?"

"Just like we don't know what kind of obsession is motivating him, we can't say with any certainty when this obsession will be fulfilled," Mason answered. "I think it's safe to say that you're dealing with someone who is very smart and very cautious but also completely insane and I see no reason why he will stop doing what he's doing."

"History doesn't suggest a motive?" Jodi asked.

Mason sighed; "The closest thing we've found to a motive are rituals used in turn-of-the-century Europe to destroy werewolves." He cleared his throat. "In Europe, when they caught someone they suspected of being a werewolf, they would put them on a rack, break their bones, hang them, and set them on fire. They did the same thing to people suspected of witchcraft. Even in this century. Even in this *country*. But we don't think he's doing all this because he suspects someone of being a werewolf or a witch. We think he's doing it because he's afflicted with a bizarre religious psychosis that is totally beyond the understanding of any sane person and probably beyond his understanding, too. We don't think even he knows why he's doing what he's doing. He doesn't know why he's doing it, but he can't stop himself. That's how crazy we think he is."

"But why do you insist it's a religious psychosis?" Jodi pressed.

"Because breaking someone's bones and hanging them from a tree are traditional religious punishments. Both of them are in the Bible. Both of them are in the Koran. Both of them are in the Torah. In a nutshell, they're universal religious means of punishment for someone breaking a religious law regardless whether that law comes from Yahweh or Allah or Shiva. Does that answer your question?"

Jodi nodded, "Yes, thank you."

FBI Special Agent Jack Rollins stood – Joe Mac heard the scrape of chair legs – and asked, "I'm sorry but I don't know your name Detective –?"

"Detective Jodi Strong, sir."

"Are you on the task force?"

"No," Jodi answered firmly. "I worked the original missing person call on Aaron Roberts when I was in uniform."

Hesitation.

"I see," said Rollins. "Well, the fact is that we don't know any more about who killed Aaron Roberts than we know who killed the rest of the victims, detective. We know this guy's methods. We have no idea who he is or why he's doing this."

"I understand," said Jodi.

She sat.

Joe Mac followed Mason to his chair on the back of the dais and listened as Brightbarton approached the podium.

"That's it, gentlemen," said Brightbarton. "Check your boxes at the end of shift for any updates. And remember: Approach this guy with the most extreme caution. And that means approach him with your gun *out* and shoot him graveyard dead if he even *looks* at you funny. Be careful out there. Dismissed."

Joe Mac didn't move as everyone rose and began filing out the three doors. He lost contact with any presence on the podium in the mulling of footsteps and conversation like one might lose sight of an eagle against the sun. He did know that Jodi hadn't moved. Neither had she opened the file she'd brought from the office. He would have heard the rustling of paper, and there wasn't any.

"I checked up on you," said Jodi.

Joe Mac's voice was a soft growl; "When'd you have time to do that?"

"When I went to the bathroom. You're a legend."

Joe Mac revealed nothing.

"The lady in the bathroom told me that you solved over a thousand homicides. She said you were a detective first grade with a gold shield, and you were one of those real guys always out there, always hunting. Then you lost your eyesight when you rescued that little boy from that house fire. And I know it sucks – I mean, don't get me wrong; I would never say I know *how much* it sucks – but you did save that little boy's life. And I bet you're still a great detective."

Joe Mac lifted his chin. He seemed to hear better that way; he didn't know why. He didn't care. It worked, and if anything worked at this stage of his life, it was good enough. "Are you thinking you could use some help?" he asked.

By the scraping in her seat Joe Mac knew she turned. "Well, Joe, you knew Aaron. And I've already talked to your daughter. She's in no shape to help me or anybody else right now. So what do you say we ride out to that daycare center and take a look around?" She stood. "Anyway, the daycare's right down the road from your daughter's house. And you live close by, don't you?"

"I live in the barn out back," said Joe Mac. "They sort of turned it into an apartment." He shrugged. "It's good enough."

"Then let's take a ride, Joe. If nothing else, I'll take you home."

Joe Mac stood.

"Bring what you got on this case."

* * *

Joe Mac didn't need eyes to know exactly where they were at any moment. His soul knew this terrain by neurological imprint. He imagined that he might have driven much of it by himself even now.

"I don't know if I told you how sorry I am about Aaron," Jodi said – the first time she'd spoken in her squad car. "I know that nothing is fair in this world but this truly wasn't fair in an ungodly, horrible way that should be damned to Hell."

Someone once said the greatest sound is silence, but Joe Mac couldn't remember who it was. He only knew he had nothing to say until Jodi finally turned the squad car slowly to the left and announced, "Here we are, Joe."

She parked and Joe Mac could feel her stare.

"You ready for this?" she asked.

Joe Mac nodded and opened the door.

"Let's do it," he said.

He extended his cane though he hardly needed it; he could remember every inch of this daycare since he'd seen if often enough when he could still see; it was a compact one-story building with three wings like a *T*. There was a playground with brightly colored plastic equipment out back. It was surrounded by mesh fence about four feet high that had a gate leading into the building. There was one exterior gate on the left. The entire facility was a half-acre surrounded by pines.

Joe Mac had already moved to the front of Jodi's car as she walked up and said, "Do you remember the layout?"

"Yeah."

"Wanna go up to the fence?"

"All right."

Joe Mac had no problem negotiating the sparsely occupied parking lot. He felt the curb with his cane and stepped up knowing the feel of grass beneath his feet; it was a half-inch deep with dry ground beneath. He estimated three steps to the fence, and he was right. He placed a hand on the top of the steel mesh and lifted his chin.

He became aware that he was waiting for … something
….

"Those pine trees back there," said Jodi. "Do you think he could have come in through those? They would have hidden him from view until he came right up to the fence."

"He could have." Joe Mac turned his face toward the back acreage as if he could still see. His voice was faint. "Still green up top. Thick enough. Dead pine needles don't make a sound when you walk on 'em … Yeah. Let's go back there. I know the crime scene boys went over it but it won't hurt to do it again."

"I'm game," Jodi said, and they turned to walk along the fence line.

The front easement had been mowed up to the steel mesh, so Joe Mac didn't have to worry about weeds. Then he felt Jodi's hand at his left elbow, guiding him gently, and he wasn't offended. Guiding a blind man by a light touch at an elbow was something people just seemed to do by instinct.

Joe Mac was accustomed to the drag of his cane on grass; it was much different than the steady, balanced, light touch he used on concrete. He had to lift it higher and touch more quickly; it was more like stabbing fish than the smooth side-to-side he normally used.

Joe Mac estimated twenty steps to the end of this fence line, and he was right. They turned to the left and resumed walking when Jodi said, "I think he used this side. The other side faces the road, and I don't think he'd use that. He'd have to stop his car on the road, jump out, run up to the fence and try to grab one of them. And the kids would have probably run away from him, screamed for their teacher, and they would have called for a unit. He would have never been able to get out of the area before one of us caught up to him. I think he knew that."

"You're right," said Joe Mac. "He wouldn't do that."

"This guy doesn't leave anything to chance." Jodi's voice took a tinge of impatience. "Sometimes it amazes me how crazy people can be so smart when it comes to killing other people. It's almost … cosmic."

They reached the section furthest from the building, and Joe Mac said, "Stop here. What do you see?"

Jodi said, "Well, this is the farthest point of the fence, and they don't mow the grass back here. It's about waist high right up to the playground. But it's been stomped down a little by the search party."

"How big was the search party?"

"It wasn't all that big. There wasn't enough time to organize a big search party or even get the word out. Aaron was reported missing at three in the afternoon, and they found his body at seven-thirty." A pause. "If he'd been missing for a whole day I'm sure we'd have had thousands of people walking the woods out here. But all they had that day was a few cops and some neighbors. Then they found Aaron's body beside that warehouse, and there was no more reason to look."

"Keep moving," Joe Mac motioned. "Keep looking down. Tell me what you see. It doesn't matter what it is."

They strolled and Jodi began "Looks like we got one rabbit hole … Rabbit tracks … There's a fresh mole hill … A coke can … "

"Bag it."

"Got it."

They continued.

"We got another mole hill … A blue leaflet … Bagging it … A candy bar wrapper … Bagging it …. I don't know why those guys didn't bag all this stuff … Amateurs … I should have come back here myself, but I was at your daughter's house …"

"I appreciate it. Keep looking."

"I don't think this is going anywhere, Joe … This coke can and candy bar wrapper look really old … I don't think they have anything to do with what happened …"

"Never assume anything, kid. Keep going."

"Okay … Well, there's some kind of dead thing … Looks like it used to be a bird … There's a piece of white string …"

Joe Mac stopped. "What?"

"What?" Jodi repeated.

"A what?"

"A string?"

"Did you say 'white string?'"

"Yeah. It's white."

"You wearing your gloves?"

"Yeah."

"Pick it up."

Jodi led him to the wood line, bent, and straightened. After a pause, she said, "It's just an ordinary piece of white string, Joe."

"Follow it."

After a moment, Joe Mac felt a tug on his arm. "This is kind of tricky, Joe. Stick close to me. It …" They took several steps, "… it leads into the woods."

"Just follow it."

Jodi suddenly stooped and stayed low for a long time. "That's it," she said. "That's the end of it. It doesn't go any further."

"What's beyond this wood line?" he asked. "Can you see?"

"Yeah. Way back there. There's a field."

"Take me to it."

By Joe Mac's count it was thirty-seven steps to the field – his entire life existed now in how many steps it was from anything here to anything there. They stood for a long time and Joe Mac knew they were in the open because the trees no longer shielded him from the wind and he could feel the sun on his face.

"Anything?" he asked.

"Joe," she said with noticeable consternation, "what am I supposed to be looking for in an empty field?"

"Just tell me what you see."

"Well," he heard her hands slap her thighs, "I don't see anything but grass, Joe. And … whoa. I can see your daughter's house from here. It's about a half-mile away. Maybe a little more. Hey, is that your little green barn back there?"

"I reckon. Unless they got two barns."

"It's cute." Jodi took a moment. "Okay, the only other thing I see back here are some crows circling something on the other side of the field. Something must have died over there. Probably a coyote or a rabbit. Nothing else would –"

"Crows?" asked Joe Mac.

"Yeah. They look like crows."

"Take me over there."

They began across the high grass, and Joe Mac got the hang of it pretty quick; he'd do fine unless he stepped in a hole. Otherwise he could move as easily as Jodi seemed able, and then Jodi grabbed his arm; "Hold it, Joe. Yeah. I can see what it is."

"Is it a dead animal?" asked Joe Mac.

"Looks like it."

"A dead cat?"

Silence.

"Joe? How could you *possibly* know that it's –"

"Is it a dead kitten?"

"God Almighty. Yeah, it looks like it used to be … a kitten."

"How long has it been dead?"

"Uh … well, I'm not really an expert at decomposition, Joe, but it looks to me like it's been dead about a week. I don't know what those crows think they're eating, but there's not much left."

"So why are they circling?"

Jodi paused. "It looks to me like this really big crow is getting the rest of them all worked up over the bones. He's, like, herding them. Or something."

"Bait," Joe Mac stated with a bitter frown. "The string. A kitten. Aaron didn't go to the fence to see a man. He was taught to run from strangers. He walked over to see a kitty cat tied to the end of a string. The man was hiding in the grass. Then, once Aaron was distracted, this guy rushed up, snatched him over the fence, and ran off with him. Quick as that. He snatched the cat up, too, but threw it down after he was clear. He probably didn't think it was important enough to take the cat. He didn't think anybody would put it together. Or maybe Aaron was putting up a good fight, and he needed both hands." His teeth gleamed. "Yeah. That was probably it. He would have taken the cat, too, but Aaron was putting up a good fight and so he killed the cat. Broke its neck. Tossed it."

"Why didn't he just leave the cat at the daycare?"

"It's too obvious. And it's probably a trick he's used more than once. If it got in the papers he'd have one less trick."

Silence and sadness seemed to overlay them, and Joe Mac could faintly hear Jodi's movements. He knew she was standing with arms crossed, staring. He didn't feel like saying anything, either, as she whispered, "How horrible."

"Yes."

Her shriek cut the air, and Joe Mac heard her jump back. She gasped before she exclaimed, "That crow flew right over my head!"

She reached down as if to pick up a rock.

"Wait," said Joe Mac.

"What!"

"Is it a big crow?"

"Biggest crow I ever saw, that's for sure! God bless! That thing scared me to death! It could have parted my hair."

Joe Mac took a slow half-turn toward the tree line. He simply stood until he heard the familiar caw and he nodded. "And you say the crows led you here?"

"What?"

"The crows? They led you to the bones?"

"Actually, it was just that really big one. The one that scared me. He was circling around the bones real high, sort of herding the other crows down over the cat. I think he's like … their leader. I mean, if crows have 'leaders.'" Suddenly she jumped back. "Look out, Joe!"

Joe Mac heard the familiar, powerful wings as Poe soared over him low enough to touch and listened until Poe was gone. Then he started forward.

"Look for some foot prints."

* * *

"Yeah!" shouted Captain Steve Brightbarton as he swung a fist through the air. "The psycho finally made a mistake!"

Jodi turned at the edge of the roped-off crime scene to see Joe Mac standing like a black harbinger of death in the middle of the field; the gigantic crow rested on the ground beside him like a faithful servant. She turned and walked forward, and when she reached Joe Mac she was curious that the crow didn't fly away.

It simply stood where it stood.

Staring at her.

"They've made casts of two shoe prints," she said. "They're way outside the earlier search grid. That's why the neighbors didn't find them, although I don't think they would have put it together anyway. They say the crow led them back to where he musta' parked his car." She hesitated. "Now that we've got a footprint, we might be able to trace the brand of shoe. If we're lucky, it's exotic. If not, we'll just run down everybody wearing Nikes. We might be looking at a billion suspects, but we'll know he's *one* of them."

"What are the prints like?" asked Joe Mac.

Jodi expelled a long breath. "They look to me like some kind of tennis shoe. Maybe a size ten or eleven. Like I say, the guys don't know what brand, yet, but they'll know by tonight." She looked at the crow, which was placidly staring back at her with almost-human ambivalence. "Do you two know each other?"

"You mean Poe?"

"It has a name?"

"Doesn't the Bible say everything has a name?"

"I don't know," said Jodi. "I don't read it, anymore."

"Maybe you should." Joe Mac paused. "Maybe we both should."

"He sure is the biggest crow I've ever seen."

"He's a raven. They're bigger than crows."

"He's almost as big as an *eagle*."

"That's what my daughter says."

Jodi knew she was scowling; it was fascinating how the thing held her gaze like a cat might do – never blinking, never looking away. It seemed to know she was curious about it and was returning the sentiment.

"He looks like the devil," she said.

"My daughter says that, too."

"Is he a pet?"

"Just a friend."

"He's a strange friend."

"Old men have strange friends."

Jodi turned toward the crime scene, arms crossed. "Well, like I said; he must be their king or something because he was herding the others over the bones of the kitten. I would have never looked over there if it hadn't been for him."

Joe Mac turned stiffly from the scene. "Take me home, if you would. Crime Scene can handle this without us. I want to check on Pamela before it gets too late."

"Sure."

As Joe Mac turned, the raven lifted off, and Jodi kept glancing up to see it circling them as they meandered across the field and through the woods and into the parking lot. And when they reached her vehicle, the raven came down with a formidable, utterly unafraid descent to land solidly on the roof of the squad car.

For the first time since she'd met him, Jodi saw Joe Mac smile. He reached up with his free left hand, and the enormous raven took two fearless steps toward him and hopped onto his forearm with a steel-vice grip. It bent its fearsome head – its hooked beak seemed sharp as black iron and much more frightening up close – and Joe Mac affectionately smoothed the glossy blue-black feathers.

"Go on," said Joe Mac.

At the words the gigantic raven erupted into the sky with a grace and fearlessness that struck Jodi with instinctive amazement. She had never seen such a powerful creature explode upward with such utter confidence and grace. She muttered, "You two really are friends, aren't you?" She realized she was gaping. "Did you say he's a wild raven?"

"He comes when he wants. Goes when he wants. Seems pretty wild to me."

"And he's not scared of people?"

Joe Mac opened his door. "Why would he be scared of people? You can't even get close to him unless he lets you."

With a grunt, Jodi opened the door.

"Yeah. I wouldn't be scared of anything, either."

* * *

Jodi waited at the entrance of Joe Mac's humble barn as he tapped a path back from his daughter's house. She wasn't surprised that the crow – wait, it was a raven – had circled over Joe Mac all the way over there and all the way back. What surprised her was that the raven seemed to have identified her individual car and could determine the difference between her squad car and all the other squad cars cruising to and from the crime scene.

Joe Mac stopped at the door and turned.

Jodi asked, "How's she doing?"

"She's been sleeping. It's gonna take her a long time." He felt for the lock using his forefinger as a key-guide. "They say you don't ever get over it. One day you just get up and start moving. But when you bury a child a part of your heart crawls down in that grave with 'em and stays there."

"Yeah," Jodi responded. "I lost a brother. But I know it's not the same. Not even close. Nothing compares to losing a child."

"Sorry about your brother."

"So am I. Drugs. We let him down, I guess. The whole family."

Joe Mac opened the barn door. "Come on. I'll make you some coffee. I learned how to do all that stuff where they rehab blind people."

"Fancy."

"Nuthin' but the good life."

Entering what was obviously a revamped barn Jodi saw – with a single glance – a recliner, a double bed, a plate of food on a small kitchen table, and Joe Mac's entire wardrobe strung along the far wall; it was a typical barn layout with added shelves and a bathroom slapped onto the back.

"You like to keep things simple, huh?" she asked.

"I got a roof. I got food. I got a bed. What more do I need?"

He began to clang around in his kitchenette as Jodi lifted and opened a lawn chair. She didn't feel the need to inform him that he only had one recliner. He knew, anyway, so she could deal with it if he could. She asked, "How come you were never assigned to this case? Seems like you would have been chief investigator for a serial killer like this."

"He wasn't killing people back then," Joe Mac called. "I retired six years ago. Back then he wasn't even a blip on the screen. It was only after I got hurt and put out to pasture that he started racking up a body count." He pulled two cups off a plywood board. "You bring the file in from the car?"

"It's right here."

"I want you to read it to me."

"The whole thing?"

"The whole thing."

"So you're gonna lend me a hand, Joe?"

He turned. Stared. "I guess that's up to you. I want to find who killed my grandson. And I can't do it by myself." Jodi saw a deep pain solidify his face. "I don't think nobody else would have me, no way."

Jodi felt a grimace. "Well, I think you've still got a few good moves left in you – you and your buddy. What's his name?"

"Poe."

the wife of recently murdered businessman, Theodore Mills, whose wealth funds the corrupt police force in the area. The local Highway Patrol is run by sexually sadistic Sam Roche and Franklin Norman and they want to put an end to Johnny's snooping. Marshall Simmons knows a lot about the goings on in the area, and has a young woman captive in a house. He is reprogramming her identity. Meanwhile Johnny discovers that years previously serial killer Donald Lake disappeared in the area while in transit between prisons. And it seems he had police help. But what is being done to the women? And who is running the criminal organisation that controls the area? Savage Highways is about lawlessness and the hunt for justice in a no man's land. Pedal to the floor all the way, the narrative speeds towards its stunning and unforeseeable conclusion.

*"The road novel from hell ... a surrealist inferno that makes Dante's version look like a Rotary breakfast."***--Castle Freeman Jr., author of THE DEVIL IN THE VALLEY**

http://wbp.bz/shreviews